THE
YELLOW
EMPEROR'S
CURE

THE YELLOW EMPEROR'S CURE

A NOVEL

Kunal Basu

OVERLOOK DUCKWORTH

NEW YORK • LONDON

This edition first published in the United States
and the United Kingdom in 2011 by Overlook Duckworth

NEW YORK:
The Overlook Press
Peter Mayer Publishers, Inc.
141 Wooster Street
New York, NY 10012
www.overlookpress.com
For bulk and special sales, please contact sales@overlookny.com

LONDON:
Gerald Duckworth Publishers Ltd.
90-93 Cowcross Street
London EC1M 6BF
www.ducknet.co.uk
info@duckworth-publishers.co.uk

Cataloging-in-Publication Data is available from the Library of Congress
A catalogue record for this book is available from the British Library

Design and typeformatting by Bernard Schleifer
Manufactured in the United States of America

FIRST EDITION
2 4 6 8 9 7 5 3 1
ISBN 978-1-59020-708-6 US
ISBN 978-0-7156-4287-0 UK

for
Philippa Brewster

Those who haven't had the pox in this life,
will get it in the next.

— RABELAIS

I
LISBON 1898
The Feast of St. Anthony

N o one sleeps the night before a *festa*. In June, when the days are long and the sea luminous, no excuse will keep the crowds from the squares or lovers dancing to the fado. The night is short before the feast of St. Anthony, with the solstice hot on its heels. It is an easy night for the beggars, fed with cups of *arroz doce*—sweet rice pudding with cinnamon—in return for favors from the saint, and a hard one for sardines, waiting to be grilled by the sidewalk and munched by revellers at the midday parade. Sardines on bread, spicy pork and chicken—as tempting as the festival queen blowing kisses in the air under the lilac jacarandas of Lisbon.

Women and sardines were on his mind as Dr. Antonio Henriques Maria left the All Saints Hospital after a sleepless night. He was hungry and cross with his undeserving patient—a man who had accidentally shot himself hunting pheasants on hilly Santa Catarina—for having wasted his superior surgical skills. It was the curse of doctors to save a man's life when it would've served the fool better to let him bleed to death. He blamed the matron for refusing to send the patient over to the bazaars of Alfama, for the Arabs to rob him of his gun before they dispatched him to his grave. In a city full of quacks, she had brought him back from the gates of hell to be saved through the miracle of Antonio's hands.

As he wielded the bone saw, stopping every now and then to unclog its teeth with a squirrel brush, he had an eye on his watch. It was to be a night with old friends—rascals and whore mongers—fans of the bullring and dance hall dandies, shedding their respectable gowns to relive their student days at the Faculdade Medicina. Doctors dressed up as pirates, drinking at taverns and singing bawdy songs, on the lookout for the merry brides of St. Anthony.

"He stumbled on a rock." The elderly matron whispered, cupping the man's eyes with her palm to stop him from seeing his blood. Antonio gave her a look of disdain.

"He'd be dead by now had it not been for the dog that stayed by his side and kept on barking."

Holding the Catlin knife like a painter's brush, he drew a circle around the crushed knee to cut it open. A stifled sob passed the matron's lips when she saw the bullet gleaming like pearl in an oyster.

"Pity the dog wasn't in heat. Maybe she was, but there weren't any males to lead her astray!" Prising out the conical lead piece with forceps, he dropped it into a pewter bowl. "There—feed it to the dog."

In moments, he changed from painter to embroiderer, taking care to sink his needle into the man's skin in a way that was least likely to leave a mark, looping the fine thread drawn from pigs' intestines over his thumb like a diligent bridesmaid. Ah, the miracle of Dr. Maria! The young lion! The pride of the Faculdade; for all of his coarse mouth and roving eye, the most precious pair of hands in Lisbon.

He sewed up the man and turned his attention to the night nurse who was standing beside him. There was something about Maria Helena's farm-sweet face and lithe Castilian frame draped in nurses' whites that had caught his eye as he sawed and scraped. Their hands had touched as she passed him the forceps, and Antonio had sensed a nervous flutter like a moth around a spider's web. He was used to fluttering women, the heat they exuded as they prepared to be trapped, responding to accidental touches with flushed necks and frozen eyes. Like a beggar pretending to be blind she kept her eyes down, but met his outstretched palm with unvarying regularity like clockwork.

The matron frowned at the give and take. She rolled up her eyes as he shot Maria Helena his lady-killer looks. In her haste to bring the patient back to his senses by warming his feet with a coal scuttle, she had missed the most scandalous bit: Doctor Maria wiping the blood off his hands on the folds of the nurse's tunic, leaving the paw marks of the predator on its prey.

Maybe I'll see her at the festa, Antonio thought, as he left the hospital, jumping over a shallow pool. Morning showers had scattered the jacaranda blossoms on the dusty avenues and added an unexpected blush to the century-old gray buildings with their balconies sprouting pots of basil—the customary gift offered by the young to their lovers at the feast of the saint. He felt his mood lifting, and imagined meeting Maria Helena at the parade. He wondered if she too would dress up as a bride, marching with the veiled horde, giving him a shy glance as she passed him. Maybe he'd meet her at a tavern, still wearing nurses' whites, breath smelling of sardines. They could disappear into the lanes and climb up the spiral stairs of a whitewashed home in the city's old quarters to watch the parade and resume their give and take.

He thought about his friends on his way over to Rossio Square, where a giant tent had been built to house the *fadistas*. They'd be cursing him for being a spoilsport. He could imagine Ricardo Silva, *Rogue* Ricardo, regaling everyone with stories of his friend's escapades. He'd be reminding them too of their teachers at the Faculdade Medicina and their verdict on the young Antonio Maria: Talent—Exceptional; Temperament—Sound; Judgment—Rash; not yet fully mature. Still drunk from the night before, they'd be laughing themselves hoarse over his judgment—the last surviving bachelor among them, guilty of letting beauty queens and wealthy heiresses slip through his fingers at more than an alarming rate. "He treats his lovers like his patients . . . cures them quickly!" They'd agree with Ricardo and puzzle over the riddle that was their friend Antonio Maria—rock steady with the scalpel, but a prize idiot when it came to women.

"What was she like?" Ricardo Silva asked him when they finally met at the grandstand in the afternoon.

"Who?" Antonio eyed the fancy dressers.

"The one who kept you sober last night."

He could smell the salted codfish in the stalls of Praça da Figueira and smell the girls perspiring as they waited impatiently for the parade to start. Everything about the festa was as it should be, about showing and watching, chasing and lechery. The young hopefuls had shed the latest walking dresses from Paris and dressed up as dolls, buxom spinsters like whores, the nuns, severe as ever, holding up statues of the saint upside down to remind him of his promise to cleanse the sinners of their sins.

He owed Ricardo an answer. There were many reasons for Antonio to feel grateful to his loyal friend, who was always prepared to throw his might behind him. Failure to succeed at the Faculdade Medicina had been a blessing in disguise for Ricardo: it had helped to secure his place among the aristocracy by simply affording him the time to spend in their company. It wasn't just that he happened to be related to every fidalgo family by a mixture of his lies and conjectures, his power to make friends out of perfect strangers made him a welcome guest at mansions that lined the glittering boroughs of Lisbon. Antonio teased his friend:

"A fool who thought himself a pheasant and put a bullet through."

"A man!" Ricardo recovered quickly from his shock. "Ah . . . the doctor was busy doctoring. You couldn't have been alone with the pheasant though."

"The matron was there."

"The owl!" Ricardo chuckled to himself. "Just a whiff of her armpits would've knocked the poor man out!"

The parade wound its way into the square, where pyres had been lit in the past to burn heretics, and the two of them waved lustily at a group of cute trumpet players dressed up as dolphins. Spotting Antonio in the crowd, the girls almost fainted. Dr. Maria. . . .! A doctor so handsome! So young and so famous! They'd have heard the scandals, the tittle-tattle, taken a moment to thank their luck and wave back.

"The pheasant, the matron and . . .?"

"A nurse."

Ricardo Silva praised himself for knowing his friend so well.

"What did she have under the whites?" He nudged Antonio. "Go on, tell me."

"A pair of kidneys, a healthy liver and . . ."

Ricardo laughed. "You mean you had to cut her open to take your baby out?"

Antonio wished he had indeed filled Maria Helena's belly. She'd be far superior to the dolphin girls, he was certain. It'd need just a little tact to prevent their secret from turning into gossip at the All Saints. The festa had begun to come alive, making it hard for him to spot the farm-sweet girl with a Castilian frame among the crowd milling into the square. The matadors had arrived to a loud cheer, and the first bets of the evening were about to be placed at the bullring. Coaxed by their fans, lazy fadistas had started to tune their guitars as fireworks would soon light up the sky and the Manueline shores of the Tagus, setting the stage for a memorable evening. It was time for a quick meal of sardines, and the two made their way over to the stalls lining Avenida da Liberdade. Smoke from the ovens stung their eyes, and Antonio cursed as he spotted the hospital matron. She was waving frantically at him over the crowd. *What's the old cow doing at the festa!* He hoped it wasn't yet another case of a half-dead pheasant. "I'll shoot her before she finds one of those again." He cocked his arm and feigned taking aim. There was a look of relief on the elderly woman's face, as if she had expected to spend the whole night looking for a truant Dr. Maria. Making her way through the throngs she reached him and passed on a letter, which he read quickly then prepared at once to break free of the crowded stalls. Ricardo tapped him on the back with a puzzled look. "Leaving so early?" he called out to his friend, unable to keep pace with his quick strides. "Wait! Don't you want to swim with the dolphins?"

Rogue Ricardo couldn't have guessed the reason for his sudden exit, or known about the unexpected letter written in the neat hand of a doctor jotting down his patient's medical history in just a few lines. More a note than a letter, it had come from his father, calling him over to his retreat at Cabo São Vicente. Antonio knew his father well, knew the true weight of his short notes. He regretted missing his chance to examine what lay under Maria Helena's whites and to listen to the fadistas who'd whip up a storm as the evening progressed. It was sad for the dolphin girls too because it had started to rain—a summer rain that was wasted on the crops, drenching everyone. The carnival's clown looked like a crab wriggling its way into a hole; the monks like bunched sardines. The brides turned into grieving widows. The crowd fled into cafés and pastelarias as if a shark had invaded a shoal. Those who'd come prepared to shed their clothes afterward made fists at the clouds for forcing them to begin so soon. "You missed it, my friend!" Ricardo would tell him later about this unintended disrobing. By the time he left the city, the waterlogged square resembled a shallow pond crawling with a bunch of ugly drunken bathers.

Antonio Maria spent the night in a carriage listening to the wheels creak, echoing the lament of the farmlands and virgin forests that had been cleared for the road and thrust back onto the horizon. His mind didn't stop for a moment. *Why has he called me back from the feast of St. Anthony?* He had a whole night to examine the letter and decipher its secret. *Why didn't he come to Lisbon for his sardines?* It took him back to the time when they'd both be on the grandstand to watch the fancy dressers, when his father would hoist him onto his shoulders at the bullring or join the crowd at Belém to catch the fireworks as grand caravels sailed out of Lisbon harbor. His destination reminded him too of the day when he had seen his father weeping among the cedars of Cabo São Vicente. He had followed him out of the house to ask about his mother, about her trip under the earth in a wooden box, tugged at his sleeves, run around him in circles, shouted into his face without an answer.

"Come, Tino, we'll visit your mother in her new home." His father would say at every anniversary of her death, as if she might still wish to return to her old home, the air in the house still heavy with her breath, waiting for her to give form to her spirit. Even during his years in Coimbra at the Faculdade Medicina, he'd get a note from Dr. Alexander Henriques Maria to come home for his mother. Growing up, he was the father Antonio never missed, even though he was already a household name, doctor to the royals and to those who could pay only with their blessings. His father took him wherever he went—to the quintas of his rich patients, or riding in Sintra's forests—the imposing Dr. Maria and his boy, both immaculately dressed like aristocrats.

He's his father's replica, friends would say, both blessed with the very same dashing looks and the air of sweet insolence. Between the two, it had been a friendship of lonely men bonded by an absence. Ever since he had understood the irrevocable journey of the box carrying his mother, an unspoken partnership had taken root in the imagination of what might've been if she was alive. If they laughed out loud while sharing their *raivas*, it was in the knowledge that no one could better her cinnamon cookies or her *pastéis de coco* or the heavenly *toucinho do céu* for that matter; none replace her in their thoughts when they heard a clip-clopping hearse go by on frosty mornings.

It was a friendship that had ripened with mischief. Teachers at the Faculdade treated the young Antonio with caution, reserving their complaints to give them to the senior doctor on his visits to see his son. He was too precious to be punished in ordinary ways, for brawling at the fencing ring or shouting down the lodge's warden or shooting the principal's pet pigeons. Their awe of his father meant that Antonio escaped the severest of punishments that were meted out to his friends, who'd wake the town at the crack of dawn on Festa das Latas, slamming on tin cans tied to their legs and marching down the thoroughfares of Coimbra to the surging Mondego for a mandatory splash. With the seriousness of a doctor noting his patient's complaints, his father would listen to the nervous principal, then leave without prescribing a treatment.

When Antonio was back for holidays, his faher would embrace him—an embrace he wouldn't exchange for those of the world's greatest beauties.

His mind returned to the festa and to the matron holding out the letter. *Did she know who it was from?* There'd been gossip about his father's absence from Lisbon. Why did the celebrated doctor abandon the All Saints where he was no less revered than Dom Manual and Dona Maria carved in stone on their pedestals? There was no shortage of lies spread by the wicked and the envious. He hadn't paid much attention to rumors. He knew his father too well. Never one to complain, perhaps the weight of his patients had at last made him weary; *he has grown tired of being a doctor*, he thought.

Arriving at their country home, Antonio slammed the carriage door behind him and felt his pulse quicken. He'd have his answer now, the mystery of the note solved in an instant by a pair of twinkling eyes. A light shone from a window, the rest of the house still as dark as the fields he had passed on his way. He marched down the corridor to the parlor, and heard the sound of breathing that came from inside.

By the light held aloft by the housemaid Rosa Escobar, Antonio saw the room had been turned into a bedchamber and a study: a desk fitted in to allow the completion of everyday tasks with minimum effort; the medicine cabinet within easy reach, a porcelain bidet, a washstand, and a dresser with knickknacks. His father was resting, and he smelled the sweet smell of juniper berries burning in a coal scuttle. Wafting smoke formed a screen around the bed, making the room seem like a crypt in a monastery. *Why has he turned his house into a hospital?* Aware of his visitor, his father shifted on his side and turned to face him, the gas lamp lighting his face. A rosebud bloomed on his temple, tumescent, a drop of milk-white dew oozing from its heart and trickling down. His lips were skewered with sores and teeth blackened like soot. Lifeless eyes stared back from the face of a skeleton dug out from its grave.

"What's wrong?" Antonio shouted at the waxen Rosa Escobar. The elderly woman started to shake.

He ripped open his father's tunic in his haste to examine him. A field of roses blinded him, the red rash that covered the body from head to knee, sparing no part except the eyes. In places the buds had dried out into ugly scabs, like leopards' spots, chafed and shriveled. Hideous lumps flattened the balls of his feet and his palms, joined his neck to his chin and sent a ripple across the chest. Pus oozed from fiery cysts. His back resembled a field of millet. A deep lesion on his forehead gaped like a dead crater. Eyebrows had disappeared, along with hair from his head and limbs; the nose turned into a one-holed flute. Saliva drooled through his gumless mouth, a tooth falling out when he parted his jaws to let out a howl. Antonio removed the covers fully and saw an abscess on the genitals resembling a flowering cactus, and testes that were far too swollen to hold in both hands. The stench of rotting flesh made him cover his nose.

His father gripped his hand, digging in his nails. Shocked, Antonio broke free, and spoke urgently. "How long have you been like this?" There was no answer.

"When did the rash appear?" The pustules seemed more than a few months old, angry and ripe to bursting point. "How long since you've treated them?" He raised his voice.

"Four months." Standing behind him, Rosa replied for his father.

"Shhh . . ." Antonio silenced her. "In which part of the body did you get them first? Go on, tell me." He took a close look at the groin, at the glistening bud on the member, and brought his face even closer to his father's ear. "What have you done? You *must* tell me what happened."

"He can't hear you." Rosa Escobar spoke haltingly. "He is deaf as dead." She started to sob.

"Nonsense!" Antonio tried to shoo her away, making her wail uncontrollably.

"He wanted to die before you to saw him like this, but I begged him to write you one last time."

"*You* begged him?"

Rosa nodded. "Only you can save him, his own Tino."

It took considerable effort for Antonio to turn away from his father and face Rosa. Then he asked her to name the symptoms, all of them, as clearly as she could, starting with the appearance of the rash. She told him about the crushing pain in the bones in the early days of his father's sickness, as if he had fallen off a galloping horse. "He stays awake all night from dreadful colic, sleeps all day then wakes up to the pain as it starts all over again. Some nights he can't sleep at all, has the sense of flames bursting through his pupils like fireballs. Can't eat a morsel of food or gulp down a drop of water. He has the tongue of an ox. And his body shakes like a rabbit caught in a trap."

It couldn't be true, Antonio thought he was dreaming an ugly dream. Even without the droning words of Rosa Escobar, he could recite the full list of symptoms: insomnia and inflammation, acute neuralgia, chronic fatigue, distress of the bowels and vital organs, paralysis and dementia.

Morbus Gallicus . . . It took him no time to add up the symptoms, to confirm his worst fears. He ran out of the room, with Rosa behind him. She begged him to stop, to give her a chance to describe the condition of the patient in full. "Your father has gone mad!" she wailed. "He's afraid of ghosts and clings to me day and night. He talks of hellfire, and of angels who are poisoning him." Rosa grabbed his arm and shook it. "He's dying, Tino!"

Antonio prowled his room at the country house, the door barred. *That's why he had run from Lisbon. . . . How foolish of me not to have known!* He remembered the storm of rumors that had chased his father all the way to Cabo São Vicente. *How could he get away with his secret?* He blamed himself for ignoring the gossip. *What can I do to save him now?* Tertiary syphilis brooked no cure, he knew too well, there was nothing bigger than the venereal pox, nothing better than to put a bullet through his head.

Back in his father's room, he smashed the bottles full of Rosa's potions bought from "traveling doctors" and amateur herbalists. Quacks! He crushed the vials of arsenic and mercury under his feet, upturned vats of almond oil and buckets full of leeches. Prize idiots! Arsenic never cured anyone of anything. Leeches simply sucked blood. Mercury gave you bad teeth. Chocolate-coated gold pills did no more than color the bowels. Quacks! Quacks! Quacks! Quacks! He went stamping over them, scattering the shards.

"Save me, Tino." His father wept like a child, when he managed to look into his son's eyes.

The one he loved most. The father who'd carry him on his shoulders at the bullring. The one who'd counsel him to shoot the principal — the old fool — and spare his pigeons.

"Save me, Tino. . . ."

Who could've infected him? An album of faces opened up before Antonio's eyes. He stared hard at Rosa. *Could she have . . . ?* She ran behind the cupboard when he took a few menacing steps toward her, as if he meant to examine her forcibly.

"No, Tino, it wasn't me. I'm clean. Look!" She pulled her bodice down and showed him her bare and unblemished breasts. "I didn't give it to him. He was sick when he came here."

"But you knew, didn't you?" He looked accusingly at Rosa. "Why didn't you write to me earlier?"

"Because your father forbade me." She pointed at the door. "He kept it locked to stop me from going out to the market even. I had to sneak out when he was sleeping. He stopped me from telling anyone. He'd mix his own medicine in the mortar, and make me rub his body with it. He thought he could cure himself, that you'd find him healthy when you came home. Then . . ."

"Then what?" Antonio looked at his father, dozing with his eyes open.

"Then he gave up. Asked me to bring him his gun." Rubbing her eyes with her apron, Rosa sobbed. "He tried to kill himself when I fell asleep, cut his wrists with his surgical knife. I threw away his box of instruments, but then he tried again with drops he had kept hidden under the bed."

"Did anyone visit him here?"

"No." Rosa shook her head. "Just him and me. Till I begged him to write you just once."

Antonio left the house to walk among the cedars. Summer's light had cast loving shadows among the trees, but he couldn't rid his thoughts of his father's ugly body, and his pathetic pleas. *He should know I can't help him. No doctor can. . . . He must know all about poxes.* Even from far away he could hear the cry of the syphilitics of Lisbon camping in the Monastery of Jerónimos: rotting whores and rogues let out of prison by their fearful guards, orphans of sick mothers, idiots and cripples. And the child monsters who had suckled the poison from their mothers' breasts and were covered from head to toe in leopard's spots. Even lepers ran at the sight of them. Shopkeepers chased them with sticks; hospitals slammed doors in their faces. Kind priests hurled rocks through their windows to keep them away.

At the All Saints Hospital they called it serpentine sickness, worse than the dark plague, than the poison of scorpions or the bite of a rabid dog. He'd flee whenever he encountered the symptoms of syphilis, make excuses, hand over the patient to fellow doctors. Let them be the ones to make fools of themselves. Shutting the door behind him, he'd put his ear to the wall and chuckle as he heard them struggle to name the mischief maker disguised as harmless gout or plain eczema, a touch of nerves, time honored rheumatism, even hypochondria. *Syphilis!* He'd want to scream his warning to patient and doctor through the wall. Call it by whichever name—French disease, Spanish itch, German rash or Polish pox—it was the same old curse Dom Columbus had brought home from Hispaniola along with gold and talking parrots.

If forced to treat a victim, he'd puzzle his assistants by advising them to take the patient to the Jesuit asylum. "But he isn't mad!" "He *will* be soon," he'd alarm them. "The patient will sing! If a composer, he'll pen a symphony, paint a masterpiece if an artist. Might even plunge a knife into his doctor's heart like a champion of the bullring."

He must've caught it in Lisbon then fled to the country. Antonio recalled his father coming to see him often at the All Saints, but never staying back to spend a night with him. *He's off to one of his rich lovers*, he'd think. Maybe he was infected by them, or by their servants. He thought of the happy ladies of Praça da Alegria and shuddered. Could his father have caught the pox from someone he knew himself, from the lot of his own lovers?

Watching the fireflies dance, he brooded over everything he had learned about the pox. The nervous face of Rosa appeared at the window to call him back. Antonio waved her away, but she pleaded with her eyes to let her speak to him just once.

Tired from his travels, he fell asleep. The tune of a marching band played in his dreams and he fretted over a million regrets. An anxious Maria Helena called out to him to cut her free from a fisherman's net with his surgical knife. Friends cheered him on as he entered the bull-ring dressed as a matador. He couldn't remember his fight with the bull, except his father picking him up from the sawdust and speaking quiet words of assurance into his ear. *One day you'll be a champion, Tino. . . .*

When he woke Antonio thought he was still dreaming about his father sobbing among the cedars of Cabo São Vicente the day his mother died. The sound seemed to find its way into every corner of the house, like a wind that has a seed of madness in its vortex. He went down to his father's room. He found him kneeling by the bed, an arm around Rosa Escobar, who was on the bed dressed up like his mother. She was lying still in the posture of death wearing an old bridal gown, the veil covering her face. Her eyes were shut, her face gripped with fear. He saw his father weeping at her feet. He turned toward Antonio and spoke in a choked voice.

"Come Tino, it's time to take your mother to her new home."

His nightmares started there at his father's bedside. Every night since the feast of St. Anthony, he woke in terror at the thought of his father among the howling syphilitics, showered with rocks and chased with sticks.

❀

From Cabo São Vicente to Coimbra, Antonio wasted no time reaching the Faculdade Medicina. He needed to consult urgently with Dr. Alfred Martin, the only one he trusted on medical matters. Waiting for the baby-faced Scot who had taught him the proper grip of the scalpel, he rehearsed a single line over and over in his mind, the one he'd offer Dr. Martin if asked why he had come to see him. *My father is suffering from syphilis.* He wondered if he should put it more plainly. . . . *My father is dying of syphilis,* given that his diagnosis indicated nothing better than imminent death. His teacher might ask him to recite the details, and he made a quick mental list of the symptoms.

Dr. Martin swept into his office, and greeted Antonio with a flourish. "Ah! the mischief maker!" He looked every bit a baby without a line on his face, ruddy cheeks and an infectious smile, the teacher who loved arguing and had the reputation among his colleagues of being a student in disguise. Settling into his deep lounge chair and lighting up a water pipe—a favorite among bohemians—he sized up his quiet visitor, and wondered aloud what had brought him over to the Faculdade after so many years, unlike his friends who were in the habit of dropping in every now and then for free consultations.

"What mischief brings you back now?"

"It's about a patient who shows signs of paresis resulting from infectious chancre. An infection that's about to enter the tertiary stage." Antonio answered grimly.

"A patient of syphilis, you mean." Dr. Martin was quick to follow. "How do you know the tertiary stage is near?"

"Because dementia paralytica has set in. All signs point to a breakdown of personality leading to erratic behavior."

"Ah! You mean he's unable to recognize near and dear ones, claims to hear the angels in his ear, thinks himself to be the emissary of the devil!" Dr. Martin sniggered. "Just like our dear principal here, don't you think?" He let out a stream of smoke from his pipe. "Might as well call the undertakers then!"

"The patient is my father." Antonio whispered.

A frown appeared on Dr. Martin's face, making him look suddenly aged. He drew quietly on his water pipe. Light through the slatted windows cut the room in half, leaving him in the dark and his student bathed in the color of green maple that surrounded the Faculdade Medicina.

"He hid it from everyone, and so there was no chance of treating him earlier." Antonio let out a deep breath. "Unless, of course, he had tried to cure himself."

"But it would be of no use." Dr. Martin sighed. "He must've known the final outcome."

"He couldn't have known of any new treatment though, something that's only recently been discovered?" Antonio probed cautiously.

Perhaps Dr. Martin, known for his blasphemous views, had a surprise or two up his sleeve.

The Scotsman shook his head. "Not since the time you were here. There hasn't been a successful treatment in four hundred years, I'm afraid." He rose to open the window and draw in the afternoon sun to light up the bookshelves and the cabinet of surgical tools. "We doctors have failed shamefully when it comes to fighting the pox. It's over to heretics now. Nothing else will do."

Antonio was upset. It was all talk with Dr. Martin, and the play of clever arguments. Sleepless from his travels, he felt cheated by the Faculdade, and was moved one last time to press on arguing with his teacher. "But there's no shortage of heretics. Why haven't they found a cure?"

"Because we distrust them." Recovering his spirit, Dr. Martin bit the stem of his water pipe and spoke vigorously. "No one even believes in a cure for syphilis anymore. The French have given up on the French disease! In Paris they're threatening to hang the victims. There's talk even of branding them with red-hot irons. In Madrid the syphilitics have been removed from the records and turned into ghosts! Mothers have been told to nurse their own children, men to avoid public baths. And Italy? The less said about the Italians the better!" He stopped to catch his breath then went on. "In Naples they've built walls inside hospitals to separate the patients from the poxies, just as in Glasgow, where the police have replaced doctors on the wards. In the lands of Calvin they've been left to die as punishment for their sins. The civilized world has simply given up."

"And the English?" Antonio was yet hopeful of the wonderfully inventive English. His teacher laughed.

"Yes, they've found one—the English cap—made of sheep's intestines to wrap around your member in case you meet the gin palace whores!"

As he listened to his teacher, Antonio's thoughts returned to his father's bedside. *I've lost him already. . . .* He had seen enough to be convinced that it was true. Syphilis had brought about a change in his character, scattering his memories like dust. He was unable to grasp his own thoughts anymore, chasing after them like butterflies. *The time has come to put him in a madhouse.*

"It's over to quacks then?" He spoke wryly and passed his hand over the trephine lying on the desk.

Dr. Martin noticed the dismay in his student's voice. Privately he chuckled at the qualities of Antonio Maria that had endeared him to his teachers. The young bull who refused to accept defeat. The streak of obstinacy that had marked him out for future success, showed all that was good and bad in a doctor.

"It depends on who you call quacks and who doctors."

"That's clear. Those who believe in the curative power of menstrual blood, gaic wood and dead lizards, those who . . ."

"They are charlatans," Dr. Martin was quick to interject, "that are fit to be locked up and put away. But what do you make of the Hopi, the Yoruba, the Aztecs and the Incas?"

"Our hope lies in spirit doctors then? We might as well trust in the Golden Mermaid!"

"Our forefathers too worshipped serpents and lizards, the moon goddess and the sea." Just as when instructing his pupils on the correct use of the circular trephine, Dr. Martin interrupted Antonio with a lengthy treatise. In the end, his student had learned much more than he cared to about the Yoruba, who expelled harmful germs—the *kokoro*—with ritual baths; about the Egyptian Imhotep, called the "prince of peace," who could treat over two hundred diseases with herbs and plants; the mathematics of Al-Kindi, used to calculate the precise nature of a sickness; about the Ayurvedic masters of India, and the *Nei ching*—the Yellow Emperor's Canon.

"The Yellow Emperor?" Antonio asked his teacher, as he prepared to leave.

"The ruler of the yellow race. His laws of medicine are older than our oldest ancestors. A Chinese doctor can tell a man's sickness simply by placing a hand on his wrist."

"So can we," Antonio shot back. "By checking the tongue, by putting a nozzle to the heart, by tapping the soles of the feet. Anyone can name a sickness, can the Yellow Emperor cure it?"

Dr. Martin smiled. "We don't know. But the heretic must believe in that possibility."

What can I do to save my father now? Rising, he spoke irritably.

"My patient will die before a cure is found." Perhaps the time had come to think the unthinkable—putting him to sleep before the devil took over his mind.

"A remedy must surely exist even if you don't find it described in the gold-trimmed volumes of the Biblioteca Nacional." Gazing out of the window, Dr. Martin followed a flock of gulls circling the banks of the Mondego. His face glowed in the falling light. He smiled kindly at his student's anguished face. "It'll take a bit of mischief, Antonio. You might have to stop being a doctor, go far from your patient in order to find him a cure."

Back in Lisbon Antonio skipped his daily rounds at the All Saints and sent Ricardo Silva word to meet him at their favorite pastelaria. His friend would be surprised, he knew, demand an explanation for his sudden escape from the festa. It'd be harder to tell Ricardo about his father than telling Dr. Martin. His favorite English tea tasted bitter as he rehearsed his opening line, ignoring the come-hither looks of a vixen who had planted herself across from him. She blew him the smoke of an imported cigarillo, but Antonio kept staring into his cup as if it held the answers to his pressing problems.

He was relieved to see Ricardo, smelling like a Parisian on a casual stroll, although he must've rushed in from his stables to meet Antonio, unable to hold back his curiosity. He poured himself a cup of the tea and patted Antonio on the back. "You've called me over to give me the big news, haven't you? Want to tell me first before you announce it to the world?"

"What news?"

How'd Ricardo know . . . ? Did Rosa Escobar write to him as well? He was perplexed by his friend's jolly mood, waving to the vixen and making eyes at her, in the face of Antonio's tragedy.

"That you've decided, finally, to get married!" Ricardo laughed out loud, drawing a few glances to their table. "I know why you left the dolphin girls and rushed away from the festa. She must've called you over? Given you just hours to make up your mind?" He narrowed his eyes and quizzed Antonio like a teacher. "What did you do to her, Tino? Don't tell me she was about to deliver your baby at the All Saints?"

Antonio sat looking at his cup. Ricardo ignored his sullen mood and delved into a plate of freshly baked *pasteis*. "You can tell me who she is. I can't let you marry a nurse, mind you, or your favorite matron, even if she's bribed you with all the sardines of the seas." A hint of anxiety crept into his voice. "You'll simply have to change your mind if I don't approve."

Antonio looked up. "My father is dying of syphilis." He muttered the line he had rehearsed for Dr. Martin, and fell silent again.

Ricardo choked on a *pasteis*, and his face turned as red as the vixen's lips. It took several cups of tea for both to recover their tongues. Then Antonio spoke with the urgency of someone who must attend to a patient in crisis.

"I want you to find me a doctor."

"A better doctor than you?" Ricardo seemed truly surprised. "There's none in Portugal, Tino."

"Not in Portugal." Antonio tried to explain to his friend what his teacher had told him about heretics. Ricardo listened in wonder as he went on about spirit doctors and shamans from parts of the world known only to sailors and unfortunate readers of Camões with his gory tales of savages.

"We have doctors here but no heretics." Antonio concluded with a glum face.

Ricardo disagreed. "There's no shortage of them in Lisbon at Alfama's pox bazaar who claim they've found the magic potion and promise their patients a full recovery: clear skin to go with a fresh crop of hair, an iron constitution and the virility of African kings."

"They aren't heretics but quacks." Antonio smiled wryly at Ricardo. Sitting at the pastelaria, both recalled how they'd once got lost at the Alfama as they strolled in the dead-end alleys listening to the melody of twittering canaries and fadistas who strummed their guitars behind the mysterious walls of the huddled tenements. Ricardo had gone to meet the master saddle maker, an Arab who supplied his private stables, and had managed to persuade Antonio to leave the hospital for a lazy walk to recount their exploits with young nurses at the Faculdade and taste the Moorish delights from the street vendors. They had passed the Thieves' Market and stopped on their way up the terraces for a few drags of the

Egyptian water pipe to blank out the stench of the open gutters. From the hilltop they could see a bustling square, queues of confession seekers before the church of Santa Engracia and throngs of brothel visitors lured by the beauties brought over from the four corners of the world. They had thought to join the throngs for a look and a laugh on their way back from the saddle maker, but the cacophony in the nearby lanes had drawn them instead to the hustling shopkeepers pressing handbills into the crowd that promised "God's cure" to all men suffering from the curse of the beauties. A toothless man in a priest's smock and smelling of the gutters had nudged them on toward the stalls, which looked like miniature apothecaries. "Couldn't you do with a few of these at the All Saints?" Ricardo had pulled his friend's leg as they took in the rows of jars under the incessant chatter of the hopeful salesman.

Ordering themselves some more tea, Ricardo tried to distract Antonio from heretics: "Call them quacks, but couldn't they have discovered God's cure purely by accident?"

"No, because even you, a failed doctor, should know that cow dung on your jewels won't cure pox but will kill your reputation at the dance halls."

It took a few more patient explanations for Antonio to convince his friend. Then, just as before, Ricardo had thrown his might behind him. "If savages know how to cure the pox, then the lords of savages would know it too," he assured Antonio. Lisbon had no shortage of viceroys and governors, bishops and members of the magistracy who had served overseas to plant the *padrões*—the cross of Portuguese sovereignty in the colonies. "You can find all the secrets that you need right here without setting foot on a ship!"

The Casa da India should be their first port of call, Ricardo announced confidently, and took Antonio to meet his uncle, Dom Salvador Correia, the chief of the Eastern trade. "It's a treasure trove, no less!" Ricardo spoke under his breath as the two waited in the courtyard of the grand building with numerous wings and gardens, laid out like a palace. "Spice, sugar, silver, tea—everything's here, crammed into the Casa's vaults waiting for greedy merchants to name their price and carry them off to warehouses."

"And the treasure keeper?" Antonio asked.

"He's a sad soul, whose only dream is to make the king the richest man in the world."

A line of stevedores waited patiently to show Dom Correia their precious bounties, for the elderly man with a monocle to pronounce their true value as he turned every item over in his hand, smelled a root to judge its power or passed a beam of light through a rock to see if it trapped it inside and glowed like a precious diamond. His conical head, bald and shining, reminded Antonio of the abbot of Santa Engracia, but his eyes spoke of the sea.

"He'll be the first to know if a ship's captain has chanced upon a native potion that could cure his poxy sailors on board," Ricardo whispered to Antonio as they waited their turn, flashing his winning smile at his uncle.

"Will you tell him who it's for?" Antonio asked his friend.

"For one of your patients, of course. Don't worry, he's used to dealing with unusual requests."

"How unusual?" Antonio arched his eyebrow.

"Magical cures for baldness, touchstones that turn lead into gold, even Amazon monkeys that can bear human babies!"

Dom Correia examined Antonio sternly, taking him for a dandy who wished to buy an unusual gift for his lady friend. He said in an imperious voice, "The Casa doesn't sell anything, for that you've got to go to the merchants," meaning the rare African sapphire that was in high demand or tiger's teeth that the recently betrothed wore around their necks to ward off the evil eye. Ricardo spoke in his ear, and the elderly man's expression turned even grimmer.

Does he have it here . . ? Antonio waited anxiously for the Casa's chief to speak. How amazing if the cure was just under their noses, not in the lands of savages but inside the pretty white mansion flanked by elegant gardens. The stevedores were unreliable when it came to delicate matters, Dom Correia announced, regaining his imperious voice, then led them to a cabinet of drawers that held questionable items. One can never be sure about syphilis, but he could offer a "possible cure" for the other great tormentor, he said, then took out a tiny root resembling a shriveled worm and placed it on Antonio's palm.

"It comes from Goa, and is claimed to cure impotence."

The worm seemed to spring to life on Antonio's palm, spread

tentacles and pierced the skin with razor-sharp fangs. He dropped it on the floor, smashing it under his boots, then stomped out of the Casa.

Loyal Ricardo didn't give up the challenge and took Antonio next to visit Dom Miguel de Sousa, a member of the Society of Jesus who had spent a lifetime in Brazil as the Bishop of Peranambuco. "Nature provides the remedy in the very same place where the sickness arises." The friar spoke wisely, giving words to the commonly held belief that only savage Indians could solve the mystery of the pox which was their revenge on the conquistadors. But he had little to offer beside tales of fornicating savages and that of the lusty Portuguese who had joined the gold rush in droves. "The old fool's a syphilitic himself." Antonio cursed under his breath, and left before Dom Miguel could finish his tales. He took pains to explain to Ricardo later that the hobbling priest wasn't a victim of gout but *tabes dorsalis*, which showed in the final stages of the pox.

"Your father won't be the first to die of syphilis, Tino. Nor will he be the last." Ricardo Silva tried to calm his friend after they had made their rounds of viceroy s and governors, bishops and members of the magistracy, after their efforts had failed to yield any result. "Search every family and you'll find a story of shame. Every cemetery will show unmarked graves, hurriedly dug in the middle of the night. The pox isn't just the disease of pickled whores and their rotting friends, but of kings and merchants. How could one more death matter?"

"It matters because he's my father," Antonio spoke gruffly.

"He is, but you can count yourself lucky that you aren't the one with pox." A cloud of suspicion passed over Ricardo Silva's eyes, and he hesitated before asking, "Do you . . . ?"

Antonio shook his head. "No." They looked slyly at each other as they recounted their own bouts of quackery: wrapping their organs in wine-soaked cloth hours before they went raiding the brothels of Coimbra on the night of a festa.

"Could your father be cured if you did find your heretic?" Ricardo Silva looked Antonio in the eye. "Can he still be saved?"

Save me, Tino. . . . He heard his father beg him.

The change in Antonio was puzzling to his friends and admirers. To the young nurses at the All Saints, it was as if he had undergone surgery to remove the most vital of his organs, or taken the severest of vows before the Virgin of Nossa Senhora. Gone were the furtive glances across crowded wards and sweet games of hide-and-seek under the very nose of the elderly matron. It affected Maria Helena the most. The poor girl had dreamed big dreams on the eve of the festa. She pleaded with the matron to be left alone with Dr. Maria when he conducted surgery on his patients. She wanted simply to feel his breath and "accidental" touches, and to die from his firm grip as he helped her carry a sick patient or turn him over on the bed. Perhaps he'd want more from her, ask her to meet him at the Avenida for a ride on the Americanos — the recently arrived horse-drawn carriages — followed by a quiet meal serenaded by the famous fadistas of Chiado. Maybe he'd ask her to visit him secretly at his home, at his doctor's chamber even, whenever they could hear the matron snoring. Seeing her condition, the "old owl" had given in to Maria Helena's plaintive requests, and relaxed her vigil. But the real Antonio had fallen far short of the Antonio of her dreams. He had barely looked at her, let alone played his tricks, when they were together during long and inviting hours of surgery. He had turned out to be no more than a pair of eyes and hands, a mere slave to his surgical box and a better doctor than before.

His father occupied Antonio's thoughts completely: his dull syphilitic eyes, syphilitic teeth blackened by mercury, scarred syphilitic cheeks. He heard his deep sonorous voice reduced to a whimper, imagined his bald head bent in shame. He'd wake up in a cold sweat dreaming that his father shared his bed, filling the room with the smell of death. It was a scent that hung over the city, filled the hollow domes and the cracks in the cobblestones, refused to be blown away by the ocean breeze. Wherever he went, Lisbon stank of rotting genitals.

He must be awake now, he thought about his father, rising from his nightmare. *Awake and delirious, battling a seizure or bleeding from the eyes. He must have difficulty speaking, begging Rosa for a drop of morphine. He might be struck next with peculiar obsessions. Like a miser, he might hide his possessions then forget the hiding place, grow suspicious of Rosa, accusing her of seducing his Tino. Might even kill his nurse. . . .* Antonio shuddered as he imagined his father in a mad fit thrusting poor Rosa's head into the fireplace. Syphilis will stop torturing its victim soon, he knew only too well, pretend to disappear as suddenly as it had arrived. *Ah! The Great Pretender!* The time will come when it'll poison his heart, choke the arteries and bring him closer to death.

He didn't blame his father but blamed his sickness, dreaded nothing more than letters written by him in the hand of Rosa Escobar. *For eleven days I haven't eaten or drunk even a sip. I wander lurching and exhausted from my chair to my bed and back again. Even if I eat something, it comes right back up. Rosa is treating me. Here is my end.* Visiting Cabo São Vicente, he returned more troubled than before. He couldn't bear to look at his father, or listen to Rosa Escobar's fearful reports. As much as she tried, he refused to examine her potions. He went instead on long and gloomy walks among the cedars before climbing back into his carriage.

"Don't let the pox kill you too, Tino." Ricardo pleaded with Antonio not to turn down invitations to game shootings and boating on the Tagus. "At this rate, you'll be taken for a monk or a poxy yourself." He tried to distract his friend with an invitation to visit Vila Franca de Xira and join the red-coated *campinos* chasing bulls on their horsebacks.

"How can a mad bull help me?" Antonio asked him.

"It'll clear your mind when you see it charging towards you. It'll remind you how lucky you are to be alive!" Like a doctor himself, Ricardo had suggested the perfect antidote to Antonio's depression, but Clara, his wife and mother of their two children, had stopped them from going to the feast of the mad bull.

Not a day passed without him wondering whether he should confide his secret to the matron and fellow doctors at the All Saints. Should he bring his father to Lisbon's Jesuit asylum? The thought of him among mad men and women troubled Antonio when he went for long walks along the Tagus, stopping only for a meal of smoked sardines by the river. The city of seven sisters glowed before him. He gazed at sumptuous quintas and dingy barrios, glamorous shops and tall cathedrals, and thought about syphilis. *Does each of them hide a victim? A wife suffering in shame for her husband, a friend for a friend, a son for his father?*

He hadn't expected to meet Dom Salvador Correia again on the matter of syphilis, but the Casa's chief sent him word for an urgent meeting. A talkative assistant rushed to the All Saints to fetch Antonio and took him to *Bom Jesus*, berthed in the Baixa docks. The ship's stevedore had brought disturbing news to Dom Salvador. Captain Marcos da Cunha had fallen mysteriously ill on his return voyage from Canton, and the dreaded Asiatic cholera was feared. A lengthy period of quarantine was being discussed, the assistant rattled on, with every sailor held prisoner till proven healthy.

The ships were a constant headache, the young man confided in Antonio, each a depot of disease. Typhus and yellow fever, variola, icterus and enteritis, diarrhea and deliriums, all year round they kept doctors on their toes. The fear of an epidemic breaking out was never far away, with the memory of the last plague, the docks deserted and warehouses aflame.

"They bring in a new disease every year and confuse the doctors." The Carreira da India and the Carreira do Brasil were both notorious for the natives infecting sailors at the ports of call, or if they had been recruited from the natives themselves. There was no greater danger, of course—the assistant had grimaced—than the southern passage—the African route—where the black gold came laced with the deadliest of germs.

"If cholera is detected, we might have to sink the ship. Shoot the sailors too as there's no cure." The assistant made a dramatic gesture with his hands.

"Nonsense!" Antonio retorted. "Cholera, Asiatic or otherwise, is treatable if detected on time."

"Didn't it kill thousands in Paris and in Palermo?" His companion seemed suspicious still. Antonio corrected him. "Madras in the East Indies has suffered most from cholera, with a quarter of its population dead. But it can still be arrested on ship if one knows the source of the disease—the rum puncheons, the water casks, or a rotting cadaver sold by crafty natives from their sampans."

Dom Salvador received Antonio on a fishing *muletta* to take him over to *Bom Jesus*, in place of the usual cutter that would've risked the lives of his officers. The captain was sinking but alive. The Casa was in constant touch with the quartermaster, who was holding the fort among the sailors. On board, they crossed over the deck quickly to enter the captain's coop.

It didn't take Antonio long to size up the old sea dog lying naked on his belly. The captain had fainted on deck as they entered the Tagus's estuary, suffering from acute cramps, unable to crawl to the ship's toilet as his bowels began to rumble with a painful burning and rapid watery discharge. Lifting up an arm, Antonio found it to be as cold as a corpse.

"Blood and rosy port," he announced. "Just a little bleeding will do. Wild pheasants are the culprit here, not Asiatic cholera, which would've finished him off even before he left the shores of Asia." He smiled at the assistant who had turned speechless, sending him off to fetch his mahogany-cased cupping set from the muletta.

"What about the sailors?" Antonio asked to see all those who'd been forced to remain in their quarters.

"They are Chinese," the quartermaster said. They hadn't partaken of the feast of pheasants, turning up their noses at the brightly winged creatures.

"They could be sick too, couldn't they?" Antonio egged the quartermaster on, expecting him to spell out a list of diseases.

"Oh, yes, they are sick! All of them. A bunch of incurable Chinamen! Come, I'll show you."

Down in the hold they entered the crews' quarters. A powerful smell rose from a sea of heads over two tiers of planks lit by oil lamps. The sailors were lying with arms and legs entwined, wedged against each other, heads nestled in the hollows of the bodies. A glowing bowl passed from one outstretched hand to another, sputtering for a moment at each stop. He heard a moaning, like breezes trapped in the sails.

"Opium," the quartermaster whispered. "It's their favorite medicine for their favorite disease. They don't want to be cured, or to see the face of a doctor. If you try to stop them, they might throw you overboard!"

The play of light on their faces made them seem both awake and asleep—drooping like a field of poppy. Antonio watched their sculpted foreheads, bone-ivory teeth and quivering nostrils. A head brushed his legs. Skipping over the mass of limbs, he tried to spot known marks of blemish—an angry rash or a ripe ulcer, an ugly abscess. It *must* be there, he thought, hiding under the loin cloth, the old fox.

"They die like flies; the ocean bed must look like a Chinese graveyard!"

"What do they die of?"

The quartermaster rolled his eyes. "Everything. Burning stomachs and feeble bones, rotten lungs and sick brains."

"And syphilis?"

In the years he had spent on the China run, there had been just a few cases of the pox, too few for him to remember, the quartermaster said. "They die from what's in and over the belly, not under it!" He let out a laugh. "For that you've got to go to the Carreira do Brasil, taste the dark honey!"

A ship full of opium but no syphilis! Antonio marveled as he rode back on the muletta. The pox was the disease of sailors, he had learned at the Faculdade. Like fine Madeira wine carried by fleets of clippers, it had spread from port to port, from the New World to the old and back. None could resist it, least of all the sailors and their shore wives. In half a mind to dismiss the quartermaster, he raised the matter with the talkative assistant.

"Those from Goa and Aden do go down to the pox and raise a scare among Baixa's brothel owners. No captain wants them back for fear of an epidemic. The Chinaman gives us trouble over gambling and opium, but not the pox."

No syphilis! Antonio sensed the veil lifting. *The Yellow Emperor . . . His laws of medicine are older than our oldest ancestors. . . .* Did they include the miracle of a cure, a secret recipe that resisted infection, capable of stopping the pustules from infesting the body like wild weed? *Is this the supreme quackery that the baby-faced Scot had spoken about?*

Antonio Maria spent the next few days stirred up and restless. *A Chinese cure for syphilis!* Four hundred years of shame erased by the miracle of the opium sod! He could imagine Dr. Martin's eyes twinkling, and the relief among fellow doctors. And his father? *There's no hope for him.* The pox had gone beyond simply scarring his skin, it had ruined his organs and nerves. He was no longer the father he knew, but a demented soul capable of causing grave harm to himself and others. It was better that he should die, end his suffering and that of Rosa Escobar.

What if he asked loyal Ricardo for his help in reaching the China coast? His friend would probably show his dismay at first. "Why China?" He'd suggest the Biblioteca Nacional instead. Antonio imagined him arguing: "The grand libraries of Florence and Paris, London and Heidelberg contain all that's known to mankind. We Europeans know as much as there is to know about the yellow race, more than they know about themselves!"

Reaching Cabo São Vicente on the anniversary of his mother's death, Antonio found the cottage empty. For the first time in years, he hadn't received an invitation from his father and wondered if he still remembered the occasion. On arrival he found the house in perfect order. Things had been moved back from the parlor, and rearranged with care. There was no sign of the medicine cabinet full of jars and ointment pots. The table had been set for tea, and a small fire burned in the grate. He called for Rosa but there was no answer. Running up the stairs he found his room empty, the windows shut and curtains drawn. *Where has she taken him?* He couldn't imagine his father leaving the house by himself and a million thoughts raced through his mind. She might've forced him out to visit her favorite quack. They must be torturing him now with enemas or singeing his skin with hot coals, bloodletting even, in the hope of draining the poison. Maybe she has passed him off to a hospice, to die in the care of nuns. A noise made him rush out into the backyard, scattering a flock of birds.

Antonio roamed among the cedars. The evergreens loomed high above the grounds covered with mature cones, crunching under his feet. A drizzle had wetted the leaves, and made them glow in the fading light. His father sat in an armchair under a tree, dressed in a woollen smock like a priest's habit. The rash had cleared and his face was clean, except for a dark spot between the eyes beneath his bald head. Antonio approached his father with caution. *Will he know who I am? Is he well enough to be outdoors?* His father smiled and made a sign for him to come closer and sit on a stool beside him.

Will he ask me to examine him? Observing him closely, Antonio prepared to tell him the cruel truth about the disappearance of outward signs, that it didn't indicate a recovery from the disease. *He might not know that he's still in danger. . . .*

"Do you remember the pranks we played on the night of São João?" His father asked him, and feigned raising a hammer to hit someone on the head.

Antonio was taken aback by the question, but his face lit up. He remembered the wild evening that had followed the parade for John the Baptist at Porto's festa that he had visited as a child. His father carried him on his shoulders as they jostled with the crowds in the narrow and winding lanes, blowing whistles, singing songs and hitting people on their heads with stalks of wild garlic and leeks following a centuries-old pagan custom.

"You were too young to know it was only a prank," his father mused.

Even to this day, Antonio could remember his panic watching the revellers as they pretended to scream in pain when he hit them—a young girl who was barely older than he was, a mulatto from the dancing band, and a dwarf who had dressed up as St. John, holding up a cross that was twice his size.

"I wanted you to be happy like everyone else and bought you a hammer made of soft dough."

"And you made me hit you with it, even though I didn't want to." Antonio recalled bursting into tears seeing his father slumped on the ground pretending to be dead.

His father spoke again. "That's when I knew you'd become a doctor."

Surprised, Antonio kept silent.

"You suffered at the pain of others, just as a doctor suffers for his patients, suffers more than them." He rose from the chair, his body straining from the effort, but he refused Antonio's help and hobbled over the slippery cones, continuing to speak in a calm voice. "I knew you'd be different and your friends might not know who you really are, that you'd stop at nothing to cure suffering, that you'd never give up."

He followed his father back to the cottage. Stopping to rest in a clearing, the smell of burning logs reached them, and they caught sight of Rosa hurrying in through the door with her shopping basket. His father held on to his arm and spoke just as firmly as he would when Antonio was no more than a child, "But I want you to promise not to come here and see me die."

Antonio shook his head vigorously. "You are my patient, and I can't abandon you."

"No, Tino, I am just your father. I am a doctor and I know I'm dying." His father released his arm and kept walking. "It doesn't matter which stage of syphilis it is. What matters is that one prepares to die." He glanced sidelong at Antonio, "If you come to see me, I'd want to get better, to recover even and be the father I was. I'd want to go hunting with you, do all the things I did when your mama was alive. I'd fight the disease, knowing that I couldn't win. I'd hope I could become a doctor again."

"Maybe there'd be a reason to hope if . . ."

"No." His father stopped him. "You shouldn't make me suffer any more by tempting me to keep on living. You must go back and do what's best for your patients, do whatever you can to help them."

His father clapped his hands to scatter the birds pecking in the garden shrubs, bringing Rosa out of the kitchen. Entering the parlor, they smelled cinnamon cookies and his father smiled broadly at Antonio, "Ah! Just what your mama would've made if she knew her Tino was coming."

He sat with the two of them drinking tea, barely listening as they talked. The elderly doctor seemed to be in high spirits, praising Rosa for the sweet and crunchy raivas and making her blush. Shadows had lengthened over their cottage, and it was time to light an oil lamp and hang it from the ceiling. Antonio saw his father's hand shake as he turned the wick, saw his eyes light up with pain as the glass fount slipped from his fingers and went crashing down on the floor.

So this is the last I'll see of him. . . . When the sickness returns, he'd become mad again, unable to recognize his Tino. He might become blind, or bedridden with paralysis. *He might change his mind and look for me, unable to utter my name.* This could be the last meal they'd share together, he thought, helping Rosa put away the shards, the very last evening with his father.

Antonio left the table and ran up to his room, curled up on his bed and filled the house with the sound of his sobbing.

✿

Returning to Lisbon, Antonio visited Ricardo at his quinta determined to tell him all about his remarkable discovery, about *Bom Jesus*, the captain's ulcers and Chinese sailors who seemed to be miraculously free of the pox. His friend was in a jolly mood, having convinced the star cavaleiros of Lisbon to ride one of his Lusitano horses during the annual bullfights. Sitting under the shade of mature trees and drinking their favorite sparkling wine made from local grapes, the two friends were joined by Clara and Ricardo's little sister Arees. They chatted all morning till it was time for Clara to leave them for her rounds of the local markets. When Antonio finally brought up the curious case of *Bom Jesus* and its healthy sailors, Arees threw him the challenge he had least expected. A rebel among horse breeders, she was her brother's favorite despite being his very opposite—in looks and in taste; the sole republican in her royalist family, who was just as fond of arguing as Ricardo was fond of stunning the ladies at the dance halls—a rebel hard to ignore given her exquisite form.

"How do we know that syphilis isn't in all of us, a sleeping giant waiting to be roused?" Knowing her strange views about most things, Ricardo ignored her question, but it silenced Antonio.

"Perhaps it's no different to love, simply waiting to be felt!" Arees threw him a teasing look, as he kept on drinking his wine.

"My brother only feels love for horses, which can't have syphilis because they aren't allowed to mate till they're old or crippled!" Ricardo grinned at his sister's obvious ignorance of his favorite animal.

Antonio thought he'd tell her about the Berber women claimed by Alfama's brothel owners to be immune to the pox even though "they've slept with a hundred rotten sailors," then stopped himself. The Arees that he met infrequently at her favorite haunts—smoky cafés full of rebels and poets—might tease him in public for being "the doctor who was brave enough to risk the fate of his patients."

He wished he could confide in Arees, have her on his side and rely on her razor-sharp wit during his arguments with Ricardo. She was the only one he knew who wasn't in awe of the brilliant Dr. Maria, who made him feel ignorant as she chattered on about Voltaire and Rousseau and recited poetry that made no sense. He had found it hard to diagnose her symptoms: whether she teased him on purpose, or made a clever ploy to trap him with her arguments.

"Even if it did reside in us, it'd still need curing." This time, he decided to accept her bait.

"But what if it was immortal?" She gave Antonio a playful look, drawing attention to the mocking lips that she parted to let out thoughtful rings of smoke.

Immortal? Did she mean a recurring infection? She smiled seeing the confused look on his face. "Just like our royals here. What if it was cured then came back under a different name, with a suffering just as unbearable; a pain that couldn't be treated while the patient was living? What if syphilis is the price we must pay to be alive?"

Antonio wondered why they always ended up arguing—he and Arees—when half of Lisbon expected them to get married. Ricardo was keen too, he knew for a fact, putting up a merry face and playing along with Tino's indiscretions, hoping all the while that his wayward friend would settle down finally with his sister after he'd had his fill of nurses and tramps.

"Death is the price for getting the pox," Antonio said glumly, wishing he hadn't fallen for Arees's bait.

"And pox is the price one pays for rebelling and to be free"—she nudged Ricardo—"the very thought of which makes my brother weak."

"Rebelling?" Ricardo frowned, unable to follow.

"Just as Syphilus, the poor shepherd, was punished with pox by Apollo for his defiance, and gave the disease its name." She raised her glass to toast "cruel, fickle and reckless syphilis," then read the despair in Antonio's eyes and called for truce, closing her arguments with an olive branch: "Let's hope our blessed doctors can save us from our gods and cure us of heartaches too."

Ricardo surprised him when he returned to the subject of pox, riding the mustard fields later in the afternoon. The two had exhausted their mounts, trudging through the soggy land. Peasants dredged channels, crisscrossing the fields, to drain the water and revive the shoots that had drowned in the untimely rains. Their noisy calls distracted Antonio. He felt ready to argue with his friend no matter what objections were raised by him.

"The Chinese know a secret cure for pox, and I must go to them to find it."

"All right, Tino," Ricardo replied, when he had had time to digest his friend's words. "But first you must get married."

"Marry! Marry who?" Antonio thought Ricardo was pulling his leg.

"Marry and be sorry?" He recited the phrase common among bachelors.

"You'll be sorry later if you don't. Who'll want to give you their daughter if they know about your father?"

"What does my poor father have to do with . . ."

"Like father like son, they'd say. As good a doctor as his father, and as rotten as him." Ricardo made a grim face. "Once people find out about him, you'll no longer be the most eligible bachelor in Lisbon." They stopped under a tall baobab tree, brought by Ricardo's grandfather from Madagascar, where he was rumored to have been a slaving baron. Its trunk had swollen with rainwater, and Ricardo tapped it with his whip as if expecting it to break and drench them in a fountain.

He's in a hurry to marry me off to Arees. How clever of him, trying to infect me with the shame of pox . . ..

"You must marry someone you're familiar with, from a family that knows you well. Those who can vouch not only for your talent but also your soundness to produce healthy babies and lead a long married life," Ricardo announced, putting on a serious face.

He's ready to vouch for me to his little sister!

"Maybe your wife can go with you to China. She can save your stomach from their ghastly treats!"

Maybe my wife will stop me from going! Antonio smiled to himself. *That's what Rogue Ricardo thinks. Married men will do anything to please their wives. Once married, I'll forget about China.*

"You couldn't simply disappear like your father, could you? What would your friends think? Your fellow doctors and nurses? And the matron? After marrying, you can go on a long holiday to somewhere strange like China. There you can do your business . . ." Ricardo smirked. "I mean the business with your wife and your business with pox."

Does he know the way it is with me and Arees? Antonio wondered if he should confide in his best friend about his sister, how they'd stood on the brink of a courtship for months, whether he should tell Ricardo what he truly felt about her, the fact that he was drawn to Arees but confused by her ways. He didn't know what she truly felt about him, if she took him to be no more than her brother's friend. He hadn't had too many arguments with her when she'd come to see him at the All Saints and awaited her turn like a patient. She'd met him in his chamber with

her gift—a volume of Voltaire's *Candide*—then played the doctor, holding the monaural stethoscope to Antonio's chest and listening to him
breathing through the ivory earpiece. She had made fun of his surgical
box when he visited her back at the Nicola. "Behold! Dr. Maria's forceps
could rid us of the House of 'Bragança!'" Her friends were plainly suspicious of him, he could see, perplexed at their extraordinary mismatch.
Ricardo would know certainly, by the way he looked at her when she
blew smoke through her fine nostrils or when she pranced about the
room in her anarchist's black, that his practical mind was trying hard to
solve the problem of Arees, the dreamer.

"Maybe the one I know will wait till I've returned. Maybe she won't
worry about my reputation or that of my father." Antonio looked up at the
tall baobab reputed to live for five thousand years. His friend patted his
horse and turned the animal around to make their way back.

"You can try, but I must warn you about China, that you may come
back a different man."

Antonio laughed as he rode along. "You mean come back with a
Manchu pigtail and eyes like sardines?"

"You may no longer know who you are, even your friends may
avoid you like a stranger."

"Even a certain horsebreeder, the rogue who eats like four men
and dances like a deer?"

Ricardo sighed. "I don't know, Tino . . . all I know is no one returns
from China smelling of Parfum de Grasse!"

Later at night the two sat drinking, after Clara had left to put the
children to bed. The sound of Arees playing her viola came from the
garden's tree house, aching but full of inner harmonies. *Is it the sound
of love that's waiting to be felt?* Antonio wondered. *The sound she makes
when that love is near?* His friend sat quietly, having argued all evening
with his sister over royals and republicans, over the merits of a "French
Revolution" to upturn their Christian kingdom won ten centuries ago
from the Moors.

"You'll miss it all if you go now," Ricardo seemed sad at Antonio's
plans.

"You mean miss the grand opening?" Antonio thought Ricardo was
talking about Campo Pequeno, the new bullring that was due to open soon.

"No, the assassination of the king." He sighed, then looked away toward the tree house. "I know why you're going. It isn't the Chinese cure you're after. It has nothing to do with treating your father. You are too good a doctor not to know that he'll die soon. You're going away because you can't bear to see him die."

Antonio stirred in his seat.

"Every death reminds you of your mother, doesn't it? That's why you hide in your doctor's chamber when a dying patient is brought to the All Saints. That's why you never treat syphilis."

It had taken Antonio more than a few tries to win Ricardo Silva over. First at his friend's quinta, then at their favorite pastelaria and after several long walks along the Tagus, he was able to convince Ricardo that the heretic was worth at least a throw of the dice, that he'd return from China with or without the Yellow Emperor's cure before the feast of St. Anthony and seek the saint's blessings for a solid life, treating patients and fathering babies with a new wife.

Then, reluctantly, and at Antonio's insistence, his friend had taken him over to meet Bernard Danziger, the English owner of a shipping fleet. He was all set to sail for Macau and promised to take the young doctor along on his run to Little Portugal, reaching the silk fair in time before the "Japs vanished with every silkworm, dead or alive!"

II
PEKING
The Yellow Emperor's Canon

From the hull of the *Santa Cruz*, Antonio saw Macau. Rising from the mist like a ghost, it seemed a spitting twin of his very own Lisbon. Lush forests flanked a bald hilltop, and spread an even carpet of green down to the coast. White adobe homes knelt on the beach like grieving widows. "It's the city of sorrow," Marcello Valignoni, the Italian artist who lived in Macau, told him. He drew portraits of the city's hongs, the rich Chinese merchants, and vain foreigners who pretended to be their lords. "You'll see when we drop anchor." Antonio spotted a white villa sitting on top of a hill, at the highest point of the island. The Praya Grande wound its way past docks full of European homes with large bay windows and wrought-iron fences. Nearer, they saw steeples rising out of barrios in the market streets and the enormous façade of the São Paulo Church.

"In China it's called the City of God, but it's better known as the City of Sad Wives!" Marcello Valignoni chuckled. Passengers of the steamship clapped as Mr. Danziger, the owner, popped a bottle of Monopole to celebrate their arrival. The captain fired a shot into the air to alert the harbor master, and a roaring group of merchants dropped a fistful of coins into the sea to wish themselves luck.

The Italian nudged Antonio. "Coolie traders. They're here to raid the barracoons. Every able-bodied man they can find will be bought and sent over to goldmines in America." He smiled at Antonio's disbelief. "They'll pay with opium brought from Calcutta." One of them danced a gig on deck, cheered on by his friends.

"He's happy because he'll meet his shore wife soon. They're *all* happy, hoping to see the children born while they were away, raised by their sad Chinese mothers." Bernard Danziger came over and offered them both a drink of the champagne that he had stocked up on before they left Lisbon.

Standing on the gangplanks, Antonio paid close attention to the portraitist as he described the "faces of Macau" on show.

"This one's Dutch with a drop of Chinese," Valignoni pointed toward a boy with sunken chest and blue eyes selling crab apples, and his friend, who was "pure Madras, as black as a Malagasy." Antonio heard him over the din of departing passengers eager to leave the ship, none more so than those who'd spent six weeks on sea from Lisbon to the China coast. He felt lonely in the crowd, without a shore wife or a back-slapping officer of the magistracy come to greet him, even a lay brother to show him his way to the nearest mission.

"You'd be staying with the lord, I hear!" preparing to leave with his retinue of servants, Bernard Danziger told Antonio. The coolie traders fell silent as someone pointed out a solitary figure on a Chinese sedan, sitting under a parasol and holding up opera glasses to her eyes.

"Dona Elvira! The lord's wife!"

Ricardo Silva had made arrangements for Antonio's stay in Little Portugal.

"You'll need friends in China, more than you need here. They'll have to teach you everything, starting with how to speak Chinese. They must find your heretic for you, otherwise you'll spend your whole life looking for him."

Antonio had protested. It couldn't be that hard to learn the Chinese cure if it did in fact exist, he had argued, but Ricardo was quick to refute him. "If it was easy to find, it'd be sold in every whorehouse in the world." He'd need no less than a Ricardo Silva to pave his way, his friend had boasted, then offered his godmother, Dona Elvira.

"You thought she was your mother when you were a boy, didn't you?" Ricardo had chuckled.

Antonio remembered Dona Elvira. She had lived in sunny Madeira with her husband, Dom Afonso de Oliveira, the island's governor, and visited her friend, Ricardo's mother, during the period of Lent. She was the good fairy of every child's dream, arriving each year laden with gifts, and she had a special corner in her heart for Antonio, the motherless boy. He remembered coming home from Ricardo's and begging his father to fetch Dona Elvira. He must bring her back, he'd plead with him, from his friend's house that she'd escaped to from her box under the earth.

"From Madeira's queen, she has become the empress of Macau!" Dom Afonso, Ricardo said, had been sent, against his wishes, from the island of wine to the island of vice to live out the last years of his magistracy. His wife, though, had relished the change. "She dresses like a Chinese empress, smokes the opium pipe, and knows everything there is to know about China. Might even have a syphilitic or two among her friends!" He had sent word about Antonio's visit to his godmother and the governor. Looking sadder than ever before, Ricardo had advised him, "She'll be your ally. Just don't let her keep you back in Macau."

Antonio greeted the lady under the parasol and received the heartiest embrace of his life, gushing and full of scents that as a boy had reminded him of his mother. He was overcome with an instant relief from his long journey as Dona Elvira, chatting away merrily, sighed and fawned over her Tino. Leaving the port and the crowded streets behind, it didn't take long for their sedan to reach the white villa on top of the hill, at the highest point of the island.

Antonio was struck by the governor's villa, even before he stepped into the large spacious verandas cooled by monsoon breezes, or passed through the tall doors that opened into rooms with high ceilings and shuttered windows. The gardens far surpassed the most sumptuous quintas he'd seen, leading into Moorish arches at the entrance. A herd of baboons, the size of sheep and hairy like lions, sat on the elaborate columns and made faces at him. Dona Elvira called out to them, as if they were her favorite pets. A row of servants greeted them in a jumble of tongues. Dona Elvira clapped her hands for a maid to appear quickly and sprinkle them with rose water, "to keep out the street smells."

The bell was rung to announce the midday meal, and his hostess led Antonio to a large table covered in plain white cloth set with dishes and glasses, silverware and napkins, behind a brilliantly painted Japanese screen to guard them from the afternoon sun. "In the East you must get used to eating your biggest meal in the middle of the day, then sleep all afternoon to digest it." Pointing out the dishes—the pies and broths, spiced meats and curried fish—she stopped to reassure Antonio. "We do more than eat and sleep. The evenings are meant for work, when the rain comes to cool the hot heads." Dona Elvira ate with her hands like a native, rinsing them in a silver bowl at the end of each course. "You'll get used to things quickly. Most foreigners do, and then they don't want to leave! But it'll take you a while to trust your tongue!" She watched him hesitate, examining the bowls. "Your nose might not know what you're tasting. Might smell a carp while eating birds' nests, or mushrooms for camels' feet!"

"What happens to those who don't get used to things?" Antonio asked cautiously.

Dona Elvira chuckled. "They get used to opium, and forget where they are!"

Antonio rose to greet Dom Afonso, the governor, known commonly as the "lord" among the Macanese. At the age of fifty, he looked seventy—white haired and hollow cheeked, with a half-contemptuous smile—resembling more a scholar at Lisbon's Sociedade de Geografia than the protector of his subjects. Returning passengers on the *Santa Cruz* made fun of Dom Afonso, the lord who slept all day, coming alive only to show off his mastery of seafaring to his friends. His eloquence on the northwesterly monsoon and tropical doldrums far exceeded his interest in taxing the opium farms and policing the vice dens for which Little Portugal was notorious the world over. He was the sleeping giant that made Macau such a safe haven for adventurers.

"Our Tino has come to find a cure for pox." Dona Elvira seemed amused by the idea even as she presented it to her husband. "How brilliant of him to think of the Chinese, and their smelly herbs. Maybe they can teach him how to suck out the poison with their needles."

Pecking at the dishes, Dom Afonso seemed cold to the idea. "Why would the Chinese care? Why worry about a cure when they could simply chop off the rotten part and solve the problem?"

"You mean turn the syphilitic into a eunuch?" Dona Elvira exclaimed.

"That won't help." Antonio spoke quietly. "Syphilis is known to spread quickly from the genitals to the whole body. They'd have to chop off the victim's neck to solve the problem."

Dom Afonso shrugged. "What's stopping them from doing just that? Men are killed for smaller crimes here." His eyes roved around the table till they found laranja da China—sweet oranges that smelled like roses. Dona Elvira pressed on with Antonio's idea, slicing and serving fruit, while a servant cleared the table for desserts.

"But they do know more about curing diseases than us, don't they? Fewer women die of childbirth here than back home. The bazaars swarm with fleas and yet none die from the plague. Maybe he can learn from them how to cure the pox, the 'Portuguese disease' as they call it."

Antonio sipped the Chinese tea, poured by Dona Elvira. She claimed it had the power to digest even the most robust of tables, but he choked at the bitter taste. He too had heard about the miracle cures of Chinese doctors from his fellow passengers, but doubted them.

"If our Tino masters syphilis, they'll build his statue in every whorehouse in Europe!" Dona Elvira wasn't prepared to give in to her husband's coldness. "We'd be famous too, for having helped the brilliant Portuguese doctor!"

Dom Afonso gave her the sad look of a fatalist. He didn't share his wife's exuberance. An idea was simply an idea, not a fact, like gold till it was discovered in the New World, or Vasco da Gama's journey on the Carriera da India for spices a mere four centuries ago. After years in the colonies he was used to adventurers, and to his wife, who was to him the greatest adventurer of all.

"You must introduce him to the mandarins in Peking, those who can help him find a good Chinese doctor. He'll need a guide too who can take him there."

"He should stay here, before he goes anywhere." Dom Afonso rose from the table, taking over from his wife and giving Antonio a glimpse of his magisterial side. "And spend the whole of autumn and winter before he's ready. He must go every day to the Jesuit College and learn to speak Chinese."

Dona Elvira's mouth fell open. "You mean our Tino must become a *casado* before he becomes a pox doctor?"

Dom Afonso shook his head. "He doesn't have to go native, take a Chinese girl and all that. Simply know their tongue well enough"—he smiled cynically—"to understand the secret when it's spoken into his ear."

"Two full seasons . . . ?" Antonio asked. *Would it take that long to master Chinese?* His host seemed to read his mind.

"It takes much longer, but our wizard at the Jesuit College can help you learn faster."

Dona Elvira's face lit up. "You mean Joachim Saldanha?"

"He's a *christãos-novos*," Dona Elvira told Antonio, when he asked her to tell him more about his Chinese teacher. "Well, not him, his fore-fathers really. They were Jews who had converted and become Christians to save their skins during the Inquisition. Most were shipped off to the colonies along with lepers and convicts, but luck had spared his lot. He grew up in Lisbon's Judiarias cleansed of Jews and their synagogues. Then he joined the Brotherhood and traveled the world."

"A *christãos-novos* speaking Chinese?" Antonio searched for the missing pieces of the puzzle.

"Like all Jesuits, he went first to the Dark Continent, but had to return on account of poor health. Then he enrolled at the Oratorio of St. Martin, and surprised everyone by learning to speak the most difficult tongue in the world." The padre was a much sought after teacher, Dona Elvira said, popular among officers and merchants. "He knows our colonies of Estado da India like the back of his hand. Name it and he has sailed everywhere: Goa to Malacca with cotton for spices; Malacca to Macau for silk; Macau to Nagasaki for swords and silver. He has fought against the trade too, to stop the smuggling of coolies, and has a scar on his neck for going against both the Chinese and the Portuguese."

"He's what you'd call a real character," Dona Elvira said, as she strolled with Antonio on the Praya Grande. "Like Marcello the artist, and Gutzlaff the German phrenologist, who's the only one to have touched the heads of the superstitious hongs."

Unlike foreign ladies who always appeared in public on their sedans, Dona Elvira chose frequently to go about on foot with her atten-dants and urged Antonio to do the same if he wished to be truly fasci-nated by the sights of Little Portugal. Following her around, he saw more to fascinate him in a day than he'd seen in six weeks during his fifteen-thousand-mile journey on the *Santa Cruz*. Even more than the blind fortune-teller or sellers of singing birds, the butchers who imitated screaming pigs to attract customers or the tiny shops that sold offerings of dough animals for the gods, he was struck by the black raven, even blacker than those on Lisbon's coat of arms, fighting with the baboons, stabbing their eyes and stealing their crumbs.

"Foreign gentleman mustn't forget to taste the Eastern fruits," Dona Elvira smiled, as she caught Antonio eyeing the *mestizhinas*—the Eurasian women who flaunted their black hair and magnolia skin, dressed like princesses in silk jackets and embroidered shawls, eyes heavy with mascara and lips reddened by betel juice. "Come, I'll show you what the Chinese prize even more than their women." She took him past the shops of Rua do Bazarihno to see the "traveling women"— inflatable leather dolls made for the comfort of Macanese men who wished to spend a pleasurable evening without their wives.

"You must taste the golden lilies before you go. Then tell me why Western men find them so tempting?" Dona Elvira gave Antonio a naughty look. "Unless, of course, you're saving yourself for your one and only one back home."

Has Ricardo told her about Arees? He wondered if his friend was re-lying on his godmother to talk him into marrying his little sister.

"You can do whatever you want in Macau." Dona Elvira spoke like a confidant. "Then go home and be the perfect husband! Your secret will stay secure here." She laid her hand on her bosom and winked at Antonio.

Back to the villa for their afternoon tea, Antonio met Joachim Saldanha. He had come to see Dom Afonso to seek his help for the reconstruction of São Paulo Church after it had been vandalized, yet again, by miscreants who claimed the Portuguese were kidnapping Chinese babies to sell as slaves to ships' captains. The governor took snuff from his bottle and blew his nose. The padres were far too lenient with their flocks, he complained. There were reasons to believe that the crime had been committed by a native Christian who was unhappy with the church's prohibition of ancestor worship. He'll confess with just a light whipping, the governor thought, and willingly bear the expenses.

"Ever since Francis Xavier resolved to enter China in the sixteenth century and Father Metteo Ricci began his splendid work of building the mission, there's been trouble over accepting Chinese rites into Christian practices." Dom Afonso lectured the padre, who was busy writing up a detailed list of items damaged by the incident. "Why not accept their rites? A pig's head on the altar won't worry our Blessed Virgin, will it?"

With his pale face and unblinking eyes, beaklike nose and curly hair, the master linguist resembled a seller of magical potions in the old bazaars of Lisbon. Barely looking up from his notes, Joachim Saldanha answered Dom Afonso's complaint. "It's different this time. Now they're blaming us for a lot more than banning ancestor worship."

"You mean for employing Chinese men as sedan bearers?" Dona Elvira thought the padre was referring to the objections raised by mandarins over "white devils" riding on the backs of natives.

Joachim Saldanha shook his head. "Now they are blaming us for poisoning their rivers, for diverting clouds from their fields, for running our railways over lakes and trapping their ancestors' spirits with our telegraph lines."

"That's silly!" Antonio blurted out. He thought Joachim Saldanha was joking. Dom Afonso introduced the two of them, then asked the padre if he knew of a Chinese remedy for the pox. "Out of a million sinners, you must know at least one who's been forgiven and cured?"

With his pen up in the air, Joachim Saldanha thought for a while then spoke cheerfully. "No one has yet asked if the Chinese can treat syphilis. No foreigner, that is. A *Nei ching* master will have the answer to that question."

"Who?" Dona Elvira cupped her ear.

"A Chinese doctor who's mastered the Yellow Emperor's Canon, the book that describes all their medical laws," Joachim Saldanha explained.

"And why would a Chinese doctor be ready to share his secret with foreigners?" Dom Afonso quizzed the padre like a true officer.

"Because it'd cure the white devils who they blame for infecting the Chinese."

"And so it's a simple matter of finding someone and getting him to spell out the method, isn't it?" Antonio inched forward on his seat, unable to hide his excitement. "There must be hundreds of such doctors in Macau." He recalled seeing a line of sick people waiting before a door marked with the sign of a hat.

"That's the undertaker's shop. The place one goes to buy one's gravestone when they think they're about to die," Joachim Saldanha said. "Macau has more quacks than doctors. One visits temples to pray when one's sick. Few can afford to make their way over to Hong Kong to be treated in a Western hospital. It won't be easy to find a good Chinese doctor, unless one takes a sampan and goes up the Pearl River to Canton, braving the opium smugglers. Peking will be far superior, especially if a true master agrees to help you out."

"Do we know any such doctor?" Dom Afonso appeared to be in a hurry. The time was approaching for his servants to prepare his opium pipe, and he wished to bring all official matters to a close before retiring for the evening.

"There is one. Dr. Xu, the empress's physician. He's known to be the best, and she trusts him completely. He'd know if . . ."

"Would Dr. Xu accept our friend here as his student?" The governor pointed to Antonio and rose to leave. "What can the Brotherhood do to convince him and advance the cause of syphilis?"

Joachim Saldanha looked at Antonio with his unblinking eyes. Dona Elvira poked him in the side and had him bow to the padre.

"Couldn't you for once help us rather than lavish favors upon the heathen?" asked Dom Afonso, seeming a touch irritated at the Jesuit father's silence.

"*You* can help him." Joachim Saldanha circled the total under the column of expenses, and passed on the note to the governor. "Dr. Xu might be willing if you wrote to him."

"The imperial doctor accepting a Portuguese request?" Dom Afonso was sceptical still.

His mistress the empress is more open to foreigners now than ever before, Joachim Saldanha said. "Loss in the two opium wars has taught her to respect the white devils. It could even make her feel superior to us, the barbarians."

Dom Afonso nodded and smiled at him. "I shall help, if you promise to help our friend learn enough Chinese to conduct his business in Peking."

"Enough Chinese by when?" Joachim Saldanha looked worried.

"By spring, when he can safely take a barge up the Yangtze."

"In less than half a year?" the padre exclaimed. "That's impossible!"

Dona Elvira patted him on the back, and motioned her maid to enter with the tea tray. Smiling kindly at the padre, she lifted the hem of the finely crocheted cloth and urged him to take a look under it. Joachim Saldanha peeked cautiously, running his eyes over the feast of roasted turkey and pickled cabbage, ringed by bowls of fresh fruits and a steaming pot of jasmine tea. It didn't take long for the frown to disappear, and make his face break out into a smile.

Antonio hoped he'd sleep soundly at the governor's villa, but his nightmares kept him awake. On successive nights he dreamed that his father was riding on a Chinese sedan, not the type with glass windows used by mandarins, but on a hammocklike bed made of rope. His bearers were shouting to clear the road as onlookers thronged to watch him pass by. Faces peered down from balconies; shopkeepers came out of their shops to join the crowd. It seemed none had seen a syphilitic before. With his spotted face, he looked like a new species that had arrived at the docks. Everyone fell into a hushed silence at the sight of him. Then an old woman covered her face and started to wail. Street urchins ran after the bearers and pelted them with stones. Men formed a wall to guard the street shrines from his father's passing shadow, and the head priest of Ama Temple led the sedan down a blind lane to a shop marked with the undertaker's hat.

Antonio woke and heard the surf roaring. The cool breeze of the receding monsoon blew in through the open window, and the chill of late autumn made him shiver. Soon it'd be the best time in southern China, he recalled Dona Elvira telling him. Winter would calm the typhoons, and spread a glow around the horizon. It was the time for nest-building, and children enacting plays by the street side. The Chinese like to hold their weddings in winter, to have babies arrive the following year at the autumn moon festival. Macau's weather was far better than Peking's, she had boasted, known for its harsh winters and scorching summers.

Antonio was grateful to Dona Elvira. Her unexpected warmth had taken him by surprise, till he realized that she too had thought of him as her son, having lost both her children in a terrible shipwreck when they were still young. It was stranger still how the cynical governor had come alive playing Sailors' Bluff with him, a card game for hardened rogues, during evenings mellowed by opium. He wished Dom Afonso would tell him about China and the Chinese. Was it true that they were smarter than Europeans, having invented the compass and gunpowder, tea, ink and paper, even the umbrella? He hoped the governor could tell him about the secret workings of the Chinese mind, how it went about solving puzzles and inventing things.

"The mystery of the Chinese is like the mystery of the sea. It fools those who claim to know it best. No one understands them, that's the plain truth." Dom Afonso had curtailed further talk about China when Antonio raised the subject during one evening, and had returned to Sailors' Bluff.

Has Ricardo told the governor and Dona Elvira about my father? She didn't probe him about anything, except his women. "Boys become naughtier when they grow up." She had chided him for remaining a bachelor, when all his friends had already got sick of their wives. *What did she know about him and Arees?* Had Ricardo kept his father's illness a secret, to keep him eligible in her eyes?

"Why must Tino learn Chinese when you could go with him to Peking and help him with the empress's doctor?" Dona Elvira pressed Joachim Saldanha one evening after Dom Afonso had left for his opium. The padre was busy feasting on a roasted chicken, his lean frame standing in sharp contrast to his large appetite, the maid rushing back and forth to refill the fast emptying tray.

"Why can't you simply translate for Tino, which will make life a lot easier for all?"

With half the bird inside his mouth, Joachim Saldanha shook his head, speaking with difficulty as he munched on the juicy meat. "He won't need Chinese for his lessons."

"Then why?" Dona Elvira gave him a puzzled look.

"You mean the empress's doctor knows English?" Antonio asked. Dom Afonso had told him that Chinese of the highest class had learned to speak that "foreign tongue" given their dealings with British merchants and officers. *If that is true then he could get what he wanted a lot quicker than expected. A month's trip to Peking on a barge and a few more with his teacher . . . that's all!*

Wiping his face on his sleeve, the padre reached for the fruit platter. He held up a bunch of grapes to check by the color if they had ripened well. "Senior mandarins in Peking know enough English to quarrel with officers of the foreign legation led by the British. They've had to negotiate two full treaties with them, and know how dangerous words can be. English speakers are everywhere in China and the Chinese are learning fast." To prove his point, Joachim Saldanha spoke at length about the Irishman Robert Hart and William Martin from Indiana, who had won the trust of high officials and entered the inner circle of imperial advisors in Peking.

"Dr. Xu can speak to Antonio not in English but American. He has worked with the Locke Mission in China, helped American doctors treat peasants. He has known men from Boston and Chicago, known their wives too, who came with their husbands and learned to speak Chinese even better than the natives!"

"Then why must our young friend spend half a year of his life mastering a tongue he'll never use, when he could be back home sooner doing what he does best?" Dona Elvira seemed more than ready to disagree with her husband's plans for Antonio.

"Because he must talk to his servants." Joachim Saldanha bit into the white flesh of litchis after he had carefully peeled their prickly skin.

"Talk to servants!"

He nodded. "He'd have to stay in Peking in order to learn everything from Dr. Xu. He'd have to tell his servants what he likes to eat, what turns his stomach, when he would take his lunch and dinner, the 'early rice' and 'late rice' as they call it. He must scold them if his bathwater is too hot or too cold. He must instruct his sedan bearers about his destination. He must bargain with a shopkeeper if he chooses to buy a dog to keep as a pet. He must . . ."

"You can speak to his servants for him, can't you?" Dona Elvira scolded the padre for going on about trivial matters. "Nothing that you've told me so far makes much sense."

Finished with fruits, Joachim Saldanha looked around the table for more food, then grabbed a fistful of almonds and put them inside the flaps of his robe. "If I go with him, then he might have to do my work."

"What work?" Antonio was interested in finding out what Joachim Saldanha did besides putting his Chinese to the service of the Brotherhood.

"Close a church that's been gutted, for example." The padre spoke slowly. "Take stock of the damages, and collect the remaining things."

"What remaining things?" Antonio asked.

"A hacked angel or an apostle smeared with dung. Pieces of a gutted altar, the severed head of our Lord, a torn Bible."

Dona Elvira had fallen silent with a knowing look on her face.

"There might still be more work remaining." Joachim Saldanha went on.

Antonio gave him a questioning look. The padre shrugged then rose to leave. "Might have to bury a pair of nuns who'd slit each other's throat to escape their tormentors."

Antonio went for the first time to the Jesuit College for his lessons with Joachim Saldanha a few days after his arrival in Macau. He'd expected to find a full class of students. Demand had grown among foreigners to learn Chinese in the aftermath of the opium wars. "Half of China belongs to us now," Marcello Valignoni had boasted. "Our gunboats have wrested five treaty ports from the emperor, where we can do whatever we like without his permission. The Chinese gold rush has started! You can buy and sell as much as you like, if you can understand what they say, that is!" Dom Afonso had confirmed the optimism of the Italian artist. European merchants were sniffing around the country, trying to sell everything to the Chinese, from cannons to railways. Their agents, arriving by the score, had turned the fortunes of Hong Kong and Macau. "China had always supplied the West, now she's hungry for the miracles of Europe and America. It tells you what the vanquished will do to win back their pride!" The governor had pulled Antonio's leg as they played cards: "You might never hold a scalpel again, if you learn Chinese and become the richest Portuguese merchant in history!"

At the college he was asked to wait for Joachim Saldanha in his attic. Climbing the long flight of stairs, Antonio wondered where the students and teachers had disappeared to. Stories of Jesuit orphans regularly made their rounds at the governor's villa. Dona Elvira never tired of telling her teatime guests about the brave Brothers who rescued abandoned children of opium addicts and the orphans of sailors and their shore wives and raised them at Santa Casa de Misericordia—the Holy House of Mercy—before enrolling them at the Jesuit College.

Light through the open windows blinded Antonio before he could take a proper look around the attic. Signs of the padre were all around him—a tattered robe hanging from the doornail and the smell of stale food. The desk was cluttered with sheaves of papers, resembling a clerk's cubbyhole. A row of boxes lined the walls, some with their lids open, looking like coffins. Antonio walked around the desk and glanced at the papers, then peeked inside one of the boxes. A soot black face with gouged eyes stared back at him. The head seemed to have been hacked off a female figure carved out of wood, the neck showing rough marks of a blunt axe. Someone had painted the male member on her forehead, and a dark streak ran down her locks.

"She's our Lady of the Sorrows." Antonio heard Joachim Saldanha's voice behind him. "Come from the Coromandel Coast to grace our mission in Souzhou." He read the bewilderment on Antonio's face then came around to shut the lid. "She was called a baby eater after a dozen children died of typhus in surrounding villages."

A pair of wings stuck out from another box; an arm holding a quill and a shepherd's staff among a jumble of wooden bits, some old and rotting and some that showed the fresh paint of their makers.

"You'll find the archangel there, and each of the twelve apostles." Joachim Saldanha led Antonio to a largish crate arrived recently. It had the marks of the French steamship *La Gascogne* which had brought it from Peking as cargo. He unlocked the hinges and nudged Antonio to take a look.

"It's the work of the mob that looted the nunnery in Jilin province." Antonio slammed the lid down seeing a pig's head, carved neatly in rosewood on the shoulders of Jesus.

"Why do you . . . ?" Antonio searched for words.

"You mean why do I collect these things?" Joachim Saldanha filled in his question, and went about pushing the boxes around to create more room. "To remind us that we aren't ready yet."

"Ready for what?"

"To live together as brothers."

Later as they sat across the desk, Joachim Saldanha taught Antonio the Chinese symbol for God and sighed, gazing out of his attic.

In the months that followed, Antonio surprised his hosts. They had expected him to struggle with his lessons, to be frustrated by the earful of strange notes, revise his plans even, to pay a visit to Peking. Most foreigners give up on Chinese within days of starting, Dom Afonso had warned Antonio. "It's the way they use their mouth and nose to control the flow of air. Something one learns as a child, not after tissues have hardened."

Dona Elvira disagreed with him. There was no shortage of fluent speakers among foreigners. She didn't doubt her Tino's abilities, but quarreled with the harsh regimen imposed by Joachim Saldanha on his student. "He's killing him with work," she complained to her husband after Antonio had failed to make his appearance, yet again, at her "early rice," asking for his meal to be sent over to his room. "He's behaving like a child eager to please his teacher." Dona Elvira scowled as she filled a plate and thrust it into the maid's hand. Waking early, Antonio walked every day to the Jesuit College refusing the sedan as it'd give him a chance to practice his Chinese with pedestrians and shopkeepers. He spent the whole morning in the attic with Joachim Saldanha, kept his teacher on his toes with sharp questions, turning down even his offer to visit the Catholic mission's gruel kitchen. When the college filled with students, he found himself a place in Mr. Gutzlaff's phrenology studio to pore over his notes. The German head reader was only too happy to lend Antonio his room filled with plaster models of human heads marked with strange notations, as he went about visiting his rich clients and assuring them of continuing good fortune.

Back in the evening, he buried his nose in his books, ignoring the governor's call to join him for a game of Bluff. Dom Afonso shuffled the cards and waited for his young guest, till he heard the rush of the dinner table being set for "late rice."

"He can't be studying during the Chinese New Year." Dona Elvira told Joachim Saldanha sternly when he came to collect her dues to the Casa. "Even schoolchildren are forbidden to touch their books." The padre smiled. He had brought news to cheer up his hostess: "Riots have broken out again all over China with the passing of winter. The anti-Christian gangs are up to their mischief and I must go soon to Tientsin to help the mission there. Given my student's rapid progress, I could accompany Antonio to Peking and introduce him to Dr. Xu," Joachim Saldanha said, and eyed the empty dining table.

"And who'll bring him back if they get up to mischief in Peking?"

"Maybe you could ask your friends, Polly and Cedric Hart of the British Legation, to keep an eye on Antonio?"

"Polly! Of course she'll look after him." Dona Elvira's mood lifted at the mention of her friend, and she clapped for her maid to serve everyone her favorite claret.

"Is your student ready?" Dom Afonso asked Joachim Saldanha after Antonio had retired from dinner, and the padre had emptied every tray on the table. "Will he be able to hold his own among the Chinese?"

Joachim Saldanha smiled. "He's more than ready. I'd keep him here at the College if he wasn't in such a rush to solve the mystery of pox."

Dona Elvira seemed both happy and sad at the turn of events, trying her best to keep calm as she fussed over Antonio's travel arrangements. "He should take gifts for Dr. Xu and his hosts, shouldn't he?" she asked her husband. "Chiming clocks and musical boxes, the kind the Chinese love?"

The telescope might interest the Chinese more, Dom Afonso thought, but Joaquim Saldanha scotched all talk of gifts. "They might want his services in exchange. Have him cut open a stomach and remove a stone, sever a gangrenous limb, or take out a dead baby from its mother's womb."

Dona Elvira went to Antonio's room after the padre had left and the governor had started to doze. She drew the curtains and arranged the scattered notes by the bed. She sighed as she watched him sleep. It was time to fill up her Tino's traveling portmanteau. Two seasons seemed to have passed quickly, and she regretted losing him again. *Why must he leave everyone behind just on a whim? What made him learn Chinese as if his life depended on it?* His face had turned red and she stroked his forehead to smoothen the knitted brows, speaking to him gently as he muttered in his sleep. Joachim Saldana's burnt angels must be troubling him; she blamed the priest and his morbid obsession. Or could it be the curse of China that had started to affect him too, the curse that turned everyone to opium?

Waking, Antonio thought his dead mother had come to relieve him from his nightmare. He sank his face, drenched in tears, in Dona Elvira's arms just as he would when he was a boy.

❦

Real China filled Antonio's mind. Traveling by barge on the Grand Canal, which drew the Yangtze into the capital, he saw the treachery of silt damming up the river, with only short tracts left navigable at a stretch. Square sails floated over rice and millet fields. Men and boys towed the barges along the banks, earning a precarious living when the winds were favorable. Mules and women worked the fields side by side, hitched to the same plough. For the most part he was struck by the sheer frenzy of cultivation and the business of feeding so many mouths. Rivers teemed with boats that rushed about with their produce: rice boats and tea boats; dog boats bound for the butchers' block; fishing boats and flower boats. The eel fishers appeared as dark specs on the horizon: men kneeling with one foot on their sledges, gliding over the soft and slippery mud on the lookout for bubbles rising from empty holes in the earth. Opium boats plied the inlets at night, scores of "fast crabs" chased by the mandarins in their "scrambling dragons" armed with sharp spears and large guns on the bows.

Whenever he was awake on his journey, Antonio talked to Joachim Saldanha. Even as he dozed, he heard him speaking with the boatmen in a voice that had the power to draw a crowd to a pulpit. Antonio asked him about his travels, and he recited names of places that he didn't know existed, like São Salvador do Congo, where he had been sent to preach to the slaves or to Fremona to fight Ethiopians who had banished the Brotherhood.

"You can go very far with the Chinese but if you go too far they'll chop your head off," Joachim Saldanha said, when Antonio asked him about natives and foreigners.

"Going so far as building a church and reciting the Bible?" A priest was scolding fishermen for setting their fish traps too close to the temple's banks, and Antonio followed him closely.

Scratching his beard, Joachim Saldanha observed the priest too. "They hate us for luring away their flock. Curse the Chinese who've converted to our faith, call them 'rice Christians,' for having heard the call of their stomachs, not that of the Lord!"

"It's no different than fighting over rice and fish, is it?" Antonio wondered if their boatmen were unhappy slaving for the two foreigners as they battled the river's strong currents. His companion seemed to relish their company, sharing their meals without hesitation, even the dried fish that turned Antonio's stomach. It would take them weeks to cross the maze of canals that sprang off the river, dock in fishing villages, sleep under thatched roofs if they spent a night on shore or under the sail covered from head to toe in mosquito nets. Could there be trouble on their way, he asked Joachim Saldanha, like that faced by the Tientsin mission?

"The irony was that the Catholic Sisters had become Chinese." Joachim Saldanha explained to Antonio. "Not Chinese simply in the way they ate and dressed, but started to act like their faith healers, handing out rosaries to the dying, or a sprig from the Madonna's bouquet to the mother of a sick child. Their flock, of course, took them for miracle cures and were angry when they failed to bring back the dead and dying." Joachim Saldanha gazed up at the horizon as if he could see the smoldering church of Tientsin. "Then the rumors started. The Sisters were poisoning villagers, sucking out the breath of babies by their black magic. The evil foreigners were claimed even to drain the milk of nursing mothers to make wine."

"How can anybody sane believe all that?" Antonio wondered if he was hearing yet another ships' tale from the usually reliable padre. Joachim Saldanha kept silent then sighed. "It doesn't take much for the sane to believe in rumors. Just like we believed that Jews killed Jesus."

"What happened to the Sisters?" Antonio was anxious for Joachim Saldanha to finish his story.

"All but one of the thirty-nine were killed. Tortured brutally, then set on fire, with the church." The remaining one was hiding somewhere, sheltered perhaps by a kind family, Joachim Saldanha said. He was traveling to Tientsin to bring her back to safety. Antonio hesitated asking him about the burnt church, whether he would try to recover the remains. The padre seemed lost in his thoughts, ignoring the sampan that had rowed up near their barge to sell fresh dumplings.

"They are no worse than us, or savages as some foreigners make them out to be. There are bad people among us too, just as bad as these killers, those who pretend to be emperors themselves, and padres who're no better than greedy traders. They want to take China away from the Chinese. And you . . ."

Antonio gave Joaquim Saldanha a probing look. "And I?"

"You've come to take their best, if you can find it."

He praised Antonio for trying to learn from the Chinese. "It'd be good for Europeans to know the real China rather than simply buy her tea and silk. Just like we learned from them about astronomy." Antonio thought to seize his chance and ask Joachim Saldanha about syphilis, if he had heard rumors about unspeakable diseases and their farm remedies, or about drowned flower girls who had infected powerful customers and paid with their lives.

The padre couldn't tell him much about the pox, except that brothel owners routinely confided in him their fear of execution if a high official was struck with a "plum blossom disease" after spending a night with one of their girls. But the "treatment" they had mentioned was far from any sound medical practice.

"What kind of treatment?"

Joachim Saldanha's face hardened. "I don't know much about it. You'll have to ask your teacher." Then he drew Antonio's attention to the yellowish brown thrush that had perched on their boat, making the boatmen call out its name—*hwa-mei*—attracting a flock of birds to descend on the mast.

"If it's here, it's invisible, like their dowager empress," Joachim Saldanha said, returning reluctantly to the topic of pox. "Just as feared perhaps as she is. She's the real emperor rather than her nephew, who's rumored to be sick."

"Sick with what?"

Joachim Saldanha smiled. "In China a sick emperor means a dead emperor—deposed and thrown into jail!"

"Why has his aunt imprisoned him?" Unable to follow, Antonio pressed the padre for more details.

"I am sure everyone you ask in Peking will have their own opinion about that. She's known as the Old Buddha, but she's really all of Catherine de Médicis and Jezebel of Samaria rolled into one! Empress dowager rules China from the Summer Palace in the western hills more than twenty miles away from the imperial throne at the Tartar city in the heart of Peking. It's the most beautiful palace in China, with more than a thousand pavilions and a lake large enough to drown them all. Europeans sacked it during the opium wars, but the soldiers were too dumbstruck by its beauty to loot all that was worth looting. They smashed priceless jade and porcelain, took bronze statues for gold and melted them down!"

"A thousand pavilions just for the empress?" Antonio asked.

"For the empress, her entourage and for her guests like you. Special pavilions have been built to be as comfortable as possible for foreigners who visit from time to time, such as artists from Europe and America commissioned to paint the dowager's portrait, merchants who trade in sea pearls, silk gowns and white and amber Pekinese pugs. Even expert kite fliers from Japan with their enormous kites to fly at the harvest festival."

"I shall live with the empress in her palace?" Antonio thought the padre was joking.

Joachim Saldanha nodded. "Dr. Xu has made arrangements to meet you there. You'll be the empress's neighbor at the Summer Palace, but she'll be invisible. Only lesser royals and her eunuchs are allowed to enter her sight besides the occasional visiting dignitary. She let Prince Heinrich of Prussia see her because he's the grandson of Queen Victoria, who she considers to be her soul sister!"

"How can she be invisible?" Antonio was yet to believe Saldanha.

"You might be able to hear her laugh, spot her bearers as they carry her away in her golden sedan. You'll see her barge on Kunming Lake. Her dogs might become your friends, but you'd be lucky to catch her shadow."

For the last leg of their journey, they traveled by carriage, sad to lose their talkative boatmen. A camel train from the Mongolian desert followed them; half awake, Antonio listened to their bells and the thumping hooves that passed his window. Mules carried palanquins escorted by sword-armed men. The dust of the northern Gobi had turned them into ugly duck-lings—the blackest dust of all that sticks to the hair and the eyebrows. Their carriage stopped for none but the water carriers, and the long-coated sellers of oven-baked bread. As they neared Peking, beggars crowded the streets, lame and blind, parading their deformities, ready to pounce on the visitors. The jolting carriage made a dash through them, and raised a cry that scared the horses into a gallop. He thought the wheels had trampled over the beggars, that they'd be taken for murderous foreigners.

Finally, their carriage entered an arched gateway and into the Summer Palace. Twilight had turned its lofty red walls to a charming pink. The western hills hung low over the tiled roofs of gilded pagodas. There were palaces of lacquer and gold, and gardens within gardens. Children caught dragonflies on the banks of canals, and lakes brimmed with in-candescent lilies. This was the China that he never knew existed, a place unlike the one he had conjured up on his journey on the *Santa Cruz*, or from Dom Afonso's cryptic accounts. They crossed a marble bridge, and their carriage driver pointed with his whip toward a large stone carved with a pair of fighting dragons. Antonio knew it to be the imperial symbol. "Can you take us to the empress's residence?" he asked. "She lives everywhere," the man replied with a shrug. "She can't live *every-where!*" He chided the driver. "Not in each of the thousand pavilions set over seven hundred acres!" Spring blossoms had spread a canopy over a cluster of houses with a shallow pool at their center. Antonio wanted to jump off the carriage and visit the shaded grove, but Joachim Saldanha motioned to the driver to move along till they were almost on the banks of Kunming Lake. It shimmered like a mirror and stretched beyond their sight. A row of boatmen waited at the banks like a band of gulls. Antonio waved at them, and asked his companion if he wished to take a swim. Cooped up inside the carriage, he longed to plunge into the inviting water.

"You can't go everywhere or do everything you like." Joachim Sal-danha whispered to him with a hand on his shoulder.

"Why not?" Antonio snapped back.

"Because the empress has set rules for her guests. Some parts of the palace may never be visited by a foreigner. Only a few are allowed into the temples and court chambers. You'd be told where you can go freely."

"A prisoner." Antonio made a face. "Do I have to live like one?"

"No, no, not a prisoner," Joachim Saldanha hastened to reassure him. "Think of yourself as a student here, just like you were at the Faculdade Medicina."

Antonio chuckled. "Oh, no, you don't want the dowager to have a rowdy student as her neighbor!" He teased the padre: "What if she invited me over for tea at her favorite teahouse?"

Joachim Saldanha ignored his words, and told him about the arrangements he had made with Dr. Xu. "He'll come here in a day or two after you've had a chance to rest from the journey. He can tell you all about *Nei ching*—the Yellow Emperor's Canon—and you can ask him whatever question you like."

"How about the syphilitics? Where would I meet them?" Antonio had expected to be lodged near a hospital, for his teacher to take him there on regular rounds. "Does the dowager have a special pavilion here for her favorite poxies?"

Joaquim Saldanha smiled. "Dr. Xu can tell you all about that." He asked the carriage driver to take them to the pavilion that stood all by itself at the far corner of the lake. Then he spoke to Antonio as Brother to Brother. "You'll have your own place here, and can stay as long as you like till you've found your answer. You'll be on your own, but I will be near you doing my work, and might have to ask your help from time to time."

When he entered his pavilion, Antonio saw a neatly laid out lodge among the gardens. Red pillars held up a roof of majestic green tiles, and a pair of bronze lions stood on pedestals at the lacquered door. A covered corridor joined the lodge to smaller quarters for attendants. A flowering plum tree shaded the neatly swept courtyard, with a fan-shaped lotus pond at its center. He heard a dog barking, and the sound of feet rushing in.

"Wait! You haven't told me anything about your miracle doctor."

"Dr. Xu? There isn't much to know about him, except that he's trusted by the empress, and has dealt with foreigners before. He has read Dom Afonso's letter, and is ready to help you."

"Will he teach me the prison rules too?"

Joaquim Saldanha pointed at the two attendants who had entered the courtyard just then, red faced for being late. "For that you have your very own eunuchs. They'll do your work, be your eyes and ears."

"What should I call them?" Antonio was wary at the thought of being left alone in the pavilion with his attendants, having to rely on the meager Chinese he'd learned at the Jesuit College.

"You can call them by any name you like." Joaquim Saldanha turned his unblinking eyes on Antonio. "You can call them Wangs — Little Wang and Big Wang!"

❀

In Lisbon, he needed no reason to sleep well. Here he slept lightly, waking several times during the night to chase away the beetles that had silently advanced to within striking range of the bed, scattering them with a stick like a broadside fired into the enemy's flanks. A cloud of flies settled on the windowpanes, like grains of rice thrown at random on a clean-swept floor. Reaching for the stick again, he tapped on the panes and watched the grains take flight, crossing the courtyard and descending perhaps on another pavilion, one that was quiet and snoring.

After a sleepless night, Antonio was tired. Joaquim Saldanha had arrived early morning to introduce him to Dr. Xu, and chatted away with the attendants as they waited sitting on stools in the courtyard for the Chinese doctor. He had finished inspecting the kitchen, and scolded the older eunuch. The meals might fail to fill Antonio's stomach, he might have to nibble on a steady supply of food to keep his hunger at bay in between his early and late rice. The younger one rushed out to the market to fetch sweet sesame dumplings for everyone, while his senior kept talking to the padre in a low and complaining voice.

"Your attendants are scared of you," Joachim Saldanha told Antonio. "They don't know why you left your late rice untouched, if they'd insulted you with too much or too little food."

Antonio yawned. His stomach was still full from the generous helpings of rice-flour pudding scavenged from the carriage driver that Joachim Saldanha had plied him with during their ride. He had risen to unfamiliar sounds, anxious about his meeting with Dr. Xu. One of his attendants had pointed to the vat of hot water, but he had shaken his head.

"Our friends here are worried because you've refused to bathe even. In China that's considered rude. They think you're angry because they weren't here to welcome you when you came to the lodge. They fear the empress will punish them, and are begging you to give them another chance."

"I've never met a Chinese before." Antonio ignored the complaints and spoke to Joachim Saldanha about his worries. "Someone with whom I can talk as an equal. Will he say why he's prepared to help a stranger? Does he know how much we suffer from the pox in Europe?"

Joachim Saldanha tried to calm Antonio down. "He has his answers, otherwise he wouldn't have agreed to meet you. You may not know much about him, but he does about you. That's the way it is here."

The younger eunuch rushed in with a plate of dumplings, but before Joachim Saldanha could taste them they heard a sound, like a volley of shrapnel fired into the lodge's roof. The padre ran for cover toward the lodge, leaving Antonio stranded on his stool. Cries rang out from the kitchen as round green fruits dropped down from the plum tree and littered the courtyard. Howls from the lion dog kept as a pet by the attendants set the bird fluttering in its cage, and a tall shadow fell at Antonio's feet. Then the older eunuch started to laugh, and pointed at a man who was striding in briskly through the pavilion's gate. He was wearing the ankle-length gown of a court official, but had the bearing of a tribal headman with his turban. Lobbing a stone to the young attendant, he headed straight to the tree and picked up a handful of fruits and brought them over to Antonio.

"It's the plum, the best fruit in China. I've struck them down for you. It's what we give to our guests when they've come from far."

Antonio noticed a pair of animated eyes that seemed foreign to the thin and bloodless face, an elegant nose and a well-shaped head. Shamefaced at his hasty escape, Joachim Saldanha called out from the kitchen to welcome Dr. Xu. The eunuchs came over too, and kowtowed before the Chinese doctor. Sitting down on the stool facing Antonio, he kept on talking and took out a small knife from his robe to peel a plum.

"It isn't ripe yet. For that you must wait till summer. But the unripe fruit is best to make wine." He offered a slice to Antonio and asked him to taste it. "If it's sour, it means we'll be friends for a long time. But if it's untimely sweet, then our friendship will last as long as the taste remains on your tongue!"

"His attendants are complaining that he hasn't eaten anything since he's arrived," Joachim Saldanha said, sitting down beside the two of them. "They think he'll fall sick if he starves himself." The older of the two eunuchs appeared with a tea tray, and Dr. Xu poked him with his finger. "That's because they're gluttons themselves, trying to make up with their mouths for what they lack under their bellies." Sipping his tea and looking a lot more settled after his dramatic appearance, he smiled at Antonio. "You've come to find the cure for a disease, haven't you? Do you have the disease yourself?"

Antonio shook his head. *He speaks like an American*, he thought, recalling Joaquim Saldanha's words.

"Ah, it must be a rare disease then. Only a few patients must suffer from it."

Antonio corrected him, speaking slowly to sound as clear as possible. "It's a *common* disease, not rare. More common than pleurisy or scarlet fever, epilepsy or pneumonia or paralysis, even the inflammation of the spleen. More people have died of it than from tetanus or jaundice."

"So doctors must already know how to cure this common disease." Dr. Xu put down his bowl and smiled at Antonio. "Have you come to find a quicker way, or one that is less painful to the patient?"

"Syphilis has no cure." He gave Joaquim Saldanha a quick look. "No *known* cure, that is. It causes a painful death. Many call it God's punishment, but we doctors know it to be no worse than typhus or plague, nothing less than a nightmare."

"No cure?" Dr. Xu's eyes gleamed. "Who treats the patients then, or are they left to die untreated?" Joaquim Saldanha spoke to him quietly about sellers of "miracle potions," making him nod and grin. "Yes, we have those fools here as well. "Quacks," as the Americans say!" Then he turned back to Antonio. "You must tell me all about this disease. Is it a short illness or a long one? Does it bring fever or bleeding? Does it puzzle the doctor with many symptoms, and recurs when you thought the patient was all but cured?" He stopped to pour himself another bowl. "You must tell me what causes this disease."

Where shall I start? Dr. Martin's voice floated into the courtyard: *It is the disease of "congress," most unfortunate. Some call it the price of sin, when it'd be fair to view it as the fruit of ignorance. Not God's punishment, but the failure of science. . . .* Antonio mulled over the "cause." *Should I tell the Chinese doctor about King Charles of France, who entered Naples with his mercenaries in 1494 and started the pox epidemic? Should I skip over a few centuries and talk about the present? Or simply name the "cause" that was as vital then as it is now?* He rose from his seat and started to speak, as he would to his assistants at the All Saints.

"It's caused by the poison that passes during lovemaking from an infected woman to a man or from a man to a woman. A sick mother could poison her nursing child; an infected child his wet nurse. We don't know what this poison is, but once inside the body, it becomes its supreme enemy." His pulse quickened and he paced the courtyard. "It's the craftiest of enemies. The first sign almost always goes unnoticed—a small bud on the private parts, like a cactus flower. It attacks the surface, setting the skin to rot, blackens nails and teeth, then ravages the organs. A great pretender, it evades detection. Treat the patient for a damaged liver, and it escapes to the spleen. Cure the spleen and it seeps into the bones, mangling them like trees in a storm. If the victim complains of a heavy heart, it means the poison has hardened his arteries. Purge the stomach for colic, or bleed him for infection, he recovers for a day or two before suffering the most horrible fit of vertigo. Rid him of his pains and he complains of blindness. There are days when he eats like a horse, and others when his appetite . . ."

Joaquim Saldanha interrupted him. "There are reasons for us to believe that the cure for syphilis might be here in China."

"Why doesn't your patient tell the doctor what he's suffering from?" Dr. Xu had heard Antonio in silence, casting sidelong glances at the younger eunuch lighting the kitchen stove across the courtyard.

"Because he's ashamed." Antonio spoke in a low voice.

"Ashamed of what?"

"Of being discovered. Being shunned by his family. Never ever being able to love anyone except a whore."

He heard the lion dog barking and a voice scolding it. Cocks crowed, and the short tread of donkeys could be heard as they came to supply the kitchen from the market stalls outside the palace. Flies buzzed around the courtyard's shrine, which held a piece of painted rock and the offering of a pig's head, guarded by a clay warrior.

Antonio wondered if he had made a mistake. The sailors on *Bom Jesus* might've been plain lucky, perhaps the Chinese were as clueless as Europeans in treating the pox.

"Do you have this kind of disease in China?" Joaquim Saldanha asked Dr. Xu, who let out a small laugh.

"We call it by a different name. Canton rash."

"Ah, like Spanish itch! Named after the carrier?" Joaquim Saldanha seemed encouraged by Dr. Xu's answer.

"The *foreign* carriers who come to trade. In Canton it's known as Portuguese pox, spread by sailors who spend nights in Hog Lane infecting their lady friends."

"Do you know how to cure Canton rash?" Antonio asked Dr. Xu, as the sun stood above them. Still casting looks toward the kitchen as if he expected the attendants to bring over a dish or two, the Chinese doctor did not answer his question directly.

"It's less common in China than elsewhere. Here the number of victims is almost half that of Malacca or your Macau. Just the port of Nagasaki has more sufferers than all of China. There's a saying that you won't find Canton rash in Canton, but in London!"

Antonio breathed a sigh of relief. *So it could indeed be true . . . a Chinese cure for syphilis.* Maybe he hadn't erred in his judgment after all, nor wasted months on his journey. It seemed all too easy, sitting face to face with the man who might pass on the secret to him within moments.

"How do you treat a patient to rid him of the syphilis poison?"

Dr. Xu thought for a moment then spoke cheerfully. "By treating the *real* reasons for his sickness."

"*Real* reasons?" Antonio looked perplexed. Dr. Xu nodded and brushed away a fly.

"Do you mean the actual symptoms rather than the poison itself?" Joaquim Saldanha tried to get Dr. Xu to say more, to relieve the confusion that showed on Antonio's face.

"The real reasons why a man is prone to sickness ever since he's born," the Chinese doctor replied.

"You're not *born* with syphilis. No! You can get it from a whore who's got it from some fool." Antonio spoke quickly, as if dismissing the diagnosis of a novice.

"Man is born with health and sickness. To help him we must know the reasons for both." Dr. Xu continued in his cheerful tone, as if he hadn't heard Antonio.

"And what might these reasons be?" Joaquim Saldanha tried to revive their discussion. "How would you spot the most important reason? And what do you do when you've found it, by what method would you remove it completely?"

"The reasons lie in the four seasons and the five elements; the twelve channels of the body and its eleven organs. The Chinese doctor knows about these things. He is able to treat a sickness even before the patient has been struck." Dr. Xu turned toward Antonio and spoke in a kind voice, as if placating a sulking child. "Then he can treat the liver, the spleen, the heart, the nerves—*everything*, all at once."

From the silence of the courtyard, Antonio could hear a duck cackling in the kitchen yard, and his attendants laughing among themselves. He was sleepy and yawned; Dr. Xu scratched his back over his tunic with a rattan cane. Once again, it was left to Joaquim Saldanha to restore a degree of purpose to their meeting.

"And you can help our friend here learn about all that you say . . . the seasons and elements, the channels and the organs?"

For the very first time since they had met, Dr. Xu looked truly pleased with his visitors. He had received a letter from Macau's governor introducing Antonio Henriques Maria—the genius—who had left his patients back home just to be able to learn the mysteries of *Nei ching*. He isn't a curiosity seeker or an idle scholar hoping to rustle up some Chinoiserie for his friends back home, Dom Afonso de Oliveira had written, but "an adventurer like the great Vasco da Gama himself."

"It'll be my privilege to help the most famous doctor of Portugal." Dr. Xu offered his hand, embarrassing Antonio into silence with the governor's exaggerations, then spoke like a real American. "You can call me Xu. Just like what you put on your foot!"

"Will you come to teach him every day?" Joaquim Saldanha rehearsed the arrangements with him. Dr. Xu nodded.

"Will our friend have a chance to visit hospitals, to see the patients in person?"

"Yes." The older eunuch came with another round of tea, but Dr. Xu waved him away and stood up to leave.

"Will he have the chance to test his skills before he leaves?"

"If we can find him a victim of Canton rash, then yes!"

"How long will it take him to learn *Nei ching*?" Joaquim Saldanha had saved the most important question for last.

Dr. Xu stopped on his way out. "As a genius he won't take too long. It might take him just four seasons to become the best doctor in China!"

❁

The elder of the two eunuchs was almost a giant, with a Roman nose and wrinkled skin like parchment. He looked older than his forty-odd years, and spoke in a singsong as if giving a performance to empress dowager. He was a eunuch of a lower rank, not fit to present her with petitions from her subjects, and allowed to retain one tenth of the sum— the "squeeze"—that passed through his hands. "Not fit to strew sand on her path!" The younger one smirked behind his back. Gossip had him addicted to *ya-pien*—opium—to the dowager's horror. She had spared his life but banished him from her entourage to serve lowly visitors to the palace. Snorting snuff in the kitchen, he bossed over his young friend and made fun of his stammer—'Chu, chu, chu, chu . . . shi, shi, shi, shi . . . !" —imitating the clucking of a hen. He'd stick out his tongue at him, who was young enough to be his son, at his grinning face unmarked by even a single line. At times he showed the skill of a mind reader and spoke for his partner, who stood with his mouth open, nodding rapidly at the precise delivery of his very own words.

Finished with his morning meeting with Joaquim Saldanha and Xu, Antonio left for a stroll around the pavilion and entered the kitchen. The eunuchs were busy with their morning supply. "You must make friends with the Wangs," Joachim Saldanha had advised him. "It is they who'll keep you alive." By his tone, Antonio knew Big Wang was scolding Little Wang as the day's produce had turned out to be below par. They dropped their voices in Antonio's presence. He heard a pot boiling on the wooden stove, spreading the aroma of some unknown species. "A nation of a thousand smells!" Dona Elvira had prepared him for his visit. Besides *Pékin-les-odeurs*—the smell of gutters—he was likely to discover countless bouquets unfamiliar to his European nose. His attendants took his visit as a prompt for his hungry stomach, and rushed to bring over a plate of shrimp eggs. He stood with them in the kitchen and spoke the Chinese he had learned at the Jesuit College, making them laugh with his well-rehearsed lines.

Big Wang was less keen when it came to talking, kept his eyes lowered before Antonio, while Little Wang wasn't shy to correct his Chinese or ask him a question or two.

"Have you to come to repair the empress's clocks?" Little Wang asked Antonio, who was busy eating the shrimp eggs with his chopsticks.

"Clocks?" The empress loved clocks, Joachim Saldanha had told him. The kind that showed singing birds and flowing waterfalls; men and women poking out their heads and bowing at the strike of the hour. Foreigners bribed her with ingenious pieces to win her favor.

"Shut up!" The older eunuch hushed his young friend before Antonio could answer. It was rude to ask such questions.

"Can you make the clock people take off their clothes?" Little Wang ignored his partner and giggled. Big Wang slapped him on his cheek and made him run from the kitchen.

Antonio laughed, but Big Wang shook his head. "His name is a mistake. He doesn't have any gifts to speak of, none whatsoever to merit the name Tianfen—the gifted one—that his mother gave him. Better to call him Tianzhen, the fool!"

So he isn't Little Wang but Tianfen, or Tian in short. . . . Antonio finished his bowl and asked for a refill. "And you? What's your real name? It isn't Big Wang, is it?"

The eunuch's face broke out into a smile. "Wang is the emperor. I'm just Wangsheng—the strong one."

"How strong?" Antonio tapped his muscles, making him turn serious again.

"Strong enough to strangle our enemies."

Leaving the pavilion, Antonio crossed the bamboo bridge to wander in the gardens along the tree-lined path dotted with stone animals.

Gardeners in blue smocks and wide-brimmed hats swept away dead leaves, and glanced up as he passed. He stopped by a rosebush. The empress allowed none to pluck flowers from her garden, he remembered Joaquim Saldanha telling him. She loved to wear natural blooms in her coiffure, and had a keen eye in choosing the right hue. *You'll be neighbors at her Summer Palace, but she'll be invisible.*

He was tempted to visit a tiny island on the lake that he had seen on his way over, ringed by a fleet of barges and streaming with flags. Perhaps his attendants would come running after him, and he'd have to outrun them to cross the marble bridge. The hill at the back of his pavilion seemed more inviting than the island. Shrouded in haze, it took a hard climb to reach the temple on top. It was empty; a rusted bell hung over a vacant seat. The Buddha was once there, the giant Buddha of the Temple of Ten Thousand Buddhas, before it was hurled down by foreign invaders from the hilltop to the bottom of the lake with a splash of ten thousand ripples and rising tides of great blue waves.

Antonio thought about Xu's words. *Man is born with health and sickness. . . .* It'd be hard for him to forget what he'd learned at the Faculdade Medicina, the certainties that had given him the strength to cut open a man's stomach or to shed his blood. *The Chinese doctor is able to treat a sickness, even before the patient has been struck.* He wrestled over the mystery of such a power. Sitting on the hilltop he sensed the spirit of the heretic as he peered down to spot the sunken Buddha among the lotus leaves. He thought his journey had finally ended, from the far corner of Europe to this unknown land.

Xu arrived next morning with rolls of parchment under his arm. Without his turban, he looked different, resembling more an elderly courtier in his cap and gown. The attendants helped him lay out the China ink drawings on the courtyard, holding them down with rocks stolen from the palace gardens. His sharp orders woke Antonio, and emerging from his lodge he found the ground covered in brushstrokes like a giant painting: the delicate drawing of the gall bladder, like a fine China vase; the small intestines resembling a puff of cloud; an upturned lotus for the liver; the spleen like a fanged serpent. His teacher walked him along the parchments, pointing at each with the end of his stick, and they spent the whole morning going over the courtyard like two peasants inspecting a plot of saplings.

Raising his voice, Xu scolded Wangsheng for his careless handling of the medical charts and Tian for spilling a pot of tea over them, adding a delicate wash to the milky parchments. "They're just bums, as my American friends would say."

"Tell me about your friends." Antonio asked him. "And what you do for the empress. Is it true what they say about her?"

"What people say about our empress is false, because no one's seen her except a handful," Xu replied with a twinkle in his eye.

"But who's she hiding from and why?" Antonio thought to tell him about the King of Portugal who had banned the carrying of firearms for the fear of assassins.

Xu grinned and patted Antonio on the back. "You are just like an American, asking questions that shouldn't be asked! It's better that she remains invisible. There might be trouble if you saw her. It's better for all of us, who can go about our business without worrying about the empress."

"But she knows that I'm here, doesn't she?"

"Yes, yes . . ." Xu tried to get him back to the medical charts. "You'll have all your answers, but we must start with the question that's brought you here." He called the younger attendant over to roll away the parchments and clear up the courtyard. Settling down on his "teacher's chair," he asked Antonio to hold out his hand.

"The pulse tells the health of each organ. To feel it correctly, you must place the patient's hand on a cushion with the palm facing up. Then press down with your middle, ring and index fingers. Force should be light at first, then moderate and finally heavy." Xu checked Antonio's pulse then asked him to hold his fingers of one hand on the wrist of the other.

"A normal pulse is neither shallow nor deep, neither slow nor quick. It beats unnoticed." He cocked an ear as if encouraging Antonio to listen carefully. "The Chinese way is different from the European. You must tell me what you hear, if it's the same kind of sound that I've heard. If you aren't careful, you might miss it completely. Might hear your breathing instead!"

Antonio heard his own throbbing head. He had spent yet another sleepless night battling insects. Crawling ants had marched like explorers drawn by the taste of spilled wine, braved the sudden drop of the shoulders to reach the deep well under his throat. The touch of feathery antennae had woken him and he had risen quickly, disappointing the ant army with his undulations.

"You should hear a different note if you press harder." Xu edged forward on his stool. "Go on, check my pulse." He thrust his hand toward Antonio.

He heard the low growl of the lion dog, watching the two of them through the kitchen window. The superiority of a race, he believed, lay in its power to invent machines. A European doctor didn't have to rely purely on his own senses, there were smart devices to help him read the signs accurately, such as the percussor to amplify the rhythm of the heart and the lungs; ophthalmoscopes to check the retina for damage; the dynamometer, the thermometer and many more.

"In Europe we've heard our patients' pulses for centuries. But we have the sphygmographs to help us record the arterial wave, which is much better than relying simply on one's ear."

"Ah, but does your machine tell you which disease makes what kind of sound?" Xu looked at him playfully. "Can it tell when the pulse is groaning under an excess of blood, when it's roaring because of a fiery liver?"

"What do you mean by a *kind of sound?*" Antonio sounded sceptical.

"Let me show you." Xu called Wangsheng over from the kitchen and made him sit beside Antonio. The older eunuch gave a nervous smile. "His pulse, as you'll see, is different to mine." Xu placed Antonio's palm on Wangsheng's wrist. "With me you heard the *Fumai*, the floating pulse, the pulse of an elderly man whose only sickness comes from his eyes. With him though, you'll hear the irregular *Xumai*—like a knife scraping bamboo—that worries the doctor about a hidden disorder."

"What kind of disorder?"

"A lump in his stomach that prevents digestion."

Like a knife scraping bamboo . . . . Antonio listened carefully. He heard the cackle of gulls around the lake, the eunuch's labored breathing and the rustling trees.

Scolded by Xu, Wangsheng ran back to the kitchen. "If, on the other hand, you examined his young friend, you'd find a . . . ."

Shouts from the kitchen broke the treatise on palpation. Escaped from its captors, a duck streaked across the courtyard, scattering feathers and chased by Tian. Coming to a full stop before them, it stretched out its neck and arched its head to one side, like a diligent student. Xu patted the duck with his stick and gave a short laugh. The pair of dark eyes lit up his lined face. Waiting for the young servant to catch the bird and carry it back to the kitchen, he sighed then resumed.

"It takes months, even years to learn the different sounds. Practice makes the head go empty, without a single thought left inside. The doctor is then able to touch the suffering organs like a blind man, smell his patient, *see* what's inside him without the need to cut him open."

"What if he never hears what he's supposed to hear?" Antonio was miffed by Xu's dismissive view of machines. "What if he ignores the pulse totally?"

"He must keep trying. That's what learning the art of medicine is all about—sharpening the senses till they're perfect."

"Nonsense. Learning medicine means learning facts. Facts about the body that are indisputable." Sitting under the sun in the courtyard, Antonio's head ached from the sleepless night. What would Ricardo have said if he'd heard the Chinaman? *You didn't have to go so far, my friend . . . could've got all that at the Alfama! We've no shortage of shamans.*

"You can hear if you try." Xu didn't seem too upset by Antonio's outburst. "Once you've had a good night's sleep, you'll be able to hear all the different sounds."

"How do you know I haven't had a good night's sleep?"

"Because your pulse says so. It beats like a *Semai*, a sure sign of fatigue."

"It's the insects." Antonio threw up his hands in a sign of despair. "They've taken a special liking to the foreigner!"

Xu showed surprise. "Insects! Do you have a lot of them here?" He called Wangsheng over and marched him down to Antonio's lodge, barking out his orders: windows must be shut properly and camphor burned to chase away the flies. A trough of weeds must be left outside the lodge to stop the beetles from foraging inside. There was no better repellent for ants than ground nutmeg scattered on the floor to resemble the ants themselves. Twigs shed by the plum tree must be cleared daily to prevent them from becoming mating groves of ferocious scorpions.

Before they could resume their lesson, a messenger came to the pavilion and whispered something to Xu. He got up to leave, and bowed to his student. "I must go now or lose my head!"

After Xu had left, Antonio wrote down his teacher's instructions on the nature of the pulse. *Fumai* is the floating pulse, pressed lightly it appears under the index finger. Pressed heavily, it disappears and portends the onset of a cold. *Chimai* is a deeper pulse; it speaks about the vital organs. *Sumai* is the fastest of all, and proof of excessive heating of the blood. *Semai* and *Shimai* are irregular, the sign of fatigue. If the pulse is smooth like pebbles, it indicates excessive phlegm and the slippery *Huamai*. If uneven like scraping bamboo with a knife, one would call it *Xumai*. It worries the doctor about a hidden disorder. *Hongmai* is full just like a rising wave, *Ximai* like silk, yet both are marks of excessive strain. A loss of blood gives rise to *Koumai*, the pulse feels hollow like an empty vessel. With pain, *Jinmai* becomes taut like a stretched cord, and it points to an injury of the stomach. The liver is the culprit if *Xuanmai* twirls like a musical note. The soft thud of *Daimai* is the mark of fear.

He placed his right hand on the silk cushion palm facing up and pressed down on the wrist with three fingers. He heard the duck shriek and the attendants laugh.

He doesn't like answering questions about what he does at the palace, Antonio thought after Xu had left. Coming over on the *Santa Cruz*, he had heard rumors. Peking's imperial court was full of intrigues; it was a closely guarded world where a doctor was as important as a general, killing off opponents or turning them mad with their evil medicine. Was it true or was it simply the overblown imagination of foreigners? He made a mental note to ask his padre friend.

A whole week passed before Antonio met Joachim Saldanha again. He arrived on a mule cart looking more disheveled than before, and asked the attendants to help him carry a large wooden box inside. The older eunuch grimaced. The box was heavier than a coffin. Maybe the palace guards could help the padre? He pleaded to be let off given his sore neck. Joachim Saldanha grabbed his arm and dragged him over to the cart. "I'll wring your neck. It won't hurt you anymore!" Tian started to laugh. Between the two eunuchs there seemed to be a contest going to see who could avoid the heaviest of chores. Wangsheng glared at his young friend and complained to the padre. "In China all burdens must be borne by young eunuchs and animals."

Joachim Saldanha praised Antonio for settling in quickly, for having made friends with his attendants, for having "learned their real names even." After the box had been unloaded, he started on his early rice, keeping little Tian on his toes with repeated calls for more helpings.

"A padre must eat well, especially in this country, where he doesn't know when his next meal will be."

"I thought all the Chinaman does is worry about his stomach." Antonio was happy to see his traveling companion back at the palace.

"He does, but only for his own stomach, not that of a foreign devil! Even if you turn Chinese like our poor Tientsin sisters."

"Do you have the thirty-ninth inside?" Antonio pointed to the box. His friend smiled. "The surviving sister's safe, rescued by the captain of an opium ship after she managed to escape to the coast. But Jeffrey Cook, our pastor in Shanxi, hasn't been that lucky." Between gulps of rice, Joachim Saldanha told Antonio the story of the Iowa pastor who had angered villagers by refusing to install *Cai Shen* and *Tu Di*—Chinese gods of wealth and the earth—on the church pulpit beside child Jesus and the Virgin. "The reverend was accused of black magic: plucking out the eyes of babies to make potions, and vices that ranged from incest to orgy. Village elders announced that he had poisoned the well. Gardeners and servants were forbidden to serve him, and the sign of a bleeding hand appeared on the church door. On the night of the carnage, he was attacked by a mob armed with swords. The fields were white with snow, but he was stripped of his smock, kicked and butted on the head then bound in chains. He had tried to ransom himself with silver and almost managed to escape, only to be cut down barely paces from the pulpit."

Joaquim Saldanha had seen smoke billowing when he reached the spot. The church façade was damaged, its steeples in ruins. Steps leading up to the altar were smeared with excrement. He had discovered the reverend's corpse in a gully, chains cut into his arms, worms crawling in the wounds and the flesh eaten away to the bones, urchins poking it with sticks.

He had built two coffins from the pulpit's carved wood, one for the reverend and one for the scorched Madonna and child.

"Why didn't he run before troubles started?"

"Because that's not what priests are supposed to do."

Before the padre could start yet another story, Antonio held up his hands to stop him. "If you don't help me, I could be just as unlucky as your reverend. I could end up wasting my whole life here without any success."

Joachim Saldanha narrowed his eyes. "You mean you've had a fight with your teacher?"

Antonio scowled. "He wants me to know each of the eleven pulses, and I can't even hear one!"

"But you've only just started, haven't you? How long did it take the Faculdade to make you a doctor?" Joachim Saldanha didn't pay much heed to Antonio's mood.

"Why don't you ask Xu to teach me quickly? Why can't we forget *Nei ching* and simply learn how to cure pox?" Antonio fidgeted impatiently with the pulse reading cushion, then his face lit up with an idea. "Maybe he can come to Lisbon with me. We can spend as many seasons together as he wants. He can treat my patients too, cure them of syphilis!"

"No!" Joaquim Saldanha smiled. "To take their best, you must give them our best. The best of Europeans, our ability to learn faster than others. You can't expect to find your answer so soon. It might even take you some time to understand the answer that you're given. You must be patient. There's no other way in China."

Beyond the boundary wall, Kunming Lake had turned itself into a mirror. Within days it'd take on the color of marble used to build the camel-back bridges and the terraces that hung over it like birds' nests. The lake and the gardens were about to recede into natural wilderness, leaving the pavilions behind, the teahouses and the court of Her Majesty the dowager.

"I have to ask you a favor," Joaquim Saldanha said as he prepared to roll out his sleeping mat on the lodge's veranda.

"Anything that our two friends here can provide." Antonio thought the padre wished to have his sack filled with food for his onward journey.

"Just a bit of room for the box, for just a few days before I return."

"Of course." Antonio prepared to lie down too. "As long as it doesn't hold the bones of the dead reverend!"

They went for a walk by the lake in the evening. The light of early summer had cast a glow on the gilded roofs, and reflected brilliantly on the water. Smoke from the teahouses floated up in a cloud. Plum trees had blossomed, and the fruit hung low on the branches inviting to be picked. Antonio asked Joachim Saldanha about foreigners who lived in Peking, and he talked at length about the Legation, which was nearly twenty miles away from the Summer Palace.

"Foreign officers are no friends of padres. They take us for trouble-makers who waste their time. They have to fight with mandarins to release a priest if he's arrested, or to seek clearance for our plans to build new churches. They don't like missionary wives either for complaining about starving orphans and scarce supplies."

"So that's why you don't leave your treasure with them!"

"They'd burn the box for wood in their fireplaces!" Joachim Saldanha didn't hide his disgust for the Legation officers.

"Do they do what Europeans do?" Antonio asked his friend. The thought of others like him living not too far away made him curious. "Throw banquets and balls, bet on horses, cheer at bullfights and hold festas?"

"That and a whole lot more!" Ministers from eleven nations — Britain and France, America, Germany, Spain, Japan, Russia, Italy, Austria, Belgium and Holland — had founded a little Europe within the Tartar city, with the British as their natural leaders. Mansions nestled in the leafy boulevards, homes to diplomats and merchants, with tennis lawns and stables. Office of the Maritime Customs, a post office, the Hong Kong Bank, the expats' club and the Hôtel de Pékin made up the quarter. Shrubs of Chinese rose peeked from behind the well-guarded walls. "But don't be fooled by the roses," Joaquim Saldanha reminded Antonio, "there are enough thorns there as well! A bitter wind blows over the bickering mansions. The Spaniards hate their American neighbors, the 'Flowery Flag Devils,' for their troubles in Manila Bay, for the loss of Puerto Rico, Guam and the Philippines. The French are yet to forgive the British for their reverses on the Nile.

The British despise the plucky Boers. Everyone hates the Japanese 'Dwarf Bandits,' and looks down on lazy Italians, drunken Russians and grim Germans."

"It's Europe divided then!"

"They are united only against the Chinese. A Europe of gossip and rumors, held together by garden parties. Not much is expected from the Portuguese, except a steady supply of Goan cooks for their kitchens!"

"Do they know I am here at the Summer Palace?"

Joaquim Saldanha nodded. "Dom Afonso hasn't taken any risks with your safety. He informed the British minister as soon as we left Macau."

"Why British?"

"Because of Cedric and Polly Hart, the deputy minister and his wife." The Harts had recently arrived in Peking, stopping in Macau as Dom Afonso's guests and the couples had become friends. "You'll find them to be the kindest at the Legation. Two lambs among the lions! They might even take an interest in your ambition."

"Should I go over then to have some tea?" Antonio was amused at the prospect of tasting his favorite drink in an English home in China.

"They might save you too from shrimp eggs!" Joaquim Saldanha grinned as he prepared to leave. "And from your teacher who has been tormenting you with pulse readings."

"Will palace rules allow the prisoner to cross the gates?" He wondered if the Europeans were freer at the Legation than he was in his pavilion.

"You'll have to find that out yourself." Joaquim Saldanha patted Antonio on the back. "You'll need more than two eunuchs and a teacher to pass time in Peking. More than a gravedigger to bring you the news of the world."

He felt his father's hand on his forehead. Unlike a man's, it was soft. As a child he knew it from the smell of ether used to clean them after surgery. Whenever he was sick, they'd stroke his feverish cheeks. His father didn't refuse him anything, not even the *pastéis de nata* made of rich almond paste or the *ovos moles* in little candy shells, when his appetite returned. He didn't stop him from lighting candles at his mother's grave or bursting crackers on All Saints' Day, even though he knew that his little Tino would cry afterward. He dreamed his father was reading him a story in their carriage to Cabo São Vicente, but his rich voice had dropped so low that he couldn't hear it clearly over the squeaking wheels. He raised himself onto his knees to nudge his father, to touch his face then tumbled on his lap as the carriage took a sharp bend. A toothless mouth gaped down at him, with a half nose and a rotten gash giving off a sickening smell.

Antonio woke with a start. Insects, millions of them, were crawling over his body. Sweat trickled down his arms and legs, and he tossed back his blanket. It was the same nightmare. On the ship, they thought he was suffering from delusions, which was a common symptom of seasickness. A nervous ship's doctor, aware of his reputation, had hesitated offering him the surefire cure of bitter lemon that worked with sailors and passengers alike. In Macau, he forced himself to stay awake at night. He'd yawn all day and invite Dona Elvira's jokes about the "lovesick doctor."

Awake, he shivered in the cold breeze. The lantern flickered inside the bedchamber, and yellow dust blew in through the window. He felt a storm rising. The rice-paper panes creaked and split open under the force of the wind that moaned on the curved roofs, breaking loose a tile or two and sending them crashing down onto the courtyard. The bell tower boomed, silencing the crickets. An inexplicable urge brought him out of his chamber into the courtyard, where the wind was churning up a bed of leaves, setting them off in an upward spiral as if they were a band of dervishes swirling in the divine music of the storm. Through an open arch in the boundary wall he could see the embankments of the moat that circled the pavilion, and a frail bamboo bridge resembling a handful of stalks, almost invisible, rising from the water.

Four seasons of nightmares! Four seasons with insects! *Why must you?* The voice of Ricardo Silva argued with the heretic. Syphilitics have been dying for centuries. It was the curse of the lower downs on the higher ups. Search every family, and you'd find a story of shame. *Do you want your statue to be carved in stone like Dom Manuel? The Saint of the Poxies!*

The heretic won during daytime. He started his explorations after his morning sessions with Xu. The Chinese and their ways appealed to his practical mind: the automatic door opener that flung open curtains and swung back doors without the need for hands. The perfect rice steamer with two vessels that allowed the heat to spread evenly. Fishermen laying traps on Kunming Lake that required far less effort to catch fish than the sweeping nets he had seen on the Tagus. Back from his afternoon stroll, he'd watch his attendants play *mahjong*, a game with more than a hundred pieces, a far cry from the simple dominoes he had learned on ship.

As he probed the mysterious things around him, he found each part related to something bigger, each minor detail wrought by the pain of invention. He solved the mystery of the steamer, the magic doors and *mahjong*, but sunset scattered gold dust around him and brought him back to his purpose.

Evenings belonged to crickets, and the memory of a carriage bounding to Cabo São Vicente. His father sat before him as he drank sweet plum wine with his late rice. *How is he now? Is he delirious again? Driving the fear of death into poor Rosa? Or is he still as clear in his mind as he was when I left him, suffering from supreme clarity, the most dangerous condition of all?* His father must've foreseen a horrible death. *That's why he's forbidden me to visit him.* Did he miss his Tino? He felt guilty having left his father behind. As a doctor, he should've stayed back, tried to relieve his pains even if he couldn't cure him. *I should've disobeyed him, made him angry just to be near him.* The fear of yet another nightmare kept him up all night as he battled the insects.

Antonio thought of starting the letter he had promised Dona Elvira. "How will you spend your evenings there without a friend?" she had asked him with a mischievous smile. Dom Afonso had offered to lend him the *História Trágico Maritima*—a report on drowning and butchering at sea—to weather the nights he'd spend alone. Stroking his face like a mother, Dona Elvira had told him to write letters. "Words will keep you alive even if the Chinese bore you to death!"

On most evenings he summoned the power of distraction, the pranks they'd play at the Faculdade. Friends in carnival costumes and nurses in white paraded through his courtyard. Memories of his adventures kept him occupied every night. He recalled carousing in the bars of Chiado where they'd befriend young Englishmen, the Inglesinhos, pretend to be secret republicans and ask for their help in overthrowing the House of Bragança. Ricardo Silva would go even a step further: promise a cache of the guns to the young innocents if they wished to assassinate the English queen.

His racking laugh woke the pavilion's attendants, made them scurry over with another pot of wine. He summoned horses, Alfama whores, bulls of the bullring. Drunk, he went strolling in the courtyard as if on Avenida da Liberdade—Lisbon's Champs-Élysées—from Rossio to the Praça Marquês de Pombal, with a stop on the way to ride the new Americanos under the even newer gas lamps. Hats were raised to him at the theater hall where a crowd had gathered for a matinee, the hospital's matron among them, hiding her face as he walked by. He saw himself enter a smoke-filled salon, order a glass of crusted port and watch Arees among her friends, chatting on about Voltaire and Hugo.

Did Ricardo try to stop me on behalf of Arees? Does he hate me for keeping her waiting?

Days before leaving, he had met Arees at the Tower of Belém. They'd gone up to the Moorish sentry box to stand with their backs to the city. The Atlantic current blew in a stiff breeze and it seemed as if they were at the bow of a ship cruising along over the waves. He had told her about his visit to China, that he'd be away for months, even for a whole year. "Syphilis?" Her gaze had strayed toward the monastery of Jerónimos as if she could hear the cries of the syphilitics in the cloisters. Her eyes had lit up in a way he hadn't seen before. "Ah! Candide leaving his Eden for an adventure!" Then her face had clouded over and she had fallen silent. Almost seven thousand miles stretched between the two of them standing on the tower and the China coast, fifteen thousand or more on the sea. What did he know about ships and ships' fevers? She had asked him about storms and murderous slavers. Blessed steam had shortened the journey from the days of Vasco da Gama, he had assured her, touched by her worries. *Should I ask her to come along?* His doctor's mind had run through the course of things. He had wavered between certainty and doubt, never as close as he was that night to breaking his indecision and asking for her hand.

"What if it takes more than a year to find what you're after?" Arees had asked. He'd kept silent, not knowing what to say. She had sighed, and spoken under her breath, almost to herself, "It'd better be soon, or I'll come to bring you back."

Swaying on his feet in the courtyard, Antonio heard Dom Afonso de Oliveira. "Why must *you* save the world from pox? Let the upstarts do it if they can—the English and the French, greedy Castilians, the Dutch. Portugal's day as the leader of seafarers is over," the governor lamented. "Once caravels and carracks ruled the waves from Estado da India to Estado do Brasil. Now it's the turn of steamships. The new masters have taken over the spice trade, the gold, the slaves and opium, let them take the pox too. Let them do their work."

Antonio smashed the pot on the courtyard's ground and raised himself on his toes to peer over the palace walls. Beyond the gates the Foreign Legation lay in darkness.

❁

His body behaved strangely after the first month at the Summer Palace. He missed his morning habit: regular drills with wooden clubs and barbells, or a game of *jogo do pau* with his friends, fighting a friendly duel with fencing sticks. In Lisbon, he'd run the whole length of the Jardim Botânico and arrive at the All Saints panting like a race horse. Morning exercises prepared him for his long hours at the hospital and even longer evenings. He missed the sparring, the grind of bones and muscles, and invited the attendants for a wrestling match.

Tian laughed like a child and ran to tell his friend when Antonio explained to him the rules. "You can fight me with your hands and legs any way you like. But you can't poke my eyes or kick between my thighs." He pointed to the folds of his robe.

Wangsheng came out of the kitchen looking ashamed and apologized on behalf of his "stupid junior."

"If he has insulted you, you can punish him." He handed a broom to Antonio and forced Tian to get down on his knees. "You can hit him as many times as you like, even if he starts to bleed." The younger eunuch made a whimpering sound, as he raised his tunic and bared his back, looking fearfully at Antonio.

"No, no, he's done nothing wrong! I just want to play a game with him." Antonio was taken aback seeing the distress on their faces. "He can hit me too!"

Both eunuchs fell silent. Then Wangsheng got down on his knees and bared his back as well.

"I don't want to punish either of you. Just fight a wrestling match. It's a game like your *kung fu*. You fight to win but not to hurt your opponent." Antonio went around his two kneeling attendants, and imitated the sparring he'd seen in Macau's Ama Temple. "Some even fight with weapons, but we can simply use our arms and legs." He drew a circle on the ground with the broom, stood in the middle and coaxed his attendants to join him inside. "Whoever wants to fight me, can step in now!"

Wangsheng stood up and cast a sad look at the circle. "What will happen to him who loses?" Straightening his back, Tian slunk away toward the kitchen.

"Nothing! We can fight again tomorrow."

"And if he loses again?"

"No one really loses, it's just a . . ."

The older man shook his head. "We can't win against a guest or lose to a foreigner."

"Then let's just fight and forget about winners and losers." Antonio made a dash toward Tian, hoping to infect him with the fun of wrestling. The young eunuch ducked under his arms and ran around the courtyard with Antonio chasing him. Wangsheng scampered into the kitchen and slammed the door. Antonio thought he could catch Tian easily, but he showed great skill evading his grasp, jumping over the pool and running round the lodge. The lion dog kept up a steady barking from the kitchen, scaring the chickens in their coop. The songbird called in a shrill note.

"Stop!" Antonio shouted, as Tian started to climb up the plum tree, wrapping his feet around the branches like a monkey. "I won't hurt you!" Maybe there was a reason after all why he was called Tianfen—blessed at birth with the gift of tree climbing! Antonio tried to go up the branches too, but slipped and fell. Looking up, he saw the young eunuch's eyes among a bunch of fruit, glowing down at him from the top.

"They won't fight with me, or let me swim in the lake, or visit the empress's court, just feed me rice and watch me grow fat!" Antonio complained to Joachim Saldanha when he stopped by his pavilion the next day, on his way to the Legation to baptize the newborn son of the Italian minister's aide.

"But they are looking after you very well, aren't they?" Joachim Saldanha sounded unconcerned. "Last time you were complaining of insects, but not anymore, I think?"

"A well looked after prisoner you can say." Antonio glared at his padre friend. "Not free like you to risk my life."

Emptying his pocket of scraps of food that he had picked up from his well wishers, Joachim Saldanha gave Antonio a stern look. "The important thing is to keep learning. That's why you're here, aren't you? Just like your time at the Faculdade."

Antonio thought about Festa das Latas, and the burning of ribbons at Queima das Fitas; the drunken fights, the whores, and lampooning their teachers at the yearly ball. "It wasn't all work at the Faculdade, but mischief too."

Joachim Saldanha screwed up his nose fishing out a rotten pear that had taken on the color of a dead rat. "No one's stopping you from playing your mischief outside the palace. Why don't you ask your eunuch friends to take you to the market, or to one of the villages? You'll find no shortage of festivals there, no dearth of rascals to remind you of your friends." He spoke to reassure Antonio. "As long as you come back here, your teacher doesn't need to know where you've been."

Antonio went down to the lake after Joachim Saldanha had left promising to be back soon to collect his box. He thought about Xu, the way he had rushed off at the call of the messenger. *The empress must've asked for him. She must know where I live, know my pavilion. She could be watching me. . . .* Her barge lay waiting at the foot of marble steps, but the boatmen were absent. The empress liked to take her afternoon tea there with her ladies-in-waiting, Tian had told him. It was her favorite spot. She'd call over musicians and poets, even actors from the palace theater to perform scenes of a play. Antonio took a quick look around, then went down the steps to the barge. A few strides took him up to the deck and into the cabin. He expected to find ladies-in-waiting or a head concubine preparing the room for the tea service.

I'd be stopped and asked who I am. . . . Her guards might force me out. . . . He felt drawn to enter the empress's sight.

A thronelike chair stood in the middle of a raised platform, beside it a couch covered with cushions. Curtained windows and painted walls gave the cabin the appearance of a private chamber, complete with a mirror and fresh lilies in vases. Remnants of a meal lay on a table, with silver teapots. Cream from an upturned saucer ran down the tablecloth into a pool on the wooden floor. *She's left after her tea . . .* he thought, picking up a fine jade bowl and smelling the rim for a whiff of the invisible lips. A pale lamp shone on a mantel, and swayed with the boat. Antonio sat down on the couch. *This is where she comes to rest after she's visited her sick nephew.* He thought of the young concubine Yehonala who'd become the dowager empress, the cavalryman's daughter who had charmed the emperor with her singing. She had jumped rank to become his favorite consort and had borne him a son. When her young nephew ascended to the throne after the emperor's death, she became his guardian, and had ruled China ever since from behind the scenes. Her beauty would captivate young and old alike, Marcello Valignoni had told him, like a flower that never dies.

Ye-ho-na-la . . . He rolled the word on his tongue. The planks creaked under him, and he heard the muffled sound of returning boatmen.

Antonio left the barge quickly and went up to the Palace of Clouds, which bordered the lake. She might've come here to watch the sunset; maybe he could glimpse her playing with her dogs while they were being groomed by her maids. He went up the steps and heard murmurs. Her consorts were likely to sight him first, raise a cry to attract the guards. They'd rush in from all sides, wrestle him down before they dragged him over to the empress.

I must be ready to answer her questions. Take Xu's name if needed. I must tell her I am a doctor.

The sound of chanting came from the room. He smelled the rare Chinese orchid that he'd seen in Dona Elvira's villa. A voice called everyone to attention, and recited a few lines in a singsong. *Is it the empress. . . . ?* Antonio inched closer to a window and pressed his face against the pane. A smoke screen covered the circle of women dressed in white, sitting around an open box with gold trimmings. They were strewing it with petals and fanning the incense burner. One of them stood with her back to Antonio and started to wail as guards came into the room carrying an old concubine in their arms, her face painted white, dressed in a white robe and wearing a garland of white lotus. Only her lips were as red as a ripe plum.

Moving away quickly from the window, he ran down the steps of the Palace of Clouds.

Back in his pavilion, Antonio surprised his attendants. They had lit lamps around the courtyard and swept the ground clean of twigs and dead leaves. Wangsheng and Tian stood inside the circle that Antonio had drawn, and were wrestling each other with their arms and legs.

❀

"Heart stores the spirit
Lungs harbour instinct
Liver holds the soul
Spleen is home to ideas
Kidneys fuel ambition"

Antonio noticed a woman dressed in the common blue of a peasant with a black band around her head. She had come with Xu, and sat listening to him in the courtyard like an actor ready to make her appearance. He thought he was dreaming of one of the many gardeners he'd seen clearing the dead leaves. His appetite had died after a week of specialties prepared by his attendants and he longed for the soothing tea to calm his restlessness. Glancing impatiently toward the kitchen, he caught her looking at him.

Xu cleared his throat, expecting Antonio to ask a question. "Do you agree?"

Antonio kept silent. His teacher waited for him to speak, then called Wangsheng over. "Ask your master which of your organs is at fault." The older eunuch stood before the two of them with a shamefaced smile, while Xu egged him on. "Is it an organ or something else, something more important?" Waving the poor eunuch away, he smiled mischievously at Antonio. "Going by *Nei ching*, one could say it's the heart that warms the spleen to drive the lungs to help the kidneys to nourish the liver. So it's not his liver that's at fault but his heart!" He looked expectantly at Antonio. "Don't you want to argue with me?"

"It doesn't matter if I do or I don't. The most important thing is that I learn enough to cure pox."

"Ah!" Xu scared off a fly soaking up steam from his tea bowl. "But to cure a patient you must believe in the principles. Learning the rules simply isn't enough. You must believe in *qi*, for example, trust the *zang* and *fu* organs to transmit it through the body. Otherwise . . ."

"Otherwise what?" Antonio stopped note taking and looked up.

"You'll fail as a doctor." He gave Antonio a teasing look. "Like you had to believe that our empress might wish to meet you before you went looking for her."

He knows . . . ! Antonio was stunned by his teacher's words, spoken with just the right tinge of warning. *He isn't just a Nei ching master, but a spy . . . .*

"I can't believe things that are untested and unproven." He rose and walked to the lodge to relieve himself, holding his hurting stomach. When he returned he found a plate of shrimp eggs by his stool. Antonio pushed it away and grimaced. His teacher studied him closely, then spoke in a friendly voice.

"In your case it might indeed be the liver that's at fault. It sleeps during winter and wakes in the spring. That's the general rule. When it's ill with a hot disease, the urine become yellow, the stomach aches, sleep vanishes and the patient becomes restless. Summer troubles the liver, while winter keeps it calm."

"A liver is a liver, summer or winter." Antonio smashed the plate on the ground. "The shrimps are the culprit here, not the liver." Tian rushed in across the courtyard and scooped up the broken pieces.

"It's a *zang* organ and stores the *qi*. It harmonizes emotions. Anger is injurious to the liver, sadness results when it's weak. If unprotected it harms the heart."

"Nonsense!" Antonio rose from his seat and prowled the courtyard, throwing back his words over his shoulder. "Its job is to supply blood to the heart. A job it does very well till attacked by an enemy. We must kill the enemy, not worry about emotions."

Xu's thin face broke into a smile, having succeeded, finally, in provoking his student into an argument. "Ah! What if the liver itself is the enemy?"

It was a question an assistant wouldn't have dared ask Antonio during his rounds at the hospital. He stood still, controlling his urge to scold the elderly man, then delivered his stern lecture. "Yes the liver might indeed become corrupted, by alcohol, for instance. It could suffer too the yellow atrophy, or from a saturation of copper. For each condition, one must select the right treatment. Even surgery can't be ruled out, especially if . . ."

"What if I were to tell you that to cure the liver you must first treat the kidneys?"

He thought Xu was teasing him. Maybe he should've heeded Dom Miguel's advice and gone west on the Carriera do Brasil, spent his days in snake-infested jungles rather than in a palace, coaxed the Amazon savages to reveal their secret of curing the pox. He was tired and angry. His teacher motioned him to sit, placed his palm down and noted his pulse.

"It's not the shrimp but your stomach. It doesn't wish to see the sight of food." He advised Antonio to rest for a few days before they resumed their lessons. "The liver is the first to complain as summer sets in. When the water dries up and the earth cracks open. It's time to store. The liver speaks for all the organs."

Holding his side and bending over, Antonio spoke hoarsely. "It has nothing to do with the liver. Just the shrimps and the plum wine that . . ."

With a quick gesture, Xu called Wangsheng over and spoke to him in a low voice. The older eunuch glanced over to the kitchen with a nervous look.

"I've told him to stop the shrimps, the starfish and the seahorse and stay with plain dishes. Also to stop quarrelling among themselves and let you sleep longer in the mornings."

The kneeling form rose and left with Xu. *I should've asked him about nightmares. . . . Maybe he can stop them, make me sleep along with my liver.*

Tian surprised him by announcing a visitor when he brought him his late rice. The girl in blue stood at the door of the lodge. She had come to fetch him for Xu.

He's found a syphilitic, a victim of Canton rash! He wants me to observe the treatment. Antonio was thrilled. His stomach recovered instantly, and he changed quickly out of his robes. The girl was telling him to bring something along, making a shape with her hands. *My hat!* She pointed under the bed. He followed her gaze to the surgical box.

Why would he ask me to bring it? How would Xu know what was inside, under the lid? Perhaps the patient needed a little treatment while he recovered, he thought, like removing a long-suffering abscess.

Antonio followed her out and into a part of the palace he hadn't visited before. Lamps had lit up the terrace by the lake, forming shadow rings on their path like ripples. The trees and pavilions were shrouded in mist, and gave him the feeling of walking along a cliff's edge as he followed his fleet-footed guide.

Xu met them on the steps of a pavilion far grander than any Antonio had seen, and they entered a private chamber. Wicks had been dimmed on the cloisonné lamps, but he noticed the fans of peafowl feather and an altar full of clocks. Xu brought him to an antechamber, with silk curtains and satin portières on the windows and doors.

A young woman lay on a divan, her face as white as the covers. Xu checked her pulse then spoke to her in a low voice. She started to whimper, shaking her head, drawing up her knees to her chin like a scared child. As the whimpering grew, Xu scolded her. She shut her ears with her hands, and swayed onto her sides like a beached carp. Why would a victim deny treatment? Anything was better than the suffering of pox, he'd heard, unless, of course, the Chinese treatment was more painful, the antidote more frightening than the disease itself.

"Maybe you could help us." Xu turned away from the patient and faced Antonio. "Can you treat her with your special instruments?"

His guide held up the surgical box. *Curing syphilis with a knife!* He thought Xu was making fun of him. He took a pair of obstetric forceps and held them out. "Why don't *you* do it? Go on, catch it with these if you can. If you're lucky you might find the syphilis poison in her belly!"

"Syphilis?" Xu looked surprised. "No, no . . . not syphilis. She doesn't have Canton rash. Maybe you can clean up her belly with your instruments."

"What's inside her belly?"

In the few moments Xu took to settle the patient down, Antonio understood. He scolded himself for not diagnosing her properly right at the beginning—the bloodless face, emaciated limbs; the heaviness with which she moved from side to side, holding her stomach as if guarding it from all the troubles of this world.

"How long has she been with child?"

Xu shrugged as the girl's moaning grew louder.

"Why don't you do it yourself?" Antonio spoke roughly. "You have enough poison, haven't you?"

"Yes, but it's too late for that. What we can give her will kill her, not just her child."

"Kill her then." Antonio turned his back on Xu. "It's common practice here, I'm told."

He was angry, called in to do the job of a quack. At the All Saints, the matron would shoo the tramps away, send them over to shady barrios of the Alfama. Sometimes she'd plead with Antonio, swayed by tears, to save a poor girl savaged by the quacks.

A shadow appeared on the silk screen—a woman's face—frail in profile with a small but well-formed nose and an apple chin. Her hair was held up in a bun, and smoke curled from the lips. The shadow spoke to the sick woman. A few crisp words stopped the moaning. *Is that the dowager empress!*

"We hope you won't disappoint us." Antonio heard Xu's voice behind him. The woman under the sheets looked at him beseechingly.

Was she the empress's favorite? The maid who combed her hair, helped her in her toilette? He remembered Joaquim Saldanha telling him about little girls carried like chicken in baskets to be sold in Peking, a cartful of them waiting at the palace gates for an audience with the empress. She'd choose the best and turn the rest away. Pimps slaughtered the unlucky ones. Chosen maids won the privilege of spending ten years with their mistress and were rewarded for their loyalty with the farewell gift of a wedding dress. Only a few had the right to age and wither away inside the palace, fewer still the fleeting horror of being carried by a eunuch and sprung naked onto the emperor's bed.

Why didn't she order her killed? He recalled old China hands on the *Santa Cruz* gossiping about the mischief of eunuchs, the monsters, "half men, half beast." Most have their jewels intact, Marcello Valignoni had claimed, to please the ladies of the palaces. "Can they grow them back after their little operation?" A foolish merchant had made everyone laugh with his question. Did the empress wish to save her maid only to offer her the "silk cord"? To have her strangulate herself for her sins?

"She may still live if you try." Xu pleaded with him.

"Let her keep the baby then."

By the silence, Antonio knew it'd be impossible to save them both. Snatching the surgical box from his guide, he barked out his orders and arranged the instruments in a neat row beside the bed: French forceps designed specially for a risky operation, the perforator to pierce the uterus if needed, the curette for cleansing, the carbolic spray pump to prevent infection, a spouted flask for inhaling ether to dull the pain of incision.

It took him just a few moments to rediscover the power of action and the comfort of holding a knife in his hand. As he dipped the instruments in warm water, he noticed his guide, now turned into a surgery nurse, a pair of amber eyes under the black band on her forehead.

He didn't hear Xu whispering to the shadow or the sighs of his patient after he had started his work, till the dilation had been completed and the fetus expelled without the need to cut her open. He could feel his own breath of relief as his patient slept, a cushion of tea leaves crushed under her shapely palms.

Xu escorted him back over the marble terraces that shone under the moon. They walked in silence. The doves shuffled their wings as they passed under their nests, and the fireflies danced, putting on a late-night show for the benefit of the hooting owls.

Sleepless, Antonio thought of the girl in the peasant's smock. Her hands had trembled at the sight of the bloody fetus, eyes aglow as she kept her gaze fixed on him.

Next morning he saw her having tea with the attendants in the kitchen, poking out her head through the window like a duck. The courtyard had darkened under clouds, and a flash of lightning lit up the pavilion. She dropped her bowl and rushed out as it started to rain. The storm had shed a harvest of yellow bottle-shaped gourds from the trees, and she ran around to gather them up in a pile, her blue smock floating over the mist.

He waited to see her again, and in the days following went looking for her along the serpentine paths and the temple gardens. He climbed the barren hills dotted with haystacks and trespassed into the Tower of Fragrance, coming face to face with the grand deity, the ten-armed Bodhisattva. Standing on the Jade Bridge, he kept his eye on both banks of the lake to spot her entering or leaving the pavilions. Gardeners were surprised to see him loitering at the lotus pond that was visited by the empress to play cards with her consorts.

She might be among the palace attendants, eating her early rice. He waited for a gust to blow off their wide-brimmed hats. A dozen eyes reminded him of those he'd seen in the empress's antechamber, eyes that didn't match the lips or the nose; or arms like lotus stems, slender and sunburnt.

"The air of yin—the feminine flavor—comes from the lower orifice. It tempts the yang. If healthy . . ."

Listening to his teacher with one ear, Antonio thought he should ask Wangsheng and Tian. Perhaps they could help him find Xu's assistant.

"If healthy, the yang enters the yin, the flavors of both float like clouds around the sun and the moon."

Maybe his teacher has sent her to the empress, to take the place of her fallen maid. Antonio imagined her in the antechamber, surrounded by the curtains.

"Forget the flavors. Tell me about your assistant."

Xu seemed surprised. "My assistant?"

"The one who helped me to do the dirty work."

"Ah!" A strand of hair flickered on Xu's face as he considered Antonio's words. "You mean Fumi? She can tell you all about herself, if you like."

"If you can bear to bring her back from wherever you've hidden her." Antonio snorted, and pointed at Xu's stick—"make her appear at the wave of your wand."

Folding up the parchments, his teacher smiled. "As a matter of fact, I was thinking of asking her to be your teacher."

Teach . . . ? He read the question on Antonio's face, then added, "Yes, she knows *Nei ching* very well."

He'd have to go away to the north for a few days, Xu said, to attend to the wounds of a cavalry captain. He gave Antonio a broad smile. "I'll be going home to escape from Peking's sun!"

Antonio thought his teacher wanted to tell him more about himself. The antechamber incident had loosened their tongues. Even without words, they shared with each other a greater comfort than before.

"You mean to the grasslands?" Antonio asked him.

"Yes, in Mongol territory. That's where I was born." Xu made a neighing sound with his tongue.

"So you must know all about horses." Antonio was excited at the prospect of discovering a fellow equestrian. Maybe he wouldn't feel so lonely after all, if he and his teacher shared their common joy. Happy to take a break from *Nei ching*, he put his notebook down and told Xu about his friend Ricardo Silva's stables.

"In Portugal we have two breeds, the Sorraia horse and our very own Lusitano, which is most popular among bullfighters. My friend Ricardo has both types. He thinks the Sorraia has come to us from China. Maybe it's a cousin of your Mongol horses."

"I was born among horsemen," Xu said with a distracted look on his face, "who tamed wild horses and sold them to soldiers."

"Did you want to be a cavalry captain yourself?" Antonio asked him. "There must be nothing more exciting than growing up with horses!"

"There wasn't much excitement killing them." Xu spoke with a sad face. "My father was butcher among horsemen. We killed the ponies that couldn't be broken in. And camels and goat for meat." He kept silent. "I wanted to get as far from horses as I could."

Antonio wondered what made the butcher's son turn to *Nei ching*. "Did you run away from home then?"

Xu shook his head. "Locusts and droughts drove us from the grass-lands, with the animals dying for lack of water. My father died too, and I was sent away to a monastery. The priests there taught me *Nei ching*, and saved me from becoming a eunuch." Xu smiled and pointed to the kitchen. "I could've become just like them!"

A horseman, a butcher, a doctor, an abortionist and a spy who keeps an eye on the empress's visitors . . . Antonio wondered what else was left to know about Xu.

"Your new teacher is the same as me."

"A horsewoman?"

"No, no . . . she has learned *Nei ching* the hard way too."

Unable to follow, Antonio asked Xu to tell him more. "What will you ask her to teach me?"

"She'll start with the twelve channels and the flow of *qi* through them. She'll tell you how the organs are connected to one another."

"How will I understand what she says?" Antonio complained about his meager Chinese, hurriedly acquired in Macau and yet to be put to a stern test.

"But your Chinese is very good. And it's getting better every day. Your attendants can understand you, and you them. I'd say it's almost as good as your padre friend's."

Antonio shook his head. "No, I'd need much more than I've got to understand what she'll say about the channels and organs."

Xu smiled mischievously and rose to leave. "She won't speak Chinese but use a different tongue, you'll see . . ."

"Wait!" Antonio tried to stop him. *A peasant using a different tongue? How many more surprises does Xu have up his sleeve?*

"You must tell me more about my teacher."

"She worked with a Dutch missionary who came to China with his printing press. She helped him print Bibles in Chinese and some in English too. She can tell you anything you want to know about printing blocks and ink."

"From Bible to *Nei ching*!" Antonio exclaimed.

"She had no choice but to leave when the press was burnt down and her master killed."

"Killed by whom?"

His teacher looked surprised. "You mean you haven't heard about the Boxers yet? Those who are going around burning churches and killing foreigners?"

Wangsheng's eyes danced as Xu gave him his orders. He ran back to the kitchen to tell his young friend. Kowtowing before the elderly man, the two turned to Antonio and each gave him a broad grin.

He sat before the mirror and held up the scissors, the surgical box open on his lap. The face seemed unfamiliar, as if the features had rebelled against their owner. The mirror showed the sea, the sun from his travels and the battle with insects, not the blue-eyed lady killer with strong jaws, a proud nose, and a pleasing cleft on the chin. The scraggly stubble and burnt skin made him look much older, like a traveling monk. A *shipwrecked Candide in El Dorado!* Arees would've teased him. He called across the courtyard for a bowl of warm water, and picked up the pocket scalpel instead.

Antonio imagined the peasant girl's hand on his face. It traced the jaws till her fingertips brushed his lips. Plaits of hair fell onto her shoulders as she leaned forward, her force greater than his, leaving a mark of blood on the scalpel. Will his new teacher teach him everything about syphilis? *I must tell her to hurry.* Antonio wondered if he should confide in her about his dying father.

Finished with grooming, he sat in the courtyard in the full finery of a gentleman. Lanterns flickered; the breeze blew in the song of the boatmen on the lake. Plum wine simmered in the brazier, and it felt like a festa.

That night he dreamed of the awful things Xu had told him. A mob had gathered before his pavilion, calling for the blood of the foreigner. Burning haystacks filled the courtyard with smoke, covering the kitchen and the lodge. A voice exhorted the men to set everything on fire and he saw himself, dressed like Joaquim Saldanha in a priest's robe, dashing about to find a way to escape. The lion dog cowered behind a shrub, its tail between its legs, and he whistled for it to come out. But there were no signs of his attendants. Soon the mob was all over the pavilion, smashing windows, ripping up the plum tree by its trunk, torching the kitchen and building a fire in the middle of the courtyard to burn him alive.

Awake, he looked for the insects, but they weren't there. A quiet night cleared his mind of the usual things, and for once he didn't think about his father, wondering instead about the new nightmare that had replaced the old. *Boxers.* . . . He mulled over rumors he'd heard on ship and in Macau, the gory accounts of rioting that he had dismissed as plain hysteria. "The noose is tightening around our necks," a nervous man had commiserated with his fellow merchants on the *Santa Cruz.* "It won't be a repeat of the opium wars this time. This time they'll strike first, catch us by surprise." Mr. Danziger had tried to calm their nerves. "We won't sit idly by and kiss the empress's arse, will we?" He had reminded everyone of the sacking of the Summer Palace—"We can hit where it'd hurt her the most"—but no one was impressed, merchant or priest. "This time there'd be no war"—a miner from Edinburgh had made his gloomy prophesy—"They'll trap us one by one, and kill us like geese."

You've come to take their best. . . . Antonio remembered Joachim Saldanha saying. Did his hosts resent him for that? What if they were no better than the Boxers themselves, Xu and the eunuchs, fooling him with the Yellow Emperor's Canon?

He started to compose his letter to Arees in his mind. She'd want to know more than her brother. *Don't write me about horses,* she'd say. *Or how much it costs to buy a Mongol sword.* She wouldn't be interested in boat races on the Pearl River, or in the pretty mestizhinas. What if he wrote her about the songbird that refused to sing, or his mysterious teacher? *Tell me about the empress,* she might ask. Was it true that she'd imprisoned her nephew because he wished to surrender his throne to foreigners? He wished Arees were here for the two of them to spy on the invisible empress. What could he tell her about the Chinese? His mind went over everything he'd heard and came up with a simple phrase, *They know as little about us as we do of them.*

Perhaps Arees would want him to write about his "adventure." *When will Candide come home?* He hoped she'd be waiting to read not simply about China but about him.

Dozing, Antonio eyed Joaquim Saldanha's box. He had almost forgotten about it. *Does it hold our best, the reason why so many have been slaughtered?* How many more were left to collect? He imagined his attendants groaning under their weight, spurred on by their triumphant owner.

As dawn broke, he opened the box, which smelled of the dung that had been used to seal the lid. A few knocks with his surgical mallet were enough to crack the crude lock. The lashings had almost come apart, and needed a tug or two to snap. Before he could take a peek inside, Antonio heard a sound, a steady rap like a carpenter tapping wood with his hammer. It stopped for a moment, then resumed, changing its pitch as if starting afresh.

He laid his ear against the box and followed the source that seemed as human as he could imagine. Whoever was inside was aware of him outside the box, responding with silence if he moved and with a flurry of sounds whenever he stood still.

Armed with the vicious bone saw, he flung open the lid and waited for the dust cloud to settle. The morning haze darted rays inside the box like spring showers, lighting up the burnt Madonna with her soot black feet and her crown strangling her like a serpent. A pair of blue eyes ringed with ash gazed pitifully from her cradle.

He slammed down the lid and turned away. The sound stopped too as the fat woodworm wriggled out of the box and scurried for cover under the bed.

Gunshots woke him, and Antonio thought his dream had come to life. It was impossible to tell from the sound if soldiers were firing blanks or fighting an enemy. He noticed Tian poking his face through the door. The young eunuch had come with his early rice, instead of the breakfast of lotus porridge. New replacements had arrived at the palace, he told Antonio, to relieve the garrison, and were testing ammunitions. The volleys would stop soon. The troops had strict orders not to disturb the empress's afternoon nap.

He scolded Tian for bringing his early rice too early, then realized that he had slept through the morning after the sleepless night. His new teacher had come and left, his attendants too scared to wake him up. His heart sank, but he stopped himself from flaying them, knowing that he'd need them to stand by his side.

He must use the day to write to Rosa Escobar, Antonio thought. Arrangements had been made to pass on his letters through the British minister to Macau and on to Lisbon. "Cedric Hart will help you,"

Joaquim Saldanha had assured him, "to do your business with Europe."
He had cautioned him though, not to mix up the two: "Favor neither
side as you flit between the palace and the Legation."

*When the symptoms disappear, the patient might think himself
lucky,* he wrote to Rosa. With the rash disappeared and his hair grown
back, Dr. Alexander Maria might think he had returned to full health.
He might even resume a normal life, go hunting, or ride the carriage to
Lisbon to see his friends. Young men often bragged about beating the
pox, let off with just a scar on their vitals to flaunt as a souvenir. Antonio
reminded Rosa about its supreme trickery: feigning a cure when the poison was up to its greatest mischief inside the body.

As the day wore on and his regret grew at missing his chance to
meet Fumi, he began his letter to Ricardo Silva. Even without thinking,
he filled a whole page with questions about Campo Pequeno, the new
bullring; about the miracle funiculars that could float on air and lift passengers from the depths of Baixa to Bairro Alto. He asked his friend if the
king was still alive, and whether his carriage had been attacked again
with objects more lethal than stones.

Dona Elvira would've informed her godson about Antonio's passage through Macau, and he resisted writing him about the palace. His
friend would be angry at the arrangements. *Why must you, the star of
the Faculdade, spend a whole year learning to read pulse from the Chinaman?* He'd question the wisdom of having a padre as his guide—"fools
who've made a virtue out of dying at the hands of savages." Why couldn't
he ask Dom Afonso to demand the cure from the Chinese? Foreigners
were powerful in Peking, everyone knew. Hadn't the British smacked
the Yellow Emperor's bottom with their gunships? Europe should
demand what it wants from China, not pretend to be a humble student.

Antonio also resisted writing him about the Golden Lilies. His
friend would snigger at him, "An Eastern empress! You'd do better with
a Nubi, my friend, even a Brazilian mama. She'd bear you more babies
than you can father!"

He missed his friend, and as he drank plum wine with his late rice
Antonio wrote about everything he'd found unbearable since stepping
into his pavilion, including the shrimp eggs and the insects.

Are books still being written? he asked, like a marooned sailor. *And music? Do you still dance and drink, ride in the marshes? What do clean sheets feel on a soft bed? Do women still love to be loved?*

The young eunuch hushed him with a finger. Stepping out of his lodge into the courtyard next morning, he thought the mob of his nightmare had arrived and they had but minutes to escape. Both his attendants were peering up at the plum tree, and circling it like predators about to pounce on a prey. A yellow bird perched on a branch looking down. It had flown its cage inside the kitchen, turned a few circles chased by the yelping dog before it escaped through the window. It was a rare songbird, he'd been told by his attendants, although he had never heard it sing. Just like Antonio it was fed a special diet of cooked rice wrapped in egg yolk, which deceived it into thinking that it was feasting on a little insect. His attendants spent more time on their pets than on their guest, Xu had complained, threatening to move Antonio over to another pavilion. Wangsheng closed in on the tree and gave it a good shake as if expecting the bird to drop down like a ripe fruit, causing it to shift to another branch and arch its neck to catch a better view of its captors.

"All is paradox in China," Antonio recalled Dom Afonso saying. "Worrying over domestic details, when the house is on fire!" He thought of shooting the bird with the handgun the governor had given him, and presenting it to Wangsheng to throw into the kitchen pot.

Fumi joined the hunt, holding a wand like stick. The eunuchs gave way as she made a twittering sound with her lips. She kept her eyes fixed on the bird, circling the tree and calling it down from the branch. Rooted to the spot, Antonio heard her sing a lilting tune, the bird giving off a sudden flutter as if called by a greater force. Then it started to descend branch by branch till it swooped down on the crook of her wand like a docile pet, hopping onto her outstretched finger. She led it back into the cage being held up by Tian.

Antonio's heart throbbed, observing the rarest of sights.

After the courtyard had been swept, he sat before his new teacher with the dog at his feet. The *hwa-mei* started to call, and Fumi spoke in the English she had learned from the Dutch printer of the holy book.

"If you want to know about *Nei ching*, you can ask me." She waited as if expecting a reply, then drew back her sleeves baring her arms. "But first, you must wake early and prepare yourself." She gave a quick look toward the kitchen. "Wangsheng can bring you tea when you're ready."

He observed her opening and shutting her lips like a pantomime. A blue form floated like a cloud before his eyes, with a dancer's twirl of the arms.

"The body is cold and the mind open when the morning star appears, before the sun has risen fully. That's the best time for *Nei ching*."

Ah! Xu has sent more than a replacement! She wants more from her student, wants me to change my ways. She has conspired with the eunuchs to rule over the mornings when I'd be at my weakest.

"Body and mind are willing at dusk," Antonio spoke in an even voice, not wishing to upset her, "when the evening star has risen, a time for learning new and useful things."

"But how will you see in the dark?" She threw him a challenging look.

Her gaze fell like a raindrop from his shoulder to the tip of his finger as he pointed at the lamp behind the rice panes.

Fumi smiled. "In the evening you can go over what you've learned during the day. But to master *Nei ching* you must . . . ."

"I don't want you to teach me *Nei ching*," Antonio whispered.

She arched her eyebrow. "No? But aren't you here to . . ."

"Teach me about nightmares, if you can." He spoke quietly. "Tell me why I haven't slept a wink since I've come here. Why do I dream of death every night?"

"But you were sleeping when I came last time!" Fumi looked uncertain.

He held out his palm without a word and laid it down before her. Reaching forward, she paused over it as if to examine the shape, then held the wrist lightly between her thumb and the middle finger. A dead worm came to life, crawling under his skin. The force doubled as she added the ring finger.

"Why do I hear voices when I'm alone?"

With the ring, middle and index fingers, she pressed down hard, and the worm turned into a dragon, surging through his veins. He closed his eyes.

An eternity seemed to pass, before he heard Fumi's voice again. "It's your mind, not your body." She kept her eyes on Antonio's wrist, as if she could see his pulse beating. "It's not the rapid *Sumai* that shows a hardening of the arteries and a loss of blood to the brain. Nor *Jinmai*, which is proof of your stomach fighting with the nerves and creating confusion. The organs are all healthy, and they don't know why you're suffering. It's *Daimai*." She nodded. "The soft and frightened one, which hides under the rest."

"What does *Daimai* say about nightmares?"

"It says you're afraid of something." She seemed to recall Antonio's account of his dreams. "Maybe you're afraid of death."

He could hear the birdcage twittering, and a pair of fine nostrils inhaling and exhaling.

"But you're young and strong, maybe you're afraid for someone else. You are dreaming of someone who's suffering." Fumi spoke evenly, without taking her eyes off his wrist.

Antonio withdrew his hand. She drew hers back too and dropped down the sleeves. "Maybe it's someone you love."

Tian brought over tea. A fly joined them and circled the bowls.

"If I tell you what he's suffering from, will you teach me how to cure him?"

From the look on her face, Antonio thought she hadn't understood him properly. "If you can cure his disease, I'll stay. But if you can't help me, you must tell me now."

A storm had risen, driving a mad squall into the courtyard. Fumi rose from her stool, placed her closed right fist under her chin and bowed. "Stay here." She spoke calmly, then moved away.

"Stop!" He called out just as she was about to vanish through the arched gate, making her turn back. He wanted to ask her about the night at the antechamber. Ask her why she had given him that look.

"You must help me save him, just as I saved someone the other night."

She glanced up at the storm clouds then dropped her gaze back on Antonio. "I saw you kill someone the other night."

He woke early to eat his lotus porridge and prepare himself to meet Fumi. She'd be less forgiving than Xu, he was certain. He'd have to learn quickly and surprise her by his brilliance. Then grit his teeth and bear her *Nei ching*. He'd be taught all about strange diseases, and their even stranger cures. Whatever their disagreements, he'd have to be ready to accept her views.

He had been overwhelmed by Fumi's presence, but also stung by her unfair accusation. *I saw you kill. . . .* "And you did too!" he could've snapped back. "You helped me kill the child to save the mother." He had fretted over her words long after she'd left. *Why blame me, the foreigner, when even a fool knows that it's impossible to overrule the empress?*

Waiting, Antonio thought of the bird that had given up its freedom and become her prisoner. What gave her the power? He had bribed Wangsheng with a Venetian pocket mirror to find out more about Fumi, but he didn't say much about her. "She is a better doctor than Xu," the older eunuch said with a straight face.

"Has she managed to cure you?"

Wangsheng shook his head. "No doctor can! God has filled my belly with something, for what he's taken away from below!"

He's hiding the truth about Fumi . . .. Antonio thought, and wondered what that truth was.

When she arrived wearing a loose robe clasped at the neck, Antonio didn't recognize her. She had the air of a princess who knows her place in the court, confident of presenting herself before the dowager. His attendants too seemed to treat her differently, not as Xu's assistant but as an important visitor. She couldn't be what he was told she was, not someone who'd learned *Nei ching* the hard way. Antonio wondered if Xu had misled him on purpose. Sitting down on the teacher's chair in the courtyard, she issued orders to Tian and Wangsheng to shut the kitchen window to stop them from eavesdropping. Antonio surprised her with his question before she could start.

"How do we know what a disease is unless we see it?"

"We'd know because we're all sufferers," she said, settling down. Seeing the mischief in Antonio's eyes, she added, "Our sages didn't teach the sick, only the healthy. Students were taught to *imagine* sickness, and those with the most vivid imaginations became masters of *Nei ching*."

Antonio smirked. "And so they became doctors without ever seeing a patient!"

She hushed him with her eyes. "Sick or healthy, we all have twelve channels, six starting at the feet and six at the hands."

As with Xu, he prepared to face the boredom of his lessons: to drink tea and stay awake, and remind himself to calm his impulse for an argument. With Fumi, at least, he'd have distraction. He'd be able to put his vivid imagination to work. He thought about Wangsheng's caustic answer when he'd asked him if Fumi was doctor to the empress as well. "The dowager needs her only to kill," the eunuch had said with a straight face.

"Of the twelve channels, the first starts at the stomach then rises to the tip of the middle finger." She laid her palm flat against her navel and passing her right hand through the valley of her breasts, held up the middle finger above her head. "The second from the heart to the inside of the little finger." She smiled at Antonio, and parted her fingers to give him a glimpse of a secret nook. "The third . . ."

She danced before him, sitting with his notebook open on his lap, lifting up her arms, twirling on her toes, as if she was performing for the empress.

"The channels transmit *qi* and carry disease. To know them is to know the body's secret passages." She waited for him to ask a question, then bade him rise. "Show me how well you've learned the third channel that we call *taiyin*."

Antonio knelt before her. He touched the small toe of his left foot, then drew his forefinger straight over his leg to the groin. A change in direction took it past the liver to the base of the throat, ending up at the tip of his outstretched tongue.

Fumi applauded, bringing the attendants out of the kitchen and they joined in the applause too.

"Tell me what happens when the third channel is blocked."

Antonio repeated what he'd learned from his teacher. "It causes pain."

"What sort of pain?"

"Like childbirth, a deep distress all over the body. And vomiting, and heaviness of the limbs, and a feeling of sinking under ice . . . ."

"And how would *you* know the pain of childbirth?"

"By my vivid imagination, of course."

His teacher laughed and called for a round of tea.

Antonio wished they could be elsewhere, by the jade fountain of the lotus pavilion overlooking the lake; or at the very top of the hill, just the two of them, rehearsing the dance of the twelve channels. After weeks of boring lessons, finally, he sensed the exhilaration of *Nei ching*, like a young student discovering the human form for the very first time.

"The fourth channel is the hardest." Fumi spoke between sips of tea.

She seemed to read his mind, stopping to give him time to finish his bowl. Then called Wangsheng over to remove the pot. "It's easy to learn if you can think of yourself as a germ that passes blindly through it. If you can learn with your instinct rather than your mind."

She knows I'm waiting . . . to show her how easily I can master the fourth channel. He looked steadily at her, mindful of noting down every detail. Fumi rose from her stool, took a few steps back and stood before him.

"The fourth channel starts at the heel of the right foot and ends at the pupils." Turning her back to Antonio, she raised her robe to her waist and leaned back to trace the curve of her snowy calf with an index finger, tracing a silken thigh, naked hips and an arched back, reaching up to her closed eyes. She held her pose for him to take note then dropped the robe back.

"The fourth channel gives force to blind impulse." Back on her seat, she spoke slowly.

Antonio sat before an empty page, barely listening to Fumi. His mouth turned dry and his breath quickened. A curtain of still air seemed to fall around them, and he heard neither the birds nor the trees. The courtyard seemed as still as the lake with the two of them alone on a barge.

"Who gives orders to the channels?" She looked stern, as if expecting the answer instantly. "How long have you been studying *Nei ching*?"

His mind went blank, and he turned his gaze back to the notes.

"The body is nothing." There was a glint in her eyes. "Once awakened, the yin and the yang rule over everything—order and disorder, health and sickness." She leaned toward him as if to pass on a secret. "To find the cure, you must first know what excites the disease."

He blamed himself after Fumi had left for not asking Xu more questions about her, for letting him get away with his mysterious answers. How did the Dutch printer's friend become a *Nei ching* master? How did she end up at the Summer Palace? What did she do for the empress? His curiosity grew with every passing moment. *Who is she? Whose daughter, whose wife, whose mother?* Was she a concubine of a special rank, or simply someone who'd taught herself the Yellow Emperor's laws? He rued the missed opportunity when he could've asked her to tell him enough about herself before he agreed to be her student. He could've pretended to be a haughty foreigner, a proud doctor who needed to know everything. *She is just like Maria Helena,* he had thought in the antechamber. Someone who'd watch and admire his moves, fancy the work of his skillful hands on her healthy body. He knew his power to win over the ladies, the power he had had to cultivate as a boy following his famous father around. He was embarrassed, recalling his earlier thoughts. It was she who had the power, putting him at her mercy.

"Bring my porridge and bathwater." Antonio surprised the eunuchs early next morning even before the kitchen fire had been lit. In the time it took to light up the oven, he memorized his lessons, reading them aloud, pacing the courtyard. Just like Xu, he laid out his drawings of the twelve channels on the ground and poked them with a stick, made Tian laugh by calling him over to pose as his student.

When they met, he surprised Fumi with his question: "What does your empress suffer from?"

"Empress?" Fumi seemed taken aback, as she settled into her teacher's chair.

"You must know, mustn't you, if you've spent time with her here?" *Will she say who she really is, or keep on pretending to be an assistant?* "Xu's the empress's doctor, we know. Do the two of you look after her courtiers as well? Her concubines and maids?" He thought he'd remind her of the abortion. "Who asked for the child to be killed?"

Ready to flout the rules, he heard Joachim Saldanha in his ear . . . *You must keep to yourself, never ask questions about the empress. . . .*

"What if she had died with her baby?" He made a sign for Wangsheng to bring them tea. "Would it have saddened the empress?"

"The palace is no different from the world outside." Fumi seemed to have regained her composure. "There are as many sick people here as anywhere."

"And can you cure them all?" He tried to probe her again. "What if there was an outbreak of plague?"

"*Nei ching* has a thousand cures for a thousand diseases. A master will know how to treat it." She looked quickly over Antonio's drawings of the twelve channels, and continued, "Unless, of course, there was only a novice to look after the patients, one who made silly mistakes like you." She pointed to the lung channel "that mustn't encircle the throat, otherwise it'll throttle the poor thing to death!"

He asked her to show him the seventh channel. Fumi had described it as the "great traveler." "This one goes all over the body. Starts from the forehead, then drops down to the bladder, sending out branches everywhere including the toe. From headache to sore muscles, it governs all pain, including the sweet pain of intercourse."

"Show me where it begins and ends."

Fumi asked him to rise from his stool and remove his clothes. She watched him closely as he stood naked before her in the courtyard. Then traced the seventh channel on his skin with her forefinger.

Sipping his plum wine in the evening, Antonio couldn't think a single thought about Fumi. Image after image invaded his mind, preventing it from examining her properly: the image of Fumi with the yellow bird or dancing in the courtyard before him. She seemed to be no more than a well-crafted form. Unlike anyone he had met before, she'd made him feel overcome by a strange sensation, unwilling to ply his charm and win her over.

"You will suffer from oriental sicknesses," Dom Afonso had warned him before he left Macau. "They'll affect the mind before they affect the body. Your medicines won't have an answer to them." Was this his first brush with an oriental sickness? The sickness of images that were more vivid than any he could remember?

He had promised that he wouldn't think about women. Like a fish entered into new currents, he'd alter his breathing. He'd planned to disguise his instincts during his travels, to avoid the flower boats and brothels on shore. He had had to remind himself of his resolve whenever Dona Elvira tempted him as they strolled on the Praya Grande. "You must taste the yellow beauty before you return home!" As he sat alone in his pavilion, his old habit returned to trouble him. Restless, he paced his lodge, reminded of what he missed most.

What would she do if she knew my thoughts? He had been on his best behavior with Fumi, hadn't cast even a single amorous glance at her. He had stayed away from the usual games: staring needlessly into a woman's eyes and unleashing a devastating smile; passing her a secret note, even touching her "by accident." He didn't know what Fumi would do if he did unleash his devastating smile. *Will she ignore me and simply go on? Will she stop?* She seemed impervious to his attraction. He wondered if her indifference came from a deep attraction, if in fact it was the cleverest of ploys to keep up her guard with him.

Was the dead Dutchman her lover?

He must prolong his morning sessions with Fumi, he concluded, to test that indifference. Calling Wangsheng and Tian over to the lodge, Antonio explained his plan to them.

"The early rice mustn't come too early." He stopped, hoping his attendants would understand him. "Otherwise, it'll cut short my lesson. My teacher will leave in the middle of our discussion. You must wait till I ask you to bring it."

Wangsheng looked confused. "But the early rice must be served when the cooking is finished. Otherwise it'll turn cold." He nudged Tian for support. "If it's cold, it'll taste bad and hurt your stomach."

"Then you mustn't start to cook too early."

"But . . ." The older eunuch appeared unable to follow his argument. "The vegetables and the meats will spoil unless we cook them soon after we've brought them from the market."

Antonio scolded him. "Then go to the market late. It's as simple as that." He was annoyed with Wangsheng.

"Unless we go early, the shops will sell out. We'll have nothing left to buy," Tian said in a small voice.

Antonio overruled their objections, and laid down his strict rules about early rice. When Fumi arrived next morning, he prepared for a long and uninterrupted session. *I must make a deliberate error or two,* he thought, *to hold her back at the pavilion, have her go over the lesson with me once more. I must argue with her, even make her angry.* Tian came over frequently to fill their teapot with boiling water, and he reminded him each time with stern eyes to obey his plan. His stomach growled for food, but he pressed on, surprising Fumi with his persistent questioning.

"Your attendants must've grown used to you by now." She watched Tian running back to the kitchen. "Their lives are the saddest in the palace, saddest in China." She seemed to be waiting for a cue to leave, and Antonio praised himself privately on his cunning plan.

"And concubines? Aren't their lives sad too?" He thought he'd ask Fumi about the old concubine he'd seen. *What did she die of? Why was she brought to the Palace of Clouds? Did they wish to preserve the body. . . . ?* He shivered, imagining a palace full of embalmed corpses. A waft of pleasing smells came from the kitchen. Fumi raised her nose, and smiled at Antonio.

"You must be hungry to be thinking about things other than your lesson!" Then she left him sitting on the student's stool.

Antonio entered the kitchen and smashed the pot on the oven. He shouted at his "empty-headed" attendants for failing to keep the kitchen window shut while they cooked early rice, just as his teacher had ordered.

He grew impatient if Fumi arrived late. The tea turned cold by his elbow; he paid no attention to Wangsheng, who begged him to eat. A whole day seemed empty and wasted, and he'd send Tian over to the palace's forbidden parts to find his teacher.

"But the empress is asleep, no one can enter her quarters now," the young eunuch would protest.

"Damn the empress. Go find Fumi."

Tian hid in the kitchen and Wangsheng scratched his head on days when Fumi didn't come for the morning lessons. Antonio drowned them with questions. Did they know if she was sick? Was she with another student? Did they know her little secret, that she'd gone away like Xu? Or worse, that she'd resolved to stop teaching the foreigner?

His anxiety grew manyfold when he thought how easy it'd be for her to simply leave him and disappear. Once Xu returned, she'd be reduced to a kneeling form in the courtyard, the silent form that no longer danced or laughed or caught birds with her bare hands. *How hard will it be for her to stop being my teacher?*

After a few weeks with Fumi he felt light in the head but possessed of a dead weight. Her image recurred day and night, as heavy as a dream that refuses to leave, as real as the rats biting his toes and keeping him awake. Alarming himself, he'd rush out of the lodge as he imagined her sitting on the teacher's chair and waiting for him long after she'd left. He thought less about insects, growing fond even of the ant army and the yellow moth that circled him like a devout pilgrim.

Awake in his lodge, he asked the questions he wanted her to ask him, then worded his replies carefully. Perhaps she'd want to know about Lisbon, about ships; how could it be possible for him to come this far? She might ask him if he was married, then question the reasons behind his lingering bachelorhood. *You must have several wives if you haven't found one yet. . . . Men find it impossible to live without any!* He could hear her laugh. *Don't you have someone special waiting for you?* He didn't wish to tell her about Arees. Perhaps she'd ask him about his mother. Even now he could hear his mother singing in the kitchen as she baked her pastéis . . . *é varina, usa chinela* . . . imitating the Varina of her song, moving about like a cat . . . *tem movimentos de gata . . . é varina. . . .* He remembered her mostly through his father, who had a habit of bringing her up whenever they had to decide about something important. "Your mama wouldn't want us to leave the marzipan cake behind but take it home." Or make him obey a house rule without having to scold him. "If you sleep with your boots on, poor Mama would have to clean the sheets for you." The *bombas* won't hurt him, his father would assure him on the night of fireworks, as his mama couldn't bear to see her Tino cry. Even when he was older and at the Faculdade, his father would remind him to wear his gown to the annual ball or risk being taken for "just a rotten drunk," as his mama would've said.

He wished he could sing Mama's song for Fumi. *What if I take her back with me?* He imagined them in Lisbon, arriving at a lavish ball thrown by his friends. A commotion would surely follow them, heads would turn and glasses drop to the floor at the spectacle of the dashing Dr. Maria accompanying a pair of slanted eyes. They'd escape the gossip, and head for the gardens to see the seven hills of the city risen like giant seahorses from the Tagus. How far was the China coast? She might ask him. They'd hear the steamships bellow at Baixa harbor, bound for Estado da India.

> . . . *na canastra a caravela*
> . . . *no coração a fragata*

He'd hum his mother's tune as they roamed the Alfama, still smelling of the sea from those who had come over on caravels and frigates. What if they went to Praça da Alegria, where half-naked ladies cursed their clients and drunks sang odes to their favorite whores?

And Arees? What will she make of Fumi?

His nightmare returned, just when he thought he'd been cured. It was the very same band of syphilitics but without his father, joined by a woman with alien features. She was taking off her chemise that came down to her knees, and a scarf folded like a turban around her head, each movement clear and languid like a dancer's steps. Her luxuriant hair sprouted like foliage under the shade of a giant tree, as if she was a flower blooming that very moment. Following her to a river, he caught a glimpse of her naked body covered by a thousand rosebuds. She waited for the howling band to pass before she stepped into the water. Like a swan, she turned a few majestic turns then disappeared under without a ripple. In his nightmare he saw himself raising a cry and charging into the river, fighting the waves in vain as she slipped further away into darkness.

Antonio woke with a start and found Tian at the door. Fumi had come for him and left. She'd be gone for a few days now, he said, smiling nervously.

"Why didn't you stop her?" He leaped from his bed and took the eunuch by the throat, rushing blood to his face.

❁

With Fumi away, he persuaded his attendants to take him to a village outside the palace. "You're only a prisoner if you think like one," Joachim Saldanha had reminded him during his last visit. Antonio called Wangsheng to the lodge and asked him to fetch bearers to take him out on a sedan. The eunuch looked uncertain. Dr. Xu hadn't left him any instructions, he said.

"I don't need Xu's permission to go out," he told Wangsheng firmly.

His attendant closed his eyes to think up a suitable excuse or propose something to divert his master. "We can take you for a walk to Suzhou Street by the lake." Then he tried to offer an even better plan. "You can go to the Peony Terrace to see the flowers."

"I don't want to go to the lake, or anywhere else only to be told that I can't be there because your invisible empress might catch a glimpse of me." He made as if to go out of the pavilion himself to search for bearers. Wangsheng followed him to the courtyard, and made a valiant attempt to stop him.

"Our Tianfen can play a wrestling game with you." Overhearing them from the kitchen, Tian fled the pavilion.

"I just want to go to a village to see things for myself," Antonio tried to explain to Wangsheng. "How the villagers keep their animals, how they build their homes, how they spend their evenings. We might have some fun if there's a festival going on." He made faces and jumped all around the courtyard. "You've seen clowns, haven't you? And jugglers?" Picking up the camphor pots, he tried to juggle them—crashing a few onto the ground—danced like a demon and made shrill noises. Wangsheng started to laugh. "Ah! festival!"

"Yes! Just think what fun there'd be!" Antonio grabbed him and twirled him around.

"Then we must go to the festival of insects." Wangsheng slipped out of his hold and called Tian over. Together they went looking for the bearers.

Antonio sat on his sedan chair with the dog on his lap, and thought he was riding a magic carpet with a sea of heads under his feet. His two attendants struggled to keep pace as the bearers moved quickly. Reaching the village, he was struck by the lotus lake and the full moon that floated over it. Lanterns shaped as insects buzzed in the breeze—beetles, dragonflies, ladybugs, silverfish and moths—casting shadows on the shop windows that lined the streets. Children chased after butterfly-shaped kites fluttering over their heads, dangled from the balconies by women in silk. The butterfly chasers waved their nets wildly to catch the pretty kites. The catchers will be rewarded, Wangsheng whispered into Antonio's ear, tempting him to have a go. It was a good omen to catch one of these in the festival of insects. A lady will throw down sweets if a child manages to capture her pretty butterfly. "She will give you more!" Wangsheng pointed to a smiling face on the balcony. "Grown men can't be rewarded simply with sweets. She'll call you upstairs!" He smirked at Tian, who followed them carrying their pet dog in his arms.

A group of widows huddled before a fortune-teller's door. Wangsheng made fun of them. "What can he tell them except when they'll die?" Each woman had a chit of paper fished out from a wicker box, each marked with a character. "The fortune-teller will tell them to pick another one. The two chits will make up their fortune. If one chit has the sign of the sun, the other that of a rooster, it means the owner will have a long life. If a man picks two chits, one marked "woman" and the other "roof," it means he'll have a good wife."

"What if one chit says man, the other dog?" Tian called out to his friend.

"It means the man will have a dog's life!"

Eyes reddened by smoke from the street lamps, Antonio gave his attendants the slip and entered a tent full of groaning and cursing men to watch a singsong show. A few foreign faces dotted the crowd, among them a blond man with rough features who was cheering on the actors. Antonio spotted Xu in the front row. *Has he returned already from his little trip?* his heart skipped a beat. A young man greeted him and started to polish his boots, another pushed a pipe into his hand. An usher offered to find him a seat in the front row, and named his price with his fingers.

Two young boys bumbled on before a bored crowd to the beating of drums, like a pair of chimps, both of them viciously maimed, unable to stand upright on their crushed knees and twisted ankles. They followed their master with sad eyes as he went about collecting money from the cheering men. "The animals! You'll see plenty of them in China," Antonio recalled Joaquim Saldanha telling him in the carriage. "Our orphanages are full of them—little boys maimed by their masters and forced to earn a living as dancers and clowns." His eyes narrowed as he considered the deformities, reaching instinctively for the absent surgical box.

Tian was in tears. Like Antonio the dog too had escaped, and he'd searched for him everywhere before giving up. Maybe a lady in silk has scooped him up like a butterfly in her net. "Maybe he's sitting happily on her lap now, in his new home," he grumbled. "Dogs or men, it doesn't matter, both ready to jump at a woman's smell!" His eunuch friends led Antonio back to the butterfly street and handed him a net.

Which butterfly? Antonio scanned the balconies, setting off a roll of laughter.

He imagined Fumi among the women, her painted face gazing down as she swept her butterfly over his head. Bright amber wings tinged green at the tips fluttered like a kingfisher's wings. Clearing a space before him, he started his chase, keeping his net down to avoid catching the wrong kite by mistake, resisting the temptation to go for an easy win. Shrieks and sighs filled the balconies as he ducked under a team of butterflies, and stalked his favorite. She teased him, pulling up her kite to a speck in the sky then dropping it down to his nose; had him fooled, standing still in the middle of the street like a shipwrecked sailor. Her face appeared on several balconies all at once, made him swear and dash across the street, ignoring her friends who begged to be trapped in his net. He disappointed the children, catching each of the butterflies barring the one he was after, and letting them go without claiming his prize. The cheers started to die. Someone tried to snatch the net away from his hand. The disappointed ladies pulled up their kites one by one, and left him under the empty balconies on the deserted street glowing with lamps.

Cries came from the kitchen after the sedan bearers had brought Antonio back to the pavilion. Wangsheng sat in the courtyard, head in hand, a trail of blood before him. Antonio rushed into the kitchen to find the young eunuch holding the dog in his arms, a leg almost severed and bleeding as it lay frothing in the mouth. A village cart had run him over, and the driver had thrown the animal into a ditch. "Dunghead!" Wangsheng growled. He tried to take the dog away from his friend, but he refused to let it go. "Of what use will he be now?" He tried to reason with Tian. Without a leg he wouldn't be able to catch the kitchen rats, he'd be no match for the ugly beetles even, grow fat eating and sleeping all day till he died. "Better to . . ." Wangsheng brought out the knife used for slaughtering ducks and chicken. Antonio snatched it from his hand and ordered him to bring the surgical box from his lodge. It'd take no more than a simple cut to amputate the damaged leg then sew up the wound.

As he dipped the knife in warm water, Tian shook his head and spoke to his friend. He doesn't want the dog to be amputated, Wangsheng whispered to Antonio, for it to be incomplete, like a eunuch, live like a wingless moth, flutter about all day without the power to fly. The poor dog would be sad all his life if he couldn't chase rats, if he couldn't fulfil his purpose. Tian laid the whimpering creature on the kitchen table and drew the slaughtering knife as Wangsheng looked away.

It took Antonio a few moments to grasp what was about to happen, then he pushed the young eunuch away from the kitchen table and took out a different instrument from the surgical box, the stone crusher used by doctors to pierce a patient's bladder and crush the stones inside. He held the dog down on its back, and plunged the crusher deep into its heart, till it stopped breathing.

Tianfen was his favorite nephew, Wangsheng said. He had brought the little boy over to the palace to save him from hunger after their family had been devastated by floods. He had chosen his nephew's future—a sad life over certain death. Antonio sat with Wangsheng in the temple's shade while Tian knelt before the priest with the dog's coffin. A sad life with a dog for a friend, a minor eunuch serving the empress. An empty head couldn't take him very far, Wangsheng whispered; he was too weak to be a soldier, bereft of talents except the urge to sing in a shrill voice. The palace would keep him safe and alive.

"Did you. . . . ?" Antonio made the sign of scissors and pointed at his loins.

"No." The older eunuch shook his head. It wasn't him. But he had made the arrangements, discussed it with the chief eunuch and sought the empress's blessings. He had consulted with a priest to know the auspicious hour and paid with his savings for offerings of paper money and a pig's head, tried to prepare his nephew's mind by telling him what was about to happen.

"Did he know what it meant?"

Wangsheng shook his head again. "He thought he'd have trouble peeing, that he'd feel better in a few days. That it'd become normal."

"Did you want him to change his mind?"

"Yes, I wanted him to run away, and make me angry. Wanted him to die of hunger, or become a soldier and be killed. . . ."

"Was there no other way left?"

Wangsheng fell silent. Antonio pressed him to say what happened after the arrangements were complete. If there was anything more to be done.

"I held the boy down, just like you held the dog." Wangsheng raised his troubled eyes to Antonio. "And then the doctor did his job."

"Doctor?"

"Dr. Xu."

The sun shifted the shade and made them come out of the temple to the graveyard of pets, Tian trailing after with a forlorn look. Small tombstones dotted a sloping hillside. The empress had her favorites buried there—horses and dogs, along with the peacocks which died every winter once it started to snow.

His bout of oriental sickness started the day after the festival of insects. For months he'd seen it coming, yet it struck him with an unexpected fury, gnawing at his inflamed stomach, which felt dull and heavy like an abscess. When not on his back, Antonio sat with his knees drawn up to his chest. His tongue tasted bitter, and he breathed heavily. The fever would come soon, he knew, with vomiting and rapid discharge. He tried to stay calm as he ground the medicine from his traveling cabinet in a mortar and swallowed it without a drop of water.

Wangsheng and Tian were kept busy all day, after he had unknowingly relieved himself on his bed. They applied hot and cold compresses to his stomach when the pain became unbearable. Ants crawled all over the warm saliva drooling from his mouth, as he was too weak to brush them away. Periods of unquenchable thirst followed nausea. Restless all night, he slept all day, forcing his worried attendants to check his breathing under the nostrils with their fingers. Nothing troubled them more than his deliriums, when he seemed a different man altogether, slamming his fists and cursing, killing them with his murderous looks.

Xu had poisoned him, he thought, when he emerged from his nightmares. Baby killer! Master of castration! He must've hatched the plot in the kitchen, added something to his porridge. Was he jealous for Fumi? He tried to bribe Tian, begging him to rescue Fumi, imagining that she lay helpless in the empress's antechamber, then cursed him the curse of sailors as the young eunuch stood by and shook his head sadly.

"You might go mad or fall sick in China," Ricardo Silva had said. He cried out in his sleep, dreaming that his friend had turned into a bumbling animal.

One night he woke to find an arm, like the stem of a lotus with five petals holding out a cup. A light force raised him up on the bed. The lip tilted toward him, and he smelled water—the kind that has lived inside a jar and acquired its smell—with the sound of heartbeats encouraging him to take a sip. As the evil-smelling potion burned his throat, he screamed, "Poison!" smashed the cup and struck out at the invisible form.

He was woken again and thought a moth had entered the room and perched on the bridge of his nose. Weakened by fever he struggled to speak. A cloud stood over the courtyard, the trees dead silent, everything as still as the pair of eyes that kept staring at him. A jade cup hung over his face like an unripe apple. Someone nudged him on his back.

"Poison," he whispered dryly.

The shapeless form leaned closer to catch his words. "What did you say?"

"Poison!" He shouted into her face.

"Anger is injurious to the liver," she murmured, shrinking from his side, "as wind is injurious to fire."

It became the nightmare of nightmares, kept him awake even as fever shut his eyes under a burning forehead. Much against his attendants' wishes, he forced them to leave the lodge to allow him to spend the night by himself, to have the measure of his torturer, who was bound to return. Yet, his sickness prevented him from knowing who it was when it did appear: a pair of almond eyes, plaits coming down the back, the white folds of the dress like a sculpture in ice. He noticed a blue flower behind her ear. She walked across the courtyard and stepped into his room holding an ivory cup, dressed not as a peasant girl but like a courtier. Coming up to the bed she gazed down, then let her plaits fall as she knelt facing him. *Ah! The torture of poison.* He closed his eyes and sensed the still air between them, the drizzle of moonlight through the window. With the rustle of silk he found Fumi bare to the waist, the robe unclasped at the back to fall from her shoulders, arm raised for modesty. He saw her pour the drink down on herself, and offer him the golden slurry glistening on her breasts.

As his fever fell he wondered who he was and what he was doing in the oriental pavilion. What on earth had brought him to China from thousands of miles across the seas? He tried to recall his nightmares and mad dreams, wondered too why his body, flushed and glowing, smelled so sweetly of love.

III
LITTLE EUROPE
The price of knives

"Our Ellie has been worrying about you," Polly Hart mentioned the letters her friend Dona Elvira had written to her while she led Antonio on a tour of her house. It was a lovely Chinese villa shaded by mature trees of an English garden, with a bell tower at the entrance to commemorate the jubilee of Queen Victoria. Inside, expert eyes and deft hands had arranged everything in perfect order: walls showed photos of the Harts in the company of Indian nawabs and dead tigers; corollas of lily floated with jasmine in shallow bowls; the fireplace was crowned with sporting trophies, and a silver opium pipe gleamed inside a cabinet of curios.

"That's why we're here, aren't we?" Polly pointed to the pipe. "Without opium, we'd all be happily home!"

Antonio wanted to ask her about Dona Elvira and her menagerie of friends and domestics, but his mind was still full with the journey from the Summer Palace to the Legation. Leaving on the shoulders of sedan bearers, he had been reassured by the sight of jostling crowds after a whole month spent alone in his pavilion. The farther they went from the gently sloping hills and grand imperial arches, the more the spectacle of bustling lanes and smelly markets captivated him like a child at a festa. He was amused by the private acts that were performed openly in public places, like masseurs plying their trade at the roadside, dentists scolding screaming patients, and a team of barbers shouting down each other as they fought for customers. A leper band trailed dangerously close to the sedan, but he was unruffled by their maddening gongs and frantic pleas for alms. A naked lunatic tossed a watermelon at him as they slowed for a funeral procession, missing him narrowly, and Antonio shouted at his

127

bearers to speed up to catch a glimpse of the brilliant headdresses of the mandarins who passed him at galloping speed. They had started early to reach the Legation in time for afternoon tea, but the twenty miles or so went by in the blink of an eye, leaving him hungry for more of the real sights of Peking.

Noticing the absent look in his eyes, Polly Hart changed the subject. "How did you manage to escape your prison?" She sat Antonio down in the reception room and ordered the domestics around as they made final arrangements for the garden party. "We have been expecting you ever since you arrived." She waited for him to answer, then added merrily, "Lucky the dowager doesn't fancy you, otherwise it'd be mighty hard to get away. She allows none to escape barring the clean shaven . . . you know!" She made the sign of a knife slamming down on a chopping board.

Without a touch of paint or powder, she didn't look like a Legation wife but like someone who dressed up just enough to remind everyone else to dress properly. She'd make a real contrast with Dona Elvira, Antonio thought, imagining them giggling over the fate of palace eunuchs. "Polly is the perfect friend," he remembered Dona Elvira telling him. "She makes no demands except that of total confession. If she speaks ill of others it's because it'll do them good. Her gossip is the gossip of angels!"

"Ellie has told me everything about you, even about your . . ."

Her eyes sparkled and there was a hint of laughter when she spoke, lifting her average looks to something extraordinary and giving the impression that there were two Polly Harts—the finicky housewife, and the impish prankster.

"She thinks you're mad, of course, leaving behind a glittering career for China! *Why must he waste his life simply on a whim?*"

He didn't answer Polly's question, which was worded as cleverly as Dona Elvira's, and kept staring instead at the bouquet of red flowers on a carved table.

"*Why must he live among strangers when he can live freely among friends?*"

"Maracujá," he said, pointing at the flowers. "That's what we call them in Portugal. The passionflower. Brazilians use it as an aphrodisiac."

"Ah, passion!" There was more than laughter in Polly's eyes. "I've heard about your passions as well, about a whole choir of lovers waiting in Lisbon to trap Dr. Maria! And about a *special* passion too."

He was saved from confessions as guests walked in through the hallway ringing the doorbell for good luck and greeting fellow guests with a raised hat or a polite bow. Everyone seemed to know each other, fanning out easily to circles gathered on the lawn with drinks in hand. Servants dashed around madly, dressed in black like an army of busy ants. Standing at the patio door, Polly introduced her guests to Antonio and whispered her *real* introductions into his ear as if confiding secrets to an old and trusted friend.

"He's the most important man at the Legation," she dropped her voice, smiling pleasantly at Monsieur Darmon and raising herself on her toes to receive his kisses. "Without him and the *Messageries Maritimes* there'd be no champagne in Peking. He brings in the bubbly and takes back opium like a *beau garçon*, under the very noses of our Chinese mandarins!"

There was a false laugh in Polly's voice as she greeted "Casanova" next, Mr. Pinchback, the Hong Kong banker, carrying an ominous black portfolio under his arm. "He's a closet pornographer, whose pen is sharper than his withered limbs and frozen tongue!"

With a wave of her hand at the "rugby boys"—the young and unmarried under secretaries, deputy secretaries and customs inspectors—she drew Antonio to the veranda, from where he could have a full view of the guests assembled like the cast of a grand opera under rows of colored streamers and Chinese lanterns. Antonio was struck by the sight of so many Europeans gathered together, just like passengers on the *Santa Cruz*. The din of voices made it hard to catch Polly's words, and they stepped behind the patio doors.

"You'll find only eccentrics here." Polly chuckled. "Even if they were perfectly normal before, they become eccentric once they come over. Back home they call it Eastern fever, but it has more to do with the boredom of garden parties, I can assure you!"

Turning his back to the garden, Antonio peered inside the rooms and spotted an elderly woman sitting under a glass mirror. Her florid face and unruly mop made her look tired and worn, her arms hung listlessly by her side. "That's Norma." Polly sighed. "You've heard about Reverend Cook, haven't you?"

"The Iowa martyr?" Antonio remembered Joaquim Saldanha's gory account of the murder. Polly nodded.

"She's the widow."

Sarah Hollinger, the deaconess of the Anglican Mission, slouched on a sofa by her side and sighed constantly—the two women sitting obtrusively like a pair of mourners among the jolly crowd.

"She's still quite raw, you know . . ." The tragedy, Polly said, was the greater because she had never wanted to be in China, never wanted her husband to take up the assignment at the pioneer mission in Shanxi. The farthest she wanted to go from Des Moines, where Reverend Cook studied for his divinity degree at Oberlin College, was Chicago, to become a portrait painter. She had thought they could work among the poor blacks, recently arrived from the slaving South after the Civil War. "She draws faces of children that she never had." Polly sighed again. On her ship from Honolulu to Kobe, Norma had met Sarah Hollinger returning to China from a congress of missionaries in Boston. The ocean breeze was still fresh in her hair when they docked in Tientsin, only to be received by the first secretary of the American mission with the tragic news.

Antonio thought of Joaquim Saldanha's box in his lodge. The dried blood he had seen on the lashings could've been Jeffrey Cook's.

"It's a funny place we've got here, a top venue for parties and funerals." Polly Hart led Antonio to her "trophy guests": the eleven ministers of the eleven nations that had a permanent home at the Legation. They received Antonio with polite nods. The Italian minister sat with his beautiful wife on a chaise longue looking like a pair of leopards, beside the Japanese consul who was the proud owner of a remarkable aviary in his garden. "He has his men scrambling all over China, ready to pay in gold for rare birds. Looks like one himself, doesn't he?" Antonio agreed with Polly, and observed the bird-faced man, his eyes darting as if he were expecting his flock to descend any minute.

Where are the Chinese? He looked around the garden, failing to spot any except the domestics who moved about, filling up glasses with great speed.

Locals aren't welcome here, are they? Antonio thought to question Polly, but she gave him her answer even before he could ask. "We've had rotten luck with the Chinese, I'm afraid. They make everyone very stiff, as if we were negotiating a treaty or declaring war. Their ladies never quite know what to make of us, and in any case they think we foreigners smell badly! Except, of course, our . . ."

A Chinese man, his arm around a tall German woman, made his way past the throngs at the drinks table. "She's Helga, the unofficial correspondent of the *Nord-deutsche Allgemeine Zeitung,* and he's Yohan, the resident spy." Catching Polly's eye, Yohan left his heavily pregnant wife and came over to greet Antonio with a flourish.

"Ah, finally a Portuguese minister in Peking! The last time we had one was during the Ming dynasty."

"Not a minister, a doctor." Polly tried to cut in, but Yohan seemed confident of his facts. "A doctor can be a minister too, can't he, even if he's only here to study Canton rash?" He smiled seeing the look of surprise on Antonio's face. "I hope I haven't let out your little secret. Maybe you could bribe my wife not to report it in the *Nord-deutsche,* that way the Germans won't know anything about it!"

"You must tell me who's paid you to keep an eye on our Antonio?" Polly assumed the tone of a fake conspirator. "Why should the mandarins care when half of them have the rash anyway?"

"Is he really after Canton rash or Peking fever? That's what they want to know. The fever that scares foreigners, not the Chinese."

Polly scolded Yohan for speaking in riddles. "Why bring a doctor from Lisbon to protect us in Peking? Could've got one from Goa, if we wanted a Portuguese, couldn't we?"

"Who does he spy for?" Antonio asked her, after Yohan had excused himself to fill up a plate for his wife, who was busy gossiping with Mr. Pinchback. "Who's given him that name, anyway?"

"He's a spy, it's his job to know everything. In any case, everyone knows why you're here. You've no place to hide, Dr. Maria, not with Ellie writing plaintive notes to her friends to keep an eye on her Tino!" The Chinese, Polly said, have set Yohan up in a villa at the Legation to keep an eye on foreigners. "But he's great fun. You should hear his stories, changing his faith and his name whenever he gets into trouble — from Anglican to Baptist to Catholic!"

Her final introduction was reserved for her dearest friend and she ran across the hall to fetch him. Stepping into the garden Antonio found a small circle of men gathered around an archery range, testing bow-strings and the nocks on the arrows. He wondered what Polly would say to her friends in private about him. Just like her other guests, she'd think of something suitably colorful, describe him perhaps as *the doctor of the unspeakable disease!*

Ferguson, "her best friend," Polly had told him, was a gypsy. One of few foreigners who didn't live in the Legation, he was most often found in the company of lower classes. "Not among ministers or merchants, but artists and actors of Chinese opera, even rebels." He wasn't just a clever linguist and a bookworm, a master forger of precious manuscripts, the best mahjong player in Peking and an avowed homosexual, he could see through everyone even though his clear brains didn't go well with his dirty clothes. "His only fault is that he's a cynic, doesn't spare anyone, not even me!"

A peacock eater! Antonio smiled, thinking about the young men of Lisbon who had eyes only for other young men, as they danced to the Moorish guitar or with mulattos singing the *modinha* of the Amazon.

Arms entwined, Polly and Ferguson swept into the portico, with the gypsy acting like the star of the show, smiling through his curly mustache and speaking in a mocking voice to the guests.

"You're the only one he can't make fun of," Polly had told Antonio, smugly. "He knows nothing about curing patients. You can teach him a lesson or two, slap his face in public. That'll make you the most popular foreigner in Peking!"

But before she could introduce the doctor to the gypsy, a voice called her from the garden making her jump. "How smart of me to have left out the best for the last, my husband!" Cutting short her introductions, she led Antonio and Ferguson out to the archery range.

Antonio knew Cedric Hart the moment he saw him. He was the blond man cheering the maimed dancing boys at the festival of insects. A small group of guests waited silently as he stood erect, chest expanded and head held high with the bow poised just at the right angle for the flight of the arrow. Without taking his eye off the target, he asked his wife to call everyone over to the tables set up under the trees lit by Chinese lanterns.

"He has risen like a rocket given his perfect 'aim'!" Dona Elvira had made no secret of her disdain for her best friend's husband, putting his success down to "party-manners" rather than the true instinct that marked out all those who had proved themselves in the tricky business of foreign service. "Servility is his secret weapon!" Unlike Dom Afonso—a *real* historian—he had acquired everything about the East from encyclopedias voraciously devoured for the sole purpose of impressing his party guests. The Harts, as described by Dona Elvira, were a perfect match, "his towering ambition sweetened by the mousse of her delicious gossip!"

Relaxing the fingers of the drawing hand, Cedric let go of the arrow, which flew level with his bow shoulder and hit bull's-eye to great applause. Handing the bow over to his compatriots and acknowledging success with a routine flick of his head, he came over to join the party, making it his business to get everyone talking, drawing out the quietest among them. Taking advantage of the thinning crowd that had started to move over to the tables, he caught Antonio standing alone under the lanterns and led him to the Japanese consul, Mr. Itami.

"Let me remind you, gentlemen, of your past hostilities, of the embargo imposed by the Shogun on Portuguese traders in 1630 that led to the Nagasaki massacre."

"In 1640, you mean." The consul smiled.

"Yes . . ." Cedric Hart corrected himself. "You haven't seen a Portuguese since then, I suppose?"

Before Mr. Itami could begin to explain the Shogun's strange decision, Polly reappeared to hurry along the stragglers. "Our Chinese chef will feel terribly insulted if you prefer talking to eating!"

Hungry from his journey, Antonio started to nibble from the table of cakes. Joaquim Saldanha had told him earlier about the "fat tea" at the Legation—a late-afternoon meal that was more sumptuous than early rice. "It's enough to fill your stomach for the whole day!"—he had patted his own—"enough even for a padre!" Antonio thanked his good luck for getting a break from his attendants, as he joined the queue of guests led by the Japanese consul, who was pecking at the dishes with his chopsticks like an overfed bird.

"Our Cedric knows as little about the Nagasaki massacre as he does about most things!" Antonio heard Ferguson cackling under his breath.

"He pretends to be a wise Manchu noble, but has brains the size of a bird's!" The "gypsy" edged closer to him, flashing his gray eyes and gold bracelets, keen to test the new foreigner in Peking.

"So you've come to find quacks for the pox!" Looking around the garden as if he might just spot one of them among the guests, Ferguson spoke to him like a confidant. "Why don't you pay someone? This is a marvelously cheap country! Shouldn't have to spend too much or wait too long to find what you're after."

"Pay who?" Antonio parried the question. He wondered if Polly's best friend was indeed the cleverest man in Peking, or just a plain gossip. He motioned with his eyes toward the guests.

"Oh no, I wouldn't trust Cedric or any of the respectable officers. Or for that matter the bunch of dejected jackals." Ferguson pointed at the young archers, and narrowed his eyes. "Try Pinchback. He deals in secret matters! He could help you raid a withered eunuch's treasure of *pau de China*."

"You're in the wrong place, Doctor!" René Darmon, the champagne merchant, had overheard their conversation and joined them, bringing his friends over with him. "You should be in France, at the Hôspital Saint-Louis, the capital of syphilis. The famous Dr. Fournier has already found a way to cure all skin diseases including the pox."

"Rubbish. Syphilis isn't a dermatological disorder." Antonio's loud voice drew more guests to their group. "All the French have done is build a waxwork museum in Saint-Louis showing ghastly models of pox victims."

"But thanks to Fournier we know that not just whores but even "happily married" bourgeois women get syphilis." Mr. Pinchback's quiet words, uttered with just enough indelicacy, expanded the interest beyond medical matters, causing Polly to seize the perfect moment to liven up the party.

"Why just women, can anyone really be safe from the pox?"

"If you've been unlucky enough to miss the pox in this life, then you'll surely get it in the next!" Monsieur Darmon made a valiant attempt to revive his standing, sending a chill down everyone's spine. Helga agreed with him, adding, "Even Bavarian nuns are known to get it, and shipwrecked sailors. Virgins, even!"

"Syphilis without sin? That's impossible!" Unknown to them, the American first secretary had come over, the big and blustering John Harris, one of Polly's trophy guests.

"Not impossible," Ferguson teased him. "Depends on what you consider sinful in America. It can be spread by a kiss even, a touch, a whisper behind the curtains, by a glass shared between lovers . . ."

"By a flutter of the eyelids!" A laughing Polly joined in, making the first secretary frown.

"And yet, not everyone who goes to a prostitute ends up with the pox!" Ferguson shrugged, drawing a puzzled look all around.

Fidgeting with his glass, John Harris said glumly, "It's not a bad punishment for sinners, I'd think," inviting yet another barb from Ferguson.

"Just as the Jesuits thought the earthquake was a divine act of punishment for lascivious Lisbonites. Even today there's no shortage of those who think that syphilitics should be burnt at the stake, married men with the pox castrated and their wives locked up in chastity belts!"

With everyone going on about syphilis, Cedric Hart tapped Antonio on the back. "I thought I'd ask you about your teacher. Has he taken you to visit his hospital yet? Has he asked you to try your European treatments on his patients?"

Before he could reply, Mr. Pinchback offered his measured advice. "I wouldn't worry about treating the Chinese, curing them of their sicknesses. There are too many of them anyway—seven times the size of the British population, and four times that of America."

"I don't think he keeps his patients in his hospital." Yohan had come to join them late and appeared, as usual, to have more information than the rest. "He hides the rebels there, lets his patients die."

"Who?" Mr. Harris asked Yohan, busy balancing a pair of wine cups for himself and his wife.

"Dr. Xu, the empress's physician, among the few non-royals allowed into her court, a master of *Nei ching*, the "Horseman," as our friends from Locke Mission named him."

"Rebels?" Antonio was eager to probe and find out more about the real Dr. Xu, but Cedric called everyone into the reception hall to avoid catching the evening fog in their lungs, before the precious oolong tea turned stale and the heavenly padre souchong lost its virginal whiff. As Antonio left the garden, he saw a shadow behind the trees stealthily approaching the tables—his friend Joaquim Saldanha, ready to wolf down the feast of fat tea—and heard Polly cackling on with her best friend about the queen of all diseases.

"Tell me how did our Casanova get the pox?"

"From a Manchu princess, of course," Ferguson sniggered. "Who had caught it from a Franciscan, who in turn had only a Legation lady to blame and she . . ."

"And she?"

"And she a savvy merchant, the result of his misbehavior with a gardener and a houseboy, the long line of lovers going all the way back to a sorry sailor on Columbus's *Santa Maria!*"

"Really!"

"From the land of our very own John Harris."

"God bless America!" Polly burst out laughing.

They settled back into plush armchairs with tea and cakes, but the shift to the interior seemed to darken everyone's mood. Linda Harris, John Harris's wife, from New York, was first to touch on the topic that was topmost in everyone's mind by mentioning a small domestic incident that had assumed sinister proportions. Her pantry maid had failed to return from a home visit even after a month, and she was preparing to write her off as yet another case of unreliable domestics when word came of her unusual troubles.

"The Boxers are holding her against her will." Stirring her teacup, Linda raised her voice beyond the ladies to include the officers as well. "She's been accused of recruiting natives to serve foreigners, using her feminine charms. They've given us an ultimatum to leave China. As long as we stay here, they'd hold her prisoner and punish her for her sins."

"What sort of punishment?" Mr. Pinchback narrowed his eyes.

"For every week we spend in Peking, they'll cut off one of her fingers and send it over to us here at the embassy. That's a grand total of twenty weeks for both hands and feet, give or take a fortnight for the Chinese New Year."

The spoons stopped stirring and the room fell silent. Mr. Pinchback held his nerve to ask the next question. "And how many fingers have you received so far?"

"None yet. John has been over to the Foreigners' Bureau to demand her release, and we're keeping more than our fingers crossed." Linda's voice had a steely edge.

Even before the American first secretary could start to narrate his encounter with Chinese officials, voices came alive with more accounts of Boxer mischief.

"The maid's lucky. A Russian man and his wife have already been plunged into boiling oil." Plump and nervy, Sarah Hollinger spoke in an alarmist's voice. She had gone out with her servants to buy curtains, and heard the shops buzzing with rumors. News had come just a week ago about the sad plight of the Belgian engineers held hostage in Fengtai, as the locomotive shed built by them was set ablaze before their very eyes. The Boxers hadn't spared the dowager's special coach even, hurling it into the fire, chanting slogans against Western devils and their evil machines.

"Boxers," Polly explained patiently to a shy Mary McKinsey, the recently arrived wife of the young Scottish telegraph engineer, Roger, "are spirit soldiers, a ragtag bunch of bumpkins passing themselves off as god-sent saviors of China. There are eight million of them, or so they say, each capable of flying in air and spitting fire, immune to bullets and bombs."

"That's why they're called Boxers," Linda Harris added. "Because they fight their enemies with their bare hands. And their ladies, called Red Lantern girls, are no less vicious, thought to be equal to their men in ferocity." Mary's eyes widened as she listened to Polly and Linda.

"The Red Lantern girls can pull down a two-storied house with cotton strings, like expert seamstresses!" Ferguson quipped, but everyone else was dead serious.

Sarah Hollinger repeated what she'd heard from the domestics, that the Boxers were threatening all those who were close to foreigners: cooks and washermen, gardeners, guards and sedan bearers. "They're butchering the poor Chinese Christians, dragging them out of their homes and killing them on the spot, or torturing them at their Boxer temples, gouging out eyes, skinning them alive . . ." Her voice fell, as an agitated Helga spoke up from her reclining chair, "They'll attack the Legation after they've finished with the converts."

"Just the yearly spring riots, I suppose, arriving a touch earlier than usual." Roger McKinsey tried to calm his newly married wife, smiling kindly at her. Their honeymoon was due to start in a few days at the British minister's private bungalow in the western hills, with acres of lush grounds and clear lakes brimming with goldfish and lotus flower.

"That's nonsense." John Harris spoke calmly, and lit his pipe. "Even half of the eight million Boxers can wipe out the entire imperial army. The dowager might have to face the fate of the emperor, imprisoned in her own quarters. Even "invisible soldiers" might be too much for an un-paid, ill-fed, ill-armed and badly led army to save her let alone protect us here at the Legation."

Despite his gloomy appearance, the American first secretary in-spired confidence in others. Pouring Antonio another cup of the oolong, Polly whispered to him, "Boxers for breakfast, Boxers for lunch, Boxers for dinner . . . that's all we have here. Thank God for syphilis, for sparing us Boxers at afternoon tea!"

Monsieur Darmon spoke seriously. "The sign of a bleeding hand has started to appear on the doors of the 'unwanted.' It's the Boxers' death warrant, more feared than the plague. Merchants and innocents are bound to suffer before our complacent officers wake up." His ill-disguised contempt for the Legation ministers showed in the way he addressed his comments to Mr. Pinchback, the banker.

"We haven't been idle," Cedric Hart piped up against the unwar-ranted jibe. "Along with the Americans, the French and the Italians, we've petitioned the dowager to suppress the Boxers." Polly gave her hus-band a quick look, to warn him against an open argument with the king of the bubbly.

"But she's too rotten a reed to lean upon." It didn't take Ferguson long to add his two bits to Monsieur Darmon's caustic remarks. "She's behind the Boxers, their 'invisible spirit'!"

Tapping his pipe, John Harris agreed. "We must guard our house ourselves. The British warships moored off the mud bar of the Peiho River are a better guarantee for everyone, merchants included, than the mandarins. Plus we have Roger to reach a quick word to our bosses if we get into hot water."

"I don't know if the bosses would care," Sarah Hollinger said in a moaning voice. "Not the English ones, at least. Our lives are cheap. Think how many were killed in the Indian Mutiny."

"But we mustn't stop doing business as usual." Cedric tried to change the topic, reviving the memory of last year's tennis competition that had thrown up the gypsy as the unlikely champion. The soiree afterward though had failed to live up to expectations. "We must encourage Sir Robert to whip his assistants into shape," meaning the young agents who served at the imperial customs department and volunteered, "by order," to add singing voices to their boss's amateur operettas.

"And let's not forget the strawberries." Polly beamed at the nervous Mary McKinsey. The strawberry growers among the Legation ladies did brisk business each summer, their order books no less healthy than Monsieur Darmon's.

Polly and Cedric tried their very best to make everyone cheerful, but the talk slipped back to dead missionaries and a possible siege of the Legation, with the men going on about guns—Nordenfeldts, Maxims and Krupps—and the ladies about saving a turkey for a rainy day. Mr. Pinchback had the most reasonable plans when it came to self-defense. Foreign troops would take forty-eight hours to reach them from Tientsin if a distress call was issued, a week even, if the Boxers mined the rail tracks and the troops had to march in over boggy marshes. The canal from Tungchow would provide another route into Peking, and it'd be fair to expect medium to heavy fighting on the way. Besides stockpiling food and guns, the Legation would need a healthy supply of sand.

"Sand?" Even Ferguson seemed surprised.

"For sandbags to guard against the enemy's shelling." Showing the instinct of a soldier, the Hong Kong banker looked up at the silk curtains and made the sign of scissors.

Antonio's eyes wandered through the glass doors to Norma Cook, sitting all by herself in the adjoining room, face shaded by a faint light.

"It's too early for her," Polly whispered, "to go on with business as usual."

He saw her sobbing frame bend over an open sketchbook on her lap.

The noose is tightening around our necks . . .. He recalled the nervous merchant on the *Santa Cruz*. What on earth has gone wrong between Chinese and foreigners, he wondered, thinking about Joachim Saldanha's accounts of burnt churches and slaughtered nuns. *There's never a good time to go to China. . . .* Ricardo had urged him to change his plans even as he prepared to board his ship. Listening to the guests, his friend's words came back to Antonio. . . . *What if you're shipwrecked in China with your miracle cure?* And how about the Legation? How would it defend itself against the spirit soldiers? Polly smiled at him across the room, and he felt reassured by her presence among the mixed lot of foreigners. She'd know; she was more than a gossip. She could read what was on everyone's mind.

Polly tempted Antonio to stay back at the end of the party to "see the *real* sights of the Legation!" But he was reminded of Joachim Saldanha's counsel, "You must leave before others do, before it's too late to return to the palace." Making his way out of the Hart villa, he found his bearers dozing as they waited for him. Fog had turned the barren trees into ghosts, arms outstretched to capture the innocent, the night promising more surprises than on his trip coming over. Cedric saw him out of the door, and he overheard Yohan teasing Ferguson about his rebel friends.

"Will your spirit soldiers fight with real knives or imaginary ones?"

"You bet they'd be real," the gypsy replied. "The price of knives has shot up in Peking, don't you know?"

❀

Antonio sat on the sedan on his way back and thought about Polly's guests. Just a few of them stood out from the dozens that he was introduced to as the "brilliant doctor from Portugal," the rest simply enacting roles that were expected of them. He tried hard to recall the names of the officers, who'd greeted him warmly with a firm shake only to turn back promptly to their friends. Polly had chaperoned him through the boring lot of visitors, and he had missed exchanging notes with Joachim Saldanha, who seemed to disappear as magically as he had appeared just in time for fat tea.

"You'll find a sprinkling of mysterious creatures among hordes of sleepwalkers." Dona Elvira had sought to enlighten him about the Legation before he left Macau, and teach him proper etiquette in dealing with "our own kind." "You can be yourself with the natives, but never with foreigners," she had warned him. "They mustn't know who you really are, otherwise they'll play with your mind and twirl you around their fingers. It's the game of the bored, left with nothing better to do than scheme each other's downfall." He took note of the mysterious creatures and a few amusing ones, but wondered if he had displayed proper etiquette toward the guests.

"You're quite a hit!" Polly had whispered to him before he left. "Barely two seasons in China and they think you're as good as a seasoned wolf!"

Feeling the heat of Peking's notorious summer, Antonio thought about the biggest mystery of the party, the mystery of the "Horseman." He was struck most by the fact that everyone seemed to know all about Xu, and open to sharing their gossip with others. *Is it simply gossip or the truth?* He wondered if indeed his teacher was a friend of the Boxers, or if it was just a story made up by anxious officers. *Does he really have a hospital full of patients?* Perhaps he should've stayed back and found out more about Xu, collected enough facts and gossip to challenge him when he reappeared at his pavilion. He wondered too what Ricardo would've said if he had heard him resisting Polly Hart's invitation to spend a night at the Legation. *You're dying for your Fumi!* Rogue Ricardo would've teased him. *It's her exotic ivory skin and slanted eyes, the strangest that you've had. Lips you've never had the pleasure to kiss. It'll pass, like the infatuation with mulattas or Arab women.*

Fumi had told him the same, the morning he left for the Legation. "You'll be among your own." She had risen from bed and was gazing out at the scorching sun, filling their courtyard with light. "You'll forget me."

He watched her slip on her robe, trying to shred it with his eyes. Like a phantom she floated around him, peered through the rice paper panes to see if his sedan had arrived. Even with eyes shut, he couldn't keep her out of his sight.

"Once you're among foreigners, you'll see me the same way they do."

"See you as what?" He made a vain attempt to catch her as she wafted past him.

"As a Chinese. Just another one of them, like your eunuchs." She shrugged. "You'll have your own friends there, you won't miss anything. Might even decide to stay back, and have Xu visit you at the Legation for your lessons."

He picked up her string of pearls and threw them at her. "Come with me then."

"To the party?" She raised an eyebrow. "What will you tell them if they ask about me?"

"You're my teacher, a *Nei ching* master."

"And?"

"A bird catcher."

She feigned a look of surprise. "You won't tell them *everything*, will you?"

"The one who kills with poison."

He remembered the look of surprise on Tian and Wangsheng's faces when they'd found him with Fumi at his lodge the night before. He had left the door open by mistake, and they feared an intruder had come with evil intentions. Entering, they had expected to see a battle scene: broken vases and upturned chests; goose-feather from the bloodstained beddings floating in air like clouds. A battlefield they had found; gusts through the open window had smashed the celadon bowls filled with burning camphor. The ant army had drowned and floated on rainwater in a shallow pool under the window. At the center of the storm, they had found the two of them fast asleep like a pair of dead swans.

The older eunuch had draped a robe over the lovers and bade his junior leave with a stern flick of his head.

Returning on the sedan, Antonio imagined Fumi's arms entwined with his. "Not a bird catcher, but a goose killer!" She had told him about her life growing up among peasants, learning to keep house, to weave and sew her own clothes, living far from palaces and foreigners. Like Antonio she had come to Peking on a barge with her husband, her worthless husband who had failed to please his mandarin master. "He collected more demerits than merits, and left a year later without me to go home."

"What happened to you then?"

"I had no choice but to stay back in Peking. The Ladies Society saved me from the wolves. A kind Dutch lady took me into her home for abandoned wives."

"Was she the printer's wife?"

Fumi had shaken her head. "No, his sister." Miss de Graff knew nothing about printing. She gave me and twelve others room and board, and taught us to read and write English." Her teacher, she said, scared them with her blond hair and deep-set blue eyes, but she was motherly toward her wards although she had never had children of her own. What she taught them was good enough to find them work in foreign shops, teach Chinese to Western wives, or help missionaries at their field hospitals, even join the empress's service to keep her apprised of the happenings of the world. The opium wars had just ended and Peking was full of travelers—diplomats, reporters and petty merchants—and the society's students were much in demand.

"Why didn't you go back to look for your husband and help him with his merits?"

"Because Miss de Graff sent me off to her brother to learn to work with my hands."

Reaching his pavilion, Antonio searched for his two friends but the kitchen was empty. He wondered if they'd return to serve him his late rice. The brazier's wick had died, and the plum wine tasted cold. He remembered Fumi's words.

"I'd have gone wherever she sent me, but with Jacob I stopped worrying over my daily rice."

The mad printer had become her teacher and friend. He came to China, the birthplace of printing, with his European gift, a Koenig's machine capable of churning out hundreds of pages daily. Jacob de Graff dreamed of producing the Bible in numbers large enough to fill the appetites of the traveling missionaries. He had taught Fumi everything he knew about the secret recipes of ink and the magic art of making pictures by lithography.

"Did you love him?"

Antonio didn't know what to make of her reply. "How do you love someone who has no need for love?"

You're dying for your Fumi! He smiled, nodding his head and agreeing with his absent friend. How quickly she had become *his*, barely a

143

month after they had met in the early days of summer, which was now
reaching its peak. He knew of men who suffered from love and went
into profound depression as they floated down the currents of hell. At the
hospital they'd be bled, especially if the patient was delirious, then dispatched to an asylum as there was no cure for heartaches. His teachers
hadn't taught him a cure for lovesickness, a disease no less mysterious
than the rarest of female disorders. The symptoms alarmed him, whenever he was alone without Fumi. He felt hardly more alive than the stone
animals on days when she failed to meet him at the pavilion or in the
palace gardens as planned, as lonely as on nights when he'd stay awake
hoping to see his dead mother, filled with a strangeness that matched
his surroundings. Watching the royal sedan rush past the palace gates, he
wondered if the empress had decided to take Fumi away with her, if he'd
ever see her again before he left Peking.

She cured all his symptoms, became the empress, the invisible
revealed in flesh, turning him into a willful prisoner. They'd been lovers for
just a short while, and it puzzled him to think how quickly he had fallen
into suffering for Fumi; how much he sought the relief of her simple cure.

Back from the Legation he recalled the very first day when he had
faced her in the courtyard and listened to her birdlike voice. He'd had
to draw his mind back from his daydreaming to answer her sharp questions. It was Fumi who had brought the courtyard into the lodge soon
after the night of delicious poisoning. Now he woke to her voice as she
scolded the attendants for delaying his morning tea, for forgetting to
empty the vats and refill them with warm water for his bath. She'd pull
down the sheets, and rub his feet to circulate blood in the veins. Like a
morning bird, she talked to him incessantly about things he could hardly
remember. He'd trap her in an unguarded moment, draw her under the
covers. They'd puzzle the eunuchs, staying indoors for hours, scare Tian
with their cries, and the deathly silence that followed, turning the bathwater cold in the vats.

She taught him how best to please her, how to regulate his breath
and keep still, how to read her without even touching. "A woman's right
pulse indicates disorder; her left, order." She slipped her right hand
into his palm one morning after the lessons. "Tell me what's suffering,
which organ?"

"The organs are healthy." He played along, reciting her words back to her. "It's the extreme heat in the fourth channel that has woken the yin, causing fever, thirst and sweating."

She gave him a worried look. "Heat?"

"Like fire." Antonio nodded gravely.

"What should the *Nei ching* master do then?"

He feigned alarm. "It's the severest of troubles, and requires the boldest treatment." Then he traced her fourth channel with his fingertip, from the heel of her right foot up the snowy calf and the silken thigh, paused at the base of her hips and made her squirm, changing course suddenly to explore yet another mysterious channel.

"Wait! Let me show you. . . ." She drew him out of the lodge after the attendants had left, and made him lie on the bed of leaves under the bare trees, pulling off his robes and mounting him like a horseman, determined to ride her charge through gusty winds and the blinding sun. She shut his mouth with her palm, and stroked him with her pointed fingers, holding him as firmly as she'd hold the staff of a sword, stretching her arm behind her back and whispering words of consolation that grew into a continuous flow of nocturnal sounds. A dead leaf fell on his forehead as she kissed his eyes and eyebrows, his lips, kissed his heart and the hollow under his neck, holding the throbbing vein between her teeth. As she started to gallop, he thought he'd die of the heat that burned every channel and set fire to the bed of leaves.

He didn't remember how and when Fumi had turned into his lover, the memory of his sickness holding no clue to that single episode that had changed everything since his arrival; how quickly she had melted his resolve, how easily the barrier had been broken between the courtyard and the lodge, drawing in the pond and the flowering plum that turned the pavilion into a secret garden within the walls of the Summer Palace.

Tired after his journey, Antonio drank the cold wine out of habit and slumped on the bed that still smelled of his absent lover. He imagined her teasing him with kisses like the solitary beetle that climbed up his toe.

"Do you know what they're saying?" Fumi nudged Antonio, and pointed at Tian, who was feeding the birds.

"What?"

"They're talking about us."

Antonio thought his attendants were complaining over his morning habits made worse by Fumi's visits. He knew they were being watched, because the kitchen fell silent as they emerged from the lodge. Two pairs of eyes burned their backs; the birds too stopped twittering in their cage. Calls for tea brought Wangsheng and Tian scrambling back to life. They filled and refilled the bathroom vat with warm water, ignoring the fact that their guest preferred to take a dip in the pond to keep cool in the hot mornings. Modesty prevented them from entering his bedchamber, and they rushed about to finish their errands as swiftly as possible to leave their guest alone with his teacher.

"They can stop worrying over my bath." Antonio spoke gruffly.

"They're saying we are the only lovers in the thousand pavilions of the Summer Palace. Wangsheng is telling his young friend what to expect."

"To expect more trouble?" Antonio guessed.

"With lovers no one knows anything for certain. Not even they know themselves. He's telling Tian to be prepared for nothing, just like in a circus. *Don't expect to see an elephant, for you might see the clown instead!*"

"What if they don't like what they see? What if word reaches the . . ."

"You mean the empress?" Fumi stopped to think for a moment, then went on. "She was once in love too, betrothed to her cousin before she entered the palace as a concubine."

"And Xu?" He had avoided bringing up the Chinese doctor. How long would it be before he returned from the North and resumed his lessons with him? He thought he'd tell Fumi about the festival of insects, about catching sight of him in the singsong. Was he really away? *He hides the rebels in his hospital. . . .* He wondered if he should ask Fumi about Yohan's remark.

"Xu shouldn't mind as long as you're busy with your lessons." She dismissed his worries with a shake of the head. "He'll be proud to know how much you've learned in such a short time."

"Unless, of course, he's too busy himself to care about his student." Antonio quipped.

Fumi gave him a surprised look. "Too busy with what?"

He thought he should confide fully in Fumi about what he'd heard at the party. "With the patients of his hospital. Maybe others even."

Fumi gave him a questioning look. "Which others?"

"He's known to be friendly with the rebels. Maybe he's left to help them fight foreigners."

"Rebels! You mean the Boxers? Is that what your friends have told you?" Fumi scoffed at the thought. "To foreigners every Chinese is a rebel. Have they told you I'm a rebel too, that you're in love with a Boxer?"

Antonio burst out laughing. "Yes, they've advised me to escape with her before trouble starts."

"Escape?" She exclaimed. "Escape where?"

He made the sign of a sailing ship riding the waves, and a captain peering through his telescope.

"You want to take me back with you?" Fumi looked out of the window. "Why don't you live here, become a *Nei ching* master and treat your friends at the Legation?"

Antonio shook his head. "They don't want to know." Lying back on his bed, he started to tell Fumi about the Legation characters, the men and women "of his own kind" who had appeared even stranger to him than the Chinese. "There's a merchant who pretends to know more than a doctor, a champion archer who thinks he's a scholar, a banker who's really a soldier, and a spy who can't keep a single secret to himself."

"And your hostess? Was she pretending to be someone else too?"

"No, she's more than what I thought she was, surrounded though, as she is, by her masquerading friends." He smiled at Fumi. "Not even your *Nei ching* could cure Casanova's itch, straighten Cedric Hart's spine or turn Mr. Itami into a bird!"

Fumi sighed. "All the foreigner wants is rhubarb to soften his bowels."

It'd be far better taking her back with him than suffering the Legation's garden parties, Antonio thought. Dona Elvira would approve, he was certain, her Tino turned at last into a proper Eastern gentleman. "You aren't a real *casado* until you've taken a native woman as your wife," he could hear her say—feel her hand on his cheek as she mothered him with her delicacies. "She'll be more than a "sleeping dictionary," more than a "traveling woman" made of soft goat leather. She'll be mother to the mongrels who'll carry your name!" Even Dom Afonso wouldn't object, used as he was to sailors jumping ship to marry fiery Malabar women, and lowly paid officers paying back their debt to kind Chinese merchants by tying the knot with long-suffering spinsters of their household. "The future belongs to mongrels." He'd bless Antonio and Fumi with his tired eyes then return to his cartographic readings. Antonio's face clouded as he thought of Dona Elvira's counsel that'd surely follow her blessings. "Whatever you do, don't take her back home. Even your friends will sneer at her, disapprove of her looks and the cut of her evening dress. She'll kill your reputation the minute you step off the boat."

"Why don't you then teach the Chinese how to use your tools?" Fumi pointed to the surgical box. "Just like Jacob taught me how to work the printing press."

He looked at her closely at the mention of Jacob de Graff. *What else did the printer teach her?*

"You can teach Xu how to use a knife. Do you know what the Chinese say about a wounded soldier? Why save his life when he'll eat a full man's meal and live like a cripple? Maybe you can . . ."

"Tell me about Jacob. What did he want from you for saving your life?"

Fumi smiled. "To be a good student like you, and learn as fast as I could. He was in a hurry to teach me everything, as if he knew what was going to happen, that there was no time to waste."

Jacob, Fumi said, was more a linguist than a pastor. A linguist and engineer who believed in the power of science to quicken the spread of the gospel. Living among villagers, he had formed his own system for learning the local dialect and devised a script to teach the Chinese their own language. "He taught grandmothers to read for the very first time, taught illiterate peasants and their children, wanted to convert their minds along with their souls." Fellow pastors complained over his neglect of church work, as he devoted himself to translating Western books to Chinese, starting with mathematics, the mother of all knowledge. "Mechanics, optics, chemistry, astronomy . . . he wanted to teach everything to the Chinese, but printing the Bible got him into trouble."

"Is that all he wanted?" Antonio asked.

"It took me seven years to understand what he really wanted, but his enemies weren't prepared to wait that long."

His preaching drew fewer converts than his mathematics, she said, but aroused bitter opposition from the mandarins. "They accused him of damaging China with the West's vulgar knowledge. Even his friends thought he had crossed the line."

"Did the mandarins kill him in the end?"

A shadow passed over her face, and she shook her head. "There were more rumors than facts about his killers. It was easy to blame the Boxers, but they hadn't warned him with the sign of the bleeding hand. It wasn't the work of a riotous mob, but men he may have known. Maybe . . ."

"Were you there when he died?"

"No, he'd sent me away from the Press to my hovel nearby. He gave me his favorite books to keep. I thought he wanted to save them from rats that raided the ink vats drawn by the sweet smell. Maybe he knew what was to happen that night."

"How did you find out?"

She held her breath for a long time, then sighed. "I knew something had gone wrong from the smell."

"Smell?"

"The smell of burning wood that woke the neighborhood up. I ran to the press. It was covered under a dark cloud. There was no one on the streets, and the residents had kept their doors locked."

"What did you see?"

"The room was dark, and I had to hold my nose to keep out the burning smell. The floor was flooded with ink, and bits of paper floated on it. Things had been tossed around, and . . ."

"Where was Jacob?"

Fumi made the gesture of slouching down while she held her head with both hands.

"Was he on the floor?"

"No. I found him sitting at this desk. Just like every day. He'd been shot through the head, and his body was covered in black ink."

Antonio and Fumi sat holding each other, unmindful of the hot desert wind that blew in through the open window. Shadows had lengthened over the courtyard, and it was time for the lamps to be lit. The temple gong silenced the birds, but Antonio didn't hear the pattering feet of his attendants coming to a nervous halt outside the door. It was getting late for their fat tea, and he wondered if the eunuchs had left them to attend a palace ceremony. Stirring in his arms, Fumi whispered, "When I met you, I thought Jacob had returned to me."

He looked at her surprised. "You saw the Dutchman in me?"

She nodded. "The same urge to know everything, and arguing everything to death. Getting to the heart of the matter like a real scientist. The two of you are like twins, just as obstinate, just as foolish when it comes to telling enemies from friends." She patted Antonio's chin and spoke like a wise teacher. "I knew you wouldn't like your Peking friends. Jacob didn't like them either, he thought them silly and cruel, too busy with themselves to care about what really matters." She gave him a teasing smile. "I knew you'd come back to me."

"Was he just as good a lover as I?" Antonio traced her neck with his finger.

"No . . ." She sighed. "He didn't know what it meant to love; cared for nothing but the smell of fresh ink on paper. He took everything I did for him as nothing more than kindness."

Antonio rose and paced the lodge, looking out of the window at the fading twilight. "Was it kindness that made you bring me your poison?"

"Poison?" She laughed. "If it was poison, how could it have cured your rotten liver?"

He spoke as if he hadn't heard her. "Was it simply the kindness of a *Nei ching* master, keeping her patient alive?"

She rose too and came up to him, lifting herself up on her toes to fold her arms around him. "I came because I was afraid of losing you."

With Fumi he no longer felt like a prisoner. In the days following his visit to the Legation, they left the pavilion for the palace gardens, ignoring the attendants who kept a close watch on them from under their hats. Boatmen raised their oars in greeting. The marble bridge glowed like a rainbow with its crown of arches. Suzhou Street was empty of visitors, the shopkeepers dozing behind closed doors. They walked up the hill, and rested under the ancient evergreens of the Temple of Clouds. Then they sneaked into the empress's private nursery, blooming with her favorite yellow rose, and the narcissus called the fairy for its magical powers. Fumi played the empress and Antonio her loyal attendant. She pointed at the blood red plum flower, ordering him to pluck a bunch for her hair. He remembered the whores who dressed up for festas, offering to pluck for their clients flowers from their shining braids. Playing the part of a disobedient servant, he ignored the plum but delighted her with the dainty juniper.

She took him to all the forbidden parts, even once to the teahouse at the Garden of Eternal Harmony, where the empress came to taste the first flush of the tea harvest. Like the empress, she had brought a jade bowl filled with dried peonies and jasmine to sweeten the tea with the flowers' honey. She stirred their porcelain cups with a pair of cherry sticks and circled the rims for good luck with the tips of her fingers.

Then she asked him to teach her how to dance like the foreigners. Jacob had taken her once to the Legation, to collect old clothes donated by the members of the European Club for the Charity Ball. Her curiosity had got the better of her and she had peeked into the hall to catch a glimpse of dancers gliding over the floor, twirling like butterflies and clutching each other like crabs.

"In China one pays others to dance for them, like singing girls and acrobats." She stood in the tea garden and waited for Antonio to hold her like a crab and twirl.

Antonio smiled, remembering his days at the dance halls. Then he told her to stand perfectly still facing him.

"I'll show you my steps, and then yours. You must follow me." He danced the leader's steps, starting slowly then going a little faster. "You mustn't mix up the right and the left," he cautioned her, taking her through the follower's moves. "Step back on your left foot, take a turn then step forward on your right."

She stood like a wooden doll, eyes fixed to the ground.

"Come, hurry!" He held her arm and pulled her forward, hoping she'd fall into rhythm. "It's the waltz, the dance of lovers." Then he started to laugh seeing how clumsy she was, quite unlike the *Nei ching* teacher performing the dance of the twelve channels.

"You must give me one more chance," Fumi said with a serious face, like a student who has disappointed her teacher. Clearing a space before her, she tried to rehearse the follower's steps, watching Antonio from the corner of her eye to catch his nod of approval.

"You must learn to waltz properly. It marks the celebration for newlyweds. If a couple dances well it shows they're suited for each other."

She laid her hand on his arm and started to move, mixing up the leader's steps with the follower's, tangling up their legs and falling down together in a heap. Rolling on the wet grass, she landed on top of him with tears of laughter on her cheeks.

"I must tell you a secret," he whispered to her after they had returned to his lodge and finished with late rice. A cool evening breeze swayed the plum tree and spread the smell of the ripening fruit. With the attendants gone, they sat on the lodge's steps, gazing up at the stars lighting up the summer sky. Fumi had started to hum a tune she'd learned as a child, and laid her head on Antonio's arm.

"I didn't want to tell you before as it might upset you."

"You couldn't tell me earlier that you were married? That it'll be time soon to return to your wife?"

He shook his head. "I have no wife."

"That your friends are concerned for your safety and have asked you to move to the Legation; that this will be our last night together?"

"No." He rose and paced the courtyard. "My secret has nothing to do with you, but with why I've come to China. And I haven't told anyone, not even Xu." He paused to take a quick look at Fumi. "It's the secret I've brought from home, the secret of my father."

"He's sick, isn't he?" Fumi spoke quietly, following him with her eyes. "Your father has Canton rash. That's why you dream of death, that's why you have nightmares. You've come to China to find a way to cure him."

He stopped at Fumi's words. His mind went back to the day she had checked his pulse. . . . *You're dreaming of someone who's suffering . . . someone you love.* . . . Back on the steps, his eyes shone in the dark and he held her hand to his heart. "Do you know the way to treat . . . ?"

She shook her head even before he could finish. "You must ask Xu, he's the one who'd know."

"I thought a Chinese doctor knows about these things . . ."

"Only a *Nei ching* master can teach you that. I'm just an assistant." She hushed him with a finger before he could ask more questions, then led him back into the lodge and lit the lamps that surrounded their bed like a ring of stars.

❁

Wangsheng brought him a letter the next day as he settled down to eat his early rice. Sitting cross-legged on a silk cushion, he held up the envelope against the sun, expecting to see the scrawl of Rosa Escobar's hand. Cedric Hart had made arrangements to have his letters delivered to the Summer Palace, leaving it to the eunuchs to hand them over to Antonio.

He expected Rosa Escobar's monthly letter to bring the sad news of his father's falling health. *He has turned blue!* She had written not long ago. Blue from the little blue pills of mercury, ground and applied as a salve on the suffering skin. *He cries all night as the devil bloats up his stomach to the size of a hill. . . .* His father had made his nurse write to him about "floating on the wings of madness" when he had left his cottage for a walk in the meadows, overcome suddenly by the urge to throw his arms around the neck of a galloping horse. It had dragged him for a mile before he dropped down on the ground, saved miraculously from the hooves.

Stories of his syphilitic father would be all over Lisbon by now, rivals gorging themselves with the details. Every one of them would claim to know the deep secrets of a fallen Dr. Maria. His friends must've disclaimed their friendship, or offered feeble and unlikely explanations at best: perhaps the noble doctor had infected himself with the poison to test the miracle vaccine he had discovered, sparing monkeys and rabbits to take on the ultimate risk. It was a sickness without sin, a brave sacrifice—they'd have argued, then given up as the gossip redoubled.

They'd be blaming me for running away, leaving him all alone to die his horrible death—the ungrateful son, the coward, who couldn't face up to the shameful truth about his father.

There were Chinese characters and red chop marks on the envelope along with the sender's name. He wondered what the gypsy might have to say to him, as he skimmed Ferguson's letter written in a careless hand that betrayed the flair of the writer. Like an old friend, he hadn't bothered with greetings, assuming that Antonio knew everything about everyone at the Legation, airing freely his opinions about them. It didn't take him long to grasp the running theme: the stupidity of the foreigner trapped within the walls of Peking's Little Europe. *I know why they come . . .* He had written. *To sell to the Chinese what they don't want; to teach them about a god they hate; to spy on other Europeans; to steal precious items from the empress's palace by bribing the eunuchs; to bed the Legation ladies who'd rather die than sleep with their husbands; to smoke the best Indian opium that a pipe can hold for a fraction of the cost in Europe.*

Within the span of a few paragraphs he revealed the most intimate secret of the *stiff, tight-lipped and old-maidish* Mr. Pinchback, of his ongoing liaisons with a pair of nubile twins who worked in his household, along with the latest scandal at the Legation. The Austrians had gone on a little river party on the Yangtze, a dozen officers and their wives. They had got rid of the boatmen to steer the junk themselves, but caught in murderous currents their *Viennese Ball on the Danube* had met with closely averted disaster, only to be saved miraculously by fishermen. The near tragedy proved what he had been saying all along about the foolish Europeans, that they owed their existence to *Fu-Hsing,* the Chinese god of good fortune, who kept a special eye on the bumbling residents of Little Europe.

You are most welcome to my home, Ferguson wrote, and promised to show him *something to interest your curiosity.*

On his way over to the gypsy's villa next morning, Antonio made an effort to recall everything Polly had told him about her best friend to prepare himself for the visit. "Thank God for Ferguson!" Polly had muttered under her breath as they saw him speak to a stooping Mr. Pinchback at the Dutch minister's farewell party, making the grave banker blush. "He makes us all look pretty pious and sane by comparison!"

Following his first visit, Antonio had become a regular at the Legation, a frequent guest at Polly Hart's "at homes," choosing to escape from his pavilion whenever Fumi was away tending to the royals. The prospect of fat tea in Polly's garden watered his tongue. He accepted invitations from the other mansions as well, delighting his hosts with riding tips and tales of gory bullfights. The only Portuguese among foreigners, he was pressed to confirm the Goa gossip that reached them regularly. Was it true that married Konkani women left their windows ajar for the roving Portuguese men to watch them make love to their husbands at night? Was it true that they shaved their private hair on the first day of the lunar moon? His ignorance about Goa or Macau didn't worry his hosts too much, who were quick to discover his talents as a doctor. To one and all the verdict was clear: Dr. Maria was the best thing that had happened to the Legation since Lord Elgin raised its walls to keep out the *Pékin-les-odeurs* after winning the opium wars. The fat tea had turned into his hour of consultations. With the resident medical officers of the missions hiding behind the bushes, he heard a litany of complaints, ranging from innocent sunstroke to Helga's swelling ankles as she neared childbirth. Troubled residents flocked around him if there was a rumor of cholera doing the rounds in the bazaars, or if a gardener had gone down to typhus. Polly Hart looked on proudly and demanded due gratitude as each complaint received a thorough hearing followed by Antonio's unwavering diagnosis, with just a few escaping her eagle eye—the anxious young officers who ambushed the Portuguese doctor, deathly scared of infections they might've picked up at the infamous Turkish *hamams*.

"They only send quacks and flunkies to the East!" Sally Hollinger pointed her accusing finger at the resident doctors, seeing the way Antonio was with his patients. "Even the Americans don't care about their own stock," she added, meaning the Locke Mission doctors who visited the deep interiors to treat the heathen Chinese while neglecting their god-fearing brethren.

His crowning glory had come with Patty, Mrs. Harris's niece, who was visiting from Pennsylvania. She had come out to meet Doug Walters, her fiancé—"tucking in some sightseeing"—and to add an Eastern touch to her trousseau. At the gate of the Tartar city a beggar's pet dog had bitten her as she stopped to drop a few coins into the poor man's bowl. "It was frightened by her white skin," Polly Hart said, "which is a common problem in China, plaguing bird, beast and man." The poor girl had waited for Douglas to return from his snipe shoot and treat her, waited for her fiancé's healing touch, but he was beyond the reach of Roger

McKinsey's magic telegraph machine.

He wasn't fussed about her fever but her headache, Antonio said, as he took charge of the patient. If it was rabies, it'd last for days then turn into acute dysfunction.

"What sort of dysfunction?" John Harris hid his nervousness behind the usual diplomatic mask. The China trip was his suggestion and he hadn't slept a wink since Patty's fateful trip to the Tartar city.

"Anxiety, confusion and delirium." Antonio replied, bathing Patty's head with drops of eau-de-cologne in freezing cold water.

"How long could she hold out till medicines arrived?" Blunt mental calculations gave John Harris little comfort, knowing that even the power of steam wasn't enough to bridge the gulf from Kobe to Tientsin in under a week.

"If rabies, there'd be no medicine." Antonio told the American minister in private. It was too early to tell if the French chemist Pasteur's vaccine could indeed control the rabies poison, although in Europe it was already being heralded as the miracle of the century.

"All dogs in China have rabies," Ferguson had announced, drowning the Legation in sorrow, then proceeded to crown Antonio as the new Pasteur after the young woman recovered, her fever and headache turning out to be nothing more sinister than a case of prenuptial exhaustion.

"He exaggerates," Polly had told Antonio after the episode. "He lives by stretching the truth to suit his pocket."

He was struck by the depth and breadth of Ferguson's pocket when he arrived at Ferguson's garden house in the middle of busy native quarters, guarded from street noise and gutter smell by lovely casuarinas that served as a natural wall. From outside, the house resembled a palace pavilion with an arched green roof, lacquered pillars, and imperial dragons perched on the cornices. At first sight it seemed like the private residence of a minor royal or an important minister at the court, even a distant Manchu relative of the empress herself.

"It's a museum of treasures," Polly had said, "full of jade and ivory, rare scrolls and old silk."

"A gypsy with a house full of treasure!" He looked at Polly, disbelieving. Pressed for details, Polly recited a pocketbook biography of her friend, starting in the middle and shuttling back and forth, confusing Antonio.

"He deals in manuscripts, precious ones that none can lay their hands on but him. He buys them cheap or forces their owners to give them to him as gifts under a variety of threats, then sells them to the highest bidder."

"Who buys?"

Polly rolled her eyes. "Rich men with money to burn, I suppose. Japanese aristocrats and English opium merchants, Oxford and Cambridge — eager to flaunt their Eastern holdings — even the odd mandarin ready to take Ferguson's word that they were autographed by the empress herself."

"A gypsy with a merchant's knack!"

"Wait, there's more! Every time he buys a manuscript, he claims it'd cause a sensation in London when published, under his superior translation, of course!"

"*His* translation?" Antonio stopped Polly and asked for the full story, starting from the beginning, inviting a caustic remark: "You doctors are all the same, fiendish for facts and sorry for imagination."

Ferguson, Polly said, came from an English family of soldiers and admirals, but had rebelled in his youth to go against family tradition. Unlike gentlemen soldiers, he didn't believe in good manners and his oriental affectations might have come down from his mother, who was raised in Malaya by a widowed planter. A grammar school boy, he read Classics in Oxford and Chinese in private, and had picked up several European languages as easily as a summer hobby. Fluency in Chinese along with a touch of Japanese and Mongolian made him the greatest Western linguist to the east of the Himalayas. But unlike traveling missionaries turned linguists for survival, he bore the curse of a perfectionist. "He isn't your Joaquim Saldanha, master of the gutters, but a real scholar." Antonio had resented Polly's unflattering view of his friend. It was easy for a foreigner with a grasp of Chinese to find work in Peking, but he had chosen the life of a gentleman adventurer over that of a highly paid hack. "He leads an interesting life behind the scenes." Polly had sounded envious. "He has more Chinese friends than American or European, and entertains himself with local affairs. He holds a high standing at the Legation too, not for his malicious tongue, but for his precious links with the imperial higher-ups."

"A few old manuscripts give him that much power?" Antonio was sceptical.

Polly had nodded. "He is more than capable of bending their ears."

"A gypsy, a scholar, an adventurer, and a merchant rolled into one!"

"And that's only half of our Ferguson." Polly beamed. "He's a man of extravagant fantasies, blessed with the cunning of a fox."

On his arrival, Antonio was received by a young servant who led him through the gates into a lovely courtyard shaded by young plum trees and dotted with stone animals like those at the Summer Palace. A row of birds hanging from their cages started to twitter as soon as they entered the main pavilion, as if to announce the visitor and Antonio caught a glimpse of a row of porcelain jars on a windowsill making the loud noise of whirring looms. The servant smiled and called him over to examine the jars, lifting one of the lids for him to take a peek inside. It was a fighting cricket of the kind that owners prized for biting off the head of its opponent and scraped its wings to keep warm, producing a loud cricket song.

Ferguson sat on a throne chair inside the parlor, dressed in a long gown looking like an early Jesuit at the Manchu court, and casting his reflection in multiple mirrors that lined the walls. An elderly Chinese man with a flowing beard held up an exquisite silk scroll before him. Tapping his fingers on a pile of books on his knees, the gypsy looked sceptically at the scroll bearer and motioned Antonio to take a seat. The two men spoke in low voices, while the young servant packed a trunk with piles of tattered manuscripts and dog-eared folios. A cup of tea arrived at Antonio's side unasked for, and he smelled the padre souchong. Although windows had been left open, the heat of the brick floor warmed his feet.

"It's dated circa 746, and would fetch a large sum in the Peking book market." Ferguson spoke to him conspiratorially, just like Polly. "The calligraphy is from the pen of Huai Su, the Buddhist monk whose 'grass characters' were typical of the Tang style." Clearing his throat he spoke to the Chinese man in an authoritative voice, holding up a chit of paper with scribbled characters. The man shook his head and started to unroll yet another scroll, laying it out on the floor.

Antonio admired the cranes flying over a snow-clad peak ringed by wispy clouds, brought to life by just a few deft brushstrokes. The elderly man gazed fondly at the painting and drew Ferguson's attention to the artist's signature at the bottom.

"Fake! Just a piece of rubbish!" Ferguson growled under his breath, ordering his attendant to roll it up and return it to the seller, who drenched his robe in agitation and started to argue in a long monologue.

"I wish the fool would shut up and sell me the Tang scroll." Taking a quick look at the elderly man, Ferguson continued talking to Antonio as if he was his trusted partner. "The old fox doesn't want an outright sale, but a large chunk of the profit after it has been sold to someone who can pay handsomely. He wants me to do all the dirty work, while he sits idle and skims off the cream!"

"How would he know who you've sold it to and at what price?" Antonio asked. "Specially if it leaves China and . . ."

"Oh no, they'll know." Ferguson sniggered. "Can't go too far with the Chinese and their ring of spies, I'm afraid, surrounded as one is by unfaithful servants and treacherous friends! They'd burn down this house if they found out that I've fooled them."

After a vigorous round of bargaining, Ferguson ended up triumphant with his arms around the Chinese man, stroking his flowing beard in a show of affection. The servant rolled up the scroll, while the seller gave it a loving look as if parting with a long-held heirloom.

"Lucky bugger, he's got more than he expected. He knew I was in a hurry to finish with him, saw us chatting and seized his chance." With the morning purchases safely put away, Ferguson rose and asked Antonio to accompany him to his library. "Come let me show you what we've got there."

Antonio smelled the dust of old libraries as he entered the "holding room." Unlike the parlor, it was dark, with mahogany shelves and drawers rising from floor to ceiling, lit by their brass handles that glowed from the human wax of frequent handling. The young servant held out a fan to stir the desiccator's fumes in the warm air.

"The Chinese are selling off their grannies at dirt-cheap prices!" Ferguson opened a drawer and peeked in. "Take the Yung-lo Encyclopedia, for example, a work of great rarity in six volumes. In London it'd fetch five thousand pounds easily, even more if auctioned at

Sotheby's. And here . . ." His voice trailed off, leading Antonio to another set of shelves with cutlery drawers to hold scrolls. "You can see what only a few could hope to see with their mortal eyes—the autograph of the Manchu emperor K'ang-hsi, who ruled at the same time as Louis XIV. It's more precious than everything put together in the British Museum's oriental collection, but the *Institut National des Langues et Civilisations Orientales* has set its sight on it and it might well end up in Paris."

He opened and shut the drawers one by one, stroking the old and tattered manuscripts like a lover.

"For just five or ten pounds you can buy an immaculate copy of a Sung or Ming book of poems, inscribed by the poet. For a mere five hundred pounds an entire library of two thousand books. With a bit of luck a palace collection might fall into your lap and barely lighten your pocket! No wonder the vultures are out there waiting!"

"Anyone can get rich then,"—Antonio shrugged—"on the back of rotting paper!"

"Not *anyone*. For that you've got to know the real from fakes. Peking is full of master forgers. They'll sell you whatever you want, pass off yesterday's doodles for century-old treasure. Your buyers don't know either. In paying for these, they're really paying for your word, paying for you!"

A stack of crates stood at the lighted opening of the holding room, marked with their destinations. Ferguson pointed at a largish case. "This one's off to the Findlay estate in Chicago. You know about them, don't you? Descendants of a famous slaving family from Alabama"—then to another—"This one to Oxford's Bodleian Library, packed meticulously as per the orders of the librarian. And this to Penang, to grace the home of a Peranakan trader who's made his wealth from gambier farms."

They returned to the parlor with Ferguson insisting on a glass of whiskey prescribed by his English doctor for raising his blood pressure. Back to his gossipy self, he chuckled over the hottest topic at the Legation following Patty's miraculous recovery.

"You're the new star! Poor Roger has bitten the dust, your stethoscope triumphed over his telegraph. Too bad you're Portuguese though." He chuckled. "If you'd been American, John Harris would've brainwashed Patty into marrying you instead. You'd have made a far better addition to the clan than that scoundrel medical officer."

Antonio recalled a feverish Patty holding on to his arm as if he was her missing fiancé.

"Could try the Italians though." Ferguson smirked. "They might need a good Portuguese doctor!" Taking a large sip from his glass, he spoke about Antonio's marriage prospects at the Legation with as much assurance as he had about old Chinese manuscripts.

"Everyone's worried about you. *What's he doing in China, wasting his life with the Chinese?*" Ferguson's imitation of Polly mimicking an agitated Dona Elvira made Antonio laugh.

"No, seriously. Sooner or later you'll fall into the clutches of a Manchu temptress, they think. The longer you stay at the Summer Palace, the greater the chance that the Old Buddha will capture you for her secret pleasures. You'd be lost to civilization."

"Is that why you have called me over?" Antonio said, finished with his drink and ready to leave.

The cry of a water seller came from behind the wall of casuarinas. Smoke from a mud furnace rose in a steady column from a smaller pavilion at the back. Colored banners hung limp from the arched gate, and added to the eternal moment of stillness at the Chinese villa.

"I wanted to show you something." Ferguson opened the lid of a jade box and brought out an elegant case holding an old manuscript. "This will answer the question that has brought you to China."

Antonio turned the parchment pages marked with Chinese characters and drawings of human organs that were similar to the medical charts that Xu had brought over to his pavilion.

"It's an old palace edition of *Nei ching*, the Yellow Emperor's Canon." He paused, waiting for Antonio to turn a few more pages. "What you are holding in your hands is two thousand years old, contains forty thousand ideographs and is the oldest medical book in the world. It describes everything the Chinese know about the human body and the cosmic order. Surely it'll tell you how to cure syphilis."

From the drawing of the second channel, Antonio could recognize the passage of *qi* that excited the veins and regulated blood pressure. A Chinese doctor would've warned Ferguson against the whiskey that stirred the yang, opting for the gentle tea of dandelion roots that came with the additional quality of purifying the blood.

"Take it. You can have it for a nominal price, practically free. It'll save you from wasting your time here. You can read for yourself and judge if your doctor friend is lying to you or not. Better to have the answer from the yellow emperor than a horseman who's a secret supporter of rebels and pretends to be a *Nei ching* master, don't you think?"

"Read . . .?"

"Ah, I see your difficulty." Ferguson rolled his eyes. "I should've known. What you need is a translator, not a teacher."

"To translate *Nei ching* you mean?"

"Yes, then you can kill two birds with one stone!"

Antonio smiled. "Which two did you have in mind?"

"Fame from curing syphilis, and fortune by selling this ancient copy to a European prince!"

Antonio set down his glass and stood up as Fergusson looked on quizzically.

"It'll be harder than that."

"Harder?" Ferguson raised an eyebrow.

"Simply reading the *Materia Medica* doesn't make a doctor. Or *Nei ching* for that matter. For that there must be more, cultivating the ear to listen to the pulse; unlearning what we've learned in the West and accepting what seems absurd to the mind." Walking toward the arched entrance he spoke to Ferguson, who followed a few steps behind. "It means taking different views about the liver, for example; or knowing when to treat the yang to cure the yin, and its opposite; learning the color of each disease, and judging the difference between men and women when it comes to causes of pleasure and pain."

"Different views about the liver!"

A faint smile appeared on Antonio's face. "Their liver is like the maple leaf—green in summer and red in autumn—while ours is evergreen."

"Did your teachers tell you that?"

"Yes, and they haven't finished yet. There are three hundred sixty-five parts in a man's body that'll take three hundred sixty-five days |to learn."

Ferguson stood under the arched gate of the villa and raised his voice to reach Antonio, sitting on his sedan. "Better hurry! You may not have that many days left before the Boxers cut everyone's throat and burn everything down!"

He mulled over the Boxers on his way back from Ferguson. What if they were to descend suddenly on Peking? What if all foreigners were forced to leave at short notice? Even long-term residents were planning to evacuate their homes within weeks, he had gathered from Polly's guests. He could see himself seasick and crestfallen on the *Santa Cruz*, returning empty-handed after his long trip. *I must see Xu immediately. I must remind him of his promise to take me to examine the pox victims.* Simply "imagining the disease" won't do, he must learn the Chinese cure firsthand, otherwise it'd be no better than the gypsy's plan. After almost four months with his teachers, the eleven notes of the pulse rang clearly in his ear, and he was able to name the illnesses that rose from the blockage of each of the twelve channels. He was certain that he knew enough to begin the hardest part of his education. He must speak with Fumi urgently, he thought, to find out when Xu would be back from his trip.

Antonio's pulse quickened as he entered the pavilion and heard Tian chattering in the kitchen. Perhaps Fumi had returned earlier than planned from her medical visits. He expected to see her sitting cross-legged on the floor, playing mahjong with the eunuchs.

In the kitchen, Antonio found Wangsheng lying on the floor without his loin cloth, needles stuck into his bulging stomach like the hump of a porcupine. Tian sniggered and made fun of his nakedness, while Xu crouched on a stool and smoked his pipe, scolding the elder eunuch for his gluttony. Seeing Antonio, Wangsheng tried to get up, but Xu ordered him to lie still.

"He's receiving his treatment," Xu said, greeting Antonio. "I've been forced to use acupuncture needles to disperse the storm brewing inside his rotten belly." He looked wryly at Wangsheng. "His channels are choked with the shit of dead birds!" Tian giggled. "That's why he hasn't been able to poop for three days!"

Antonio left the kitchen and sat under the shade of the plum tree.

The north wind blew in from the desert and stung his arms, and he drew them into his sleeves. Waiting for Xu to finish with Wangsheng, he thought over Fumi's words about treating pox. *Only a Nei ching master can teach you. . . .* Did she know that for a fact, or was she simply guessing? Why couldn't she ask her master and learn the cure for him? Xu must've mentioned to her the reason for Antonio's visit, the reason why he was prepared to spend a whole year learning *Nei ching*. Now that she knew about his father, she'd understand why the very mention of syphilis made him tense. A dying father was worse than a dead one, every letter carrying the scent of a rotting corpse. She'd know why he sometimes seemed cold and remote; why on certain days his lodge smelled of burnt paper; why he seemed anxious when Tian ran to fetch a lamp from the kitchen as he waited to read a newly arrived letter.

Is she hiding the cure from me? He wondered if it was a simple ploy to hold him back in the pavilion.

"You've surprised us!" Xu said, coming out of the kitchen. "It takes years to learn what you've learned in just a few months. Your teacher claims you've already mastered the twelve channels."

The old doctor seemed a bit leaner than before and walked with a slight limp. With the box of needles under his arm, he made the usual enquiries about Antonio's meals, and if insects were still keeping him awake at night.

"Most of them die in the summer. Those that live become more ferocious than before." He smiled kindly seeing Antonio squint at the sun. "You must have your lessons inside the lodge rather than in the open courtyard."

"Lessons for what?"

Xu closed his eyes to recall. "After the twelve channels you must learn about the eleven organs. Mastery of these and the pulse will prepare you to understand how the five viscera bring perfection to bodily functions. You must start now to study the first of the five, and it might be best"—Xu paused for a moment—"to have Fumi continue to teach you, given that you've learned so quickly from her."

"I must start now with syphilis." Antonio spoke gruffly.

"Syphilis?"

"Yes. That's why I'm here. Have you forgotten? Syphilis, also known as the pox, Portuguese disease, Canton rash, or whatever you call it." He stared into Xu's eyes. "You must take me to see the victims now, teach me how to cure them."

"But that can wait. It's better that you learn the principles first."

"You *must* take me to your hospital. You've pox patients there, don't you?" His voice hardened.

"*My* hospital?" Xu showed surprise. "There are several hospitals in Peking, which one do you want to visit?"

"The one where you can show me your trick." Antonio waited for Xu to answer, and continued when he did not. "I've waited long enough for you to treat your cavalry captain, or whatever you were doing while you were away. It's time now to learn the treatment of pox that you promised me."

"I promised to teach you *Nei ching* in four seasons if you so wished."

Antonio rose from his seat and came up to Xu, standing barely inches from him. "Do you think I'm a fool? That I've come here to throw my life away? Your canons are worthless at home. Worthless, unless they can teach me how to cure the pox. Didn't Dom Afonso de Oliveira of Macau write to you just that?" He brought his face closer to Xu's. "Were you lying when you said "The Chinese doctor knows how to cure a patient even before the illness has struck'?"

"No," Xu whispered, shaking his head.

"Then show me how."

Wangsheng poked his head through the kitchen window and asked if Antonio was ready for his early rice. Running across the courtyard, Tian handed Xu a needle he had left behind, its arrow head crusted with blood.

"Very well. I'll take you to see a patient of Canton Rash. Fumi will bring you word in a few days when we're ready." Wiping the blood off the needle on his robe, the Chinese doctor bowed and disappeared into the mist beyond the pavilion's gates.

Walking along Peking's silk market under a large parasol, Polly ignored the hawkers to steer Antonio past the jumble of shacks. Without shop windows, it was hard for him to know what the keepers were selling, if the promised treasures were nothing more than items of master forgery as Ferguson had claimed. Polly seemed to know her way around the narrow alleys that smelled of filth, covering up her nose as she trotted along merrily. "Fine feathers don't make a fine bird." She hurried him along. "You're never 'done' with Peking till you've examined every shop. The darker they are and filthier the lane, the better it is for the treasure hunter."

He had been called over to the Legation, not to yet another garden party, but to tend to Cedric's grumbling tummy. It had turned out to be nothing more than a swollen liver, and Antonio had calmed him with cold compresses and a single dose of medicine to ease the flow of bile. With her husband resting, Polly had seized upon Antonio's company to go shopping, offering to teach him her superior bargaining skills.

"It's a pity not to go to the shops." She scolded Antonio for "hiding like a eunuch in the palace." Where else would you meet the Chinese? she asked. "You won't find them among our domestics that we've trained to behave like butlers and manor maids. Not their officials either, who'd rather we disappeared like jinn into thin air. Only shopkeepers love us and our purses."

"The feeling is mutual, I thought," Antonio said wryly, watching a hawker wink at him as he held up a jar of ginseng roots and made a rude gesture with his fingers. "The foreigner cares less about China than her products and the Chinese have no option but to put up with us."

Polly looked surprised. "You can say so. But it doesn't have to be that way, does it?" She knitted her brows as if thinking of something important. "What's the use having us here then, better to station a battalion instead."

"Yes, better. Then we don't have to pretend we're friends. It'll save our backs too from their spirit army."

Polly leaned over and patted Antonio. "Come, Dr. Maria, you must be more hopeful. Couldn't we still be friendly with the Chinese, if we try?"

They had reached the end of a dark lane, and Polly opened an old rusty gate to enter a building that resembled a barrack. Generous layers of moss covered the cracks on the walls, and white linen curtains fluttered from the windows like a row of sails.

"It's the best shop in Peking, the most expensive," Polly whispered, entering the modest gardens that led up to the front entrance.

"Shop?" Antonio looked around unable to spot a sign or a hawker loudly announcing his wares.

"This is the Ladies Society's home for the elderly, the place where they give shelter to those nobody wants."

They stepped into a hallway leading to a largish room with many windows that gave Antonio the feeling of being out in the garden. Despite the breeze blowing in, the room was still, set out like a ship's deck with the Society's residents sitting on chairs. Each had the appearance of a statue carved out of translucent jade, faces marked with wrinkles; each frozen in their own posture. Eyes followed him as Antonio walked around the chairs, but he didn't hear a shuffle or a whisper. A pair of hands held up a glass bottle with a dead butterfly inside. He drew in a sharp breath catching sight of a set of stone eyes bent over an abacus. They all seemed alive yet unmoved by his presence, like a forest of ancient trees lit by cones of light from the windows.

Polly spoke to a young attendant and passed on an envelope to her, receiving a flurry of grateful bows in return.

They rode back on the sedan, reaching the Hart villa just in time for afternoon tea. Cedric had recovered sufficiently to go out for a game of cards with Monsieur Darmon, and they settled down in the parlor with their favorite padre souchong. Antonio wanted Polly to tell him more about the Ladies Society, when her maid brought in something for her.

"Ah, a letter from Dr. Alexander Maria to Dr. Antonio Maria!" She exclaimed, then eyed Rosa Escobar's scrawl on the envelope. "But it isn't a man's hand. Maybe he asked a friend to send it over to you?"

Antonio kept silent with Polly probing away gently between sips of tea. "Perhaps a *good friend* who takes his letters and . . . it's always the same hand on the envelope, isn't it?"

"Not a friend, his nurse," Antonio spoke abruptly.

"Nurse! Is your father sick? You must be anxious . . ." She edged closer to him on the sofa. "Shouldn't you be home looking after him?" Then she relaxed, unable to prise out an answer. "How silly of me. Perhaps your father is simply convalescing, well on his way to recovery."

He kept his eyes down and peeled the envelope. His jaws hardened as he read the letter, face turning red. His lips started to quiver.

"What is it . . . what's wrong?"

. . . you have left me to die in the company of a whore. He read his father's letter slowly. *She torments me with purges, leeches and enemas, eating me away with her rotten teeth. I am a prisoner in my own house. I shall kill her and kill myself soon. . . . Bring me a gun when you come Tino.*

"It's bad news, isn't it?" Polly touched his face. "Shall I call Cedric back?"

He passed on the letter to her without a word, and shut his eyes. She read the pages quickly, then hugged Antonio, drawing his head into her arms. "Poor Tino . . . Your father is sick, very sick. These are not his words. You mustn't take them to heart." She stroked his head, and comforted him like a child. "He'll recover soon, you'll see."

"He'll never recover. He'll die before I return."

"A bout of delusion won't kill him surely." Polly spoke calmly. "Sooner or later he's bound to return to his senses."

"Not delusion." Antonio spoke between sobs. "It's syphilis. It has turned him mad."

"Syphilis?" Polly sounded stunned. She turned around to take a look at the letter, eyeing it with suspicion. Then her eyes lit up, as if the shroud of a mystery had lifted finally. "That's why you've come here. You've come to save your father, haven't you?" Her face clouded over once again. "But isn't it too late already?"

"Too late to save his life, you mean?"

"Will he last that long, till you've found the Chinese cure?"

"He'll die before that." Antonio spoke grimly. "The disease has already spread beyond repair. It has damaged his body and his mind. There's no hope for him."

"Then why . . . ?" Polly fidgeted with her cup, unable to find the parloursing piece of the puzzle. Pouring Antonio some more tea, she tried to comfort him one last time. "Why don't you ask Rosa to take him to an asylum? Maybe he can find some peace there."

Cedric sent word that he'd be late returning from Monsieur Darmon's, and the domestics set the table for the two of them. Polly had the windows opened to let in the refreshing breeze, making the candles dance over their wicks. Antonio felt relieved at having told Polly about his father. He mustn't let his letters upset him anymore, he thought; it was only a matter of time before the secret would be out. He wished to return to the Ladies Society, ask Polly if she knew about a certain Miss de Graff. Stirring her soup, his hostess seemed to have no appetite left for dinner, brooding over an unanswered question.

"Whatever be your reasons to stay back in China, how can you be sure that your teachers are telling you the truth?"

"Teachers?" He noted the plural.

"The Horseman and his young assistant." Polly spoke with a straight face. "What if they are simply leading you on?"

"What would they gain from a Portuguese doctor?"

"One never knows with the Chinese, the games they play with foreigners, blowing hot and cold all the time. Maybe they're holding you hostage to use as a pawn."

"Tell me about the Horseman. Is he really what gossip makes him out to be?"

Polly shook her head. "There isn't much that's known about him. The American doctors thought him strange. They knew he was keeping an eye on them. He's the dowager's confidant. There are rumors about him doing her dirty work. He's known for his sudden disappearing tricks, and skill in turning boys into eunuchs." Polly grinned. "if you can call that a *skill*!" She stopped to gather her thoughts then stared into her soup. "I'd worry more about his assistant, if I were you?"

"Fumi, you mean?" Did Polly know about him and Fumi, he wondered.

"She's not unknown to the Legation. But we know nothing about her doctoring and teaching, how she became what she is now from what she was. How did she manage to find her way into the palace? There are those who think she's the real master and Xu her assistant.

Does she know that the young assistant has become my lover . . . ?

"You're wondering about all this gossip, aren't you?" Polly smirked. "Wherever there's life, there'll be gossip!"

He woke early and heard the attendants sweeping the courtyard and talking rapidly. Tian came to his door and asked Antonio to excuse the two of them for the day. They'd be off to celebrate the Qixi festival that fell on the seventh day of the seventh lunar moon on the Chinese calendar.

"It's the festival of love." Tian smiled impishly. They'd be off to watch newly married couples sing songs and make offerings to the gods.

"The festival of domestic skills," Wangsheng corrected him. "Skills to find a suitable match and keep the marriage happy." The kitchen would serve him his meals while they were away, he assured Antonio, pointing to a row of bowls.

When he was alone, he thought about Polly's words. *I'd worry more about his assistant . . . ..* It was true that he knew nothing about Fumi beyond what she'd told him. *She's spoken about Jacob but not Xu.* He knew how the abandoned wife had ended up at the Dutchman's printing press, but who had brought her to the palace? He was surprised that not even Polly had answers to her questions about Fumi.

He'd need her to prepare him for the hospital visit, Antonio thought. Maybe she could come along with him and observe the treatment herself, prompt him even to ask Xu the hard questions. When she came to the pavilion in the afternoon to share his early rice, Antonio passed her a drawing of a syphilitic man, his face covered in spots.

"What do you know about Canton rash, even though you might not know how to cure it?" He asked Fumi.

She looked a bit surprised. "It's the plague, Jacob said, that afflicts sinners."

"Sinners?"

"Yes. Soldiers, sailors, fallen men and women. They deserve their punishment, he told me, but their suffering is hard to watch."

"So why didn't you learn to cure their suffering?"

"Because . . ." Fumi seemed taken aback by the question, searching for an answer. "Our *Nei ching* describes ten thousand diseases and their cures. A Chinese doctor doesn't know all ten thousand, but only those that he treats frequently." Working at the palace she had no reason to worry about Canton rash, she said, no reason to ask Xu to teach her the treatment.

"Xu?" Antonio feigned surprise. "Who's Xu? You haven't told me anything about him yet."

She smiled. "You're angry with him, aren't you, for making you wait?" She passed the drawing back to him. "You must learn everything.

You can't become a Chinese doctor who knows how to cure just a single disease, even if it's something as terrible as Canton rash."

"Does he himself know how to?" Antonio pushed his plate away and spoke bitterly. "How can I trust him when you've told me nothing? How did you meet him? Was it he who taught you and made you his assistant? Did he bring you to the palace?"

She stopped eating and knitted her brows. "And how will the answers to your questions help you learn the canons?" Finished with her meal, she crossed over to the kitchen, speaking loudly as if she was scolding Antonio. "Your friends must be spreading lies about him."

He came up to the kitchen and faced her across the brick oven. "Tell me, what does he actually do for the empress? He can't be her personal physician if he disappears so frequently, can he?" He waited for Fumi to answer, then brought his mouth close to her ear: "Let me help you remember. He's a eunuch maker, that much we know, maiming little boys and ruining their lives forever. And a baby killer. What else?"

She made no effort to move away, set her plate down and spoke in an even voice, "He's a *Nei ching* master who follows the empress's orders, nothing more nothing less."

"A doctor following orders to kill?" He mocked her.

"Why not!" she shot back. "Better than some of your friends who kill for profit." She stared hard at him, then stepped out into the courtyard to pick up her wicker hat and walked out through the open gate, leaving him alone inside the kitchen humming with flies.

Antonio fretted in his lodge after Fumi had left. *She doesn't want to talk about Xu, or tell me about her past beyond Jacob.* He wondered why. Who was she protecting, Xu or herself? Why didn't she answer his questions? Why hadn't she pressed Xu to take him to a hospital, even after he had confided in her about his dying father?

As the evening progressed, he began to feel bitter about having quarrelled with Fumi on the festival of love. It was wrong of him to have hurt her, and insulted Xu. Polly would've reproved him for his bluntness. There were better, *sweeter* ways of finding out the truth, she'd have said. He regretted losing his chance to tell Fumi about the Ladies Society, and ask her about the elderly residents. The late rice tasted stale, and he retired early with a bottle of plum wine, hoping to make up with Fumi when he saw her next.

The sound of laughter woke Antonio, and he thought he was dreaming of a garden party. Loud shrieks and the patter of running feet made it seem as if a game was being played outside. Tumbling out of bed, he peered out of the rice paper panes. Tian and Wangsheng were running around the courtyard, plucking plums from the fruit tree and throwing them at each other. Both were bare-chested, with Tian wearing a pig mask and squealing like one as he chased his uncle. They looked drunk, swaying on their feet and making gurgling noises that made Antonio laugh.

Wangsheng came up to the lodge's door and knelt before Antonio, carrying Tian on his shoulders. Both at once started to tell him about the festival, jumbling up their words and making fun of each other. There had been a contest at the end of the evening, Tian said, to test which among the young unmarried girls would make the best wife. "The best cook, the best singer, the best gardener, best everything." They were told to float their sewing needles on a bowl of water. A floating needle would mark the one who'd make a skilled seamstress.

"Every girl tried and every one of them lost, their needles sinking as soon as they were dropped into water," Wangsheng announced gravely. The contest was then opened to the public. "Even eunuchs were allowed to join, with the winner rewarded with a pig mask." Tian held aloft his needle proudly and danced around Wangsheng.

"Your needle won?" Antonio asked, unable to hide his surprise. Wangsheng nodded and patted his nephew on the back. "He knew about the contest and had kept his needle ready." He made Tian show Antonio the winning item—a twig from the plum tree, polished to resemble a needle.

Maybe his mother was right after all—about her gifted son, turned out later to be a gifted eunuch!

"You're lucky there weren't any Boxers at the festival, otherwise they'd have sunk you both in a boiling pot!" It was well known that the spirit soldiers despised eunuchs for being cowards, hiding inside palaces and doing the work of women. But the talk of Boxers failed to dampen the spirits of a usually nervous Wangsheng.

"If the Boxers come we'll be prepared," he said, flexing his muscles.

"Prepared to fight them?" Antonio looked on amused.

"No, to become Boxers ourselves." Wangsheng said proudly.

"But . . ." Antonio hesitated before blurting out, "I thought they hated men who're incomplete, those who've had their . . ."

"We won't be incomplete when we join them," Wangsheng interrupted him. He made a private sign to his nephew, the two ran back to the kitchen and emerged moments later, each carrying a clear glass jar which they brought over to Antonio. Wangsheng nudged him to take a look at them, "When Boxers see us with these, they'll know we are complete like any other man."

Antonio gazed in wonder into the jars, each holding a severed male member. He remembered Polly telling him about the precious part that every eunuch guarded zealously and took to his grave in order to become a "whole man" in his next life.

"It's better to live among rebels than to die with the dowager." Wangsheng clapped his hands, urging Tian to join him as he leaped in the air like a flying Boxer, landing on the ground with a thud, crushing a pile of fruits underneath him.

His mood lifted after his eunuch friends had left, and it was too late to fall back to sleep. Despite arguing with Xu and Fumi, he was comforted by the thought of the hospital visit, longing to become a doctor again. He could see himself at a patient's bedside, checking pulse and examining the symptoms, just as his teacher had taught him to do. His thoughts strayed, and he remembered the troubled face of Rosa Escobar nursing his father. *She has suffered the most. . . .* He must bring Rosa back to Lisbon after his father's death, he resolved, have her look after his children after they were born.

Sipping plum wine, he began composing a letter to Ricardo Silva then changed his mind and started one instead for Arees. She had wished him a speedy return after his "adventure." The adventure was about to begin, he wrote . . . *to solve the mystery of Morbus Gallicus.*

❋

Wangsheng woke him. He looked frightened. A message had come from Joachim Saldanha, urging Antonio to come at once to Fengtai's Marco Polo Bridge, where he had been injured in an accident.

Splashing water on his face, he jumped onto his sedan chair and rushed to Peking's railway terminus. Fengtai was only an hour's ride away and he thanked the Belgian engineers for opening the line in such a short time, as it would've taken him at least half a day on a mule cart to reach the Marco Polo Bridge. Chris Campbell, the young *Times* correspondent, met him at Fengtai's station, standing all of six feet and six inches, visibly shaken. Antonio remembered meeting him at Polly's, among the big, blond and bearlike rugby boys. He hurried Antonio off the coach and into a covered mule cart.

"Where's Saldanha?" Antonio expected to see him brought to the station.

"Shh!" Chris quietened him with a finger on his lips. "There'll be trouble if word gets around that one more foreigner has come to Fengtai." He whispered to the cart driver, instructing him about their destination.

"What trouble?" Antonio peeked through the covers to catch a glimpse of the crowded street they were passing through. He heard more than he saw. A bullhorn blared out slogans, and marchers stomped on the road, banging on the doors of closed shop-houses. The sound of shattering glass mixed with Chris's trembling voice.

"Boxers have stirred everyone up against us. One small mistake and we'd be finished." He pushed Antonio's surgical box under the seat. "They mustn't catch us with this, or they might take the contents as dangerous."

Antonio thought the reporter was suffering from an unfortunate attack of anxiety. "Don't be foolish. How can anyone think a syringe or two could hurt them?"

"They'll believe anything. They might take your tools to be the tools of black magic." He drew Antonio away from the covers. "Nothing can be ruled out after what happened last night."

They felt trapped as the marchers surrounded their carriage, slowing it down. Their driver got into an argument with some of them. Sitting inside, they sensed they were being spied upon through the slats by a set of eyes. The carriage started to shake as if the crowd was trying to force them off the street.

Antonio tried to calm Chris down, by getting him to talk about Joaquim Saldanha. "What brings you here?"

"I came to check if the rumors being spread by the Boxers were true." Chris twitched nervously on his seat.

"What rumors?"

"That the Pascals, Simone and Jean-Paul, the owners of the French orphanage, had insulted their servants by cutting off their pigtails."

"Is it true?" Antonio asked.

"No! Their Chinese servants were all converted Christians who had rid themselves of their pigtails long ago. It was a ploy really, to scare away the French couple and recruit the orphans into their army."

"Did they attack the orphanage last night?"

Chris nodded. "They incited a mob and surrounded the compound, lit bonfires, stormed the gates, and hurled rocks that narrowly missed the orphans inside. We didn't know if they were bursting bombs or firecrackers, but the sound scared the children and made them wail all night."

"And the Pascals?"

"They were scared too. All of us huddled inside the building, and waited sheeplike for the end." Memory of the night made him shiver.

"And then?"

"At midnight they sent in an emissary. He demanded money in exchange for the children. Money and guns, that the French were claimed to be hiding in the orphanage."

"Where was Saldanha in all this?"

"He was our only hope. He was known to be visiting Fengtai, and the Pascals sent him word through a secret network of Christians."

"Word for what?" Antonio tried hard to follow Campbell.

"They wanted him to negotiate with the Boxers and secure their release."

Antonio caught a glance of the Marco Polo Bridge through the slats. He was relieved at the nearness of their destination. Chris Campbell seemed to recover from his nervous twitching, but just as they were about to cross the bridge a bomb exploded a few yards from the carriage. A huge cloud of dust engulfed them. The mule let out a sharp neigh, lunging to one side, and almost toppled the cart over. In the mad dash that followed, their driver managed to turn the animal around and cross the bridge, shouting at the top of his voice to warn the marchers in front of him. Keeping their heads down, Campbell and Antonio held on to each other to steady themselves inside the hurtling carriage. Once they were on the other side of the river, the crowd seemed to thin and they left the banks to enter a road that was quiet except for the distant sound of fireworks.

"They're celebrating the Boxers' victory over the French." Chris Campbell muttered, after he had recovered from the shock.

"Did they kill the couple?" Antonio asked with a grim face.

"No. Their lives were spared in exchange for the orphans."

"You mean . . ." Antonio clenched his teeth, expecting to hear the report of a grisly massacre.

"It was agreed that the children would be set free, the orphanage turned into a Boxer temple, and the Pascals pledge never to set foot on Fengtai again."

Antonio breathed a sighed of relief. *So no one was killed* . . . Chris went on with an ashen face. "The crowd wanted more. They demanded blood; tried to set the orphanage on fire. Rumors went around that Saldanha had been killed, that he had confessed to planting the cross in Chinese temples, tricking the innocents into praying to a foreign god."

"Did the French couple manage to get away in the end?"

Chris chuckled bitterly. "Yes, but first they fought over what to take with them and what to leave behind, getting angry at each other and throwing their favorite things around."

"What happened to Saldanha?"

"He managed to save us all, but suffered some injuries himself."

"What sort of injuries?"

"You'll see . . ."

When they reached a makeshift camp near the Marco Polo Bridge, Antonio found his friend sleeping. Jean-Paul had injected him with morphine. Dead exhausted, Simone was sleeping too. A young Chinese servant kept watch on the iron bridge for a sighting of the Tientsin train steaming its way to Peking.

"He said he had cut himself on rubble and rocks at night." Chris Campbell whispered. Jean-Paul puffed on his pipe and gazed wistfully at the orphanage across the river. Antonio unwrapped the bloody strips of cloth. His friend winced in his sleep. They appeared to be more than accidental cuts. Second degree burns had blackened the soles of his feet, going up to the ankles and calves. The flesh looked raw where it had split from the bones. On the priest's back, he found a maze of razor cuts like a beehive of dark blood.

"Not an accident. He has been tortured."

Chris Campbell gasped. "So this . . ."

"*This* was the price paid." Antonio looked up at Jean-Louis, who stood outside the tent and peered in. "Did you know that he'd negotiate with his body?"

An angry welt circled Saldanha's neck like a necklace. *This one must've saved the orphans . . . .* A hot iron had singed the hair on his chest and arms. *And this for Simone, saving her from certain rape.* The padre must've clenched his teeth and vouched for her innocence, then spelled out the terms of surrender.

His patient must be moved urgently where he could treat him properly. Antonio barked out his orders to the young attendant to fetch a litter—the typically Chinese box carriage supported by poles on the backs of two animals. Simone woke up and started to argue with Antonio over the timing of the Peking train.

"It's easier to take the train." Simone scowled. Jean-Paul agreed with her. "It'll take five hours on a litter, whereas . . ."

Antonio cut him off. "You go by train. I can't risk my patient by waiting for a train that might never come." Chris had mentioned reports of Boxers blowing up rail lines and bridges. "Can't let gangrene set in, which will force me to amputate his legs."

"Why don't we all go on litters then?" Simone pressed Antonio. "Why should we be stuck here while you disappear with your patient?"

"Because he almost died saving you. Can't let him die a second time." Antonio wrapped Joachim's legs in a blanket, and raised him on a mule litter with Chris's help then jumped up to sit next to the driver. "You can follow on foot if you like or wait for the train," he shouted back at the quarrelling Pascals and the *Times* reporter looking as confused as ever.

The five-hour journey seemed to last five days. The litter plodded through dried swamps studded with corn shoots, like a minefield of spears sticking out from the ground. They passed villages deserted only a short while before, wooden stoves still burning in abandoned kitchens and tea warm in the kettles. Talking to the few invalids forced to stay behind, it was unclear if the residents had fled the advancing Boxers or for fear of European soldiers who were thought to be on their way, marching into Peking from Tientsin to guard the foreign Legation against a rebel attack. With wells too few in number, the short supply of water alarmed Antonio. His patient would dehydrate very soon, and a cold compress was the only way of keeping the fever at bay. Passing the empty fields, their driver was scared of being fired upon by scared villagers from tree-tops and spurred the mules on. It would also be unwise to travel after sunset for fear of bandits roaming the lawless country. The river slowed them, turning a bend when it was least expected, and forcing a change in direction that added more miles to their journey.

They reached Peking finally and made their way over to the Summer Palace. His attendants helped Antonio carry Joachim Saldanha from the litter into the lodge. Tian screwed up his nose, smelling the pus-filled bandages. Wangsheng ran back and forth to the kitchen with pots of boiling water, and set fire to the soiled wrappings. His friend hadn't lost consciousness, Antonio was relieved to see. Burn shock could've set his temperature roaring, and spread infection throughout the body. For a whole week, he bathed and treated the wounds, taking turns with his attendants to stay up at night. He was happy that he had brought the antidotes along, fearing a fire breaking out onboard ship. "The doctor must be prepared for burns, cuts and broken bones!" Dr. Martin had taught them at the Faculdade. It was no use treating him for a serious condition, if the patient bled to death from a simple cut.

Joachim Saldanha slept fitfully, staying awake during the night, muttering to himself but didn't complain of pain. Antonio knew he was suffering. It was the worst kind of pain, worse than a deep cut or shattered bones, and he debated whether or not to help him with morphine. The recovery could take a month, and he wished to avoid sedating his patient too much lest he should become weak. The padre didn't speak much, simply nodding at Antonio when he asked him if the pain had lessened with the treatment. Within a fortnight, he showed real signs of recovery, regaining enough strength in the legs to hobble around.

"The litter saved my life!" Joachim Saldanha said, giving a glimpse of his tiger's appetite as he gulped down Wangsheng's specialty—bowls of noodle soup smelling of herbs. "You were smart to bring me over on one. The train to Peking wouldn't come. Rioters burnt it down not far from Marco Polo Bridge. They'd looted the brass nuts and bolts, torn up and buried the rails and sleepers. I learned all this while they were busy torturing me."

"They didn't know, of course, that they were dealing with a padre who was easy to torture but impossible to kill."

Joachim Saldanha grinned. "It was closer this time than before." He stroked the pink baby skin covering up the ugly blotches on his legs.

"And it'll be closer still, Boxer or no Boxer, if we don't cure your rotten tummy." Antonio warned him.

Living rough and going without proper meals had given the traveling padre a condition or two, and Antonio took the opportunity to examine him as he rested in the lodge. He had started by placing his friend's left palm down on the pillow and applying pressure on the wrist with his fingers. A low cough made him look toward the window. Fumi was watching him. As he continued with his pulse reading, she came in and sat beside him, observing his patient. Then, without speaking a word, she placed her fingers too on Joachim Saldanha's wrist to confirm what Antonio had heard.

"It's the *Chimai*," he whispered to her, meaning the deeper pulse. "It seems to have lost its rhythm. The flow of *qi* through the liver is weak." She nodded. "The stomach channel is blocked too," he went on.

"And so?"

"So not enough bile is being released for digestion. That's why he complains of cramps, and his belly swells up after his giant meals."

"Could the spleen be injured as well, given his irregular habits?"

"No," he disagreed with her. "The spleen is simply suffering in sympathy with the troubled liver. It's nothing but a coincidence." He released Joachim Saldanha's wrist. "One mustn't mistake the accident for the essence."

Fumi smiled, hearing Antonio recite her very own words back to her. She looked on approvingly as he spelled out the medicines for Wangsheng to fetch from the palace's store. Joachim Saldanha raised his hand to greet Fumi, and offered her the bowl of grapes by his side. She refused politely, and praised Antonio for bringing his patient back to the pavilion quickly. Burns were a nightmare for the Chinese doctor too. She was surprised that Joachim Saldanha's were healing so well. Then she rose to leave, closing the lodge's door after her.

"Wait!"

He breathed a sigh of relief when he found her under the plum tree, waiting for him and looking just like the peasant girl when he'd seen her first. *Does she hate me for my loose words?* Maybe she'd become wary of his moods and his acid tongue, scared even for her own safety given how close she'd become to a foreigner.

She shut his mouth before he could say anything. "I know why you're angry with Xu. He hasn't kept his promise to you yet. But he's not what your friends think. He won't betray you, not even if he had to die."

"Why did you stop coming to the lodge?"

"Because your friend is here with you. You must look after him now."

He ran his finger along her chin, "But I *must* see you too. How'd I know if you're safe?"

"It was risky for you to go to Fengtai," Fumi said. "It's a Boxer stronghold. Your attendants told me when I'd come, and I wanted Xu to go with me to find you there."

"Boxers could've killed you both if they'd known you'd come to save me."

She took a quick look at the kitchen. "I hope your attendants aren't telling others about us, or scheming with your enemies behind your back."

Antonio started to laugh. "You mean Wangsheng the Boxer!"

She scowled and moved away from him. "One day you'll know. . . ."

"My friend won't mind you coming here. He needs you more than I do. Maybe you could teach me how to use the Chinese needles to open up his stomach channel."

Fumi beamed. "Acupuncture is best to help the body heal itself."

"It'll help my body too, if you stop your self-imposed exile."

She kissed him and left quickly before he could go on any further. When Antonio returned to the lodge, Joachim Saldanha lowered his head in a mock bow. "You've become a *real* Chinese doctor, I see." He had managed to get up and eat the early rice, shoveling it down expertly with his chopsticks. "Your friend thinks so too, doesn't she?"

"A Chinese doctor who's ignorant of the pox." Antonio spoke glumly.

Saldanha tried to cheer him up. "It'll take you four full seasons, as I recall, and we aren't past two yet. Didn't Fumi say that you're doing even better than a Chinese doctor?"

He knows about her . . .. Antonio wondered if it was his attendants who had told the padre about Fumi, or if he had heard about Xu's assistant from another source. *He must know about us too, how could he not, seeing us the way we were together?*

"What if I have to leave before the four seasons are up? What if Boxers cut short my lessons?"

Joachim Saldanha stopped eating to think. "It's a different China now to the one we've known, but some things haven't changed, will never change."

"Like what?"

"Xu has promised to teach you the cure for syphilis. He'd rather die than go back on his word."

Antonio was struck by his friend and Fumi both vouching for Xu. "But he's rumored to be more than a doctor. Some claim him to be a Boxer in disguise, and the empress's spy. He's known too for his disappearing tricks, and hasn't kept his word yet taking me to see a pox victim."

Joachim Saldanha thought over Antonio's complaints, then offered his advice. "He might well be all those things, but without Xu it's impossible for you to achieve your mission. You must become his friend. You should go to his home and see for yourself how a Chinese doctor lives. If you fight him, he'll fight back. It's best to take from him what you want, and leave the rest behind." He smiled at Antonio, "Fumi can tell you what his weaknesses are, for you to be aware of your strengths."

Weaknesses . . .? He stopped himself from pressing on about Xu, and asked his friend instead about his treatment at the hands of the Boxers, unable to control his curiosity. "Is it true that foreigners had cut off Manchu pigtails in Fengtai?"

"Yes!" Joachim Saldanha laughed. "It wasn't the pigtail of a servant though, but Simone's. She had cut her hair and flung the locks from her window only for them to be discovered by her neighbors!"

With Fumi visiting regularly, the pavilion was transformed into a happy family home. The day started with Joachim Saldanha waking everyone up with his loud calls for breakfast porridge. A cold wind howled across the lake, making Tian shiver as he stoked the oven and muttered curses under his breath. Fumi came early and helped the attendants prepare medicine for the patient, boiling herbs that spread a pungent cloud over the courtyard. Antonio would rise to find her chatting with Joachim Saldanha. She dressed his wounds and advised him on his eating habits, making the padre laugh.

"I'll take you with me when I leave. That way you can rule over my stomach!" He teased Fumi like a kind uncle, teased Antonio too for growing a monk's beard. "They'll take you for a pirate if you return home looking like this! Your patients, especially ladies, will be afraid to visit you!"

Wangsheng reminded everyone of the rites of the Chinese New Year that was fast approaching. Paper cut-outs of the fortune gods had started to appear on the kitchen window, red silk tassels hung from door hooks and bowls of mandarin oranges appeared with the meals. Much to Antonio's dismay, the eunuchs began to open every door and window of the pavilion to expel the stale air of the past year and fill the rooms with the icy breeze of the new, serving fresh air with dumplings to sweeten the year of the rat.

"You won't mind the winter when the Chinese New Year comes around," Joachim Saldanha told him. "It's much grander than Christmas. Even our Legation brothers and sisters observe it with much pomp, dress up as emperors and empresses, or the mischievous red-tailed monkey of the Chinese legend."

For a whole month Antonio and Fumi examined their patient. They read his pulse and went over the symptoms, discussing the twelve channels, the five viscera and the eleven organs, to cure the padre's lingering conditions.

"Of the nine kinds of needles," Fumi explained, "those made of yellow metal have the power to stimulate the body, while the white ones have a calming effect."

Antonio examined the arrow-headed, blunt, and spear-pointed needles, testing them for sharpness and drawing a drop of blood on his forefinger. Joachim Saldanha gave him a fearful look.

"You must know when to use which needle. The one made of cold silver is best whenever the patient suffers from an excess of yang." Fumi drew out a long silver needle and warmed its head in a lamp's flame.

"When the yang subsides, it'll restore yin, balancing the two," Antonio was quick to recite the principle, drawing a look of satisfaction from Fumi. He was excited by his first practical lesson in China, helping his teacher treat a patient.

"But you mustn't drain the yang during a new moon." Fumi looked out through the window at the bright crescent, and called Joachim Saldanha over to lie on his side on the bed. He looked nervous, as if he was being summoned to yet another bout of torture, then obeyed meekly. Tian yelped with excitement.

"One must start by feeling with the hand." She ran her fingers up Joachim Saldanha's ribs, tickling him on purpose and making him laugh. "Then trace the whole body to mark the three sections and nine subsections to insert the needles."

"What if there was a mistake?" Antonio asked. "What if a needle pierced a vein and caused bloodshed?"

The padre looked alarmed, and tried to get up. Fumi stopped him, pushing him firmly down on the bed. "To guard against that, you must raise the skin like a piece of silk and hold it between your thumbs. Then wait for the patient to inhale before you puncture the skin."

Joachim Saldanha drew in a sharp breath as Fumi inserted the first of the needles, and waited for him to exhale before she turned it with her fingers and drew it out slowly.

Lying on his side with a dozen needles stuck into him, the padre recovered his humor to tease Fumi. "The Boxers could learn a trick or two from you. With torture such as this, I'd have told them anything, including the most important secret of the Summer Palace!"

At the end of his treatment, Joachim Saldanha gazed fondly at Fumi as she draped a woollen wrapper over her peasant's smock and left.

"What did you mean by the 'most important secret'?" Antonio

asked him. His friend sighed, then patted him like a kind uncle and said quietly, "If only you were one of them, or she was one of us."

With Tian as his guide, Antonio set out for Xu's village home. But they lost their way after they'd traveled just a few miles from the palace. A steady stream of peasants herded water buffaloes to their fields as his guide stood in the middle of a bamboo bridge and scratched his head. He had expected the Chinese doctor to live in a pavilion within easy reach of the empress. Wangsheng looked uneasy when he'd brought up the matter of visiting his teacher.

He needed Xu more than ever, Antonio had concluded after speaking with Joachim Saldanha. He wished the padre could come with him, but he had recovered just enough from his wounds to set off once again to an important mission. "Don't worry, I'll be back soon." He had hugged Antonio and the eunuchs before he left. "Just pray that I don't return in worse condition than last time." He had left a gift for Fumi, a lucky charm made of jade and shaped like a peony, to wear around her neck.

Antonio wanted to surprise Xu with his visit. He was taken aback by the modest home set among rice fields and chicken farms. Sitting on high stilts, it resembled a fisherman's hut. Only a sedan chair on the courtyard marked it out from its neighbors. A *Nei ching master living like a peasant!* Xu came out to meet him in the courtyard. He looked as if he had just returned from his field with his buffalo.

"You're a master already!" Xu smiled broadly, praising him for treating Joachim Saldanha "just as a Chinese doctor would. It was right of you to have relied on the pulse. A patient is bound to imagine things, while the doctor must trust his own readings." Calling Antonio inside, he offered him a high-backed royal chair that was the only mark of luxury.

"I was expecting you earlier, but you were away." Xu spoke kindly. "Fumi went over to fetch you. We had found a sick man for you to examine, a man who showed symptoms of Canton rash."

Antonio expressed his regret at the missed opportunity, but Xu brushed it aside. 'Your chance will come again. At the end of winter there'll be many more to examine.'

"Many more?" Antonio showed surprise. "Do you expect a higher rate of infection in the cold season?"

"No, no . . . not higher." Xu corrected him, pouring a cup of tea for his guest, and lighting up his pipe. "In spring we round up the victims from all parts of China and bring them to Peking. It tells us how many have been struck by the disease. You can come and see how we treat the patients, if you're willing to wait a little longer."

Surely he doesn't mean treating all patients the same way? Antonio was confused. Syphilis didn't strike two victims alike. For some it lay dormant for years, while for others it spread at a gallop from the very onset of the infection. It was just as common to find the grave of a young victim who had barely reached his prime, as that of an old man who had lived to a ripe age with syphilis.

Sipping tea, his host seemed more interested in Antonio's visits to the Legation than the pox. "You're the most popular doctor among foreigners in Peking, I hear. With you around, they must feel less worried than they did before."

"Worried about Boxers, you mean?" Antonio shrugged. "I can't save them from bullets and rusty spears. No doctor can."

"Why would they be afraid of Boxers? With British warships in Tientsin barely a few miles away, they must feel safer than everyone else in China!" Xu dismissed his concern.

"A few battleships taking on a million spirit soldiers?" Antonio heard voices across the walls of Xu's mud-thatched home. The power of China lay with the peasants who fed her millions, he recalled Joachim Saldanha telling him.

"Why not? Last time the foreigners fought the Chinese over opium, English and French soldiers came over from their ships and brought the emperor to his knees. They looted and destroyed the Summer Palace too."

Antonio kept quiet. Marcello Valignoni's vivid accounts of the sacking of the Summer Palace went through his mind.

"Perhaps Mr. Mckinsey has already sent a telegram to the English captain to ready his troops." Xu looked searchingly at Antonio. "Maybe the soldiers are on their way to Peking to protect the Legation. There'll be war when they come, between the Boxers and foreigners, maybe even with the empress's army." He stopped drawing on his pipe and cleared his throat. "You are free to leave the palace and go to the Legation if you like."

Antonio shook his head.

"No? Wouldn't you feel safer among the foreigners?"

Xu watched Antonio closely, taking his silence as a mark of doubt. "You don't have to decide now. You can make up your mind when you hear more about the Legation's plans. You'll know before us. You can tell me then." He smiled kindly. "We must do everything to keep you safe."

"I'm willing to tell you what I know about foreign soldiers, if you tell me everything you do about treating pox." Antonio finished his tea, and rose. "We can be friends, helping each other out."

Xu looked surprised. "You mean . . .?"

"Why don't you teach me how to cure syphilis right now? That way we can save us both a lot of trouble." Antonio persisted. "You must know how to deal with the symptoms, don't you?"

"Ah! the cure." Xu nodded, as if he understood Antonio perfectly. "That's why you've come to China. Pox is your enemy, and you want to kill it. The human body is pure, you think, the disease an evil intruder. And the doctor must act like a soldier, learn the secret of winning." He moistened his lips, and lit his pipe again. "Pox to you is what Boxers are to your foreign friends, isn't it?"

"But there must be cures for both." Antonio spoke firmly. "Boxers or the pox, ultimately they will be defeated the same way."

"Same way?" Xu raised an eyebrow.

"By force." Antonio waited for Xu to speak, but he remained silent. With a final glance at his teacher, he rose and climbed down the steps of the house on stilts.

On his way back to the palace, Antonio went over Xu's prodding about foreign soldiers and the Legation's plans. *He wants my help, but isn't prepared to help me just yet.* He recalled Joachim Saldanha's warning to keep clear of Chinese and European intrigues. Wangsheng stopped him at the pavilion's gate and pointed to a visitor waiting for him inside the lodge.

Antonio was surprised to see Ferguson at the Summer Palace. He was dressed formally in a black suit, very different to the Jesuit gown he'd worn when they'd last met. The older eunuch had served him tea, and he raised his cup to toast Antonio's arrival.

"Ah! The dowager's prisoner!" He sneered at Antonio's muddy boots. "Has she turned the Portuguese doctor into a peasant?" He was visiting the palace to negotiate the sale of a precious vase, he said, one looted by the allies from the Summer Palace only a few decades back, now offered back to its rightful owner by an anonymous collector for a small price. "I came to leave the item with the chief eunuch and thought to pay you a visit."

Antonio knew Ferguson was lying. He was certain the gypsy had come to meet him unannounced just to surprise him. It wasn't the simple matter of selling him the palace copy of *Nei ching* that he had shown him, but something more important, and he expected the usual volley of gossip before the real business started.

"Pinchback may have to leave soon. It's a pity given all the good work he's done with the Hong Kong Bank. His bosses have got wind of his mischief! As long as Casanova frolicked with the domestics it was fine, but not with a Legation minister's wife!" Ferguson waited for Antonio to egg him on then continued. "The Italian minister has threatened to kill him for making a pass at his wife." He chuckled, adding on the juicy bits, "I bet the bugger will describe his tête-à-tête with the signora in the smutty memoirs that he's been writing for years. Bet you, though, he won't mention his 'French' problem, the same one that has brought you here!"

"He shows no outward sign of syphilis," Antonio said coldly.

"He's been seeing Chinese doctors in private, my sources tell me."

Antonio called out to Wangsheng to bring him his early rice. Ferguson changed tack and told him about the head eunuch of the Summer Palace and his escapades with the palace maids. "He's a eunuch only in name, whereas . . ."

"You haven't come to see me about Pinchback or the eunuch, have you? Nor to sell me the manuscript. You're too good a dealer to know I'm not a collector. Why don't you tell me why you've come?"

Stung by Antonio's reaction, Ferguson stuttered. "It's Polly. She's worried about you. She thinks you might be in danger, and has asked me to warn you."

"What sort of danger?"

Ferguson shrugged. "Could be anything really. It has to do with your 'judgment'," he explained. "Not your medical judgment, of course," Ferguson hastened to add. "In that you're superb, everyone knows that, but your judgment about people. She thinks you might make mistakes when it comes to those that are around you here."

"You mean my two eunuchs? My judgment about them was accurate the very first day we met, that they're good for nothing!" Antonio offered to share his early rice with his visitor, but he declined.

"And how about your teacher's assistant? Do you know much about her? Has she told you about her foreign lover?" Ferguson took advantage of Antonio's full mouth. "She has printer's ink in her blood from sleeping with the Dutch printer, the weirdest foreigner to have come to Peking." He lit his pipe as Antonio ate his meal. "No one can tell you more about Jacob de Graff than me. Ask anyone and they'll say he was a priest. Priest! My foot! At best they'll know him as a Bible printer, the one to have introduced China to modern printing. But if you ask me . . ."

He's lying again . . .. Fumi never slept with Jacob. Antonio felt angry at Ferguson for spreading lies about her, but decided to keep calm and hear him out.

"How did you know Jacob?" He asked the gypsy.

"From Oxford. He was a Balliol man like me. Read mathematics and did nothing else. No girls, no boys, no drinking, no cricket. If ever there was an egghead, he was one. One would expect him to end up at some university in Europe and drive his students mad, but wonder of wonders he ended up in China."

"Maybe his sister brought him over." Antonio recalled Fumi telling him about Miss de Graff.

"Margaret? She was your typical spinster, doing penance for the sins of Europeans. What she didn't know was that her brother was neither priest nor printer but a pure mathematician."

"How do you mean?"

"He thought like one. Always demanded proof for everything. Argued for the love of arguing. But in China the arithmetic was too messy for him to solve. He was a proud man, it wasn't easy for him to take anyone's help, not even from his old Balliol friend. But he surprised everyone with his golden lily." Ferguson let out a cloud of smoke. "She had run away from her husband, and Margaret was her savior. She passed on her little gem to her dear brother. It didn't take long for our Jacob to forget his maths and lose his mind."

"What happened then?"

"His troubles started to grow as he fought with both Chinese and foreigners. The mandarins hated him for printing the Bible, and the foreigners for the secret bulletins of the rebels. Harassed by both, he became a recluse and then . . ."

"Then?" This time Antonio showed interest in Ferguson's gossip.

"Bad stories have sad endings. Our priest and printer finally threw in the towel and died by his own hand."

"Own hand?"

"He set fire to the chemicals stored at the printing press and was gutted with the machine, blocks, paper . . . everything." Tapping his pipe Ferguson looked around the lodge suspiciously. "I don't know how she met Xu and entered the palace, but only she could tell you more about Jacob than I."

"Who do you mean?"

"Jacob's golden lily."

Antonio controlled his urge to slap Ferguson and throw him out of the pavilion. Instead he called out to Tian to bring him tea. "And so you've come to warn me about Fumi."

"She's had the taste of a foreign man, but doesn't fit the role of the typical Chinese mistress. *She*, not Jacob, is the mystery of the story. Perhaps she had as much to do with his sad ending as he did himself." Rising, Ferguson cast a final glance around. "We wouldn't want anyone to misjudge her character as our poor Jacob did, would we?"

"What does Polly recommend as cure for my 'misjudgment'?"

"I shall let her tell you all about that. She'll have more time on her hands, now that Linda Harris has usurped her role as the queen bee! The Chinese New Year will be celebrated next week at the American minister's mansion rather than at the Harts'. Linda will call you to her fancy dress ball. There'll be singing and dancing through the night, and fireworks imported from Hong Kong by the lecherous Pinchback." Leaving, Ferguson returned to his favorite theme, "Damn foreigners know nothing about Chinese astrology. If they did, they'd be afraid of celebrating the year of the rat, which is the year of death!"

Tian came running in with the rumor that was on everyone's lips. The dowager empress was leaving the Summer Palace. It wasn't her annual pilgrimage to the temples in the high mountains, but to some place unknown. No one knew why she was leaving and for how long. Among shopkeepers of Suzhou Street the word had spread that she was fleeing yet another invasion by foreigners. "They'll kill her this time," they whispered among themselves as they boarded up the shops fearing an outbreak of looting. Those who remembered the opium wars spread gory tales of the sacking that had followed the allied victory. "They won't repeat their mistake. This time they'll take the whole of China not simply her treasures."

Even the head eunuch didn't know where she was going, a puzzled Wangsheng confided in Antonio. Her attendants have been told to be ready to leave at short notice, carrying nothing but precious jewels with them.

"Is it foreigners or Boxers she's afraid of?" Antonio asked him.

"It could be neither. Maybe she's afraid of someone inside the palace, someone who's close to her nephew, the emperor."

Antonio asked him if Xu would leave too, but the eunuch had heard nothing about that. He waited all morning for Fumi to come, then left with his attendants to join the crowds that had gathered outside the Temple of Clouds. The empress always visits the temple before leaving the palace, the guards were telling those who had come to catch a glimpse of her. Some of them were crying. With all the talk about war that was going around, it could only be an evil omen. An old man started to kowtow before the temple's deity, followed by others.

Antonio searched for Fumi among the throng. Passing quickly through the temple gates, he looked for her in the gardens; poked his head into private courtyards and tearooms. *What if she's left already with the empress?* He entered halls and towers, ran from one pavilion to another along the winding galleries, and came up to the Great Opera. The empress's seat facing the stage was vacant. He parted the curtains to take a look inside. There were no signs of the actors and singers. Only the opera masks hung from the racks like a row of severed heads.

The terrace by the lake was empty and he strolled along aimlessly, overcome by a searing pain. *I've lost her now. . . .* He was certain that he'd never see Fumi again. He blamed himself for ignoring the danger signs, even after Joachim Saldanha was tortured. *I should've left Peking with Fumi.* For the first time, he questioned his strange obsession with syphilis, asking himself all the questions that friends had asked him, from Ricardo to Dona Elvira and Polly. *I've hung on to pox and lost Fumi. . . .* Unable to think any further, he started to weep as shadows loomed over the lake turning to gray its icy waters.

A boatman tapped him on the shoulder and smiled through his toothless mouth. He pointed toward the horizon with his oar, at the empress's barge floating like an island in the middle of the lake. Lanterns had lit up the deck and the cabins. The sound of music wafted across to the shores, and it seemed that a tea party was in progress with the dowager's favorites, her ladies-in-waiting, actors and musicians. He strained his ears to catch the notes and heard the song of a dying swan, too weak to fly away with its flock.

❀

The American first secretary's mansion was lit up with Chinese lanterns for the New Year and the masquerade was in full swing when he arrived with Fumi. Antonio had assured her that it was customary for single guests to bring along a friend, that neither Linda Harris nor her husband would mind her presence at the ball. "Jacob never went." Fumi had looked at him accusingly before they left the pavilion. "They are vulgar, he used to say. Men and women act like animals, get drunk and vomit all over. Married couples do naughty things behind each other's backs. Jacob thought them a terrible waste of time."

"I'm not Jacob," Antonio told her, slipping on a tattered robe that Joachim Saldanha had left behind. Fumi asked him to shave off his long beard. "You can't go looking like this!"

"It's a fancy dress ball. You must go dressed like someone you're not."

"And who have you dressed up as?"

"A padre." He told her to wear her white silk robe. She looked startled. "You want me to come along with you? A priest accompanied by a courtier! What will people take us for?"

"Lovers. They'll take us for what we are." He had shut her mouth with his palm and asked her to hurry as the bearers were waiting.

Their hosts John and Linda Harris, dressed up as Mad Hatter and Gooseberry Fool, received them in the hallway of their mansion, which was lavishly decked with plum-blossom bouquets. A giant paper rat hung from the parlor's ceiling. Distracted by their guests, the American couple didn't ask too many questions and as Antonio started to introduce Fumi, Polly arrived to whisk her away. "We know about your teacher, Tino, know *all* about her!"

They entered a large room full of light but chilly for the breeze that blew in through the porch where a bunch of athletic men, dressed as gladiators, had gathered to smoke cigars. Monsieur Darmon in an explorer's jacket and leaning on his *fusil de chasse* was entertaining them with stories interrupted by bursts of laughter. Mr. Pinchback hovered around the room, dipping his Roman headgear to the ladies, battle-axe perched firmly on his shoulder. Antonio caught sight of Linda Harris's niece Patty and her fiancé, the two dressed appropriately as bride and groom. She didn't recognize him at first in his priest's smock, then nudged the junior doctor to come over and thank Antonio for his timely help and extend a warm welcome to visit them in their future home in Philadelphia. He held up his hand to bless them, making Patty giggle.

"You should've asked for more than a measly night's stay in bloody Philadelphia." Antonio could see Ferguson's dancing eyes behind a Venetian mask. He moved away to find himself a drink. Drawing his magician's cape around him, Ferguson followed him and brought his face close to Antonio's ear. "It's brave of you to bring her with you! For a moment I thought it was Jacob who's come with his golden . . ." He stopped, noticing Antonio's icy gaze. "She came with him once, but that was different. She even looks different now . . . like a proper guest."

"What did she look like before?" Antonio glanced around the room to catch the eye of some one he knew, just to be able to shake off an obviously drunk Ferguson.

"Like an ordinary Chinese. Now she's extraordinary!"

He saw Fumi through the glass doors, sitting next to Sally Hollinger at the kitchen table and reading her pulse as her patient, dressed as a Welsh farm girl, waited nervously. Antonio smiled. It wouldn't take her long to captivate the guests. She'd win over the neurotic lot with her accurate readings and sage advice. They might even forget that she had come on the same sedan as him and take her for a senior mandarin's wife invited by the American diplomat. He looked for Polly and found her conspiring with Yohan, her snake-like Medusa braids contrasting with the wide-brimmed mariachi hat of her Chinese friend. She gave Antonio an impish grin and continued chatting with the spy who was without his pregnant wife. Cedric was engrossed as well with John Harris, the pirate and the Gooseberry Fool catching up on important matters as Sir Robert's band played the opening number of the evening.

"Let me tell you why you won't find syphilis in China." Mr. Pinchback edged up to Antonio and spoke in his usual measured voice. "Men with longer foreskins are more easily infected than others. The germ hides under the tender skin and breeds easily in its moist nest. The Chinese are born with shorter hoods on their weapons than Europeans. You can say they're born circumcised, with fewer than one in one thousand getting the pox even when they're severely exposed to it."

Antonio dismissed Pinchback's theory, which he knew to be false from watching the peasants relieving themselves by the river from his barge on the Yangtze.

"How many Chinese hoods have you examined?"

Mr. Pinchback wasn't ready to give up. "It's a well known fact. Most women who've had the taste of both Chinese and European types will confirm what I'm saying."

He was saved by Polly. Making her way through the gladiators, raising battle cries and crowding the dance floor, she reached Antonio and dragged him away to the cozy corner between the hall and the dining room. "Come, or you'll miss out on Ferguson's treasure, the most precious book in all of China!"

Heads crowded over a coffee table with Ferguson hovering around, like a proud father showing off a newborn. The Italian minister's wife turned the pages of the old manuscript gingerly with her long fingernails with Hanna Mueller from the German mission holding down the parchments for everyone to see, accompanied by spirited commentaries from Ferguson, speaking like a true Confucian expert.

Hanna gasped as she eyed an illustration: "To think that a primitive people could produce something so extraordinary!"

"Who are you calling primitive?" Ferguson shot back. "The Chinese are the fathers of pornography, with the oldest books in the world. It goes back to 200 B.C. The Han emperors were even buried with their favorite 'recipes of the bedchamber' and the 'secret arts'."

"Just so they could please the angels!" Polly laughed.

"The yellow emperor slept with twelve hundred wives and concubines and ascended to heaven a pure soul," Ferguson boasted, then lectured on the virtues of having multiple partners over an entire lifetime. "By sleeping with many women a man has an infinite supply of yin energy. It prolongs life, cures illnesses, gives him the power to father children even when he's eighty."

"And what do women get by sleeping with multiple men?" Linda Harris asked with a look of disapproval even as she stole glances at the illustrated book on the table.

"Sagging breasts and heartaches, what else!" Polly announced as gravely as Ferguson amidst peels of laughter. "For men it's medicinal and for women fatal."

"Tell me what it says." The Italian minister's wife drew Ferguson's attention to the Chinese characters underneath a sketch of a man stroking his lover's face.

"It starts with a 'reddened face,' it says, the first of the five signs of desire. It advises a man to prepare to unite with his lover."

"Unite!" Someone in the group murmured under her breath.

"Yes, to be ready for her nostrils to flare, for her skin to burn and nipples harden, which is the second of the five signs."

"What's the fifth?" With an eye on the dinner table, Linda tried to hurry him along."

"Wait! Let him take it slowly . . ." The Italian lady had her eyes glued to the illustrations.

"American men go from one to five in five seconds, unlike us Europeans." René Darmon had crept up to the group and offered his vast expertise on cultural mores based on his extensive travels.

"European, American or Chinese, the third step is the most vital." Ferguson kept everyone in suspense then read out the characters, translating them with his usual flair. "The third stage is about the opening, the most precious one, the lips. When a woman is ready for love her lips moisten naturally like ripe cherries, and her lover must be brave to pluck them without asking."

Antonio saw Fumi through the glass doors, talking to an elderly Chinese woman wearing a maid's apron. Is this how it'll be when they were back in Lisbon, Dr. Maria and his oriental wife visiting the quinta of one of his friends or that of a rich patient? Would they ignore her as she chatted with the domestics or show kindness, allowing her to lay her fingers on their wrists? He could imagine the looks of reproach among those who had had their eyes on Dr. Maria for their daughters or sisters, and the gleam of revenge at his sorry state of affairs, turning down a "proper match" for a piece of yellow trash.

His heart throbbed, and he couldn't take his eyes off her lips ripe like cherries and waiting to be plucked.

Ferguson finished his treatise on the five signs of desire, and moved on to the best parts of the *Memories of the Plum Cottage*, which was a rare find even by his standards, a book "he'd almost had to kill to lay his hands on." One might call it a "harlots' manual" of the kind used by madams to train their nubile recruits. It contained instructions for giving the greatest enjoyment to the clients, and the serious matter of sexual hygiene. "Those outside the brothel were never allowed to cast their eyes on what you're about to see." Flipping quickly through the pages, he stopped at one with pictures of the thirty most enjoyable "postures of intercourse," then read aloud the note that accompanied each for the benefit of everyone.

"This one's called the *Butterfly*, where a man lies on his back with his legs wide open and his lover sits lightly on his thighs resting her weight on her feet. This the *Flying Pigeon*, which is the very same as the *Butterfly*, but the woman chooses to sit with her back to her lover. Then there's the *Dance of the Phoenix*, *Merry Turtles*, and the *Cat and the Mouse Sharing the Same Cove*, which is the most demanding of all, where a woman takes in two lovers at the same time."

"*Two* at the same time?" Hanna Mueller gasped even louder than before.

"Yes, the first man lies on his back, while the lady climbs up to . . ."

Not willing to be outdone by Ferguson, René Darmon raised his voice to drown him out. "You can see all this and more in pure flesh in Peking. Just have to go to the 'lookie shows' at the Tartar market where peasant girls are kept in cages behind the stalls. You can pay and look under their skirts, or pay their owners to take up the thirty positions with them." Scandalizing the ladies, he smirked and nudged Antonio. "Dr. Maria, of course, doesn't need a filthy Chinese book or a lookie show. He can see all he wants every day in his pavilion—free!"

Antonio punched and bloodied his nose, the blood spilling out in spurts and dropping down on the pages of the *Plum Cottage*.

"Go home, Tino. The world will die of poor French jokes before it dies of syphilis." As she bandaged his bruised and bleeding knuckles in the bathroom, Polly spoke almost in a whisper. "Look what you've done now. With one blow you've scotched all the gossip I'd whipped up about you and kept going for so long. Who's going to believe me now?"

Polly had quickly led him away before the men could gather around, preventing them from catching the sight of blood that would've excited them surely. Her quick glance at Cedric was enough to have him keep the party going with his usual wisecracks, and instructions to the band to play the liveliest of tunes.

"He isn't like the others, I'd told everyone, not Casanova's cousin, collecting golden lilies. There's someone waiting for him back home." She gave Antonio a look of reproach. "What will happen to Arees, now that you've got Fumi?"

He jerked his head up. "What do you know about Arees?"

"Everything. Everyone knows about you two. That you're to marry soon, that she's waiting for you to return."

She cleaned the bloodstains off his shirt. "You should've told me."

"Told you what?"

"That Fumi has caught another one of us now. How smart of her to spot the love-starved foreigners."

He wrenched his arm away from Polly and rose. "You make her seem like a man eater on the prowl. It wasn't she who made the moves.

I did. I chased her, begged her to teach me; I followed her at the palace; I dragged her here against her wishes to this vulgar lot of foreigners." He took a swig from the glass that Cedric had brought over, and smashed it on the floor. "And I shall leave with her now."

"Wait." Polly stopped him before he could open the door. "It's going to be tougher than you think. Taking her away from China won't be as easy as leaving on your sedan. You don't know who's behind her, none of us do." She came up to him and laid a hand on his face. "I knew you were trouble the moment I met you. I knew you wouldn't like it here at the Legation, that your mind was elsewhere. It'd be easy for you to go astray." She sighed. "Do you know what Ellie wrote about you?"

Antonio shook his head.

"She wrote to say that I must keep you safe even if I had to fall in love with you." She sighed again, then opened the door for him. "Now I must help you get out of your little trouble."

The party had taken on a harder edge when he returned. Voices rang louder across the hall, champagne corks popped like gunshots, and the gladiators stomped on the dance floor as if pounding an arena with their iron-clad boots. Everyone greeted each other with the Chinese greetings for the New Year they had learned from their servants. Pinchback had dropped his Caesar's axe by mistake on a Ming vase, and crawled on the floor looking for broken pieces of the priceless item; Ferguson plied everyone with his usual stories of "stupid foreigners," with more than a touch of malice. Past sufferers of his barbs kept a safe distance, secretly wishing for the sign of a bleeding hand to appear on his door.

Antonio looked for Fumi, unable to find her anywhere. Maybe someone had said something rude to her and she had left by herself. His skirmish with Darmon seemed to have set off alarm bells among the guests. The telegraph operator smiled nervously when he enquired about his chronic indigestion, his wife pretending not to recognize him in his priest's attire. A gloomy Linda Harris avoided eye contact, drifting through the room with her Chinese maid and ordering her to clean up the mess on her rosewood furniture and Persian carpets. The *Golden Waterfall* brought everyone out onto the lawn as the first of Pinchback's fireworks bathed the night sky with sparkling mist. A hushed silence greeted the *Spring Peony*, opening petal by petal around the bud, followed by *Heaven's Rings* in colors of the rainbow. A roar went up with the deafening boom of the *Red Chili* crackers.

Herr Mueller's voice rang out from the balcony as the guests were about to leave: "Boxer!" followed by shrieks and shouts. All eyes turned upward, as if expecting a mythical beast to descend from the clouds. The gladiators dashed out to fetch their swords and daggers, tumbling on the slippery lawn. Sally Hollinger screamed at those trying to open the hallway doors for a look, warning them against the barbarians who might be waiting in force outside. Several of the guests ran toward the fence of trees at the far end of the garden, looking for the servants' gate that'd allow them to slip out through the back. No one expected the dreaded attack on the Legation to begin so soon, and wondered if it was a false alarm. "Surely our spies would've warned us!" Polly too seemed confused by the unlikely turn of events, until a measure of calm was finally restored by John Harris, who appeared on the balcony and made an announcement.

A Boxer soldier had slipped in through the Legation's cordons and was found loitering the streets. The German guards had captured him, and taken away his country-made rifle. "He's a village lad, and looks pretty harmless," the American minister assured everyone. He had come to buy chickens at the market, the boy had confessed on interrogation, and lost his way in the Legation.

"Liar!" A seething Sally Hollinger raised her voice to catch Mr. Harris's ear. "Must've come to raid a mansion or two while everyone was busy with the party." Several others joined in with strong views about the intruder's intent, forcing John Harris to invite everyone to come up to the balcony if they wished to have a look at the Boxer boy.

Julius Caesar led the charge up the stairs followed by the pirate and the vampire, Mad Hatter and Medusa, the entire cast of the masquerade following suit with the gladiators bringing up the rear as the guests thronged the balcony and strained their eyes beyond the mansion's walls to catch a sight of the Boxer soldier in his comical hat and rags held by the scruff of his neck by a German guard brandishing his Mauser, each as scared of the other as bullfighter and bull.

"Why did you fight for me?"

Inside the sedan, he lay on his back with legs wide apart, resting his head on Fumi's lap. A gray mist sped past them. Grunts of the bearers reminded him of carriage horses, letting out a scream every now and then to warn those who stood in their way.

She stroked his injured fist. "What's the use? People will always say what they think." She spotted a bloodstain on his priest's smock. "Can you stop them?"

He nodded. "As long as they're within reach."

"Silly! And what if they're not? If they spread lies behind our backs?"

She kissed him where the cross would've hung, and parted the robe to stroke his chest and tickle the sides. A breeze blew in through the coupe's curtains. She loosened her hair, leaned forward to press down on him, reached with her hand to hold him between the legs and match the trot of the bearers as they bumped up and down along a ragged path.

"Wait!" She stopped him as he tried to rise. Light from passing lanterns turned her into a shadow. He could hear the rustle of silk freeing her undulating form turning and twisting to perch herself over his waist, resting her weight on her feet. He waited for that infinite moment of aching to pass as she lowered herself, settling down like a butterfly on her stalk, holding him still as they sped along.

The bearers grunted even louder crossing a bridge, and they entered a village glowing with lamps. The sound of screaming children followed them. The flash of a firecracker lit up the two shadows—now turned to one—inside the coupe, moving to keep pace with the bearers. Changing from butterfly to dove, she asked him to imitate the ox, the force of his fury almost shattering the sedan's weak planks.

By the time they'd left the village, the ox had turned into a spider folding its mate firmly into its legs.

Reaching the pavilion, the bearers left, setting the sedan down in the courtyard with the two of them fast asleep under the weak moon of winter.

IV
FRAGRANT HILLS
The pulse of spring

"I've come by ship, rice boat, rickshaw and mule cart, by chair and by foot to see you, Tino."

Ricardo's unexpected visit caught Antonio by surprise. Seeing him arrive at his pavilion, he thought he was still dreaming after a long night with plum wine. Why didn't Dona Elvira write to Polly, announcing her godson's visit to Macau, and to tell her that he was on his way to Peking? He noticed the usual marks of long travel on his friend, and his awkwardness in the new surroundings, just as Antonio had felt himself when he arrived at the Summer Palace. Without the wise companionship of someone like Joachim Saldanha, China and the Chinese seemed to have left an unfavorable impression on his friend during his journey. He noticed a shadow in Ricardo Silva's eyes.

"It's a land of ditches and swamps. If you've seen one village, you've seen them all, just dustbowls and morgues for dead animals, hardly the oriental paradise it's made out to be. Everyone's a liar when it comes to China—sailors, merchants, even my own godmother! There's no treasure here, but the sight of walking ghosts."

Antonio said nothing.

"They're ugly as none other! If it isn't goiter, it's a squint! A bump on the forehead. Eagle's claws for nails!" He took a sip of the tea and made a face. "A day here is like a season in hell."

Antonio took a good look at his dearest friend. Rogue Ricardo—the one who drank hard, slept well and ate like four men. The friend who always disagreed with him, but ended up helping him all the same. The man who held the memory of himself, of his mischief, his extravagant bets at the bullring, his late nights and late mornings, and of his many indecisions. Ricardo opened his traveling case and took out a letter for Antonio. He hesitated for a moment or two before handing it to him. Antonio recognized the familiar hand of Rosa Escobar. It came in a different envelope to her previous letters, without the address of Peking's British mission, with simply his name written on it. He held it in his hand without opening it.

"You can read it while I wait outside." Ricardo spoke to him in a low voice. Antonio gestured him to stay.

Your father had to be taken away to Lisbon's Jesuit asylum before his death, Rosa had written. Then she went on to describe his last days. It wasn't his health that worried doctors, as much as his sudden spurts of vigor. After months of crushing pain and dizziness when he couldn't even stand upright without Rosa's help, Dom Alexander had displayed the strength and madness of a young bull. It was hard to keep him indoors. He'd jump out of the window and escape to the woods before Rosa could grab him and pin him down. He roamed about like a mad man, raided the markets to steal freshly slaughtered animals, scared the children by hanging from branches like a ghost. He had cleared the cottage to fill it with new things that they'd need once he married Rosa Escobar. He had reduced the poor woman to tears by announcing that she was none other than Tino's mother reappeared in flesh decades after her death.

"I am sorry, Tino." Ricardo Silva stole a quick glance at Antonio after he had finished reading the letter. "In the end there was nothing that could be done except to keep him in chains. Death, fortunately, came soon after."

Antonio's face hardened and turned rigid, as if he was wearing a mask. Ricardo stopped, seeing his reaction, then spoke gently. "He'd be buried like a prince had he died any other way. Maybe a statue would've been built in his honor, or a street named after him. But now . . ." His voice trailed off as Antonio rose and paced the lodge, then continued. "We know he wasn't to blame, no matter what others say. It must've been an accident. It might not even have been the pox, but something else more dreadful." He came up to Antonio and laid a hand on his shoulder. "I'm glad you didn't have to see his end."

Antonio could smell his father dying. Leaving Ricardo back in the pavilion he went for a walk in the gardens, and climbed up the hill to the temple of Ten Thousand Buddhas. Smoke from the incense burners carried the stench of rotting flesh mixed with the whiff of juniper berries that burned in the scuttle of his father's cryptlike chamber. The lotus at the feet of the deity had shriveled up, and the bronze peacocks arched their graceful necks away from the flame that sputtered on. The curtains on the arched windows were stained in the color of blood. The sun glared on the thawing lake. He thought about the face that had given him nightmares; how easily it had turned from father to patient on the feast of St Anthony. He hadn't written to his father about his journey. *Did he wait for me in his cell? Did he weep for his Tino?*

He felt empty like the temple, robbed of its Buddha. Walking around the vacant altar, he tried to imagine the moment when it was unseated. It must've taken a dozen soldiers to lift up the stone idol, and carry it over to the open window. How quickly would it have fallen from the hilltop to the lake, sunk to the bottom without leaving any trace? He wondered why the empress hadn't filled up the empty spot with something else. Even without the offerings, he could imagine the Buddha as if it were still there, eyes dancing in the flame of the incense burner.

Sitting in the temple, his mind rose from the gloom of Rosa Escobar's letter. His stomach growled for early rice, and he wondered if Wangsheng had been brave enough to serve Ricardo his favorite shrimp eggs. On his return to the pavilion, he found his friend sleeping, tired after his journey, covered from head to toe in a blanket to ward off insects.

"Why didn't you write to me from Lisbon and save yourself the trip?" Antonio asked Ricardo when he woke, the two sitting in the courtyard.

"Because a letter wouldn't have brought you back." Ricardo smiled. "I know you, Tino. You're not the one to give up easily. You'd rather die than fail. A letter would've done no more than sadden you. Then you'd have pressed on just as before."

Antonio was surprised at his friend's words, at his clear view of his character. He knew Ricardo to be quick and headstrong in judgment, pliable to robust arguments, especially those of a friend. In the end he'd give in, accept a contrary view if only to be faithful to his friendship. You never really win with Ricardo, he had thought, simply bend his will by appealing to his love.

"How much longer are you planning to be here?" Ricardo asked him gently.

"I've agreed to spend four seasons, of which one and a half are remaining."

"That long?" Ricardo looked surprised. "But it isn't necessary any-more, Tino. The pox is dead now. There are doctors in Austria who've found a cure. The miracle has been tested on hundreds. The Pasteur Institute in Paris is close to announcing a vaccine."

"Rubbish!" Antonio waved aside his friend's arguments.

"Not rubbish. You're wrong. Let me tell you about Sebastian Heller, the famous German chemist, and what he's saying about the poison."

"No, let me tell you about the Sebastian Hellers, about the rascals!" Antonio cut him short. "Let me tell you what they do to their patients, bleed them and feed them the witches' brew that kills them even before pox can finish its job." He stopped to catch his breath, and gave Ricardo an angry look. "You treat me as if I've lived here all my life, as if I don't know what's going on in the world. I'm no idiot . . . syphilis isn't dead. It's still winning against us all."

The two sat quietly, leaving their plum wine untouched. Then Ricardo resumed. "So what have you learned in the three seasons here?"

What can I tell him about Nei ching? Antonio thought for a moment, then asked for Ricardo's hand, placing it on his pulse reading cushion. His friend looked on suspiciously. Antonio applied three fingers to the wrist and listened carefully.

"I can hear the *Sumai*. It's beating like a hammer, and warns of excessive blood in your heart channel. That's why you find it hard to fall asleep, and sweat like your horses after they've run a race. It has caused you to faint after heavy meals." He smiled reassuringly at his friend. "It's your condition. You've been born with it, just as every man is born with health and sickness."

Ricardo wetted his lips and searched for words. "Is that what the heretic has taught you?" He took a quick look at Tian sitting in front of the kitchen, sharpening a knife for slaughtering ducks and chickens. "Has your teacher taught you the cure for pox too?"

Antonio shook his head.

"No?" Ricardo seemed surprised. "I thought that'd be the first thing you'd learn."

"It takes a lot more than reading pulse to cure a disease."

Ricardo rolled his eyes in apparent disbelief. "But you're the best, Tino. Nothing's too hard for you. Why must it take so long?"

Antonio shrugged. "Because my teacher doesn't think it's time yet. I must wait till I'm ready."

They were distracted by shrieks coming from the kitchen, and watched the young eunuch run out with a basket of ducks' heads.

"What if you don't find the cure in China?"

Antonio sighed. "Then I shall return knowing there's no hope. That there's no point being a doctor."

Ricardo tried to soothe his friend. "Only a child thinks like that. Maybe there'll be a cure in a hundred years. Why must you abandon those who haven't been as unlucky as to have contracted the pox? You should return and do what a good doctor does."

"You mean get rich by selling lies? Tell a tottering fool that he's young enough to father a child; promise a dying spinster that she'll live a hundred years?"

Ricardo laughed. "No, my friend, you must go back and help young mothers give birth to babies, and father some yourself!"

The two spent a strange night lying awake in the lodge with Ricardo smoking his opium pipe — "the only good thing to be found in China!" — having acquired the taste from his godmother. Along with the sad letter he had brought two gifts for his friend: a box of cinnamon cookies and a daguerreotype of Arees dressed as a gypsy in a feathered cap.

"Who's the nurse?" Ricardo asked him next morning, spotting Fumi as she chatted with the attendants in the courtyard.

"I'm not a doctor here, and she isn't my nurse."

"So what is she?"

"My teacher."

"Ah! Is she the one who teaches you to read pulse?" Ricardo grinned at him. His godmother had told him all about Chinese doctors and their tricks while he was in Macau. "Dona Elvira swears by their smelly herbs for every imaginable disease on earth, but her husband doesn't believe in them at all."

Antonio smiled at Dom Afonso's stout opposition to all things oriental that his wife found so fascinating. "But he has taken to opium, the most potent of all Chinese medicines."

"Is she just your teacher, or?" Ricardo kept an eye on Fumi through the latticed window of the lodge as they talked.

"Not just a teacher but a demanding one too. And the very best I've had from the days of the Faculdade."

"Let's hope she's not too demanding." Ricardo sighed. "I don't know whether the Chinese have the cure for syphilis, but only God can cure you, Tino."

He found it hard to confide in Ricardo. For months, he'd craved his company, dying to tell him everything he'd seen in China. The friend whose voice he heard in his head whenever he was alone, the one he laughed and argued with in his mind, shared all his secrets. *I'll have to tell him the whole story or nothing at all*, he thought. A story that seemed at once clear and unfathomable. He'd have to tell Ricardo about Xu, the rumors about the Horseman and about his own suspicions. Undoubtedly, his friend would want to know about Xu's assistant. How could he tell Ricardo about Fumi without mentioning Jacob and his mysterious death? How could he argue in her favor, without confessing his love? Even without saying a word, Ricardo might suspect something between him and Fumi if he saw them together. It'd be hard to fool Rogue Ricardo. He'd know what was going on, and blame Antonio for lying to him. *You aren't staying back for pox but for your Chinese lover. I knew she was more than your teacher.* He'd blame him for hiding in China, for misleading him, his godmother and his sister.

With Ricardo sleeping, he reread Arees's letter that she had scribbled on the back of her daguerreotype. She had started in her usual mocking way, then confessed to her boredom, *dying among the meek and weak-hearted, among dreamers who are simply happy to dream.* It was strange to read her praise him. . . *The seas around your new world must be choppier than our calm European seas, and you must be sailing bravely along, my dear Candide. . . . Come back soon and wake us up!* She had added a postscript: *More than a year has passed since you left; it'll be time soon to fulfill my promise.*

He wondered what he'd say to Arees, if he wrote back to her or confided in her brother about his choppy seas.

Polly saved him by inviting them both to a snipe shoot. Her favorites would join them—Yohan and Chris Campbell—but not the gypsy, who was busy foraging old manuscripts. Traveling from the Summer Palace to the Legation, Ricardo ignored the street sights to fill Antonio in on the latest from Lisbon, prattling on about their favorite sports and friends. The royals were at their last gasp, he said glumly. Sinister plans were being hatched against them. Antonio resisted asking about Arees, but his friend brought her up unexpectedly.

"My sister has decided to become an abolitionist, even after slave trading has been outlawed, claiming that our merchants have been secretly flouting the ban in Brazil."

"She'd have a lot on her hands if she were here," Antonio mentioned, recalling the coolie traders arriving in Macau on the *Santa Cruz.*

Ricardo gave him a quick look. "I'd rather she were here than in the Amazon, that she threatens to visit. Mind you, it isn't safe here either. Not with the Boxers, who my godmother hates."

Antonio was relieved to move on from Arees, and impressed his friend with stories about the spirit army. By the time they reached the Legation, words had started to flow again between the two.

"I'd love to see a Boxer fight a bull with his bare hands!" Ricardo said.

"It must be a *foreign* bull then, and a Christian as well!"

Ricardo reminded him of the Alfama Arabs who considered themselves to be true natives of Lisbon and every Portuguese a foreigner, charging them a tax by robbing them blind.

The hunting party got off to a good start with Cedric passing on to the guests rifles and cartridges from his personal collection. Chris Campbell made everyone pose with their weapons and took photographs. Reaching the western hills in their sedans, they left in two groups of three to trudge through the fields awash with spring rains. Ricardo had struck up an instant bond with Cedric and Yohan, and the three of them marched ahead of the others sharing their hunting tales. Meeting him for the first time since Fengtai, Chris Campbell seemed a bit overawed by Antonio, having witnessed his medical skills firsthand. He had had trouble with the Pascals after Antonio had left with Joachim Saldanha on the litter, with Simone insisting that they return to the Boxer-occupied orphanage to collect a few more of her belongings. Jean-Paul had managed to stop her after hours of pleading.

When Chris fell back to take pictures of spring blossoms, Polly whispered to Antonio. "Has your friend met Fumi yet?" Antonio nodded.

"But he doesn't know who she is, does he?"

"She's my teacher, I've told him," Antonio replied stiffly.

"But not your lover." She looked at him knowingly. "That could complicate matters, raise a few problems for you back home, couldn't it?" They walked in silence, neither of them looking for snipe to shoot, till Polly returned to the subject. "Why don't you and Ricardo spend a few days with us? It might help you avoid talking about touchy matters with your friend. He doesn't need to see how you live in the palace among your eunuch friends and your lover, does he? He can keep Cedric company, given how well they've hit it off. You can go back when he leaves Peking."

"He has come to take me back with him," Antonio said with a look of resignation.

"Back?" Polly exclaimed. "But you can't leave now. Not with Helga about to go into her confinement!" She patted him encouragingly. "You just have to think of a good reason to stay here, Dr. Maria."

The party returned empty-handed from the hunt but in good cheer. The news of the Portuguese friends staying back at the Legation made everyone happy. True to form, Ricardo had won over his host and others with his stories of crazy bullfights and hunting rabbits in the Algarve.

"Don't you have anything bigger than rabbits in Portugal?" Yohan teased him, sitting in the garden and enjoying the evening breeze.

"Yes, they do." Cedric joined in too. "It's called the Cachena cow."

"There's nothing bigger than a rabbit when it comes to hunting," Ricardo boasted. "Not because it's faster than most other animals, but because it tricks the hunter by sitting as still as a rock."

For once, Antonio was happy not returning to his pavilion. With

Fumi out of sight, Ricardo would have no reason to be suspicious. His friend would be happier too among Europeans than living with the eunuchs. He could enjoy the sights of the Tartar city that many thought the most fascinating in China in the company of Yohan, who knew the secret behind every wall and alley.

"How long do you plan to be in Peking?" Antonio asked Ricardo, at the end of the long evening before they retired to their rooms. His friend finished his claret before answering.

"I had come to take you back, Tino. The annual races will start soon at Hong Kong's Jockey Club, the very best in the East. I wanted you to come with me and cheer my horse. It'll be the first time for a Portuguese thoroughbred," Ricardo said proudly. "I'll leave now and go alone to Hong Kong, but return soon when your four seasons are up. Then I'll carry you back home on my shoulders, to get you married on the feast of St. Anthony." He stopped to take a long look at Antonio. "Don't worry, you won't have to go looking for a bride anymore. It'll be my turn to find you one."

A storm had risen, and spread a haze over the lake. Sitting on a bench, Antonio and Fumi watched it gather force and stir up the waters. The boatmen chattered on, keeping their eyes on the horizon. Storms were a common occurrence in late winter, and they didn't feel the need to moor their boats.

"Does Xu know about your father?" Fumi asked, breaking the silence.

Antonio shook his head. He hadn't thought of telling Fumi about his father's death, but she knew it seeing Antonio after he returned to his pavilion. "Your friend brought bad news, didn't he?" She listened in silence as Antonio spoke. "I knew he'd die before I returned," he said, confessing that he read every letter from Rosa Escobar hoping against hope that it'd bear the news of his father's passing. "I wished he'd die before he turned mad."

It was harder for him to explain that he had lost his mother yet again. His healthy father had kept her alive for him. Father and son had learned to live in peace with an invisible spirit in a home that still carried her smell, her laughter and songs. Syphilis had struck down his mother too. He could no longer hear her humming in the kitchen, or smell her freshly baked pastéis. He couldn't imagine her anymore as she once was, her face beginning to fade rapidly as soon as he'd finished reading Rosa's letter.

They sat by the lake and followed the imperial barge as it rode the choppy waters with cymbals and flutes playing the empress's favorite hymn. "I saw Jacob after he died but not when he was buried." Fumi spoke quietly.

'Where were you?"

"Hiding from those who killed him." Rising from the marble bench, she looked sadly at Antonio. "Just like you, I was far away."

Why would they want to kill her? Unless . . .

She stopped him before he could ask more questions. "You must tell Xu about your father. He'd understand why you're so eager, so impatient, if he knew you were more than a doctor."

Later, as Antonio lay awake in his lodge, he thought about Jacob and Fumi and wondered why Ferguson had lied to him. *Bad stories have sad endings.* How could his vast store of gossip contain such a vital error? A lingering suspicion returned to nag him. Was it Fumi who was lying? Had she simply made up the story of Jacob's murder? She must've known the gypsy well if he had anything to do with the Dutchman. Why hadn't she brought up Ferguson's name? Why was he absent in Jacob's story? He wondered how much of herself she had revealed to him, how much lay buried under the ashes of the printing press. As his mind sifted through the details, he was struck by the strangest of thoughts, that the mystery of Fumi might somehow be related to the mystery of syphilis, like two symptoms both arising from the same condition.

He decided to visit Ferguson to test his suspicion about him. It'd be hard to get a straight answer out of the gypsy, but Antonio hoped to trap him through his own devices. *I must make him tell me everything he knows about Jacob's death, then challenge him with Fumi's story.*

When Antonio arrived at the villa, Ferguson greeted him from his massage bed sprawled out naked on his belly with the young servant working on him vigorously. The bittersweet smell of opium rose from the silver pipe and bowl by the bed, the dark mud sputtering as Ferguson stoked it with a fine bamboo quill. Antonio took his seat facing the gypsy, a cloud of smoke shrouding them both.

"I thought you weren't interested in books." Ferguson spoke with an eye on the smoldering bowl.

"Not any book, just a few special ones."

"There's nothing available on the treatment of syphilis in particular, I should warn you."

Antonio shook his head. "Not syphilis. I don't need a medical book."

Ferguson showed surprise. "Then just name it. My friends can sniff it out for you, if it's still here, of course, not shipped off already like most old manuscripts."

"Not old manuscripts. These would be quite new." Antonio waved his arms to part the smoke and watched Ferguson.

"New! Then why don't you send your servants to buy them from the Tartar market? They should know where to find them. You can go yourself too." He gestured at his masseur. "Take him with you if you like."

"I don't think you'll find what I'm looking for in the market." Antonio looked Ferguson in the eye. "Can you find me the books that Jacob de Graff printed on his press?"

"You mean the Holy Bible?" Ferguson narrowed his eyes.

"I mean the other kind of books he printed for the Boxers."

Ferguson raised his hand and ordered his servant to leave the room. Sitting up on his massage bed, he wrapped a towel around his waist and offered Antonio his opium pipe. "You've dug deep into China, I see . . . must've developed a taste for this too?"

Antonio shook his head. "You had told me about Jacob printing bulletins for the rebels. Can you get me a few of those?"

A slow smile spread over Ferguson's face. "Ah! I see. You want to surprise your lady love. Even better, you want to call her bluff, don't you? A little lovers' tiff we have on our hands!"

Antonio rose and paced the room. "Never mind what it's for. If indeed they were printed on Jacob's press, then there must be a way of finding them."

"It isn't as easy as that. The Boxers are the empress's enemy. Officially that is, although secretly she's their patron too. Any mention of the rebels could get you into trouble with the mandarins. They don't want foreigners meddling in their messy affairs, which will soon become our affairs, mind you. You could be jailed and tortured if suspected to be a Boxer or their supporter."

"So who would be reading these bulletins?"

"They're printed for the lower-down clerks and district officials, calling on them to "observe their duties" to protect China from the foreigners. Also to teach peasants about deep-breathing exercises that'd make them strong and immune to bullets, along with instructions on what to eat, how to do up their hair, what to wear, how to burn incense and all that nonsense."

"But if the dowager is their patron, why should these bulletins be secret?"

"Ah! It's simply a matter of strategy. The dowager is keeping her options open. If indeed the Boxers succeed in rousing the masses, she'll throw in her lot with them and oust the foreigners, who she hates for burning down her Summer Palace during the opium wars. But if they fail, she can wash her hands clean and come to the Legation's rescue as their guardian angel. She's running with the hare and hunting with the hound as the English say!"

Picking up a bronze measuring weight for opium from the side table and turning it over in his hand, Antonio appeared to have digested the dowager's intrigues. "And who could've been behind our Jacob?"

"A senior mandarin perhaps, acting on behalf of the empress. The Dutchman would've been the perfect cover for this sort of thing, don't you see? A padre printing the Bible by day, and the Boxers' manual by night!"

"But why would he have done it?"

"Who would've done what?" Setting down his pipe, Ferguson quizzed Antonio.

"Why would the mathematician risk his life to print the manual of spirit soldiers? He, more than anyone, would've known that their claims were untrue, that men couldn't fly through air or stop bullets by deep breathing."

Ferguson started to scratch himself absentmindedly. "Could've been the money that he got . . . having the Boxers pay for the Bible."

Antonio shook his head. "From all that you've told me about Jacob de Graff, he was anything but a shrewd merchant."

Ferguson's eyes danced. "Maybe he did it to please someone he cared for, someone he couldn't say no to."

"A mathematician violating natural laws?"

"Why not?" Ferguson shot back. "Men will do anything for love, won't they?"

At Antonio's insistence, Ferguson named his price for Jacob's bulletins. Not only would he have to pay the finders handsomely, he'd have to pay them off to keep their mouths shut. "I'll do the dirty work for you if you tell me why you want to dig up Jacob from his grave." He gave Antonio a mischievous smile. "It must be for your friend."

"Because I want to know if you were lying to me."

The Harris mansion was full, not simply with the residents of the Legation, but those who lived beyond as well: student interpreters, visitors, even deserters who'd been lured away from the missions to work for foreign merchants. Governesses shepherded children, looking as anxious as their parents waiting for John Harris to deliver a briefing to all foreigners to prepare them for upcoming events. Chinese domestics ushered in the crowd, but there was no sign of the champagne table routinely found in these gatherings.

Waiting for John Harris to begin, Antonio called Polly over to tell her about his visit to Ferguson. The gypsy was making up stories about Jacob de Graff, he was certain, and asked Polly if she knew why.

"Why would Ferguson lie to you?" Polly brushed aside Antonio's report. "You've become a real Legation animal, seeing smoke and mirrors all around you!" Fanning herself at the first hint of summer, she ignored Antonio's interest in "silly intrigues," chiding him for wasting his time.

"Because you said it's his pleasure to lie and invent gossip."

She spoke sternly. "You should be in Lisbon taking care of your father's affairs. Ellie is upset with you. How could you have left him behind when he was so sick? The father who had brought you up? Ellie thinks you are just as selfish as all men are." She ignored Linda's call to assemble under the American flag, and asked Antonio why he thought the Dutchman died a mysterious death. "It's not unnatural for foreigners to die. The padres die like flies from harsh winters and killer summers."

"But they aren't usually burnt to death inside their homes, are they?"

"Boxers have killed missionaries like that, we know. But who's to say it wasn't an accident?" Polly shrugged, leading Antonio toward the podium, smiling pleasantly at Linda as both women dabbed their faces with their handkerchiefs. "Men see unnecessary conspiracy when the truth is plain and simple."

"The fact that his body was taken away and buried god knows where doesn't make it all that plain and simple, does it?" Antonio told Polly what he'd heard from Fumi, her account of the murder and the burning of the press. She heard him in silence, but continued to dismiss his obsession with Jacob's death.

"I wouldn't trust everything that Fumi tells you. How do you know that it isn't Ferguson but *she* who's lying?" Her face hardened. "I'd get her out of my mind if I were you. Half of Jacob's troubles may have started with her. He was known to be awkward but harmless before he met her. He had few friends but fewer enemies. She changed him, he stopped visiting the Legation. Rumors started that he had gone over to the rebels."

"Who do you think can give me the truth, rather than rumors?" Antonio asked her, frustrated by Polly's answers.

She threw up her hands in exasperation. "How will the truth of Jacob's death help you, Tino? How will it bring you any closer to what you're after? Or have you stopped worrying about syphilis now?" She stopped to catch her breath. "Unless, of course, you've decided to do something else."

"Decided what?"

"To be with Fumi. Unless you've already forgotten about your father, and now want to find out as much about her as possible before taking her as your bride."

She stopped, seeing the hurt look on Antonio. "Poor Tino! It's been hard, hasn't it . . . with your father, and living by yourself in the palace? In China one loses one's past, which is worse than losing one's mind. Everything becomes blurred except this very moment and the next." She sighed, then livened up to give Antonio her advice.

"To get more than rumors you must talk to Yohan. Our favorite Chinaman might be able to serve you the straight truth as only spies can."

❀

A chirpy Sally Hollinger found Antonio hiding behind the garden roller, waiting for John Harris's briefings to start. She hadn't come to listen to the American—"our very *very* lightweight boxer!"—but to find Fumi. She had expected to see her with Antonio, and wanted to ask her a few questions following the successful pulse reading at the New Year's ball.

"She told me about diseases I never knew I had! The migraine that turned out to be nothing more than a blocked nose. Then again I thought I was dying from a rotten heart, when in fact it was simply the curse of dry air!"

Antonio reassured her with Xu's words. "Western doctors deal with simple cause and effect when it comes to disease, whereas the Chinese look for reasons that might even lie outside the body."

Sally nodded. "Just like our emperor of the Legation here, the simpleton who thinks the war will start only when he's ready! He treats the padres, who are our best spies in China, as crybabies. We're just crying wolf, he thinks, whenever someone reports an incident."

Antonio caught sight of the Harts huddling with the Harrises as the other ministers maintained a safe distance. Captain Popov, the Russian military attaché, peeled a banana and smiled slyly at his Spanish counterpart, while the French minister yawned broadly making no effort to hide his boredom.

"The Straits of Dover are as wide as a sea!" Ferguson had crept up behind Antonio, and whispered into his ear. No one else seemed to be in a good mood. The alarm had been sounded last week after the diplomats had gone over in strength to the *Tsungli Yamen*, the foreigners' bureau of the Chinese government. After months of regular attacks against foreigners and native Christians, the ministers had demanded that the empress issue firm orders to suppress the Boxers. The situation couldn't be allowed to get much worse with churches around the country reporting a flood of refugees, burning and looting of foreign shops, and armed Boxers conducting drills in public barely a dozen miles from Peking. The ministers had recorded their gravest concern with the *Yamen*, urging them to secure the release of Scottish miners captured by rebels after they had struck gold in the North. Into the first week of March, there was still no news of the miners, and murmurs had grown to a loud clamor for the ministers to call for foreign troops to march into Peking in a show of strength.

"They've been squabbling," Ferguson gestured at the ministers, "over whether the timing is right to use force, or if they should give the mandarins one last chance. The *Yamen*, as usual, has responded with fuzzy edicts, making it clear that the empress is up to her old games." The Europeans, Ferguson said, were leading the cry for a show of muscle unlike the cautious British and Americans.

"We should've sent you to talk to the dowager, the Portuguese have better luck than everybody in dealing with Orientals!" Ferguson said something about cunning friars from Goa fooling the mighty Moguls as far back as the sixteenth and seventeenth centuries.

It took a while even after John Harris had started to speak for everyone to quiet down. The first secretary started on a somber note. "This might be the last time we are able to meet freely in the Legation, until temperatures cool. The *Yamen* has promised to tame the Boxers and it'd be unwise," he said, anticipating the question on everyone's lips, "to inflame the situation by calling in our troops from Tientsin." Cedric Hart nodded, while the European ministers stood motionless. "Proper consultations must take place with Washington, London and other capitals before anything drastic happens, unlike the one-woman government of China!" John Harris offered a wry smile, giving just the opening for Chris Campbell to cut in.

"Better not to inflame the situation than have us wait like sitting ducks?"

Freed at once, many voices joined Campbell's, with Sally's rising above the others. "The Boxers won't wait, why should we? How long shall we remain at the mercy of our frightened servants?" Even Mr. Pinchback seemed doubtful of the show of unfortunate restraint. He reminded everyone of the tricky journey from Tientsin to Peking. "It isn't as if our troops are next door. The ships would take half a day to reach the sandbar at the mouth of the Peiho River, where conditions are normally turbulent with high winds. From the sandbar to the Taku Forts in small dingy, and then the eighty miles to Peking by train. Eighty miles could take eight days if the Boxers blow up the tracks and the soldiers have to be force-marched to the capital. More, if they cut the telegraph lines and a man has to be slipped through the enemy's ranks to reach the British commander in Tientsin."

Mr. Pinchback's intimate knowledge of military matters hushed the crowd into admiration. "Casanova should be running the show," Sally Hollinger whispered for everyone to hear, "rather than the bumbling idiots." Abandoning the first secretary, Chris Campbell addressed his questions to Mr. Pinchback, treating him like the Tientsin commander himself.

"The risk of doing nothing is more than the risk of doing something. I'd order evacuation now," the Hong Kong banker spoke confidently. "Move the families off sharp to Japan."

The very mention of "move" stirred the crowd, with everyone talking at once. The French minister gave an amused smile, and slapped his Italian counterpart on the back as if they had just scored an easy win over their Anglo-American rivals. Only Ferguson seemed upset with the "family clause," challenging Pinchback to spell out his plans for saving the "poor singles." It took Cedric Hart's brave efforts to restore order, as he prompted his American friend to announce a set of practical tips on behalf of "all ministers."

John Harris read out the list of dos and don'ts. No woman should leave the Legation unaccompanied, even to visit the silk market or the curio shops on Flower Street and Donkey Alley. The train to Tientsin should be avoided at all costs by those who were planning their own evacuation. There'd be day and night vigil at the Legation, with the names of volunteer guards to be circulated soon. All foreigners would be given sanctuary at the missions, and the allotment of beds and provisions would be overseen by a small committee led by Linda Harris. Men and women would be furnished with service revolvers, the first secretary announced, and a self-defense class would be conducted by Herr Mueller in the grounds of his residence.

"We haven't reached the point of no return yet," Mr. Harris stated to general dissatisfaction. Ferguson gave the final tip of the evening: everyone should have a set of Chinese clothes handy for purposes of disguise, if necessary. Western women would need to add lengths to the Manchu robes to cover their legs, and the men to grow beards over their flat cheeks.

"What about our large feet? Wouldn't that give us away?" Polly giggled at her friend.

"Shh! Decent ladies only bare their feet to their lovers!"

"You are one of us." Polly tried to persuade Antonio to stay back at the Legation after the briefings. His sedan chair could return empty and bring back his things next morning. "I won't have Linda "allotting" you to one of her dodgy friends. Ellie would be so relieved if you stayed with us."

He told her he'd be safe in his pavilion. Why would Boxers attack the dowager's palace? Who'd expect to find a Portuguese doctor living so close to her anyway? He disappointed Polly by telling her that he couldn't just abandon his two loyal attendants, or leave his education incomplete.

"You are going back for Fumi, aren't you?" Polly sounded hurt. "It's foolish, Tino, and you know that. Risking your life for what? When our troops arrive they'll once again burn the Summer Palace down, and teach the Old Buddha a lesson. Your Fumi will leave you and run as soon as troubles start."

She waited for Antonio to change his mind then when he didn't, offered a diplomat's compromise. "Why don't you both come and stay with us for a few days? I'm sure Fumi won't mind. She was quite a hit at the ball. It'd be safer for her as well."

"Why would she be safer here?"

"Because the Boxers haven't been too kind to the Chinese who are close to foreigners. They've been killing gardeners and cooks, interpreters, even friends." She made Antonio promise that he'd discuss the matter with Fumi after he returned to the palace. "Come over whenever you're ready, come before it's too late!" Cedric Hart accompanied him to his sedan, and wished him well for his return journey. "You, more than us, will know when the *real* trouble starts. When you leave and come over, we'll know the attack on the Legation is soon to begin. As long as you are there, we'll know we're safe here!"

He thought about the Legation on his way back. *There are serious men there among the clowns.* Perhaps the clowns too were only pretending, hiding under their comical manners. It won't take long for party guests to turn the gardens into trenches and barracks. He wondered what'd happen to those like Joachim Saldanha. What'd happen to him and Fumi if the things that Polly said came to pass? He tried to peek through the curtains, and catch the half moon perched behind the trees, adding a halo to the streetlamps. The bearers seemed to follow a different route back, not a word exchanged between them.

Back in the lodge he drew the naked torsos of a man and a woman on a sheet of paper. He marked them both with spots, and shaded their skin to give them a withered appearance; added oozing sores to the female breasts, and a full moon to crown the male member. Calling his attendants over, he showed them the drawings. They looked away at first then gaped at the syphilitic couple in wonder.

Tian exclaimed, and nudged his uncle. Antonio asked if they had seen anyone who resembled the drawings. The spots could be greater or lesser in number, he explained, but always ripe and oozing or dark like dried blood. The female might show scars around her belly as if it was stretched by childbearing. Wangsheng stared long and hard at the male member then shrugged. They both shuddered as he drew the woman's head with a few deft strokes, showing a half eaten nose and a mouthful of rotten teeth.

"You've seen her, haven't you?" Antonio asked them.

"A mad woman," Wangsheng said, "lives at the village of the insect festival, resembling the Hungry Ghost or a *kuei-shen*, a demon born of the scorched earth. Elders know her as a whore who traveled with soldiers and bore their children, but the wounds she carried were much worse than a knife's gash or bullet holes."

"Can you take me to see her?"

The eunuch mentioned something about Xu.

"No, no, we don't need to ask his permission. Just the three of us can go to the village of insects." Wangsheng looked uncertain then nodded, disappearing quickly with a fearful glance back at the syphilitic couple.

The Hungry Ghost might be his savior, Antonio thought, if she was indeed a pox victim. She might tell him a thing or two about the

Chinese treatment, more than what his teacher was prepared to. Perhaps the poor woman could lead him to other ghosts like her, his own investigations prove more successful than four seasons of *Nei ching*.

He missed Fumi. The royals kept her busy and he saw her for just a few hours before she left him alone in the lodge and disappeared. There were days when she didn't come at all, sending word through his attendants of an urgent call to attend to the empress. Their routine of daily lessons had all but ended. Might Xu send off his assistant and take it upon himself to teach him now? On his return from the Legation he was anxious at the thought of losing Fumi before the rebels stormed Peking.

Polly had kept her word and arranged for Antonio to meet Yohan at the old monastery of the Tartar city. He'd go there with Helga to have the chief abbot of the brotherhood of Buddhist monks bless her and her child before she gave birth. "You can ask him all you want but beware, in the end he might get more out of you than you of him!"

For a consummate gossip, Polly had been curiously tight lipped when it came to Yohan. His wife had had a colorful past, she told Antonio. Her German first husband was an agent for Krupp, the makers of the Krupp cannon that the Chinese loved, and the couple's reputation as social butterflies had wafted in from Shanghai to Peking, along with rumors of debauchery.

"What kind of debauchery?" Antonio had asked.

"You know . . . couples indulging themselves with other couples; hurting and punishing each other in the name of love, even forcing their housemaids to join them. The kind that shocks normal people." The Krupp agent was the meek one, rumor went, Helga the greedier of the two, and he didn't mind it a bit when she left him for his business partner, "our Chinese spy!" and moved to Peking.

"Did Yohan know all about her?"

"Everyone knew! She was our juiciest gossip before you smacked the King of Bubbly!"

"I thought the Chinese wanted their wives to be as chaste as daisies."

Polly corrected him. "Our Yohan is really an American with a Chinese face. Don't forget that he wasn't born here in this country and hadn't lived in China till his parents brought him back from San

Francisco. Some say he had to be taught to speak Chinese the hard way by spending a whole year among poor and illiterate orphans. His brain though is the brain of a genius. He can read people's minds, predict accidents, find gold without digging an inch. He's what you'd call 'pure intelligence'!"

Waiting for Yohan at the monastery, Antonio remembered Polly's words. Why would "pure intelligence" choose to spy on bumbling foreigners, whose secrets were common knowledge among their domestics? He wondered too about meeting his debauched wife among the white pines that circled the monastery's inner courtyard like a candelabra.

"She's all changed now," Polly had told him, "as pure as a hausfrau."

Imposing walls guarded the exquisite pagoda and the monastery from the dusty streets. At the entrance, stone tablets from the Ming announced the abode of Buddhist scholars. The garden path led to the austere pagoda and the monks' residences shrouded in stern secrecy. It was built at a time, Antonio remembered his friend Joachim Saldanha telling him, when "men were willing to spend money on God instead of on themselves."

Yohan in a European suit and Helga dressed as a proper Chinese wife in a jade gown were kneeling before the chief abbot on the pagoda's steps. He was blessing them with a chant, holding joss sticks over their heads. A flock of doves observed the ceremony from the pine branches, descending every now and then to peck at the offerings brought by the kneeling couple.

A junior priest led Helga to a private chamber for an audience with the chief, and Yohan sauntered over to Antonio, holding out a cigar for him.

"In China there's a ceremony for everything! Even one for getting well after a cold! The priests are better than merchants in squeezing the people."

"Better even than a Krupp agent?"

"Ah! You've done your homework on me! What else have you learned?"

"That your talents are wasted in your current occupation, which is a mystery to most."

Yohan laughed, scattering the doves and drawing out a young head or two from the monastery's windows. "But isn't it a doctor's job to solve mysteries?" They sat under a giant catalpa tree revered on account of its size, providing the perfect shade for the peonies that would bloom under it in spring and dazzle the visitors.

"I won't tell you everything I know about you, except that your friends consider you an even better gambler at the bullring than a doctor." Antonio smiled noticing the trace of Ricardo Silva in Yohan's words, wondering what else his friend had told the Chinese spy. It didn't take long for Yohan to come to the point, like a real agent interested in closing a deal.

"You'd like to know more about Dr. Xu, wouldn't you?"

Antonio nodded, privately rehearsing the answer he'd give if asked why.

"Would you like me to tell you what he does to remain in the empress's favor, or do you know that already?"

"He's a eunuch maker, and a killer of unwanted babies."

"Good!" Yohan gave him a look of genuine regard. "He's rumored to have done more than that, although we'd never know for sure."

"Done what?"

"Got rid of her palace rivals by serving them top-grade poison as medicine. Some even claim he's the 'cause' behind the emperor's sickness."

Antonio recalled Fumi's vigorous defense of his teacher: *he's a Nei ching master who follows the empress's orders—nothing more, nothing less.* He wanted to ask Yohan if it was true that the empress kept a stable of "false eunuchs" for her private pleasure, then decided to hold back, reminded of rumors about his pregnant wife.

"He's what you'd call a loyal man, loyal to his ruler and friends."

"And rebels too?"

Yohan shook his head. "It's hard for foreigners to understand what that word means." He seemed distracted by the cooing doves, and glanced at the closed chamber with Helga inside before continuing. "If you think being critical of foreigners for what they've done to China makes one a rebel, then most Chinese are rebels. I'm a rebel too! A rebel is born every time a foreigner spits on a Chinese shopkeeper for failing to win a bargaining match, or when he pokes his servant in the ribs with his umbrella. Who isn't a rebel? One can't simply blame Xu."

"I didn't mean just any rebel, I meant the Boxers."

"That's different. Supporting the spirit army has nothing to do with hating foreigners. It's about being confused."

"Confused about what?"

"Which way the empress will go. If she sides with Boxers and they win, then everyone would want to be a Boxer! No one wants to be on the losing side, do they?"

It'll be hard to get anything out of Yohan, Antonio thought, hearing him lecture on the subtlety of court politics. Perhaps he should drop the rebels and ask him about personal matters, ask him about Xu's boyhood in the North.

"You can call him a self-made man." Yohan seemed happier talking about Xu than Boxers and foreigners. "His American friends loved him, the Locke Mission doctors who took him on as guide for their trips to far flung places. In many ways he's an ordinary man, but his mystery is not as easy to solve as yours or mine."

"Mystery?" Antonio pricked up his ears.

"Why did he betray the mission and put his American friends in danger? Why does he frequently disappear from sight, why doesn't he live with his wife, why has he never come to the monastery to be blessed for a son?"

He hadn't noticed a wife in Xu's home. "A wife?" Antonio asked cautiously.

Yohan nodded and rose from his seat under the catalpa tree. "He's rumored to have one, but never takes her name or appears with her in public. The secret of his wife makes our Xu a mysterious man!"

As they reached the pagoda's steps, Antonio knew his investigations had reached a dead end. The spy had given nothing away. He felt frustrated by Yohan's answers and cut him short when he started to tell him about the many difficulties of sifting the truth from rumors.

"It's no use then. If you, whom Polly considers to be nothing but 'pure intelligence,' know nothing about Xu, then he's probably best left alone as mystery unsolved." Helga, looking serene, emerged from the private chamber and waved at them.

"Did Polly really say that about me?" Yohan looked pleased and surprised. Antonio nodded.

"I think 'pure wisdom' will be more useful to you than 'pure intelligence,'" Yohan smiled. "I am prepared to take you to see Oscar Franklin if you'll take a look at my wife and tell us if it'll be a boy or a girl."

"You mean I should meet yet another Chinese-American spy? How do I know your Oscar won't serve me one more dose of 'unsolved mysteries'?" Antonio started to walk away toward the monastery's gate.

"No, no . . . if anyone knows the real story about Xu, it's Oscar. And he's *American* American. He's a Locke Mission doctor who married Chinese and stayed back in China, unlike his younger compatriots. He's not the type to sit around and "chew the fat", as Americans say. He was the Horseman's best friend and almost died saving him."

"Who died saving whom?"

"You'll soon find out!" Yohan patted Antonio on the back on his way out of the monastery, an arm around his wife.

Tian was in tears. "He was attacked," Wangsheng said. Antonio heard a commotion and coming out into the courtyard, found the older eunuch cradling his nephew like a child. Between sobs, Tian was telling his uncle about his troubles during his usual morning rounds at the market. A big crowd had gathered before a makeshift stage, with shopkeepers abandoning their wares to flock around it. A group of young men were swirling about, raising supernatural cries and calling on the gods to descend and possess them. The crowd cheered them on as they danced with sticks and naked swords then dropped down, one by one, strewn in a heap like dead soldiers. Everyone held their tongue, Tian recounted, and children had started to cry. "The real drama got going then. The dead men started to twitch and stir, born again as gods!" A roll of drums greeted *Lei Gong*. The god of thunder rose and banged his feet on the stage and let out a fearsome yell. The celestial Monkey King turned somersaults, lifted up his comrades and threw them onto a bed of burning coals. Led by their gods the crowd left the stage and went around the market, drawing everyone out into an open field with a bamboo cross planted in the middle. A live pig was hung from it, and torches lit all around. *Kuan-Ti*, the God of War, appeared next with his friend, the God of Archery. Together they had danced a war dance then shot arrows killing the animal, and made fun of the Christian god that was no better than a rotten pig.

He had tried to escape the Boxers, the young eunuch said in a frightened voice. But a few shopkeepers caught him and tugged at his robe. "Show us what you've got!" They had taunted him, "All Chinese men should be soldiers!" The watermelon seller grabbed him and threatened to wring his neck; the pig farmer raised a mallet to smash his head, while a band of Red Lantern girls—the female Boxers—made cruel fun of his stutter.

"Boxers at the market?" Antonio gave Tian a look of disbelief. "I thought they were doing their drills in Tungchow."

He was saved by none other than Dr. Xu. Chased by the mob, he had slipped on a banana skin and smashed his head against a rock. They were all over him in a flash like a hunting pack, and started to spit and piss on him before the doctor who was on his way to the palace stopped them with a yell no less ferocious than the gods.

Wangsheng shook his head. "Not just in Tungchow, the Boxers are everywhere, maybe even inside the palace." He glanced fearfully at the courtyard from the kitchen window. "They haven't killed a eunuch yet, but things might change quickly if their gods tell them to."

They decided to leave a scared Tian behind and travel to the village of insects, with Antonio on his sedan chair and Wangsheng running behind, begging the bearers to slow down for him to keep pace. The morning's events had discouraged the elder eunuch, and he tried to dissuade Antonio with dire prophesies as the year of the rat was upon them. From his chair Antonio saw a China that was unlike the one he'd seen on the Yangtze: a barren land, scarred by winter and waiting for spring; shriveled fields and empty rivers with boats stuck to the banks like dead crocodiles. It was as if a great storm had blown over, flattening the thatched roofs of the villages, smearing the dung of their cattle on the walls. There wasn't a dog or pig in sight, not even the cackling geese that followed the passing chairs out of habit, like orphans. The smell of rotting leaves had scented the breeze from whichever direction it blew, and gathered force as it swirled around corpses of mules that had died of thirst and were too old to serve as meat even to the starving. This was the land of beggars and robbers, broad smiles replaced by furtive and fearful looks. Few had braved the gusty winds to search for edible roots and brackish wells that still held the promise of water, hearts poisoned by the betrayal of nature. He understood why the dowager and the royals hid behind the walls of the Summer Palace in winter to escape the worst of China, to rest while the world was in mourning.

They arrived at the village of insects. The lotus lake was dry and coated with a layer of dead algae. Wangsheng led him quickly away from the huts to a communal cow shed at the back. "There's been a death," he whispered, pointing to a flag that fluttered over the headman's home, and quickened his stride. Maybe the villagers had left for the funeral. White mourning streamers hung from the doors. "The flag will fly until a child is born, when there's once again cause to celebrate." The Hungry Ghost would be inside the shed, Wangsheng said, suckling the dry teats of old cows and sharing their fodder to keep alive. The villagers hated her but were afraid to throw her out for fear of a curse.

Antonio had come prepared with his surgical box, knowing full well that the poor woman might not be a pox victim but suffering from a common disease made worse by neglect and her neighbors' fears. "Ignorance is the most glorious of all diseases," Dr. Martin would tell his students during their hospital visits, reminding them that there were hardly any new diseases left to discover, simply novel descriptions of common maladies.

They found the shed empty, swept clean as if waiting to be filled with grain. The cattle had vanished, the pigsties deserted; the dark room animated only by bats' breathing. The eunuch made a low gurgling sound as if calling an animal to a trough, then raised his voice to make an owl's hoot, stirring a tiny heap with the tip of his stick. After a moment or two, Antonio heard him speak, urging her to come out and meet the miracle doctor who'd cure her of her sickness. He heard a scream and couldn't tell if it was Wangsheng or the Hungry Ghost that had knocked the other over and made a dash toward him. Sharp fangs pierced his arm and he recoiled from the pain. Wangsheng tried in vain to grab her and pin her down. Antonio wrestled with the ghostlike form, stung by her ice-cold touch, and heard her pant like a stock animal. How could such a great force come from someone so frail? He held her back with his bleeding arm and tried to catch a glimpse of her. A syphilitic would give herself away by the lifeless eyes. Even if the sores had healed and the pus dried, she'd show blue rings around the cornea marking the tertiary stage. If bald and toothless there'd be further proof; a leper's stench would give away the rotting skin eaten down to the bones.

Like a ghost she wafted around him, stabbing at him with her nails. Then she wrenched the stick away from Wangsheng to strike his head. Roused by their tussle, the bats flew madly around, flapping their wings and letting out pathetic screeches. Breaking free, he fled from the shed with the eunuch following him. They ran pell-mell toward the lake, where his bearers were resting. Seeing Antonio and the eunuch, they too howled in fear of the Hungry Ghost, and rose quickly to carry him away.

Putting his surgical box to good use, he bandaged his arm, his doctor's instinct advising him to return later and treat his assailant, if indeed she could be persuaded to leave the shed and face him in daylight. He heard Wangsheng's teeth chatter. A bat flew in and out of his coupe like a straight arrow. From his sedan he could see a line of peasants returning to the village of insects with their cattle. He told his bearers to set him down. *I must ask them about the Hungry Ghost.* He stopped the village elder at the head of the train, but he waved his stick and ignored Antonio's question. It was the same with the rest, walking past him with eyes lowered, taking no notice of his presence as if he were a ghost himself.

"Stay with me." He begged Fumi.

She slipped on her robe and looked at him surprised. "Stay here?"

He nodded. The night had warmed just enough for them to leave the windows open, and they heard the rustling trees. "Why leave now when you'd be back in the morning?"

"Because I am not your wife. Only married couples can stay together in the palace. I'll be back, you know that, don't you?"

"We could be married if you want." He caught her hand. "Marry the Chinese way if you like before we're married in a church."

"A foreigner marrying the empress's servant?" She smiled sadly. "How can you think like that? It can't happen in China, not in a thousand years!" She tried to free her hand. "Also it's dangerous."

Antonio sat up on the bed and spoke angrily. "Everything is dangerous in China, and everyone. The Boxers, the empress, the foreigners, even the Hungry Ghost. Polly doesn't think it's safe for me to be here. Xu thinks I'd be safer at the Legation. Half the foreigners think the whole of China is dangerous. I'd rather be in danger with you."

The smell of the lake drifted in with the breeze, mixed with the scent of sap and spring buds. He wondered if Fumi was surprised by his proposal. She seemed withdrawn, her face averted while she tidied up her things.

"We can leave China if you want." He rose from the bed, determined to hear her answer before she could slip away.

"Leave?" She looked surprised. "What will happen to Canton rash? Don't you want to wait and learn the cure?"

Antonio looked exasperated. "I don't know what you think of Xu, but he's been fooling me with his promises. Almost a year has passed and I haven't seen a single patient yet. I think he just wants to keep me here and use me as he pleases. Maybe he's waiting to deliver me on a platter to the Boxers, to sacrifice a 'devil's doctor' to their gods. Maybe he wants me to spy on the foreigners to help the empress." He spoke urgently. "We can leave now and go to Macau, wait there till the troubles are over then come back."

She shook her head and left the lodge, but Antonio followed her to the courtyard. "We can leave by train from Peking and catch a steamer at Tientsin port. Cedric will be only too happy to arrange everything for us. We can leave any day we want." She kept walking toward the arched gate.

"Why, Fumi?" He shouted. He banged his fist on the kitchen door, opening the wound on his arm again. "I thought you didn't want to lose me."

"I can't leave," she whispered, and disappeared into the mist.

Striding back to his lodge he picked up the empty bottle of plum wine and hurled it through the window then dropped down onto the bed.

Joachim Saldanha greeted Antonio with a smile when he woke next morning, eating porridge and gently stroking a battered statue of Jesus in his arms. Antonio was surprised to see the padre's sedan bearers chatting with his attendants in the courtyard.

"Since when have you adopted such an exalted mode of travel?" He asked Joachim Saldanha, then tumbled out of bed holding his aching head. His friend scraped the bottom of his porridge bowl with a spoon, and called out to Wangsheng for a refill.

"The sedan is a must now, for all foreigners. No one must see us as we pass through the streets. Least of all Boxers. Traveling on the shoulders of men, they might take us for mandarins, minor royals of the court, even the dowager! Unless, of course, you were coming to the Summer Palace, where you could be mistaken for the head eunuch!"

"But how will you carry your trophies without the mule cart?" Antonio yawned.

"I won't be needing the cart anymore." Joachim Saldanha spoke in a matter-of-fact way. "I've come to take you back to Macau."

Antonio remained silent, pretending he hadn't heard the padre.

"It's an order from no other than Dom Afonso de Oliveira." The news of the Boxers had traveled all the way down to Macau, and troubled the governor. "The Macanese are too busy robbing foreigners and selling opium from their fast crabs to English ships to worry about rebels. But Dom Afonso's geographer's nose has picked up the storm brewing northwest. He has sent word to the guardians of São Paulo Church to track their prodigal son down." Word of the governor's order had reached Joachim Saldanha while he was in Hebei, escorting a group of five hundred Chinese Christians to Peking after their church compound was burned down by Boxers and several of their compatriots thrown into the flames.

"We've been fighting with the Chinese for centuries over God and opium, but this time it's different. Now *they* are the aggressors and we the target. It's their turn to spread lies about us. This time it'll get a lot worse than the opium wars, and the Legation will be under siege, not the Summer Palace."

Antonio grimaced, rubbing the back of his head. "I can't leave without my answer."

"You can leave now and return later." Joachim Saldanha smiled kindly. "A few months won't make a difference to the treatment of Canton rash. If fighting breaks out, your teacher might not be able to visit you. Chinese hospitals will be too busy with the wounded to care for pox victims, turning them away and spoiling your chances of observing the Yellow Emperor's treatment," he argued. "A war postpones everything, even syphilis! Dona Elvira has asked me to bring you back on Captain Jacque's *Warrior Queen*. It'll leave Tientsin in two weeks for Macau. That way we can avoid taking a rice boat on the Yangtze. Her Tino shouldn't be spotted in the open countryside, she has warned me, just in case a Boxer or two were lurking nearby. Her friend Captain Jacque can be trusted with the most dangerous of tasks, having earned his stripes smuggling opium from Calcutta to Canton.

"Is it Fumi you're thinking about?" Joachim Saldanha then asked him quietly. Antonio wasn't surprised by the question. The padre was fond of her, he knew. He had heard the two chatting every morning when Fumi nursed his burn wounds. Like a kind uncle, he'd ask her about her family, about her dead mother, avoiding any mention of her husband. It wouldn't be a secret to Joachim Saldanha how he felt about Fumi, from the way he followed her with his eyes. He'd know how she felt too, from the way she sneaked away to the courtyard to meet Antonio alone.

"You are, of course, free to bring her with you. But . . ." Joachim Saldanha paused.

"But what?"

"The empress mustn't know. She wouldn't want her personal attendant to elope with a foreigner, would she? Perhaps you could ask her to come to Tientsin on her own and meet you?"

He took Antonio's silence for doubt. "You're worried about you two being together, aren't you? You're thinking about others, about what they might say?" He turned his "kind uncle" eyes on Antonio, "I'd say you ought to worry less and do what your heart tells you to do. In the end there's always a way around the trickiest of problems." He wiped his mouth on his gown soiled with porridge. "I'd just leave with her, if I were you."

"She doesn't want to leave." Antonio threw up his hands in despair, and turned his back on Joachim Saldanha. For once he wished his padre friend would leave him to return to Hebei, or fall asleep after the generous helpings of porridge.

"Then you must convince her to come with you, or convince yourself to leave without her." Joachim Saldanha spoke with a rare intensity.

"We can't afford to wait, Antonio. If the empress throws in her might behind the rebels, it'd be too late to escape. China might yet witness the first massacre of the century."

He thought he'd ask Joachim Saldanha about Xu. Instead he decided to ask him about Oscar Franklin and the Locke Mission.

"James Locke was a doctor from San Francisco who came to China in the early 1890s and died of cholera. But his friends kept him alive through a medical corps named after him that spread its wings all over this country. Bright and shining youngsters come every year with their wives to show the Chinese 'how to do things the American way.' Some older ones come too, disillusioned at home and searching for a new Eden."

Joachim Saldanha hadn't heard much about Oscar Franklin except rumors.

"What rumors?"

"People say he's James Locke reincarnated, fearless and foul-mouthed. The officials are as afraid of him as his patients." The Locke Mission was the butt of jokes among Peking foreigners for their missionary zeal tending to poor Chinese, but he could vouch for the courage of the American doctors, "a blind courage that comes with innocence, not unlike the Boxers."

"We doctors can't seem to have enough of China!" Antonio mused.

"Yes, but not all are after the same thing." Joachim Saldanha paused then he said quietly, "They come to give to China while you've come to take from her." He started to scold Wangsheng for skimping on the porridge, then beamed at the sight of Tian bringing him his early rice. Crossing his chopsticks like a pair of scissors, he asked Antonio, "What do the American doctors have to do with you anyway? They wouldn't know much about syphilis, couldn't care less about the medicine of the 'savages'!"

"Not syphilis . . ."

His friend shrugged. "Whatever it is, you don't have more than two weeks in which to leave. Captain Jacque will have your cabin ready for you, and whoever else you might want to bring along."

He dreamed he was on a ship with his father. They arrived at a port, teeming with locals on their sampans, crowding the ship's hull like a bunch of crabs. Haggling buyers and sellers filled the air, along with tooting vessels, announcing their passage to those on shore. His father examined a bag of cowries sent up to the deck in a rope basket, then led him down the gangplank with a hand on his back. A set of bronze pelicans caught his eye at the market, but his father moved on to the stalls that sold live birds with phosphorescent plumes, singing songs like humans. Their owners poked them in their cages and made them dance, but he was struck most by the cormorants, taught by fishermen to return their catch in their beaks to their masters. He didn't remember if his father had bought the dancing birds or the fan-tailed pigeons, even the fighting cock that had sliced the neck of its rival and won the wager. All he remembered after he woke was his father arguing with the owner of the flower girls, pointing at a face under a wicker hat, the most shy of them all, the most beautiful. The owner was reluctant but his father insisted, then left triumphant with his catch. Antonio remembered dashing past the throngs and rescuing Fumi from his father, wrenching her free from his arms.

"Come quickly . . ." Polly had written, and from the note he could imagine her urgency. It wasn't the danger of Boxers, he knew, but a medical matter. She had asked him to come prepared with his surgical box. Antonio looked for his sedan chair but it wasn't there. Her messenger had come on a mule cart and motioned him to get in. They wouldn't have to go far, he said, not to the Legation, but to the British minister's retreat in the Fragrant Hills near the palace. Antonio knew about the Fragrant Hills from what Joachim Saldanha had told him the day he arrived in Peking, that it was once the garden of immortals, laid to waste in the opium wars.

❀

As he traveled on the mule cart, Antonio remembered his padre friend telling him how the Fragrant Hills had got their name not from the fragrance of the apricot groves or the thousands of almond trees in white blossom but from their highest peak, which resembled a three-legged incense burner on a misty day. In autumn the gardens stun the visitor with the boundless red of the smoke trees, their dense cover delaying spring and hastening the end of summer. He expected to find a replica of the Summer Palace among the gardens, built centuries ago to serve as a traveling lodge for emperors, full of pagodas, archways and pavilions. Joachim Saldanha had warned him to look out for their burnt remains, the torched pavilions sticking out of the sloping hills like an armada of shipwrecks.

"A villa in the hills is what you get for dying early in the East, and to escape the envy of friends!" Polly had joked about the sumptuous retreats of the Legation ministers in the Fragrant Hills. The British had built their own "summer palace" to escape the sizzling heat of Peking, while the Americans and Russians leased temples from priests and converted them into luxurious bungalows. A visit to the Fragrant Hills was certain to cure Antonio of his pox fever, Polly promised, and soothe the tragedy of his father's death.

"Fleshpots!" Mr. Pinchback had overheard Polly and confided in him later. "They're nothing more than private plum cottages for foreigners. The French have their orgies there, and our Italian friends hold grand balls where guests turn up in their birthday suits; the Germans too play a curious game with muzzles and whips."

The British retreat in the Fragrant Hills hid behind tall maples and resembled a hunting lodge. It was built of local stone, and the care of Polly's meticulous hand showed in the interiors: richly paneled walls were lined with six-point buck heads, the mantel gleamed with hunting trophies and a bearskin rug lay before the fireplace. It felt a touch cold from the morning mist. Chris Campbell received him and hurried him indoors. Polly stood at the top of the stairs. "It's Norma," she told him. Walking him down the corridor, she whispered to Antonio about the dead reverend's wife. "She should've returned home long ago, but stayed back to visit the gutted church in Shanxi and see with her own eyes where her husband had been martyred and to recover his meager belongings from the vicarage. Cedric wouldn't have allowed her to risk it, but the stupid Americans didn't know any better." Polly snorted. "Linda Harris encouraged her on her sentimental and foolhardy pilgrimage. As luck would have it, Chris had decided to go along with Norma, just to report for his paper on the aftermath of the murder." Stopping before a door, she spoke in a serious voice.

"If it hadn't been for Christopher, she'd be dead by now."

Entering the room, Antonio asked, "What happened in Shanxi?"

"Everybody seemed to have forgotten about the crime." Chris spoke under his breath. "We didn't meet a single villager who remembered Jeffrey Cook. The church had been turned into a granary and cowsheds, the altar's wood stripped away inch by inch. Nothing, of course, remained of the ecclesiastical items. The only visible thing being the golden inscription on the dome—*benedictus qui venit*."

Antonio saw Norma lying face down on a cot, with a Chinese maid fanning her.

"She was quite normal," Chris continued, "picking up her husband's personal items. The rioters, surprisingly, had left them untouched. One could almost smell Jeffrey inside his small and dark room, and make out the sag on the canvas bed caused by him sleeping on his side. She filled the traveling portmanteau to the brim then asked our guide for a small sack. I thought she wanted to take away the hard-dough cheddar cookies—the only luxury the reverend permitted himself— brought in jars from America. But she had other plans."

"What plans?" Antonio asked, as he checked Norma's pulse.

"She stuffed the sack with rat poison from the vicarage's store." Polly spoke for Chris, pointing to a moaning Norma, "then swallowed it on the train back to Peking."

It was wrong to have the patient lie flat; Antonio moved quickly to prop her up on pillows. Polly sang the praise of Chris Campbell: "He was smart to spot Norma's troubled eyes that had turned bleary on the train. She had started to swoon as if she was drowning. Our smart reporter persuaded the chair bearers to bring her here rather than travel all the way to the Legation."

"It's the perfect rescue, if only you can save the patient," Polly said. Antonio dragged the washstand over to the bed, and held Norma's jaws wide open, pouring jugs of water down her throat. It took special skill to avoid choking her, then he started to pump her stomach, bringing on pathetic howls and a frightening moan like an animal in the throes of slaughter. Everyone was amazed to see her bring up the poison—a glistening stream of liquid diamonds smelling of rotten milk—panting loudly and catching her breath to glare at her doctor. The room fell silent with her. The maids rushed about cleaning up the mess, while Chris Campbell held up a fresh towel for Antonio to dry his hands.

"She's lucky there's no arsenic in Chinese rat poison, otherwise she'd be dead by now." Finished with his patient, Antonio lectured Chris and Polly on the correct procedure for treating low-grade poisoning by stomach pump and enema and preventing death by acute dehydration.

Later, sipping stiff grog in the lounge, Chris Campbell let Antonio into his scoop: "It was a homegrown plan."

"What do you mean?" Antonio looked at him quizzically.

"Norma and her fried Sally Hollinger had cooked up the suicide scheme at the Legation itself."

"How do you know that?"

"Because she told me so! As she lay dying, she asked me to thank Sally for her sound advice to kill herself where she couldn't accidentally be saved by foolish doctors. Little did she know . . . !" Chris chuckled and ordered them both a refill.

"We should've left her to die then!" Antonio shrugged in mock despair. "It's our curse as doctors to save lives when in fact it'd be better to let them go."

"I bet it's rare though . . ." Chris remarked, stirring the ice in his glass and looking every bit a seasoned journalist.

"Not rare at all. Mind you they aren't always as planned as Norma's. Could be a foolish accident too, fully capable of spoiling a doctor's plans. Like I had to save a man once from his own bullet on the feast of St. Anthony, had to spend a whole night at the hospital away from the girls. Back then, of course, I considered that a total catastrophe, a curse that'd doom me to eternal bachelorhood!"

They gazed at clouds tinged by sunset flying low over the humps of the peak. After months of living as an outsider—the only European without his own mission in Peking—Antonio sensed a surprising bond with the cub reporter. The nervous and faltering Chris Campbell he had met in Fengtai during Joachim Saldanha's "accident" seemed to have grown out of his cocoon into a wry observer of both foreigners and Chinese, and of his masters in London as well with their insatiable appetite for oriental grotesquery.

"Jeffrey's story wouldn't have made it into the papers, if the poor man hadn't lost his life. Nothing moves them as much as the Mutiny, with foreigners butchered in Calcutta's Black Hole!"

"But with Saldanha's torture you must've struck gold?"

"Oh, no, quite the opposite. Our editors were miffed that I hadn't managed to interview one of his rotten torturers. Bible martyrs aren't in fashion any longer, I'm afraid, not even if they died distributing the first locally printed edition as Jeffrey Cook had in Shanxi, bearing the proud name of its printer."

Antonio stirred. "You mean Jacob de Graff?"

"Yes! The one who was killed. Not by the Chinese but by one of us." Excited to show off his investigative skills, Chris mentioned that Norma had told him about a letter she had received from her husband while she was still in the States. It was about something awful, about a foreigner killing another for profit.

"Who killed Jacob and why?"

Chris Campbell shook his head. "It wasn't a story I'd followed. Except that everyone at the Legation knew who the murderer was."

Antonio adopted a different line of investigation. "Why would anyone want to kill him?"

"It might have something to do with the many more Koenig machines he was planning to buy to expand his press and make it the largest in China. Might've troubled those who didn't like what he was about to print."

"And how do we know he had such a grand ambition?"

"That's simple!" Chris smiled confidently. "You don't have to dig too deep to know the answer to that one. Not with Mr. Pinchback going around telling everyone how the Dutchman had almost cost him his job by dying, after the Hong Kong Bank had underwritten the purchase of the German machines and paid for their freight to China."

Antonio slept badly, waking up every now and then to Norma's snoring. At first he thought she was crying, complaining to her dead husband about the unexpected actions of an irresponsible doctor. The glow of the brazier beside the bed reminded him of his running battle with insects during his early days at the palace: the beetle army that he defeated every night only to be faced with recurring assaults; the yellow moth that had chosen him as a sleeping partner, made a habit of perching itself on the bridge of his nose. And ants that refused to be fooled by the sugar trap, marching doggedly to feast on the spilled wine on his bed.

He thought about Chris Campbell's account of Jacob's death and tried to solve the mystery that sometimes seemed within his grasp, but in other moments felt as wispy as the clouds that shrouded the peaks of the Fragrant Hills. He was anxious to return to his pavilion and press on with his investigations, following up on the young reporter's clues.

"Why don't you stay here and enjoy the spring?" Polly proposed to Antonio over breakfast. "With all the troubles in Peking it might still be the safest place for us all." Chris was enthusiastic as well. He could do a story about the pavilions of the Fragrant Hills pillaged and burned by the allied troops just a few decades ago, although it was doubtful if the editors would print anything about Western mischief in China. Antonio turned down Polly's offer, much to her dismay, but promised to come and celebrate her "first step to the grave" fortieth birthday at the Legation.

On his way down the slopes he saw wild peonies budding in the tall shrubs, the flower of honor, known to calm passions and bring riches. The Yongding River wound through the woods in a silken sash, the sun chasing it down. Peasants had started a fire of dry leaves, and the blossoming apricot trees glowed like giant lanterns hung from the peaks. The driver of the mule cart started to sing in his coarse voice. He felt Fumi's hands holding onto him . . . *in spring the pulse beats like the strings of a lute* . . . heard her sigh as she laid her head against him.

On his return, Antonio found that imperial troops had entered the Summer Palace and camped in the gardens surrounding the lake. Kansu soldiers thronged the palace grounds, dragging their field guns behind them. The "Savages," as the Moslem fighters from the northwestern Kansu province were called, were the empress's favorites, decked out in black and blue with ammunition and provisions strapped to their backs like pack animals. The few who had managed to settle into their posts inside the palace were sleeping in tents, cradling their rifles like wives. The stink of unwashed soldiers mixed with rotting scraps and manure, and as Wangsheng weaved his way past the throngs to lead Antonio to his pavilion, they heard a volley of gunfire welcoming the troops from the Terrace of Heavenly Clouds.

The cavalry guard hadn't taken the invasion too well, the horses refusing to budge from the stables that the Savages intended to occupy for the pigs, goats and chickens they'd robbed from peasants during their long march into Peking. The chief eunuch was nowhere to be seen, having fled his charge of keeping order to accompany the dowager and her closest advisors to the Forbidden City, from where she was rumored to be following the movement of foreign troops. The boatmen had fled too, along with the gulls after the soldiers had raided their nests for un-hatched eggs. The terrace by the lake had turned into barracks, the marble bridge was packed with sandbags to serve as gun turrets, the giant incense burners mounted with Krupp canons against enemy attack. The empress was yet to forget the allied invasion of her favorite palace during the opium wars, and the Kansu savages had been commissioned to thwart its recurrence.

The soldiers had stayed away from the private pavilions, but their very presence had caused Wangsheng and his nephew to panic. The Savages might go after eunuchs just to pass the time, to have some fun before the killing started. Tian had locked himself up in the kitchen, singing to his favorite songbird, and refused even to come out to the courtyard, with both attendants deciding to buy the inferior produce brought in daily by donkey carts, rather than risk going out and scouting the markets.

Within moments of arriving at the pavilion, Antonio shocked them by asking for his chair and bearers. The empress might still decide to side with foreigners against Boxers, he tried to reassure his attendants, and the Savages could well turn out to be their saviors. In any event, the *Tsungli Yamen* had vouched for the safety of all foreigners and it'd be foolish of soldiers to stop him on his way in or out.

Wangsheng grumbled all along the way to Hong Kong Bank, following his master on his sedan, glancing fearfully at every soldier they passed. He was foolish to panic, Antonio kept telling him. There were no signs of disturbances on the streets. Bands of urchins had gathered around the soldiers and examined their weapons openly, touching them even to see if they were real.

Mr. Pinchback, looking relaxed behind his banker's desk, agreed with Antonio. The Orientals were quick to panic. Over his long career in the East, he had found them to be wise during peacetime and infantile in a crisis. "Unlike us, rock steady in war and barmy otherwise!" He thought Polly had sent the Portuguese doctor over to examine his troublesome acne, and seemed surprised when Antonio brought up Jacob.

"He died much before you arrived. Couldn't have saved him, I'm afraid!" He looked sternly at Antonio. "As a banker, I can't betray the fiduciary trust of my clients, even a dead one like Jacob. But I can tell you all about his fantasies."

Mr. Pinchback waited for Antonio to answer, then wetted his lips to start. "Jacob de Graff had won a jackpot with his Bibles. They were cheaper to print in China than in England, say, and ship over. Churches in Europe and America were falling over themselves to have him do their job for them, ready to pay for more machines, more paper, more of anything he needed. If a proper businessman, he'd have slept soundly, but the mathematician in him kept him awake at night." He paused to straighten a pile of papers on his desk, then went on. "Jacob had figured out a way to adapt his Koenig machine to produce Chinese books much faster and in larger numbers than using traditional ways. He didn't just want to print more Bibles, but to reproduce classic Chinese texts. He was dreaming the dream of emperors, getting a group of scholars to translate the *Analects* of Confucius, Sunzi's *Art of War*, the *Four Great Books of the Song*, and many more. He wanted to enlighten the world about our yellow brethren and stop the sharks from forging old manuscripts for grand profit." Mr. Pinchback followed Antonio's gaze to the row of banker's seals on his desk. "It was typical of Jacob to dream foolish dreams. I didn't mind at all, as long as he could guarantee payment for the printing presses from his Bible sales. His business was sound, not his fantasy, but I didn't expect . . ."

Antonio cleared his throat and leaned forward on the desk. "You didn't expect that he'd die so soon?"

"More than that." Mr. Pinchback rose to part the curtains and looked down from his window. "I didn't expect his fantasy would attract such powerful enemies. News of his plans had leaked out and threatened the mandarins and their agents. It wouldn't be possible to pass on a fake manuscript as the real one anymore if he succeeded. Jacob's scholars would catch the rotten ones. With thousands of genuine copies and translations available, the market for so-called originals would suffer too, hurting the thieves, and all those who claimed monopoly over the Chinese and their books."

Antonio picked up a seal and turned it over in his hand, then asked, "So he didn't commit suicide."

"Suicide!" Mr. Pinchback looked genuinely surprised. "Which fool told you that? Our Jacob was a true believer, if ever there was one. His zeal was the zeal of apostles." Sighing, he returned to the desk. "We don't get too many clients like that in the bank."

Should I ask him who Jacob's enemies were? Antonio wondered if Mr. Pinchback would give him a straight answer, then decided to ask a fiduciary question instead. "What happened to the machines?"

"Thank God for telegraph! We were able to intercept the ship carrying the Koenigs in Bombay port and had them offloaded. Luckily there were ready buyers in India, those who'd caught the printing fever even earlier from the 'Indian Jacob,' the Baptist William Carey of Serampore."

"And his house?"

"He left no will, of course. His sister had already returned to Holland and with no relative here, his friend, *your* friend, could've claimed his "missionary's fortune," But then she disappeared, fearing his enemies would kill her too."

Antonio unbuttoned Pinchback's cuffs and rolled up his sleeves to examine with his finger the goose bumps on his arms, then advised him to wash them without soap and use a light tincture of sulphur to dry and exfoliate the skin.

"Where did I get it from?" The banker seemed nervous. Antonio assured him that it wasn't an infection he could've picked up somewhere or from someone. *Acne Vulgaris* didn't have a known cause, it could well have been hereditary, the infection of his parents.

Antonio found Wangsheng and Tian sitting solemnly in the courtyard when he returned from Hong Kong Bank. Someone had gone through his things with a fine-tooth comb. A theft was as rare at the Summer Palace as a secret affair. The two were napping inside the kitchen all afternoon, and had woken to the sound of feet rushing about the courtyard. The soldiers had arrived, they thought and bolted the kitchen door.

The surgical box had been emptied onto the bed, the instruments heaped up in a pile. His traveling case had been dragged out from underneath the clothes rack and left on the floor with its lid gaping. The thief hadn't shown much interest in his clothes, except to rifle through the flaps of the sacklike robes that Joachim Saldanha had left behind, turning them inside out to search for things that might be hidden or left behind by mistake. His medical drawings and notes had received the most scrutiny, the pages flung about the room to resemble a captain's coupe after a storm. Nothing had gone missing, not even the silver wine bowl presented to him by the departing Patty and her fiancé.

He put the instruments back into the box, counted them to ensure that none were missing then left it to the attendants to straighten up the mess. The soldiers might be responsible, he thought, although their callous abstinence made him wonder. Maybe they were looking for precious things, believing the pavilions to be full of gold and jade, even opium.

Although Fumi hadn't visited him for a few days, Antonio started to worry about her safety. *How would she come to the pavilion now?* He imagined her surrounded by a band of Savages. The soldiers might stop her, assault her even; she could be raped, they might cut her hair and turn her into a camp whore. As he lay fretting on the bed, Wangsheng knocked on the lodge's door to announce a visitor.

A young man, a deputy prince at the dowager's court, sat on the walnut bench under the plum tree, looking like a young student at the academy for civil servants. Antonio exchanged pleasantries with him. "The empress doesn't wish to disturb her guests," the deputy prince said calmly, sounding wiser than his years. "The soldiers have strict orders not to enter the private pavilions. But they might trouble you with their loud manners and gunfire. The troops will leave as soon as things return to normal." He smiled politely, and offered Antonio a box of French bonbons, the empress's favorite.

"Would you like me to go away?" Antonio wondered if the man had come to give him a farewell gift.

"You can leave if you like, but it might be better if you stay," his visitor replied. "The palace is safe. It might even be the safest place in Peking. The empress has invited all foreigners to come over and some have arrived already."

"Which foreigners?" Antonio looked at him with disbelief. He couldn't imagine Polly and Cedric or the rugby boys rubbing shoulders with the Savages. He hoped the dowager hadn't foolishly planned to raid the Legation and imprison all foreigners in the Summer Palace.

"We have Heinz Ulrich here. He's our friend from Germany, who's come to teach us the art of modern shipbuilding. A team of Swedish explorers have arrived as well from the Gobi desert, where they've spent the last two years digging for lost civilizations. Then there's Edward Pickering, who was born to Australian pastors here in China, the editor of the *New Hunan Review*. He has brought over his two assistants with him, and hopes to keep the paper going from the palace. Do you know any of them?"

Antonio shook his head.

"And we have a doctor here as well, a western doctor. Just like you."

"Who?" Antonio thought the deputy prince had mistaken a padre for a doctor. It was common for men of cloth to travel in China with their own dispensaries and share the medicines with their flocks.

"Oscar Franklin, the most famous foreign doctor in China."

"Of the Locke Mission, do you mean?" Antonio was excited hearing the name Yohan had mentioned to him: "Pure wisdom," who was a friend of Xu.

"Yes, you can meet him if you like. If *he'd* like to meet you, I should rather say!"

Antonio took advantage of his visitor's politeness to ask him the most uncomfortable question. "So there's no truth to rumors that the empress is conspiring with the Boxers to throw all foreigners out?"

The deputy prince smiled. "Rumors spread by whom? Boxers or foreigners?"

He thought about the recently arrived foreigners after his visitor had left, about the ambition that had brought each of them over to China. He wondered if his was the sole lost cause among them. Even without the troubles he was no closer to learning the Chinese cure for syphilis. Alone in the courtyard he blamed himself. Why did he let Xu off the hook? How could he have allowed himself to be distracted by

Fumi, to have fallen in love with her? In just a few seasons he had lost the fire that had made him the most successful doctor in Lisbon, turning into a lovesick wretch. He should've kept on arguing, kept the Chinese doctor on his toes till he revealed his secret; he shouldn't have allowed Xu to disappear and pass him on to the amber-eyed seductress. As he tossed and turned in bed, he concluded that it was his obsession with Jacob's death that was to blame. One mystery had replaced another, turning him into a second-rate sleuth, sifting through idle gossip like a vulture picking bones. What had caused him to trust in a housewife's hunch? What invisible thread had he glimpsed that joined the Dutchman to syphilis?

The Kansu Savages could be his saviors. It'd be nothing short of a miracle if there was no one among the soldiers and their camp wives who suffered from the pox. Coming through the gates he had seen several of them lying under blankets in their tents, coughing and spitting blood; a great many showed gashes and tumors; the acidic smell of pus had turned his stomach as he picked his way through the festering heap of human cattle.

As doctor to the soldiers he'd learn about Chinese syphilis. The age of a chancre or a skin lesion would tell him if treatment had failed; he'd be able to judge a real recovery from one that was fake. The sick might take him into their confidence and tell him about quacks, while those recovered could reveal the mystery of the Yellow Emperor's method. His spirits lifted as he thought of surprising Xu with his own findings. He imagined Polly shrieking . . . *You examined the privates of those stinking savages . . . !* His attendants would worry, shake their heads madly like freshly slaughtered pigs at the very mention of soldiers. He must calm them down, Antonio thought. Picking up his surgical box, he called out to them. He found the kitchen empty and the gates of the pavilion shut, with him, the prisoner, locked securely inside.

"I've found a patient for you."

He woke instantly at Fumi's words, but kept his eyes shut.

"She's suffering from Canton rash, and has never been to see a doctor before." She poked him in the ribs, and tickled him. "Don't you want to see her?"

"Ask Xu." He turned over, and pretended to snore. He shouldn't show his keenness, he thought, but wait for his teacher to invite him for a proper demonstration of the treatment.

"But he's disappeared! Don't know if he's in Peking even." She prodded him again and spoke pleadingly. "Why don't *you* treat her?"

Antonio sat upright and held Fumi by the shoulders, drawing her close to him. "I'm not stupid, Fumi. I can't save her, you know that, don't you? That's why I'm here, to learn from Xu how to cure the pox. *He* should be her doctor, and I his student." He drew her even closer. "I've seen my dying father, don't need to see another one just for the sake of it. You must go and fetch Xu from wherever he's hiding."

She pulled away and withdrew from his side. "Who'll save her then?" She spoke angrily. "Jacob said there's always a way if one can think like a good machine."

"He lied. That's why he's dead, because the best machines couldn't save him."

Her eyes lit up for a moment and she said under her breath, "That's not true," then strode out into the courtyard.

"Wait!" he called after her, struggling to put on his robe and follow her out.

"I must take her to see the other doctor," Fumi shouted back at him.

"Which other doctor?" He stumbled and caught himself against the door.

"Oscar. The American. He's come to stay at the palace."

Catching up with Fumi, Antonio tried to take her hand, but she turned away and spoke without looking at him. "We can't be seen together anymore."

He didn't have time to fret over Fumi's words. Wangsheng rushed in with news of a palace maid who'd been kidnapped last night as she went about lighting lanterns by the lake. She was a concubine, a promising girl who could've risen in rank some day by bearing a royal child. The jeweled clasp of her robe was found in a nearby grove, and all evidence pointed to the gunners on the marble bridge and to their evil bed of sandbags guarded by barbed wire. "She'll be alive as long they have a drop of spunk left to fill her up. Then she'll sink under the bridge. Or she might be saved for later, dumped with their whores to follow them as long as she can bear children."

Antonio asked him about the deputy prince who had boasted that the palace was the safest in Peking. Wangsheng scowled. "Anybody who's important has already fled. Only the eunuchs and poor servants are left behind."

"What about the newly arrived foreigners?"

"They're foreigners only in name," the eunuch remarked caustically. "These men are Chinese really. Heinz the German shipbuilder is worshipped as the son of *Guan Yin*, the Goddess of Mercy, for starting an orphanage in Shandong after he lost his family in a shipwreck. Pickering the Australian has had his two arms cut off by the cruel governor of Hunan for writing against his policy of taxing the poor to profit the rich."

"And the American doctor? What's his story?"

"He's a *dizi* player, famous for playing the bamboo flute in local operas. His Chinese wife was a dancer when she was young. She plays the *konghou* harp, and has lived with him ever since his American wife left him many years ago."

Returning to the subject of the vanished concubine, Wangsheng warned him to stay out of the soldiers' sight and get his things ready. Ready for what, Antonio asked him. "To leave the Summer Palace," the older eunuch replied without thinking. "Chair bearers may still agree to take you to the Legation during the afternoon when soldiers are asleep in their camps after their early rice."

"But I don't want to go the Legation. Nor will I need a chair to go over to see Oscar Franklin."

"Oscar!" Wangsheng exclaimed. "His tongue smells worse than a donkey's bottom!"

His attendants led Antonio along the palace's long corridor that ran from east to west, with pavilions on both sides. It didn't take them long to pass the four arched gateways and reach the American doctor's quarters. After he'd exchanged greetings with the eunuchs of the Franklin household, Wangsheng offered them the gift of a dozen snipe caught by his nephew with the clever net he had devised and tested on his songbird. The doctor was sleeping, they were told, having spent all afternoon trying to calm his patient.

A naked woman lay on her back on a reed mattress in the living room. Lixia, the Chinese wife of Oscar Franklin, looking prim in her dancer's dress and wearing her silver hair down to her waist, knelt by her side and rubbed a lime green paste all over her skin. The woman lay perfectly still, and he couldn't even see her breasts lifting as she breathed. Shadows of giant cranes flying in from the cold mountains flitted through the room like passing clouds. From Lixia's smile Antonio saw that she knew who he was. Wangsheng must've told his eunuch friends about him, or the deputy prince when he presented French bonbons to Oscar Franklin and his wife. She motioned him to sit and resumed anointing the patient's skin. Acrid smell of burning leaves came in from the open courtyard and he wondered if the eunuchs of the palace were making offerings to the gods to rid them of the soldiers.

"She has two navels instead of one." Lixia called Antonio over, "Come look . . ."

The gash above her navel was wide and deep, like a recently erupted volcano. The rest of her body was unblemished, but exuded the smell of dead oysters. Not even a hint of emotion showed in her eyes, which were open and unblinking.

"The green lotion will kill the smell. It will let her sleep. When the fever returns at dawn she'll be stronger to fight off her headache and nausea."

Lixia spoke kindly, as if showing off a newborn to a fond relative. "It's her first month. She went to visit her village for a few days and returned with the Portuguese disease."

Portuguese disease! Antonio asked Lixia if the patient had been treated.

"She was brought here, because you refused to see her." Washing her fingers in a small bowl, Lixia started to fan the young woman, spreading the smell of jasmine around the room. "Her friend said she'd asked you first."

Antonio felt angry at Fumi for talking to strangers about him. "Why didn't she practice her *Nei ching* and treat her friend herself?"

"She isn't a proper Chinese doctor, and her master is away. Besides . . ."

"Besides the Chinese are shit scared of syphilis." Antonio heard the deep voice of Oscar Franklin. "One sniff of her, and they'd have run!"

A tall and muscular man dressed like a coal miner in his dungarees came over to his wife and the sleeping woman. "It doesn't take a doctor to know what's wrong with her." He motioned Antonio to kneel at the woman's feet as he parted her legs. "Just one look's enough."

An angry rosebud showed on the mount of her vulva, breaking free from the dark vines. Her eyes twitched, but she didn't try to cover herself with her hands.

Settling down beside his wife, Oscar poured tea for all three of them and resumed. "I don't blame you for refusing to treat her. I'd have done the same had it not been for our Chinese friends saving our lives. I thought I owed them at least a little look-see." They drank in silence, then Lixia spread a blanket over the sleeping girl, tucking in her toes like a loving mother.

"Could a *Nei ching* master have saved her?" Antonio asked cautiously.

"You mean like our Xu?" Oscar turned to his wife. "Why don't you tell our friend about the Horseman?" Antonio edged forward on his seat remembering Yohan's words. . . . *If anyone knows the real story about Xu, it's Oscar. . . .* From the way she behaved, he knew Lixia wished to avoid the subject. Fidgeting with the teacup, she shook her head. "You tell him, he's your Horseman not mine."

"He was the empress's spy who became our friend. It was impossible for a Western doctor in China to avoid Xu. The dowager was suspicious of *our* medicine, and wanted her favorite physician to keep an eye on us. He was imposed on the Locke Mission as an interpreter." Oscar took a quick look at his sleeping patient and continued. "He was the nicest guy you could ever meet. Never lost his cool, didn't mind us pulling his leg. He was real sweet when it came to putting up with our crazy wives who hated China and drove us mad! He learned to speak English the American way, picked up our vices—chewing tobacco and spitting on the ground—but kept us clean." Oscar chortled. "The golden lilies never had a chance with Xu around."

So he's indeed a spy, Antonio mused. *He's used to playing games with foreigners. . . .* He thought to put to rest the mystery of Xu's name.

"He was raised in the north among horsemen, but didn't fancy the animals. So who named him Horseman and why?"

Oscar roared with laughter, spilling tea on his robe. "We all did! To tease him. He had a mortal fear of being trampled by horses and lost his cool whenever he was near them."

Rising, Lixia suggested they move over to the garden to enjoy the evening breeze and taste freshly baked spring cakes, but Oscar stopped her. "Wait, I haven't told him the best story yet."

"Worst not best," Lixia sat down reluctantly.

"Our spy friend almost got us killed and died himself." Oscar seemed happy to tell his favorite tale to someone new. "It was a tricky mission in the northern steppes, where we were called to treat an epidemic of typhus. Xu came along as our guide. Everyone suffered on the way over on account of poor food and water, and sleeping in yurts on windswept nights, sharing our blankets. The typhus turned out to be a strain that killed babies faster than adults, and we spent more time digging graves than tending to the sick. Xu was remarkable, doing what we did by imitation and a whole lot more, like teaching hygiene to the villagers."

"Why didn't he treat the victims with his *Nei ching*?"

"Because he didn't know how to." Oscar paused, then went on. "All seemed to go well, till the day we were set to return. The mule carts that had brought us over went suddenly missing. There was no choice but to return to Peking on horseback. But there was another problem. Xu disappeared when he found out about the missing carts."

Antonio smiled, remembering his own story of the disappeared teacher.

"We knew we'd be dead without Xu. The road to Peking was full of dangers. Bandits would chase us down and greedy peasants demand bribes for sheltering us from dust storms."

"You must've known though, why Xu had left." Lixia seemed ready to defend the Chinese doctor.

Oscar nodded. "He had panicked at the prospect of riding horseback with us."

"So did you leave him back in the North?" Antonio asked.

"No! We weren't stupid. We couldn't risk the journey without him. Also, we didn't know if he'd be safe returning to Peking all by himself."

"And so you did the stupidest thing, going out into the desert all by yourself to hunt him down," Lixia added wryly. "Spent a whole night and a day on a one-man search party looking for him. Bandits could've got you before they got Xu. Then dug both your graves."

"I was lucky. Everyone had given him up for dead when I found him swooning on the dunes like a mad man, starved and parched on the brink of death." Oscar thumped the floor with his fists.

The three of them sat holding their empty teacups, feeling the hot breeze of the steppes. The girl snored and mumbled in her dream, smelling like a wreath of jasmine. Then Antonio brought the Locke doctor back to his question.

"Can Xu cure syphilis?"

"It's hard to know." Lixia whispered. "They have two methods, one for the royals and one for . . ."

"And one for soldiers and whores, sailors and peasants." Oscar added impatiently. "The first is mysterious, the second simple."

"What's the simple cure?" Antonio's breath quickened.

"Death." The elderly doctor passed his hand around his neck and made the sign of Cross. "Kill the patient, that's the simple cure."

"Cure by killing?"

"It's a crude philosophy really. Get rid of the syphilitic to eliminate infection. Life is marvelously cheap in this country, don't you know? Brothel owners are punished with death if they hide a sick girl, ship owners too if a rotten sailor boards the planks, a peasant suffering from the pox is kept in a cowshed to die of hunger, soldiers are drowned to save bullets." He took a long look at the sleeping girl. "They'll kill her as soon as the chief eunuch finds out, or send her back to the village where she'll be locked up and called a demon."

Antonio noticed a tear on Lixia's cheek.

"And the cure for royals?"

Oscar shrugged. "Don't know." His wife cradled the girl's head in her lap and started to fan her once again. A distant explosion sounded like a firecracker and made them look out of the window.

"Everyone who comes to China hears of miracle cures." Oscar sounded dismissive. "It's the easy way of explaining why you don't see any victims of the pox here or even the plague. They are smarter than us—haughty Europeans and foolish Americans—we're told. Inventors of paper and gunpowder have trumped us when it comes to the treatment of diseases. Rumors never die about the 'pill of longevity' meant only for emperors."

"But it can't be as simple as killing all sufferers, can it?" Antonio's mind went back to the sailors on *Bom Jesus*. Were the sick ones thrown overboard? He pressed on, "If indeed there were a royal cure, the Yellow Emperor's Canon would describe it, wouldn't it?"

"If only their Yellow Emperor wanted to reveal his secret! The Locke doctors, including myself, never paid any attention to *Nei ching*. China needs the *Materia Medica*, we believed, not the treatment of porcupines, sticking needles into bums! Xu wouldn't have told us the real cure anyway, if such one existed. He wouldn't have told even his little sister," Oscar snorted and pointed at Lixia.

She had resumed talking to the sick girl, woken by the sound of firecrackers now nearer than before. "Whose little sister?" Antonio asked, watching the patient, whose eyes had come alive with pain.

"Xu is my wife's elder brother. I met her through the Horseman. You can say he arranged our wedding."

The sound of running feet came from the courtyard and stopped in front of the door. Wangsheng stuck his head in. The Savages had started to fight among themselves, uprooting trees and setting off bonfires. More trouble was expected when night fell, and he pleaded with Antonio to return to his pavilion because they'd need to bolt the gates from inside to stop the soldiers from entering. An explosion shook the house, and caused the patient to cry out.

Xu's sister! Antonio was thrilled. It was the closest he'd come to unlocking the mystery of his teacher. She must know everything about him. He could probe her too about Fumi, get her to tell him about Xu's assistant. He ignored Wangsheng and kept on talking.

"Did you live in the monastery with Xu after your family had fled the grasslands?" he asked Lixia. She kept her eyes on the girl, and shook her head.

"We were separated when we were young. He was sent to live with monks and I with a troupe of dancers and musicians. It could easily have been the other way around." Lixia smiled.

"Thank God for that!" Oscar bellowed. "Otherwise we'd have spent half our life arguing over yin and yang."

"Did he ever tell you what he does for the empress?" Antonio thought he must be brave enough to ask. It was time for him to learn everything he could about Xu. Maybe Lixia would know where to find him; she could tell him if he was still hiding in his peasant's hut.

"Of course, he didn't!" Oscar answered for his wife. "Once you enter her stable, you lose your tongue and become a loyal pet."

Lixia gestured helplessly as the girl started to howl, throwing her arms and legs about like a buck felled by a hunter's shot. Oscar rose quickly and called his servants to fetch his surgical box. Filling a syringe with morphine, he injected his patient, holding her down with his weight. It took the joint efforts of the couple to calm her, bathing her head with ice-cold water and wiping her sores with a soothing tincture. Then Lixia invited Antonio to join them for late rice, tempting him with the rare delicacy of snipe brought over by Wangsheng and Tian.

While they ate, Oscar cursed the soldiers and the eunuch attendants let out loud moans and gasps as explosions rocked the pavilions. "Shitheads! They're brave only when it comes to a friendly fight among themselves. The great imperial army is no more than a bunch of wimps. They'd lose easily to an enemy less than half its size, like the Japanese navy. They're afraid of the Kaiser, who's threatening war unless the Chinese yield to his demand of a naval base in Shandong. Even the Italians can bully them simply with their mannerisms! The Savages are savage only in name." He mocked the eunuchs for being foolishly nervous about the soldiers, when the likes of Fumi moved about the palace without fear.

Antonio stopped eating. "You mean when she brought the girl over?"

Oscar nodded with his mouth full, and Lixia spoke for him. "She passed the very spot where the soldiers are camping. She must've seen them fighting when she went to fetch the patient from the concubines' hall near the marble bridge full of gun turrets." Washing down the snipe meat with wine, Oscar added, "Mind you, she herself was as sick as that poor girl, not very long ago."

"Fumi?"

"She suffered from chronic depression after her friend the Dutch-man was killed. A classic case of nervous breakdown attended by hysteria. Almost starved herself to death, hiding inside her home, afraid for her own life, till Xu saved her."

Lixia urged Antonio to eat, taking his silence for an aversion to the snipe. "You'll miss your late rice at midnight if you eat so little."

"How did Xu save her?" He asked his hosts, trying hard to keep his mind perfectly still.

"She came to see our Horseman and he cured her of her depres-sion and hysteria," Oscar replied. "Then he taught her *Nei ching* and brought her into the palace were she'd be safe."

"He married her and brought her here as his wife, made her look after the empress," Lixia corrected her husband.

He must've misheard Lixia, Antonio thought, clearing his throat to ask her a question, interrupted each time by Oscar plying him with more helpings and offering generous advice on the eating habits of the Chi-nese.

"It's what they eat that keeps them healthy, not the Canons."

"Who was married to whom?" Antonio spoke each word carefully.

"Xu and Fumi, the Horseman and his assistant. We too got married soon after, but it wasn't a double wedding!" Oscar replied.

"Xu and Fumi were married before us, but it was a proper Chinese wedding," Lixia said, her eyes growing fond.

"You bet it was proper! With gongs and fireworks, the groom marching in procession, accompanied by his Good Luck Man to fetch the bride from her house and all that." Oscar slurped on his bean-curd noodles, and added the details.

"Oscar was his Good Luck Man, his 'best man' as you'd say." Lixia stirred the soup pot, "But he forgot to wear red as per custom, and dressed in a white silk mandarin robe, which is the sign of mourning!"

"Did they come here afterwards to live in the palace?" Antonio asked in a choked voice.

"No." Lixia exchanged a quick glance with her husband. "Fumi came here, and he went back to his home in the village."

"And they've been coming and going ever since." Oscar patted Antonio good-humoredly, and pushed over the pot of dark *guilinggao* jelly made from the bittersweet shell of box turtles, with reputed powers to clear up the skin after an attack of smallpox.

Antonio left before dessert, feigning a full stomach and a seasonal cold. He walked briskly back to his pavilion past the lake that was freshly spawned and brimming with fish.

The songbird fell silent as he entered the kitchen. A green lizard circled his early rice left by the attendants, observing the wormlike rice noodles with curiosity. The wood oven was cold. He sat under the plum tree as if waiting for someone to appear in the courtyard, then went inside the lodge. The stillness of the pavilion set his mind racing. *Where is she now?* He imagined Fumi in Xu's hut, looking like a peasant in a broad-brimmed hat, feeding the buffaloes in the sheds. How did they manage to fool him? *Your new teacher is the same as me . . . she has learned the Nei ching the hard way too.* The vision of Fumi, kneeling in the courtyard as Xu taught him his lessons, filled him with an uncontrollable urge to scream. They must've schemed behind his back, laughing their heads off at the Portuguese doctor as he lost his mind and fell hopelessly in love. *Why . . .?* How could she have fooled him, feigned to be his lover for three full seasons? The early rice swelled up to his chest and he felt he was choking under the hard shell of a tortoise exacting its revenge on its gluttonous enemy.

Unable to sleep all night, he rose early and ran up the one hundred and fourteen steps of the Tower of Fragrance, where the empress came on the third month of every lunar year to worship ancestors. Fumi might be there, he thought, as a member of her entourage. The eunuchs would be startled to see him among the palace ladies; they'd raise a cry as if an eagle had descended on a dove's nest.

The empty temple turned his mind toward the Garden of Pleasures. Forbidden to foreigners, it was a favorite among the royals, where they came to hear Confucian tales from palace scholars. He'd be stopped at the entrance, he knew, shooed away by the guards then wrestled to the ground if he insisted on barging in and taking a close look at the visitors.

Gardeners glanced at him quick, then went back to polishing their sickles. Women played cards under a cherry tree. The sound of laughter grew as he inched up behind them. His mind raced through the possibilities. If not in the garden, she could be chatting with the dowager's eunuchs; or strolling under the weeping willows at the Island of Immortals, waiting for the sun to set before she joined her mistress on the marble boat. Perhaps she'd be on the Bridge of Floating Hearts, among the anglers who fished for pleasure and returned their catch to the lake.

It took him all morning to realize his mistake. She wouldn't be at the palace but at the soldiers' camps, treating the sick and those injured in the friendly fight. Chinese doctors and their assistants must be busy caring for the camp wives and their scraggly children. Reaching the lakeshore, he walked boldly toward the bell tower that had been turned into a small village full of sounds and smells. Sleepless faces greeted him, weary and battle scarred. It didn't seem like a part of the palace, but a jumble of huts uprooted by force and planted haphazardly around the tower.

The Savages haven't seen a foreigner before, might skin one alive taking him for a rare animal. . . . Ferguson had warned everyone during John Harris's briefings. Many of the soldiers were Boxers in disguise, Wangsheng had told him. It was their job to start a fight between the Savages and foreigners. Even Joachim Saldanha avoided the soldiers, who didn't believe in give and take, but grabbed everything they could, sparing none, not even beggars and priests.

Hell-bent on finding Fumi, he ignored all warnings. Luckily, the soldiers were dozing after early rice, and few noticed him picking his way past their sprawling bodies, lying like corpses in a battlefield. The women peered out of the tents to watch him; stopped fanning their ovens and nursing their babies. An old woman made the sign of crossed swords, forbidding him from approaching her tent, and barked out sharp orders to the children playing nearby. He quickened his steps, and peered inside the huts. *She must be here. . . .* From all that he knew about Fumi, he couldn't imagine her hiding with the empress inside the palace, while the tents groaned and moaned with sufferers.

The sound of chanting drew him to a hut, and peeking through the flaps he saw a doctor bent over her patient. A soldier with a nasty gash on his head lay on the ground surrounded by his anxious camp wives, while a frail and elderly woman swirled around him. Her lips moved, and he heard a wail. Holding a knife in her hand, she made as if to cut the man's head open.

Not a doctor, but a quack . . . Maybe she'd know about Fumi. Perhaps she'd visited the injured soldier and left, knowing that his wounds were untreatable. *I must ask* . . . He parted the flaps and entered, covering the opening and darkening the interior. One of the women noticed him and screamed, followed by the rest. The doctor drew her knife quickly back into her robe. The wounded soldier opened his eyes and glared at him. Word of his presence seemed to spread from hut to hut within moments, the sleepy camps suddenly coming alive. A rush of voices followed him as he withdrew quickly and strode out, heading toward the bell tower. The soldiers called out to him; he could hear guns being loaded and a rock landed at his feet. Breaking into a run, he saw a dark form flit across the tower, dressed in a peasant's smock. "Fumi!" he called out to her, then watched her disappear into the gardens. Someone tugged at his sleeves, and Antonio raised a hand to strike him, taking him for a Savage. It was a child. He smiled at Antonio and drew his gaze down to a handful of birds' eggs, holding them like pearls on his grimy palms.

Back in his pavilion, Antonio called the eunuchs over. They stood in front of him glumly, expecting a dressing down on account of the poor meals they'd been forced to serve without their daily visit to the market. Wangsheng had an explanation ready on his lips for the rancid meats that the donkey cart seller had brought over.

"My little nephew will go to the market from tomorrow. He'll risk his life to bring you fresh food." He looked at Tian for support.

"I don't want him to go to the market. Both of you must go immediately to find Fumi and bring her back here."

Wangsheng shrugged. "But we don't know if she's here at the palace."

"Then go and ask the empress where she is."

"But it's forbidden to speak to the empress without her permission." The older eunuch made a gesture of helplessness. "It's forbidden to enter her quarters even."

"It's forbidden to disobey your guest." Antonio spoke to him sternly. "You can go search for her in the palace, while Tian goes to Xu's home to look for her."

"Xu?" The eunuchs looked at each other.

"She's his wife. You knew that, didn't you?" He circled them like a caged tiger, spitting out his words. "Why did you hide that from me? Why didn't you tell me who she really was when I asked you? Why did you lie? *She's a better doctor than Xu . . .*" He mimicked Wangsheng, then stared hard into his eyes. "I thought you were my friend."

His attendants looked confused, then Tian spoke up. "Dr. Xu told us not to trouble you when we spoke to him about our problems. He said we mustn't worry if you didn't wake up in time for your porridge after spending late nights with your teacher; we mustn't complain if the vats couldn't be cleaned properly because we were too shy to disturb you when you were together. We mustn't be surprised if we found the bed soiled and pillows ripped up." He walked away towards the kitchen and called his uncle over to join him, throwing his parting words to Antonio: "We thought everyone knew everything—Xu, Fumi, and you."

She has deceived me for her husband, Antonio thought, sitting alone in the courtyard. He recalled Xu's words. *Maybe the soldiers are on their way to Peking . . . there'll be war when they come. You'll know before us. You can tell me then. . . .* And he felt Cedric Hart's arm around his shoulders. . . . *You, more than us, will know when the real trouble starts. . . . When you leave the palace and come over, we'll know the attack on the Legation is soon to begin. . . . As long as you are there, we'll know we're safe here!*

He regretted ignoring Joachim Saldanha's advice. *You mustn't carry the palace with you when you visit the Legation, or give away the foreigners' secrets to the Chinese.* He'd be pressed to take sides, his padre friend had cautioned him, and he chided himself for acting so foolishly. Rising, he paced the courtyard, stomped on the spring roots and scattered the sacks of birdseed brought by the eunuchs. The rustling plum tree drowned out the footsteps approaching the pavilion's gates, and it took him a while to notice Fumi. Hushing him with a finger, she entered the lodge and called him over, shutting the door firmly behind her.

"You must leave."

"Then you must leave with me," he matched her pressing voice. "I can't leave you behind with the soldiers all around us. Or do you not need me anymore?"

Standing with her back to the door, she ignored his words. "The empress is powerless now. She can't stop the Boxers. They'll strike the Legation any moment. You'll be cut off from your friends, and there'll be no way for you to leave China. The palace will turn into a battlefield. Pavilions will be destroyed, the houses set on fire and gardens uprooted. . . . It'll be like the opium war all over again. No one will be able to escape."

"What'll happen to you then?" Antonio stepped closer to her. "Will you run away to your husband's home when the war starts?" He waited for her to answer, then spoke slowly, "Why didn't you tell me you're Xu's wife?" She didn't speak, turning away toward the open window.

"Why did you lie when you said you loved me?"

She shook her head, her lips started to tremble.

"You mean it wasn't a lie? That you loved me even though you were married to someone else?" He spoke as evenly as he could. "Why did you hide the truth from me?"

"You mean the truth about syphilis?" She sounded defiant. "The one and only thing you think about day and night?"

"The truth about *you* and *me*."

"How does it matter who I'm married to?" She avoided looking at him, the spring breeze blowing her hair through the window.

"It matters because you can't be *my* wife. Because it means we can't both leave China and go away, that we couldn't marry as we'd planned."

She tried to stop him, raising her hand to cover his lips. "As *you* planned. When did we decide to leave China?"

"But I thought . . ."

She interrupted him, "If I asked you to stay, would you have stayed?"

"You mean stay here as a prisoner, waiting for you to come and go as you pleased, whenever your husband set you free?" A strange note entered Antonio's voice, a note he didn't recognize as his own. "With you I thought I'd have more . . . more than I've ever had or wanted before."

She turned and stepped out into the courtyard, followed by Antonio. He called after her, "Stop! If we go, we must go together."

The breeze turned her into a kite fleeting across the courtyard and he tried to catch her in the mist rising from the lake. The last of the snow cranes flew over their heads, crying out for its lost flock. Fumi followed the bird with a desperate look.

"To leave now would mean the end."

"End of what?" He raised his voice over the rustling trees.

"It's the only chance . . . don't you see?" She gestured with her hands to make the argument that seemed plain to her. "It's only now that they're afraid of being trapped. After years of waiting, it has finally come to this."

He caught her at the edge of the boundary wall, just before she could leave through the arched opening. Her eyes glowed like that of the peasant girl he'd seen at the empress's antechamber.

"Only chance for what, Fumi?"

In seconds they'd turned icy: "To kill Jacob's killers."

He had lost Fumi, Antonio was certain. He had seen it in her eyes, the eyes of the wild crane that had broken free and flown past their pavilion. Who could tell him what she might do next?

"Fetch Xu!" he called out to his attendants next morning. Wang-sheng scowled. "The doctor has disappeared, and no one knows when he'll be back. It's too dangerous to go out with Boxers everywhere."

"Liar!" Antonio cursed him and shouted to the chair bearers to get ready, making known his intention to go himself and trace Xu down. The older eunuch went out grudgingly and returned with more bad news: the bearers had disappeared as well. Perhaps the soldiers had commandeered them to go on a joyride. His anger grew as he heard the eunuchs chatting and yawning all day.

He heard the *dizi* and the *konghou*. Tempted as he was to go over to the Franklins', he decided not to. He might give himself away to the American doctor and his wife. It'd be hard to disguise his feelings, and they might take him for a troubled visitor. The funereal strains of the duet wafted through the breeze, filling him with deep foreboding.

The more he thought about Fumi's last words, the more guilty he felt. Perhaps she had come to ask for his help. As a foreigner he could be trusted with delicate matters rather than her husband, the empress's servant. She might be wary of Xu, unwilling to confide in him lest he should think she had simply feigned her recovery, when in fact she was still grieving for Jacob, still angry at his killers, still bent on exacting her revenge. Who was to say that she was in love with Xu, that she'd ever been in love with her husband, marrying him simply to stay alive?

Antonio waited the whole day for Fumi to return, to talk things over calmly with her. Perhaps he could stop her from following her impulse. Drunk on plum wine in the evening, he considered joining her. What did he have to lose, except Fumi? He could teach her to fire a gun. They could travel together in their sedan chair like lovers then turn into assassins. His laugh rang through the pavilion and scared the songbird in its cage. He wished Joachim Saldanha would come with a box of hacked limbs or a scorched apostle. The eunuchs would scurry to bring him his late rice, the pavilion transformed by his jovial laugh and constant demands from the kitchen. The presence of soldiers wouldn't deter his padre friend. He'd find a way to humor them even, have them carry his box for him.

You must tell Fumi to name the killers. . . . Joachim Saldanha would've advised him. It wasn't just a matter of revenge but of justice, he'd have argued. If the empress wasn't prepared to punish them, then maybe the foreigners could. What if the killers were foreigners themselves? This last question would've silenced the padre before he came up with his answer. He wondered what Joachim Saldanha's answer would've been, what clever ploy might he have suggested to win Fumi back.

The kitchen fell silent the day after. Waiting for his porridge in bed, he didn't hear his chattering attendants or the splash of water in the vats. Perhaps they'd left to chase down the donkey cart that was now busy selling to the soldiers' women in their camps. The songbird's cage was empty; the painted rock and the clay warrior had vanished from the courtyard's shrine. Looking around he failed to spot the New Year's streamers or the paper cut-outs. The pavilion bore an abandoned look, as if the residents had fled an advancing army. It took him the whole day to realize that his attendants had disappeared with their belongings.

As his stomach complained, Antonio raided the kitchen, finding nothing more than a sack of birdseed. He scraped the clay jars in vain, hoping to find surplus stocks of rice and noodles. The shelves were empty without the baskets of maize, quails' eggs, peanut buns and lotus cakes. Even the pickle jars had disappeared, along with evil-smelling strips of dried fish that hung like bats from the roof. His hunger grew by leaps and bounds as the day wore on, and he dreamed of the honeyed crab apples and rice cakes that Tian fetched for him from the kitchen to munch between meals. He remembered seeing Wangsheng bury a nest of old eggs in the kitchen garden to preserve their pungent yolks in ash and salt, and dug up every bush and shrub.

Antonio wondered what'd happen if he went out to the food stalls, if there'd be enough left for him to buy after raids by the Kansu Savages. Perhaps he'd end up having to prowl around the other pavilions to steal from their kitchens, caught by the guards and tonsured for his crime like a common thief, handed over to the soldiers even, for a more severe punishment.

I must see Fumi, even if it means risking my life. His anger had turned into a sense of unfathomable loss after just three days of waiting. It was the same distress he had felt after learning of his father's illness. Just as hunger inflamed his stomach, Fumi's absence purged his mind of all thoughts except the unstoppable urge to be with her.

He dressed carefully in the English gentleman's dress popular among the dandies of Lisbon — muslin shirt with frilled cuffs tucked under an evening tail coat, with a top hat and an ivory handled stick. If caught he'd claim to be the empress's doctor and point to his surgical box. He might need to bully the maids to enter the private quarters, and pretend that he knew his way through the maze. He must face the guards calmly if stopped, otherwise he might be taken for an intruder and shot.

Setting out from his pavilion, he knew it'd be hard to find her in the numerous teahouses and temples spread out over the gardens. She might be in the throne room even, sitting next to the dowager commiserating with her generals.

The grand pavilion and the throne room were empty, without a single guard in sight, just as before when he'd come with Xu to "treat" the pregnant maid. He didn't see the eunuchs either, those he'd expected to stop him.

He was ready to meet the invisible. The neighbor he'd seen only as a shadow; the one who prayed at the temple of Ten Thousand Buddhas, played cards in the tearooms and sailed on Kunming Lake under his very nose. He'd meet her delicately arched brows and tell her why he had entered her sight. Surrounded by glass mirrors and chiming clocks under the dimmed cloisonné lamps, he expected to meet Fumi in the most private pavilion in all of China.

The antechamber was empty as well, and the silk curtains blew in the breeze through the open window. He examined the divan, his mind returning to the moment when he had handed Fumi the fetus and seen her eyes glowing on him. Lost in thought, he imagined a shadow on the silk partition, setting his pulse racing.

Antonio returned to the throne room. A gong sounded. "Fumi!" he called in a soft voice. The clocks started to chime just then — crowing cocks and singing birds, church bells, gushing waterfalls and organs playing the music of a waltz.

V

WARRIOR QUEEN
The bleeding hand

May 25, 1900: The much feared Boxer rebellion had started, and the siege of the Peking Legation was imminent. News of the advancing rebels had brought genuine panic. With the telegraph lines cut, it became clear to residents that if the foreign soldiers didn't arrive soon, they'd be too late. Eighty miles away in Tientsin, a meeting of the rescue party on the German *Hansa* debated the considerable difficulty of landing soldiers in the dark night: lowering, manning and equipping the boats in the face of possible hostilities. If the Chinese general of the Taku Forts didn't surrender, the war might have to start right away at the mouth of the Peiho River in the Gulf of Pechihli before troops could board the cattle train to Peking and save the Legation. The possibility of Boxers dynamiting the rail link was real, and the risks of a foot charge to the capital crossed everyone's minds.

The streets of Peking's Tartar market were deserted. The screeching wheelbarrows and their noisy owners had disappeared; the jingling bells of the camel trains had fallen silent, with no signs of the abusive hordes that trailed them and poked the animals' hinds with razor-sharp stems of desert palm. Downed shutters kept the idlers away from shops, as roving bands of dogs patrolled the lanes, strangely at peace with their rivals and behaving like docile pets. Beggars had left the temples, urchins locked themselves away inside abandoned homes; the mad women who ambushed foreigners and pretended to bite their hands huddled under trees in the nearby cemetery and slept the sleep of death.

Only the Legation was busier than usual, bustling with newcomers. Refugees had poured in from the provinces to the safety of the fortified walls and the jade green canal that guarded the quarters from free contact with the natives. Terrified Chinese converts streamed in, led by their pastors through the east gate next to the Italian mission. They carried their possessions on their backs and looked like sheared lambs, having marched for days in torrential rain. Lying on waterproof sheets in the godowns of the Imperial Maritime Customs surrounded by their fowls, pigeons and ducks, they slept with eyes wide open and dreamed of the headhunting Boxers who displayed the grimacing heads of their victims in cages. They'd escaped by the skin of their teeth; many had seen their loved ones thrown down wells inside their homes; smelled the leaping cremation flames. Dark crusts of blood showed on the necks and ears of those beaten with rifle butts. The children slept the least, and kept a frightened watch on the poor adults who'd carried them on their backs for days.

The missionaries had been the last to leave their far-flung posts, although some had stayed back resigning themselves to their fates. The Mitchells had arrived on a houseboat with their three adopted Chinese daughters, dressed in European clothes to hide them from the Boxers. They were certain they'd be attacked when their boat ran aground in a narrow channel. Other boats had crowded up behind them, and the Boxers ambushed each with bricks and stones, smashing the windows and threatening to board them with guns and swords. Glen and Nancy Mitchell had saved the day, firing from their recently acquired English Webley revolvers and disproving to their frightened flock that the Boxers were immortal. In mourning for the loss of their deckhand, an elderly Chinese man who had suggested bartering the adopted daughters for safe passage, they had dug the Legation's first grave in the grounds of the Expats' Club.

The population had swelled to double its size almost overnight, and the refugees were forced to spread out their bedrolls and mattresses wherever they could find space, from the tennis courts to the aisles and vestibules of the recently built Legation chapel. They had even started to share the stables with mules and ponies. Charlie Baxter, the American mining engineer who had fled after the rebels had overrun his company's gold mine in the north, showed a special knack for building shelters out of everyday things, earning the praise and gratitude of residents and refugees. Within days of arriving, he had turned Canal Street into a row of shanties, covered with tarpaulin that he had managed to wrangle out of Monsieur Darmon's champagne warehouse. Camp cooking in the evenings was his solution for feeding so many mouths, and a large crater-like pit had been dug in the middle of the post office's grounds to serve as a common oven, sending up a great swirl of smoke that tricked outsiders into thinking that the Legation had been set ablaze by enemy fire.

Sanitation had proved to be a bigger problem, and Mr. Pinchback had come up with the practical solution of using the canal as a flowing repository, obviating the need to bury the night soil and risk an outbreak of infection.

"It's silly to invite so many inside our walls," the banker had argued with the mission officers as the refugees marched in like a tired army. "It will make it easy for the Boxers to kill all their enemies in one go. I'd be delighted if I were a Boxer! No need to search for bloody Christians when they're all congregating at the Great Basilica of the Legation!" He showed despair at the false logic of saving as many lives as possible, speaking like a mandarin himself, "How many eggs remain intact when a nest is destroyed?" No one suspected that Mr. Pinchback was a crafty general in disguise and willingly accepted him as the leader of civil defense; they trusted his novel methods of building barricades should the Boxers decide to storm the missions. Selecting the strongest from the newly arrived converts, he had them dig and fill cardboard boxes with earth and stack them up in front of the mansions; board up windows by removing the glass from the frames and closing the openings with bricks. Garden rollers were lined up before the gates by his order and bombproof shelters dug inside the walls of the British Mission, considered to be the safest spot of all.

Linda Harris's circle of ladies were kept busy with scissors and thread, sewing up sandbags which the rugby boys carried to the roofs to prevent bomb splinters from raining in, having to keep pace with deft fingers that worked at a frenetic pace. Whoever could lend a hand was urged to do so, with the first secretary's wife going around the missions and shaming the lazy ones who slept all afternoon in their hammocks. Luckily for both, Polly had gathered her own ladies circle around the tricky problem of feeding so many mouths, without the luxury of raiding the Tartar market and bribing the sellers for scarce items. The refugees arriving with their animals provided enough meat, and grains had been stockpiled by the local shops that had foreseen just such a catastrophe. Never one to serve the simplest of suppers, her instructions were no less severe than her American rival's: to save the animals for later, while making do with boiled eggs and tinned beef, Chinese biscuits and condensed milk for the babies, and fifty blows of a bamboo cane for thieves. Professor Norman Brummel, who had fled his archaeological excavations in the Gobi Desert, was entrusted with the whipping although it was common knowledge that the gentle professor could hardly bring himself to hurt a fly.

"We'll be eating mules and dogs if the thieves have their way!" Those who heard her thundering were ready to believe Polly Hart, given her reputation for fastidious attention to detail.

There was no shortage though of champagne and claret, cigars and Egyptian cigarettes. Monsieur Darmon had promised to distribute French ships' tobacco in the unlikely event that fresh supplies failed to arrive and the Hôtel de Pékin was forced to serve the awful Chinese variety meant for stable hands.

Mission officers burned the midnight oil as they waited for word from the commanders of the foreign fleet. Perhaps an advance party would arrive followed by a regiment in case a full offensive was required. Perhaps the fickle dowager would change her mind and unleash her Kansu Savages on the Boxers. Imperial soldiers were already in the capital, encamped before the Temple of Heaven, creating panic among the natives and raising temperatures among foreigners.

"The English seem to be always at war with somebody!" A few among the missionaries were secretly furious at the "war dance" of the British and the Americans, believing that not enough tact was being shown in convincing the *Tsungli Yamen* that the foreigners were the empress's allies. The troubles were caused by foolish officers and greedy merchants, with the common visitor having to pay the price. Everyone worried about the "price," if the Boxers kept their word and dumped all foreigners into the sea.

Just a few iron cots and a handful of camp beds at the Legation's makeshift hospital did little to comfort those tormented by the thought of casualties, the vast number of the sick and injured expected to occupy the floors, lying on donated mattresses and bales of hay covered with sheets. A trained nurse and a couple of cheerful doctors attended to those who had arrived in critical condition, and kept their eye on a possible epidemic breaking out. With water scarce and close contact between the sick and the healthy, enteric fever or septic poisoning, even dysentery, couldn't be ruled out.

"The Boxers will kill us with infection, not their rusty spears!" Mr. Pinchback never failed to point out the folly of the general evacuation, directing his barbs at the Americans for lording it over the Europeans despite their inexperience in dealing with colonial crises.

Riding on his bicycle, Antonio went from camp to camp to tend to the refugees. Half-starved mothers called out to him to examine their sick babies, or to revive a child who seemed on the verge of death. Men with spear gashes and bullet wounds begged for relief from ulcers teeming with maggots. Breathing in spurts due to exhaustion, almost all of them showed blistered feet and a dull gray look in their eyes from dehydration. A peasant carried his sick wife on his shoulders and tried to stop Antonio, speaking incoherently. A mother clutched a dead baby and screamed a curse after him. In places, he had to push his way past the throngs who had gathered around a man to mourn his death, when in fact the patient was still alive. There were days when he'd see a great many who couldn't reach the hospital, standing in queue to be examined, and he'd stop frequently as he rode along the lanes crammed full with shanties. Harelips to cataracts, tumors to ulcers—more than just the casualties of war, he'd treat the whole range of ailments that plagued the human race. Luckily, the missions had done admirably well stockpiling medicines and he could count on the field hospital's nurse to fill his prescriptions.

The refugees lit bonfires at their camps in the evenings to drive away insects and blood flies drawn by the scent of open wounds. Children cried all night, their parents trying to calm them with a bleating sound, like lambs waiting to be sacrificed. Familiar voices called out to Antonio when he rode by, including that of Chris Campbell. The reporter was squatting beside an old man who had lost all his fingers to the Boxers for the crime of weaving the cross on a silk handkerchief for a Jesuit Father in exchange for a few bushels of rice. Chris took notes as his native interpreter held up the man's maimed fingers. Each tale of misfortune drew another, and soon the young Englishman had to raise his arms to stop the eager voices.

"There's enough here to keep the papers going for a full year! All the blood and gore London wants, even better than the bush wars with the Boers!" Why didn't he offer to pay for his sins by weaving the Boxer slogans on their banners? Chris asked the old man, who shook his head sadly. Even if he wished to make a simple flower, the Boxers said, the devil would turn it into a cross. It was better to rid him of his evil instrument altogether. Another man showed his right ear wrapped inside a pouch, and started on his own tale. A weeping woman gestured with her eyes at her daughter, raped for housekeeping a Christian home, who was slinking away to a corner of the tent.

Chris Campbell told his interpreter to hurry up; he'd had enough stories to fill his column. But the maimed man spread out his arms before him and begged to be treated for a numbness that had followed the amputation of the fingers. "It's as if he's lost both arms, struck off from the shoulders," the interpreter said in a nervous voice. "He wants you to cure him."

"Me?" It was Chris's turn to be nervous. He sensed the crowd of victims eyeing him accusingly, as if he had stolen their stories and provided nothing in return. "He's the doctor," he said, pointing to Antonio, then babbled something about the field hospital.

It was *sanjiao*, the tenth channel, he knew instantly, starting from the tip of the ring finger and traveling up between the metacarpal bones to the wrist and onward to the upper arms and the shoulder region. The shock to the fingers had cut off the flow of *qi*, and made the victim go numb in the limbs. If untreated, the blocked channel might damage his hearing as well, as a branch of *sanjiao* forked up to the neck and ran a loop around the ears.

Antonio opened his surgical box and took out a small case of needles: gold, copper, silver and chrome tipped, and of varying lengths. He needed the gold ones for their stimulating power, to bring alive the tenth channel withered by trauma. Making room for himself in the crowd, he examined both arms of his patient as well as his body for any visible damage. Then, just as he'd been taught by Fumi, he traced the three sections and nine subsections of each arm, applied a gentle massage and pulled up the skin to free the veins. A hush fell on the crowd when he inserted the needles as the man inhaled, and turned them round with thumb and forefinger as he exhaled.

"Western doctor saving his patient with Chinese needles!" Chris Campbell chuckled under his breath, having found a better story than any he'd heard all day. "Will he recover sensation in his arms?" The reporter was more curious than the old man, who seemed to have dropped off to sleep.

"Not overnight, but if the treatment is kept up for some time." Gratitude showed on his patient when Antonio cycled away, a small crowd following him through the lanes.

"You are alive!" Hanna Mueller exclaimed meeting him at the hospital. "I thought you'd left Peking with your friend." She had come with her niece Kristin, an art student in Vienna who was visiting China to learn calligraphy. She ignored the other doctors and confided in Antonio about the young lady's female problems, with an open invitation to visit the German mission and taste the delicious Berner sausages.

The field hospital's doctors were happy to have him run around the camps. It saved them the trouble of checking the shanties for infectious diseases, and prepared them in advance to receive the critical cases. Dr. Maria was their eyes and ears. It seemed odd to have such a brilliant doctor do the job of a junior, but he seemed happy to be both a specialist and an apprentice, a surgery nurse who thought nothing of cleaning wounds and removing stitches; an ambulance driver, carrying a critical patient on his lap as he cycled to the hospital, and as the jovial matron claimed—"a Chinese quack into the bargain!"—checking pulse and sticking needles, doling out herbs that smelled worse than rotting scraps.

On most nights Antonio slept wherever he could find a vacant spot, setting up a bed with a mat and a mosquito net that he carried in a roll along with his surgical box. The storeroom of Imbeck's—the foreign shop for liqueur and general supplies—was his favorite. Here he'd lie on the wooden crates full of jam and marmalade, coffee and Stilton cheese, canned meats, olive oil and Indian spices. The oily wrappings on the crates repelled insects, and the small and dark room reminded him of his ship's cabin. There were nights when he slept on a hospital cot next to his patients, exhausted by a long and complicated procedure, or under the club's snooker table to evade Polly as she went on her rounds to track down the missing Dr. Maria.

"You must live among the officers, not refugees," she scolded him. There was nothing wrong with a doctor tending to the poor in times of crisis, and she was proud of her brilliant but headstrong Tino. "But why must you live like a gypsy?" She was troubled too by his unkempt looks: long hair and beard like a padre, and Jesuit robes that smelled of manure from the refugee camps. All her Legation friends had coped admirably well with the influx. Sally Hollinger, after she'd been suitably reprimanded for abetting the attempted suicide of her friend, had turned out to be her trusted lieutenant in the gruel kitchen. The resident spy was just as jovial as before, ferreting out gossip from the *Tsungli Yamen* about the dowager's misadventures, as Helga marched on toward blessed motherhood. René Darmon deserved everyone's praise for "keeping the parties going," Polly had mentioned to Antonio with a look of reproof, "and for reminding us why we're in China—to have fun!"

"And how about. . . ?"

"Ferguson?" Polly thought Antonio was curious about her gypsy friend. "He's hiding somewhere, waiting perhaps for the troubles to end before sending in his claims to whoever is victorious!" She didn't worry about Ferguson. "He knows enough bad people to keep safe!"

"And Joachim Saldanha?" Antonio, who was more concerned about his friend than Polly's, asked the arriving missionaries if they knew of his whereabouts. "The gravedigger?" Some knew him by reputation only: the strange Portuguese padre who worked harder at saving statues than converting heathens. The Mitchells hadn't heard of him, nor had Reverend Olaf Lundstrom, the Swede who thought the greedy Portuguese had "quit the missionary business a long time back to manage gold mines in Brazil." The refugees seemed to know more, but were afraid to talk about the priest who risked his life to bargain with the Boxers over a few pieces of burnt wood.

"He must've fled to Macau." Polly didn't know Joachim Saldanha's whereabouts either. "You worried us, Tino," she said, stroking his face just like Dona Elvira. "We imagined the worst about you . . . that you'd been kidnapped by the gangs and . . ." She gave him yet another look of reproof. "You shouldn't have left the Legation, but listened to poor Cedric who begged you to stay." She asked him about Fumi, if he knew where she was, if she'd be coming over to join him.

There were nights when he slept on a camp bed in the upstairs veranda of the Hart villa, opening the shuttered windows to draw in the breeze. Fine nets kept the bats away as well as the insects drawn to the glow of the oil lantern that hung from the high ceiling. A hooting owl kept him company from its nest on a nearby branch. He heard the rattle of the compound's watchman. Torches lit up the camps, the flames dancing in the night like will-o'-the-wisps. *Where's Fumi? Is she waiting for me in the empty pavilion?* He wondered if she was riding a sedan chair through the troubled city, on her way over to meet him. Was she in a camp herself, among the butchered and the raped, reading the pulse of a dying patient? *Is she hiding in the Legation?* Maybe she was fleeing the Boxers too, and had decided to come over to the shelter of foreigners.

He imagined her visiting the camps with him, the two of them treating the refugees, taking turns to assist each other. *Is she out on the streets stalking Jacob's killers?* A shudder went through him, and he smashed from his window the bottle of rice wine smuggled in by the peasants and sent the owl fluttering away.

You're dying for your Fumi! He heard Ricardo, his voice floating in from Avenida da Liberdade, and raucous laughter filled his ears. He heard his friends teasing him over his golden lily. The kind saint has finally come to his rescue, he imagined his doctor friends stripping off their whites and plunging into Rossio's fountain to celebrate the much delayed blessings of St. Anthony on Antonio Maria. Perspiring on his divan, he heard murmurs from the camps and the howls of the inconsolable, scaring the dogs that had stopped barking the day the tired refugees trudged into the Legation and slumped inside their tents. The Harts and their servants had fallen asleep after yet another hard day, and the house rose and fell with their snoring like a clipper cruising on topsail.

He stayed up all night and wondered why the kind saint had brought him all the way to China to offer him the gift of sweet basil—

the promise of eternal love—then shredded the leaves like a thought-less gardener.

The Legation woke to the news of the Boxer assault at the crack of dawn. A whistling bullet broke the chapel's stained-glass window, show-ering the refugees underneath with shards like a rush of raindrops. The hospital received its first dead: a young girl trampled by the fleeing crowd.

The mother cradled the dead girl on her lap after Antonio had failed to revive her. She seemed faultless with her bones intact, just the breath squeezed out of her tiny frame. A thicket of legs surrounded the three of them, other patients watching the pair of unblinking eyes, as if expecting them to come alive through the magic of the doctor, who sat there with a look of distraction.

"Pinchback was right," Polly whispered to Antonio. "It would've been better if they had stayed away. Here they'll end up killing each other."

The burial had taken up the whole afternoon, with mission officers issuing strict orders afterward on the conduct of both residents and visitors in case of future attacks. The mood in the gruel kitchen was somber despite the improvement in diet caused by the release of hand-fed ducks by the Hôtel de Pékin to mark the anniversary of its founding in China. The rumor mill had gathered force by the evening, and everyone had their own doomsday story to share with whoever was willing to listen. The dowager might order all foreigners out; Mr. Pinchback, as usual, had the grimmest prediction of all, as he played croquet with John Harris and Mr. Itami. For the four hundred or so foreigners at the Legation it'd mean a hard journey to Tientsin to board the ships home, made perilous by the Boxers they might encounter on the way unless the empress offered the protection of her Kansu guards. But what'd be the fate of the Chinese Christians, all three thousand of them herded like cattle in the camps? What if their pastors insisted on taking them along on an exodus?

"Take them where?" John Harris quizzed Mr. Pinchback. "I hope you aren't suggesting we take them home." He reminded everyone of the exclusion act of 1822 prohibiting Chinese "idiots, lunatics and labor-ers" from entering the United States, with onus on the pastors to prove that their flock didn't fall into any of these categories.

The Hong Kong banker didn't disguise his dislike for the men of cloth and made everyone uncomfortable with his extreme views. "I'd say leave the refugees here and let them revert to their own ways. Christianity is not for the Chinese. Replace Christ with Mammon, and we'll have swell profit!"

A siege of the Legation was more than likely, everyone knew. "They'll trap us like rats, and starve us to death!" — Mary McKinsey resented her botched honeymoon, and commiserated with the unflappable René Darmon. The bubbly merchant told her stories of worse disasters, had her mesmerised by mutinies on slave ships and sepoys killing sahibs and memsahibs in Calcutta's Black Hole, adding his own touch of black humor: "A siege is the rudest of all, much worse than frontal combat. It's the war of eating horsemeat and women going around with unshaven armpits!"

Siege or not, ladies didn't dare disrobe at night in case they were forced to run to the bomb shelters without notice. Mothers with children kept a full knapsack ready, and Charlie Baxter was rumored to be digging a secret tunnel to escape the ring of rebels in the manner of a grand jailbreak. Sally Hollinger kept her own counsel after Norma's failed suicide, but nobody doubted that she'd be up to her old tricks again, signing a pact perhaps with her friend to kill each other if captured by the Boxers.

A desert storm broke at night and covered everyone sleeping outdoors with a fine blanket of dust, the howling wind drowning the human and animal sounds. At its peak, it seemed as if a thousand priests were blowing their horns, sending the curse of their gods to the foreigners; as if the dunes had swept in like giant waves and were lapping at the Legation's shores. The mission officers stayed awake, waiting for news of soldiers, wondering how many lives would be lost if they failed to arrive within the next forty-eight hours. Their wives slept fitfully — lights going on and off in the mansions like blinking stars — with servants kept busy serving refreshments all night. Everyone worried about the telegraph lines being cut between Peking and Tientsin, forcing the extra risk of slipping in a messenger through the enemy's ranks, but it was none other than Roger McKinsey, the shy telegraph operator, who brought the news everyone had been waiting for. He had received a message through Russian Kamchatka that the allied guards were on their way and would arrive by train next morning, about three hundred and fifty men from America, Britain, Russia, France, Italy and Japan with Germans and Austrians set to follow soon.

"No need to turn up our toes yet!" Polly beamed at Mary McKinsey. "Long live the honeymoon!" In the time it took for the news to reach everyone, Monsieur Darmon had invited the officers and their friends to the "Great Boxer Dinner" at the French mission in honour of "our smelly saviors!" Everyone seemed relieved and happy, walking around the Legation and greeting each other with, "Thank God it's all right now!" The evening couldn't have come too soon with the "cleaning up" already under way, getting the Legation ready for the soldiers. The Sanitation Committee and the Civil Guard held timely meetings, and the Ladies Circle debated the merits of a full-blown reception for the soldiers while troubles were still brewing.

"It's that moment between doubt and certainty when most wars are won or lost," Mr. Pinchback went around the guests at the party, expounding his views about military strategy, but for once no one listened to him, busy being silly all over again.

"You should watch out for the Cossacks," Hanna Mueller was telling her friends. "They're no better than the Boxers, worse even when it comes to women." The Italian minister's wife, decked out in a renaissance hat with ribbons and lace, giggled. "None are worse than Italians! They lose every war and win every heart!" All eyes turned toward Charlie Baxter, the dasher, as he stomped in, sat down at the piano and hammered out an off-key concerto to everyone's distraction.

"Who needs guards if he keeps playing like that!" Polly was excited about the Indian soldiers who were likely to arrive with the British contingent. "Look out for the Sikhs! They're the best fighters of all!" The British had won the opium wars because of their Indian troops, she explained to the ladies. "They scare everyone by the way they look, and the way they curse."

"How can you tell a Sikh when you see one?" Linda Harris, who'd never met an Indian in her life, asked.

"By their turbans, of course," Polly made as if to wrap a shawl around her head. "And by their smell!"

The first secretary's wife looked confused, wondering if she should take Polly seriously.

"The smell of India! You'd know it when they're within a mile of our walls!" Before Linda or anyone could quiz her any further, she disappeared, making excuses about an "important visitor who'd shown up without advance notice."

"A visitor at a time like this?" Sally Hollinger exclaimed.

Sitting on a lounge chair, Antonio watched Cedric Hart conferring with Yohan, both officer and spy chirping away. Has he now chosen the winning side and decided to spy for the foreigners? The tired voice of Dom Afonso de Oliveira floated in with the evening breeze . . . *The puzzle of war is the same as the ocean's currents . . . it fools those who claim to know it too well.*

"Must leave you alone to behave yourself!" Passing Antonio, Polly smiled at him playfully. "Can't let our visitor wait . . ."

"I thought your gypsy had died and gone to hell." Antonio spoke with his eye on the ladies who gossiped around the dinner table, exchanging a sharp word or two with their fleet-footed servants.

"Not Ferguson. This one's far more important than him. More important to *you* than to me!" Polly smiled teasingly. "You'll know when you see . . ."

"Why not bring your friend over?" He called after her.

"Oh, no . . . it's too early to throw her to the wolves," Polly pointed at the rugby boys and left the room.

Antonio wondered about Polly's visitor. Maybe she was just making up a story. She'd be the last to miss out on a party, no matter how important her visitor. His thoughts returned to Fumi, and he imagined her sitting on a thronelike chair surrounded by the officers' wives, holding up their wrists in the air. He hoped she'd give him a smile across the room between her readings, even invite him with her eyes to come over. Sipping the Frenchman's champagne, he took another look at the circle of pulse reading and saw his Fumi transformed into the dowager, wearing a headdress of golden filigree representing five phoenixes with tails and wings outspread. Each of them held a tassel of pearls in its beak that hung down her face like a bride's veil. She was smiling at him now, the smile of the empress, with the ladies turned into her attendants, fanning her with peacock plumes and the bushy tails of mountain goats. As he looked away and called for another drink, René Darmon laid his hand on his shoulder.

"You can hit me again if you like, Dr. Maria, but this time there must be a proper fight."

"And a proper wager!" The rugby boys had come up as well, and everyone seemed suitably drunk for a good fight.

"A case of Monopole, nothing less!" Perkyns, the customs inspector who had spent all his years in China as a bachelor, seemed most eager.

"A case of Monopole for what?" The champagne merchant was eager, as he stood to gain whatever the outcome, win or lose.

"For blood!" Perkyns waved others around him to form a circle for the fighters.

"Blood is cheap!" Charlie Baxter had given up on the piano and bellowed. "To fight means fighting to the death! Nothing else makes a good wager among pitmen and panners." Even Yohan had left the officers and joined Chris Campbell, clapping his hands and egging Antonio on, "Come, Doctor, let's bring on the bullfighter!" The ladies turned their heads as the clapping picked up, calling the servants to come over quickly and remove the expensive porcelain from harms way. The officers too seemed mildly interested in the duel, sizing up the rivals and murmuring their bets to each other.

Dashing in from the circle of ladies, Sally Hollinger caught hold of Cedric and urged him to step in between the two. "Stop them! We can't have them fighting. There'll be bloodshed, don't you see?"

"Oh, let them fight, there's nothing wrong with a bit of a punch-up." Cedric waved her aside, and joined with the rugby boys who had already formed a ring. "We might as well have our own boxers."

Looking around the room, Sally raised her voice and called for Polly, hoping she'd come over and drill some sense into her husband.

The Frenchman had removed his coat, unbuttoned his cuffs and rolled up his sleeves. He took off a giant emerald ring from his right middle finger and slipped it into his pocket. A drop of sweat stood on the bridge of his nose, and a stream of spittle joined his lips like a spider's web. Clearing the circle with his arm, he clenched his fist and grunted.

"Come, on, Doctor . . . !" Yohan led a chorus and soon they were all chanting, waiting for the fight to begin.

"But they aren't evenly matched," Sally tried yet again to stop the fight. "Our doctor is just a shadow of himself having worked himself to death, while Darmon has been fattening himself on champagne."

"Uneven matches are better!" Cedric hushed her with his finger. "They are more fun to watch."

Antonio rose from his chair and walked across the hall toward the garden. The crowd expected him to enter the ring, take off his ungainly robe and flex his arms and legs but he walked past them. "Wait!" Perkyns called after him. "Aren't you fighting?" The rugby boys started to jeer and the clapping grew, as Charlie Baxter yelled a miner's curse and tried to stop him.

"You can run away if you like, Dr. Maria, and hide behind your Chinese cocotte if you can find her." Monsieur Darmon seemed triumphant at his easy victory. "But you must settle the wager before you go."

"You bet he'll pay!" Charlie Baxter looked disappointed at the abrupt end to the duel, wondering if he should return to the piano. "Charge his account for every bottle you have and more!"

"What account?" René Darmon sneered. "He has no account. He's no officer, just a rotten pox doctor!"

Standing behind the tall casuarinas, Antonio relieved himself in the garden. A steady drizzle drenched him, and he resembled his padre friend traveling for weeks with a soggy beard and unruly curls. The pale light of the mansion cut him in half and made him seem ghostlike. A swarm of fruit flies came from nowhere and buzzed over his head, made him turn back and he noticed Polly waiting for him at the patio's door.

"Come along, Mr. Prizefighter, I've a surprise for you!"

He expected her to be angry with him, but her eyes were shining. "I was looking for you everywhere!"

He held out his hand, hoping it would be filled with a delicacy from the table, something made especially for him, like grilled sardines for her Tino.

"It's better than you think! Come soon if you want it badly." Polly laughed and left him standing in the rain.

He arrived drunk at the Hart mansion and started to go up the stairs to the veranda. Polly whistled from the reception room and waved at him to come in. From the way she behaved, he thought she had company, pointing with her eyes at the mirror above the fireplace, at the reflection of a young woman, a cloud of smoke twirling around her. Entering the room Antonio saw Arees dressed in anarchist's black—the exquisite rebel, looking much the same as before, as if she had just stepped out of the Nicola or the Café O Greco.

"Ah, my dear Candide!" She said, blowing a kiss of smoke toward him. "How much longer will you stay in your El Dorado?"

❦

A German guard had tripped and fractured his leg on his way back from last night's party, and Antonio was called in early to treat him. Too much drink was blamed for the morning rush, the nurse running out of pills for nausea and headache, and cursing everybody under her breath. Pinchback found him at the hospital.

"Herr Mueller wants us at the firing range, to test our aim and get us ready for the spirit army."

"I thought the war was over," Antonio said, helping the guard to his feet with crutches.

"Not over, but just starting, I should say. It'll take more than a company of foreign troops to stop the mischief makers. Our bosses have ordered all fingers to the trigger, and not without reason."

Arriving late at the German mission, Antonio found the Legation officers and their wives queuing up before two garden tables laid out with handguns and long guns and belts of cartridges. The target at the end of the firing range had been built out of empty cartons from Imbeck's shop, and bore the markings of cheese makers and fine distillers. A comical tiger had been painted over the bull's-eye, the Boxer symbol reminding everyone of their real and immediate target.

Everyone seemed surprisingly steady after the party, eager to test their aim. Herr Mueller issued sharp orders to maintain silence as the shooters were given their instructions at the gun tables. Each would be allowed three tries to hit the target, then asked to return to the back of the queue and await their turn to try again. Only those who earned the title of "perfect shots" would be excused from further trials.

A round of applause greeted Perkyns, and the shy customs agent bowed to acknowledge his three-out-of-three success at the firing range. Monsieur Darmon picked up a Chassepot rifle from the table and gingerly passed his fingers over the sharp edge of its bayonet. Charlie Baxter explained the breech-loading action of the shoulder gun to the Frenchman, while Pinchback stooped over Antonio's shoulder and whispered to him, "It was smart of you not to fight him. He's a coward who acts like a bully. Must've been quaking in his boots waiting for you to accept the wager."

Arees sat at the ladies' table and taught the queue of shooters the basics. She picked up a revolver and spun its cylinder, patiently explaining its action to Sally Hollinger. The Anglican Deaconess returned the gun without firing it, and walked away shaking her head.

Why has she come? It was mad of her to visit China at a time like this. They had hardly spoken during the surprise meeting at Polly's villa. Maybe Ricardo too had come with her, he thought for a brief moment, then abandoned the idea. His friend would've come to his aid if he was indeed at the Legation, and taught the champagne merchant a lesson about fistfights and wagers. And what about Dona Elvira? How could she have let her godson's sister leave Macau with the news of trouble in Peking? Dom Afonso would've surely tried to put his foot down, then given in to the guiles of his wife, resigned to yet another misadventure. He had meant to ask her about the Macau couple, about her brother and her friends from Lisbon's cafés, but Arees had told him about Ricardo even before he could ask.

"My brother is in mourning, and has sent you his apologies. He couldn't return to Peking from Hong Kong because his thoroughbred has come down with a mystery fever and he's spending sleepless nights at the stable."

Polly had laughed seeing the look of surprise on Antonio's face. "Aren't you glad that Arees was home and resting while you were scrapping with Darmon? I should've told you she was here. That way you could've left with me, given the party a miss altogether."

Even then, he hadn't asked Arees why she had come. His mind was still full with the events of the past few weeks. Leaving the Summer Palace had meant more than giving up the pavilion that had been his home for almost a year. It meant giving up all hope of meeting Fumi again. Once he entered the Legation, he'd be cut off from the Chinese, and events might stop him from returning. He had debated with himself whether he should stay and risk starving, wait for Fumi to reappear, or hunt down his sedan bearers while there was still time. He had sulked for a few days then left feeling at odds with himself, moved to turn back several times during his long journey. The Boxers might still prove to be nothing more than a bad dream, he had tried to calm himself; they might simply disappear like pawns in the chess game between the empress and foreigners. He had tried to kindle hope from the fact that the feared siege of the Legation was yet to occur. The empty pavilion had squashed his hopes. He had missed his eunuch friends, and feared for their safety. He had left gifts for them in the kitchen before boarding his sedan: his wristwatch for Tian, the one he'd taught him to wind, and a Bengal cutthroat razor for Wangsheng.

Spotting him in the queue for men, Arees called him over. Pinchback nudged him. "Your Portuguese friend is calling you. She's new, another one of Polly's courtiers."

Linda Harris tried to wave Antonio away to the other table, but Arees overruled her objection. "It's all the same, man or woman."

He was surprised to see how knowledgeable she was, lecturing everyone about the merits and demerits of each firearm. *Did her Republican friends teach her all this . . .?* She led Antonio over to the firing range and handed him a Portuguese Kropatschek rifle popular with the royal army.

"Think of the target as His Majesty Carlos I, our favorite oceanographer, painter, bird-watcher and sailor, who's also the lord of Guinea, Ethiopia, Arabia, Persia and India."

Standing back from the firing line, he took aim.

"With one shot you can turn poor Amélia into a widow." She looked around, and dropped her voice: "you can forget the Boxers, and kill the Bragança instead."

The first shot missed the tiger's tail. He reloaded his gun, and took aim again. *She'd have known the risks of coming . . . must've read all about the Boxers in the papers. Did she fight a wager with her friends . . . ?* He hit the distiller's mark, wide of the target. A sigh went up, and Chris Campbell shouted his encouragement from the back of the queue,

"Come on, Doctor!" Antonio avoided looking at Arees, and shook the Kropatschek rifle as if to set it right for his final shot. Why doesn't she teach me how to kill the tiger? he thought, suddenly feeling like a novice after years of game shooting.

She must've come for me.

Antonio failed to hit the target on his third try. He handed the rifle back to Arees and left the firing range.

"Stop!" Polly ran after him, grabbing his arm. "Where do you think you're going?"

He pointed at the hospital, and kept walking.

"And what about Arees? Haven't you noticed her yet? Or are you blind to everyone except your patients?" She stood before him, forcing him to stop. "Why didn't you speak to her at the house? We were waiting for you to return from that stupid party. She was waiting. I could see that she was anxious, and why wouldn't she be? It isn't easy to come here at the best of times. She'd had to take a lot of risks, and must've worried everyone to death. And you? You just pretended you hardly knew her, asked a few silly questions and went to sleep like a rotten drunk." She shook her head, "And all along, I'd hoped . . ."

"What?"

"That you'd be thrilled. It'd break your sullen mood, bring you back to life after all that's happened with your father and with Fumi. They'd be up all night, I thought, talking their hearts out. You'd be relieved to find someone from home, someone who knew who you were exactly."

Antonio started to walk with Polly beside him, till they reached the hospital's compound. He saw a line of patients waiting for him.

"Why didn't you ask her why she has come? If she had missed you while you were away? If she has come to take you home?"

Polly stood at the gate and said angrily, "Treating your patients. Is that all you know and care about?"

The foreign guards, about 350 men, had arrived by train from Tientsin and marched over briskly to the Legation with bayonets fixed and ready. They were received by the residents with great applause, although opinions differed with respect to which group among them looked the smartest. The Americans and the British were the top contenders, although the Japanese, everyone agreed, looked the most menacing. Once inside, guards from all nationalities camped along the massive Tartar wall that formed the northern boundary of the Legation. Their officers wasted no time in recruiting the refugees to form gangs of coolies and build barricades around the missions particularly those that were believed to be close to the enemy's firing line. Digging of bombproof shelters took more time than expected, with annoyed residents complaining of the clouds of dust that set everyone's lungs on fire. The guards were under strict orders to ignore the Chinese imperial troops that were gathering in plain sight across the Tartar wall, and were instructed to hold their cool when a rock landed at their feet or when one of their native coolies was taunted and called a traitor. It'd be easy to lose one's head and fire off a few rounds, fall into the empress's trap of starting a skirmish. They were told to be watchful though, checking for spies, rounding up those seen to be loitering about suspiciously near the officers' villas.

The Russian guards brought over to the hospital a man, his nose bloodied. Tall and thin, with heavy features and a protruding chin, he didn't resemble the peasants, dressed unlike them in the manner of a servant who had stolen his master's clothes. The wrinkled skin made him look older than he was, and his face had swollen from the beating. The headmen among the refugees had failed to recognize him; he himself had failed, on interrogation, to spell out the reason why he had entered the Legation, except to offer the lame excuse of being a messenger.

"Messenger or liar!" Charlie Baxter, who was passing by, had stopped to join the crowd of onlookers and thrown a punch at the intruder. To everyone's surprise, the man had started to weep like a child and said something about wanting to meet a doctor and pass on his message.

Antonio recognized Wangsheng instantly, and drew him into the ward. The newly arrived Russians, unaware of the doctor's reputation, weren't prepared to take his word that the intruder was innocent. They were reluctant to let him go, and blocked the hospital's door. The eunuch whimpered as Antonio dressed the wounds and scolded him for his foolishness.

"You are stupid to come out here. What if the Boxers had caught you? You know what they'd have done to a 'tail-less man,' don't you?" Wangsheng winced as Antonio rubbed tincture into the open gash on his cheek. "If not the Boxers, the Kansu soldiers would've had fun with a eunuch surely, made you dance to their drums. Where did you leave your nephew, or has he been caught by the Savages already?"

Wangsheng raised his weepy eyes to Antonio. "Dr. Xu wanted me to come here and tell you."

"Tell me that I must return and continue my lessons?"

"No." Wangsheng kept quiet, then spoke looking at the floor. "He came to look for Fumi. He asked us where the two of you were hiding. If we had seen you anywhere in the palace. He didn't believe us when we said that you'd left, and he asked me to find you. He said he has something important to tell you, and that you must go to his house."

Something important . . . Antonio gave the eunuch a clean shirt to wear over his loose-fitting pants, and offered him a shot of whiskey to relieve the pain. The eunuch refused. There were shouts to open the door followed by loud banging. The crowd outside was demanding that the spy be handed over to them for further interrogations. Antonio stopped himself from coming out of the ward and taking on the mob single-handedly. The Legation had seen a sea change in the past weeks. He was unknown to the newcomers, and many of the refugees were in murderous mood having narrowly survived the Boxer atrocities. The other doctors and the nurse had disappeared smelling trouble, and he wished he could send word to the mission officers to come over and throw their weight behind him.

"Why did you disappear with Tian and leave me alone in the pavilion?"

"We were told it'd be better that way," Wangsheng mumbled.

"Better for whom? You mean it'd be better to starve me to death?" He waited for an answer, then pressed on, "Who told you to leave?"

Wangsheng kept his eyes lowered as the sound of banging increased. Antonio took a quick peek through the shutters to see if he could spot someone familiar.

"It was Fumi," Wangsheng muttered under her breath. "She told us to go away for a few days then come back after you'd left. She said it was the only way to make you leave the Summer Palace."

You must leave. . . . He heard her voice in his ear. It was hard for him to imagine that Fumi had schemed his removal from the palace behind his back. The eunuch pleaded with his eyes to be forgiven. "We knew you'd be angry, but she told us that it was the best way to save your life."

"Do you know where she is now?"

Wangsheng shook his head, and glanced fearfully at the door which was on the verge of breaking. Charlie Baxter's voice bellowed over the din, demanding that the "scoundrel" be let out.

Finished with his patient, Antonio opened the door and faced the American gold miner. The Russian guards flanked him on both sides, ahead of the crowd of onlookers, mostly refugees who had their own scores to settle with Boxers. A bugle sounded at a distance, and martial music played at the soldiers' camps along the Legation's canal.

"Why bother with a few stitches when you've got to do a lot more when we're finished with him?" Charlie taunted Antonio and looked past him for a glimpse of Wangsheng.

"Finished with what?" Antonio asked him coldly.

"In America we call it gouging. It'll take a tiny bit of that to get him talking."

"What if he doesn't?"

"All spies talk." The miner tried to push Antonio aside and enter the hospital, spurred on by the guards.

"He isn't a spy." Antonio stopped him, holding firm to the doorposts. "He's innocent, just a visitor here. He's come to give me a message."

Charlie sniggered. "That's what spies do! What message did he bring for you?" Turning back to the crowd, he asked them for evidence, releasing a flood of voices. The man was seen snooping around and trying to enter the Hart villa when he was stopped and turned away. The scoundrel had tried next to scale the walls, but he wasn't equal to the task. There was a roar of laughter. He tried to bribe a poor peasant boy with a few coins to show him the way to the hospital when an old lady had raised the alarm.

"He isn't a peasant like them, as you can see from his clothes," Charlie Baxter argued. "Must be a Boxer dressed up to look like a poor mandarin. Could've been a secret assassin even, looking to finish off our Cedric."

"He isn't a Boxer," Antonio said calmly. "Not even a man. He's a eunuch, and he's my friend."

Charlie looked stunned, then roared with laughter. "Your friend a eunuch?"

"He couldn't be a spy, because the Boxers hate 'incomplete men,' they wouldn't trust them to fight foreigners."

The crowd started to get restless, chanting for the Boxer spy to be handed over. The Russians seemed agitated as well, and Charlie narrowed his eyes and challenged Antonio. "How can we be sure he's indeed what you say? What's your wager? I mean a *real* one, not like last night's that you refused to pay."

Asking everyone to step back, Antonio grabbed Wangsheng by the hand. He brought him out before the crowd and pulled down his pants. A hush descended upon those gathered, followed by jeering and laughter. Charlie Baxter gave a loud curse as Wangsheng covered his face with both hands and started to weep.

Antonio sat in Polly's garden, his mind still on the day's events at the hospital. He had been filled with fury, watching the flood of tears stream down Wangsheng's face, ready to take on the Russians and Charlie Baxter and finish off last night's wager. His restraint had surprised him at that moment, and he felt guilty now for having shamed his friend to save him from the lynching crowd. Word of the incident had reached Polly, and she had called him over. Offering him a drink of persimmon fruit, known to cure insomnia, she returned to her friendly ways. "You must spend time in the garden away from the hospital and the camps, otherwise you'll fall sick like your patients." Calling Arees over, she left him sitting under the canopy of Chinese lilacs.

Antonio rose and greeted Arees. They walked along the garden path admiring the spring peonies that had just bloomed, with bees buzzing around them. A train of kites circled the flower beds, and it seemed they were strolling in Lisbon's Jardim Botânico.

"Why didn't you reply to my letter?" Arees asked him. He kept quiet.

"You were busy with your lessons, we heard, from word that came through. Waiting for your letter, I thought you're close to finding your answer. Our Candide will be back soon after his marvelous adventure!" She smiled cheerfully. "You are close now, aren't you?"

Antonio broke off a twig and twirled it around absentmindedly. *I must tell her now, tell her everything.*

"It'll take four seasons, you had said, to learn the Chinese cure. It must be time now for . . ."

"I have failed with syphilis." He spoke, looking up at the thicket of branches that covered the sky. "After all these months, I am no closer to my answer than I was back in Lisbon. If the Chinese have a cure for the pox, they haven't revealed it to me yet. And they might never do."

"But your teacher had promised to, hadn't he? Didn't you write me after you arrived here?"

Antonio nodded. "He had, and with every passing month I thought I was getting closer. I grew impatient, waiting to see him practice his cure on a patient; I wanted to try out the method with my own hands. I wished to see as many victims as I could, visit hospitals, examine corpses, do everything possible to learn what the Chinese know about syphilis. And then everything changed, I no longer knew what I'd come here to find."

They watched a squirrel run around a tree. The evening star appeared on the sky and temple gongs mixed with the sound of a marching drill.

"But there must be an answer. Maybe it's just waiting to be found. Waiting for someone brave. It could simply be a matter of time before we know it."

Antonio shook his head. "That's what I thought before I came here. A doctor must be an explorer, ready to go where no one's gone before, to learn the cures to all the sicknesses in this world. He mustn't shy away from danger. And if he's pure, he'll find what he's after. But" — he paused, then went on — "Maybe the answer he wants doesn't need to be discovered, but felt, just as we feel love when we have it."

"Is that what your teachers have taught you here?"

Antonio sighed. "They've taught me to look inside the doctor to know what makes him suffer for his patients, what gives him hope and how to go on living even when he fails." He stopped to watch the fireflies dance inside a bamboo grove. Arees tapped him on the shoulder and pointed at a tree shaped like a deer, its trunk twisted by the gardeners to resemble the animal.

"So they might've already taught you everything you need to know." Arees spoke quietly.

They walked back in silence to the Hart villa. Guards shouting orders to their native helpers distracted them from their thoughts. Creaking wagons snaked past the Jade Canal carrying supplies to the camps, and roars went up as crates of ammunition were unloaded. The occasional gunshot brought moments of stillness, only to be broken by sharper calls and louder cries.

"Did you meet a Boxer on your way here?" Antonio asked Arees.

She shook her head. "No, I wish I did; I would've liked to have seen what he looks like, if he's just as harmless as our friends in Lisbon or a real spirit soldier."

"They must be real,"—Antonio chuckled—"otherwise they won't be of any help to the invisible empress."

"Maybe the invisible is as worried as we are." Arees smiled. "Maybe she's suffering too and doesn't know how to cure herself, just as we don't."

Listening to Arees, Antonio thought about his friend Joachim Saldanha, what he had told him about the Chinese on more than one occasion, reminded him that "they weren't any different, but just as weak as us." He looked admiringly at her. *How did she manage to know so much in such a short time?*

"And you?" he asked her. "What have *you* come here to find?" He waited to see if she'd say what was really on her mind, or offer a clever argument.

She pursed her lips to blow out a mouthful of smoke, then replied, "I didn't know what I'd set out to find exactly, but thought it was time to see with my own eyes how Candide is getting on with his little adventure."

Sitting under a parasol, Polly waved at them and held up a "real drink" to toast their "reunion." Exchanging a knowing glance with Arees, she invited them over, and plunged right into the day's big story.

"The *real* spy has left the Legation. He's taken Helga to his ancestral home a hundred miles away. It's auspicious for the child to be born among grandparents, he's told everyone, but that's not the real reason."

"Which means we won't have a chance to see the Chinese-American-German baby when it's born!" Arees made a glum face.

"If the parents are anything to go by, he'll be both intelligent and greedy!" Polly whispered the story of Helga and her ex-husband to Arees, while Antonio sat quietly.

"What if it's a *she*?"

"Then she'll be unstoppable!" Polly called her maid and instructed her to make up a proper bed with mosquito nets for Antonio in the veranda. "It must be well arranged to feel like a real bedroom, with a washstand and clothes rack. We can't have you prowling the streets while we sleep in comfort, can we?" She begged Arees's pardon for putting her up in the "tiniest room of the house," traditionally reserved for a lady when she was ready to go into labor.

"What's the real reason?" Antonio asked Polly.

"You mean for Yohan leaving?"

He nodded. Polly laughed nervously. "Maybe he's got advance wind of the Boxers coming to storm our nest."

The city was unsafe despite the arrival of the allied guards, and it took Antonio a fair effort to convince the driver of a mule cart to ferry him over for a visit to Xu. He asked Chris Campbell, who by now was accustomed to his strange habits, to come along for the trip to see his old *Nei ching* teacher. "There'll be something in the journey for you as well," he told him. "You can find out for yourself how the locals are coping with the imperial army and the Boxers on their doorsteps." Chris agreed. The *Times* could do with a report from the front lines, giving gory accounts of public executions, even a sighting of the dowager as she went about inspecting her soldiers in her royal sedan.

They ran into Hanna Mueller and Kristin loitering around the refugee camps. The young woman had recovered sufficiently, and was out with her sketchbook to add a few Boxer victims to her pictorial diary of the China visit. Chris Campbell smiled at her. There seemed to be something going on between them. Antonio had seen him posing for her at the French mission's party, waiting for his portrait to be finished. He had also seen the two of them slink away from the firing range to walk along the smelly canal holding hands. Leaving the Legation, Antonio teased his companion, cautioning him against missing a golden opportunity.

"You should insist that Kristin stay back while you're here in Peking. Otherwise she'll find a German boy to pose for her when she's home."

Blushing, Chris complained of the matronly Hanna. "She's keeping her locked up under the pretense of sickness, when she's fit enough to scale the Great Wall."

"You could have London publishers salivating with your account of the Boxer revolt accompanied by her sketches. Just imagine what a great hit that'd be."

A nervous Chris Campbell kept up a constant chat as they passed through the empty streets. Residents and shopkeepers had disappeared as if in the aftermath of an earthquake. In places there were signs of looting. Well-planned fires had reduced neighborhoods to ashes; smashed doors and vacant shelves gaped at the trail of items left behind by the thieves. Boxer banners welcomed them as they entered deserted villages, their moats dammed up by bloated corpses. The mule driver cracked his whip and sped past torture grounds, guarded by dogs that prowled like wolves looking for things to eat. Midway into their journey the reporter wanted to turn back.

He smiled sheepishly at Antonio: "The trick of journalism is to be well prepared. We must come back another time with a proper escort. Cedric can help us, can't he?" A cloud of smoke appeared on the horizon and made him stutter. The mule driver gave them a questioning look, and Antonio asked him to drive on, pointing at a lane that branched off the main thoroughfare.

"Nothing can be worse than getting lost in Boxer country." Chris looked pleadingly at Antonio. "It can be a lot worse than at Fengtai. We wouldn't have a Saldanha to save us, would we?"

Should I tell him the truth or calm him with lies?

"What makes you think that your teacher hasn't fled his home? What makes you think he's alive even?" Chris showed impatience. "Why are we going on this wild goose chase?"

"Because it's something important." Antonio looked for the bamboo bridge that led to Xu's house on stilts.

"More important than our lives?" Chris threw up his hands in despair. "Why don't you go by yourself then, and let me return to the Legation."

"It could well be the most important story of your life. More important than Boxers."

He left Chris Campbell stunned on the cart and asked the driver to wait for him. Then he crossed over the bamboo bridge on foot to reach Xu's peasant home. It seemed deserted, a faint lamp casting a ghastly shadow on the barren courtyard normally cackling with geese. The Horseman has left, he thought, he's escaped up north fearing a cavalry charge. He's taken his wife along, the two of them are waiting for the empress to crush the Boxers before they return to the palace. Without a neighbor in sight, who could tell him where he'd gone and for how long? He felt bitter all over again as he regretted the time lost learning *Nei ching. Why has he called me over? Is it to tell me about the cure for Canton rash? Why has he waited this long?* He wondered if it was a clever ploy to have him leave the Legation only to be captured and killed by the Boxers. *He wants his revenge for Fumi.* A low cough broke into his thoughts. Someone was inside, and he proceeded with caution, coming up to the unlocked door to take a look.

Xu slept on his bed like an invalid with his mouth open, a half-eaten meal by his side. The room smelled of opium. He looked different, like a sick or a dying man, in an ankle length robe and a skull cap, with gray stubble on his chin and both hands clasped to his chest as if guarding himself from a painful blow. An oil lamp glowed on the silver opium pipe and the jar of black mud at his bedside, spreading its shadow play on the addict sunk into his *yen* sleep. His nostrils quivered and eyelids fluttered, then he shifted on his side and knocked the pipe off the stool. Antonio picked it up and held the warm bowl in the palm of his hand. Xu opened his eyes wide as if he had been awake all along.

"I've come to see your wife."

His teacher motioned him to sit, and held out his hand. Antonio stood still, then passed him the pipe which Xu accepted gratefully. "Will you tell me where she is?"

With a great effort Xu opened the lid of the opium jar and dipped a needle into it, holding it up to the lamp's flame till the dark mud softened like clay and dropped into the pipe's bowl.

Antonio looked at him through the smoke, measuring up the *Nei ching* master who'd promised to teach him the Canons and the Yellow

Emperor's cure for pox. The man who was the husband of his lover.

Xu shook his head. "I thought she was with you."

"Me?" He wondered if this was yet another trick played by the Horseman.

"She's not at the palace, not anymore. Where else could she have gone, if not with you?" Xu looked searchingly at him. "That's why I came to your pavilion, to find out where you'd taken her."

Antonio's heart sank. So that's why his teacher had sent him word to come. He has nothing new to tell me, except to accuse me of stealing his wife. His anger rose, and he circled the bed inside the small room.

"She can't be with me, you know that, don't you? She can't be my wife, because she's yours."

Xu watched him closely and drew on his pipe. A sudden gust of wind threw open a window, and he looked out at the fading light. Then he made a sign for Antonio to sit at the foot of his bed and spoke slowly.

"She was never mine. Do you know about Jacob, the Dutchman?"

"Yes." Antonio nodded.

"She was his. He was the one she loved. I was just her husband, the one she married to stay alive."

A gong sounded in the distance, followed by a horn. Xu cocked his head, then kept on speaking while he looked out of the window. "I saved her from her troubles after Jacob was killed. When I met her, she was grieving for him, but afraid for her own life as well. She knew his assassins—the man who had come with his Chinese servant and set the printing press on fire—and they knew her too. Jacob had told her about the danger they were both in. She couldn't live alone and needed the protection of a husband, a powerful husband."

"And so, you . . ."

"I taught her *Nei ching* and took her to the palace to attend to the empress, the royals and the visitors. As my wife, she had her mistress's trust; she could do as she pleased, come and go whenever she liked, live a life free from fear."

The sound of the horn grew louder and stoking his pipe, Xu said hoarsely, "No one knows the real story about me and Fumi. Except Oscar, my American friend, and his wife, my sister Lixia. They know that I'm not her real husband. She wouldn't have any other man but

Jacob. All I could do to save her life was to marry her."

"That's why she didn't live here, but lived at the palace." Antonio whispered to himself.

Xu nodded. "That's why she always remained my assistant, never became my wife."

"But . . ." Antonio hesitated, then decided to go ahead. "You knew about us, didn't you?"

"Yes." The elderly doctor raised himself on the bed, and looked deep into Antonio's eyes. "Wangsheng is my friend, and I've castrated his nephew. They told me everything. I knew it too from the way Fumi changed after she started teaching you. I knew that she'd stopped grieving."

"Did you know she was as good a teacher as you?"

"And I thought I could save her once again." Xu interrupted Antonio before he could go on any further. "Save her from the husband that she didn't love. When you came to the palace, I thought Jacob had returned for his Fumi."

He was astonished hearing the very same words that Fumi had said to him. "How could you save her again?"

Xu laughed quietly. "By letting my wife fall madly in love with you. By having the two of you live like emperor and empress in the Summer Palace. I wanted to disappear and let her teach you *Nei ching* so that you'd be together. I hoped. . . ." Xu fell silent, and an immense sadness spread over his face.

"Hoped for what?"

"That you'd take her away with you. Maybe you'd free her poor husband from waiting for her love."

A band of musicians seemed to be passing by the bridge, followed by marching feet. A bullhorn roared above the music, accompanied by strange howls. A swish cut through air like a whip. Clashing cymbals of a wedding procession drowned all the noise, and then the horn resumed.

Antonio strained his ears to catch Xu's whispered words: "Take her with you and leave China." Like a helpless invalid, his teacher tried to hobble up from the bed. "Find her before it's too late."

"Too late for what?"

Xu cast a frantic look outside the window. "Before she loses her mind again."

Antonio rose and held Xu firmly by the shoulders. He drew him close. "And syphilis? Are you a real doctor or a fake? Did you lie to me when you promised to teach me the cure?" The sound beat down on them like a monster, rattling the windows, the marching feet blew up a cloud of dust that rushed inside like a sudden explosion. Antonio held Xu by the neck and shouted into his face, "Tell me the truth. Can you cure the pox?"

His teacher didn't answer, but pointed to the window.

"Where? Where would I find it?"

"Look outside," Xu managed to say before dropping down on the bed.

Antonio ran out of the hut to lose himself in the crowd of marchers. The musicians were upon him, dressed in white, carrying their instruments like bearers at a funeral. A short man in a red coat shouted orders, while a mandarin sat impassively on a sedan chair behind him. Chris Campbell grabbed his arm and dragged him toward an empty lane. "Quick!" Gasping for breath, he spoke into Antonio's ear in spurts. "It's the march of death. The empress has announced her annual sentences for undesirables, and the prisoners are being marched over to the execution ground."

"Undesirable?"

"Criminals, addicts, and those suffering from incurable and infectious diseases, on their way to be hanged or beheaded on butchers' blocks."

Soldiers dragged the prisoners along bound with chains. Heavy breathing mixed with groans and sobs. They crawled along the banks of the canal like animals taken to slaughter, or an army of insects risen from the soil and turning it black. A deep bloodlike trail followed them, the prisoners' necks smeared with oil to make it easier for the executioners to chop them off. The convicts carried boards that announced their crimes and sworn confessions: a dwarf who'd murdered his parents for giving him birth; a whore who'd poisoned her lover for breaking his promise to marry her; a thief who stole babies from nursing mothers to sell to impotent lords. A pale-faced creature who could be either man or woman held up a sign with the picture of an opium pipe. Antonio spotted several carrying crude drawings of their diseases: frightening sores and ugly eruptions all over their bodies and disfigured genitals. Rows of prisoners passed him with their lifeless eyes, bald heads and half-eaten noses. He smelled the revolting smell of syphilis.

"They might take us along too if they spotted us." Chris trembled, keeping his head down behind a fence. "Maybe the empress has issued edicts for undesirable foreigners as well." He glared at Antonio. "We'd be safe if we hadn't been foolish." A snarling guard passed them a hair's breadth away, spitting on the ground barely inches from their feet.

Antonio saw the woman of his nightmare, young and suffering. Wearing a white chemise and a turban around her head, she seemed almost invisible. She had fallen behind the rest, and slipped past the guards to run away to the open fields. Her cloudlike form floated effortlessly over the slush and mud. She appeared to be a high-ranking concubine; her delicate features made her out even to be the wife of a mandarin. She could be an innocent victim, or the carrier who'd infected hundreds. He lost her among the tall reeds on the riverbank. Craning over the fence, with Chris trying to pull him down, Antonio caught a glimpse of her taking off her chemise, her luxuriant hair sprouting like spring foliage, as she moved like a dancer with clear and languid steps: a naked angel blooming with a thousand rosebuds. *Death . . . that's the simple cure. . . .* Oscar Franklin whispered in his ear, and as she entered the river Antonio shouted at her to stop. He broke free of his companion, seeing her sink under the water, and bounded through the fields. He charged after her, slipping and falling on the muddy slopes and reached the bank, then gaped at the surging stream on the verge of drowning the fields in spring floods.

Polly woke him at midnight. A maid has fallen sick, Antonio thought. Perhaps it was her asthma, or Cedric's liver that troubled him from time to time. Dressed in their nightgowns, she and Arees led him downstairs from the veranda and out of the mansion. Patrolling guards saluted as they walked along the canal, passing the Russian quarters to reach the Harris mansion. John Harris received them at the door and led them up to the attic. As he entered, Antonio heard a whimpering sound. Linda knelt at the feet of Norma Cook, holding a wash basin while a maid fanned the elderly widow, who sat on a straight-backed chair holding out her arms.

"A perfect nuisance. . . !" John Harris muttered under his breath, and pointed at the thin streams of blood that dripped down from Norma's hands to the basin.

Linda spoke without rising: "She's slashed her wrists." She glared at Norma, who sat impassively on the chair, wiping her tears with a hand-kerchief embroidered with the reverend's initials. "The maid was woken by a rat and heard her crying. If it weren't for her, she'd be dead by now."

It didn't take Antonio long to stop the bleeding and close the cuts. Fortunately, the wounds weren't deep enough. She had simply managed to scar her wrists with her husband's rusty razor that she had recovered from his Shanxi lodge. Finished with bandaging, he slung up her arms and had the maid hold a feeding cup to her lips for a shot of whiskey.

"You won't let me die, will you?" Between sips, Norma Cook spoke to him in a tearful voice.

He broke down before the widow and started to cry, sobbing in great bursts that startled Polly and Arees. Linda Harris hurried her maid out of the attic and stood with her husband at the door. Kneeling by the chair, he buried his head in Norma's lap and wept the tears for all those he'd loved but failed to save.

❋

Tensions kept mounting week after week with the Legation crammed full of refugees and imperial soldiers blocking off all exits to the north of the Tartar wall. Skirmishes had started some days earlier when a picket of Italian guards was attacked while everyone was taking a well-deserved nap after the night patrols. Heavy casualties were inflicted; the soldiers were late to react to what they thought were fire-crackers to mark the coming Dragon Boat festival. The city's churches were set on fire. The French orphanage of the Cathedral of Immaculate Conception was wrecked, as were shops catering to foreigners. Jewelers, furriers and goldsmiths had begged the rebels on their knees to spare them, but all it took for sparks to fly was the discovery of a Burma teak plaque carved with an ode to Queen Victoria, commissioned by the head of Jardines, the opium giant, among the collectibles. Reams of silk burned in the bonfire, along with lanterns and fans, and priceless furniture stolen from the royal palaces for the enjoyment of merchants and officers.

Mr. Pinchback was emphatic: "We were foolish to celebrate too soon. A mere four hundred foreign soldiers can't measure up to four million Boxers plus the imperial troops. They'll have more rats in their trap now, unless the world declares war on the Chinese soon." Last night's shelling of the missions had left more than a dozen dead and the hospital's floors were full of bodies, the stench of human blood made intolerable by the warm weather. Everyone had stayed up, ears ringing with flying bullets making a noise like crying cats, and the thud of shells.

The officers were most perturbed by the murder of one of their own kind, Mr. Itami, the Japanese consul. The short man with clean-cut looks and immaculate manners was strolling in his garden in the morning, doing what he most enjoyed—feeding the birds in his famous aviary and imitating their calls—when a volley of shrapnel cut him down. He had bled to death in front of the birds that watched him in silence through the nets. Leaving the hospital, Antonio was cornered by Mr. Pinchback, visibly agitated by the death of "important people, not simply the refugees."

"You know what's happened to Yohan, don't you?" Antonio shook his head.

"He was found in his ancestral home with his throat slit, along with his three young sisters in lovely clothes, all of them lying dead in a row." Mr. Pinchback grimaced.

"The Chinese have killed their own spy?" Antonio exclaimed in disbelief.

"Spy, my foot! Everyone knew him to be a weakling, a dandy passing himself off as someone important. The Chinese had seen right through him. The most troubling thing is that he was killed for being a foreigner, his death note condemning him for fathering a child with a white witch."

"And Helga?" Antonio asked nervously.

"She's delivered a bonny girl, who'll sadly never see her father.

Luckily, her in-laws had taken her and her child to be blessed at a Buddhist monastery when the mischief happened."

Polly came to join the two of them, looking more anxious than Antonio had ever seen her. He thought she was concerned with the foreign guards, some of whom had gone berserk at the sight of dead dogs thrown at them over the wall by Chinese soldiers and fired more than a hundred rounds. There were unconfirmed reports of a Russian guard misbehaving with a refugee girl, and a brawl breaking out between hotheads on either side. Pinchback tried to calm her even before she could spell out her worries.

"The Chinese will run out of dogs to shoot, if we manage to hold fire for just a few days more. You don't want this war to go down in history as the great canine conflict!"

"Not dogs," Polly spoke nervously. "It's Arees."

"You mean the Portuguese girl?" Pinchback took a quick look at Antonio. "What's happened to her now?"

Polly shrugged. "She left some hours ago, and should've been back by now."

"Left why, with whom and to go where?" Pinchback narrowed his eyes. *Polly Hart letting out her visitor at a time like this!* His disbelief showed plainly in his voice, at the exceptional lack of judgment from someone usually so reliable.

"She's gone out with Ferguson. He promised to show her the sights of the Tartar city before it's burnt down."

"I thought your best friend has left Peking," Antonio remarked caustically.

"Not left, but hiding."

"We're all hiding from the Boxers, but why's he hiding from us?" Antonio snorted at Polly's lame excuse. He was angry at her for trusting the gypsy and letting Arees disappear with him. "Where could they be hiding now?"

"He must've taken her home to show off his treasures," said Polly sheepishly.

"Then why don't you ask Cedric to send his Sikh fighters to rescue her?"

"And who'll rescue her from the Sikhs?" She looked pleadingly at Antonio. "You must find her . . . after all she's your . . ."

Busy with casualties at the hospital, he hadn't met Arees since his return from Xu's house, although he had caught a glimpse of her as he went pedaling to the camps. Like strangers they had exchanged greetings from a distance, and he had noticed Dona Elvira's lucky charm on her neck.

"Are you thinking of a rescue mission?" Pinchback asked him after Polly had left. "You'd be mad to play the savior. Fortunately, you don't have far to go. It won't take you long to reach Ferguson's villa, especially on the backs of my sedan bearers."

Antonio looked quizzically. Pinchback explained: "They've been smoking opium all morning, and can't tell a Boxer from a dead dog by now. They wouldn't mind taking you out on a ride." The banker held out his hand and offered Antonio his terse parting words: "Hope to see you in my next life if I don't see you again in this one."

From the outside, the Chinese villa looked intact, guarded by the casuarinas, but bore a look of desolation like all other mansions of the Tartar city. Without a guard or a servant to show him in, Antonio walked up to the courtyard through the arched gates and into the parlor. The young servant he'd met before was packing up a large wooden box and stood up to greet him. Stacks of manuscripts lay piled on the floor along with empty trunks and a variety of scrolls. The sun glinted on a broken mirror, and lit up the jumble of furniture and bric-a-brac that had turned the well-appointed room into an old and dusty curio shop. The young boy smiled shyly, and looked around to find a chair for him to sit on.

Ferguson staggered into the room cradling a pile of books, and dropped them at the servant's feet. "Where's Arees? Have you brought her here?" Antonio asked him anxiously.

"Ah, the Pox Warrior!" the gypsy nodded and motioned to him to sit. "You've nothing to worry about." He ordered the young man to bring over his medicinal whiskey, and poured a generous inch for himself and another for Antonio.

"You'll meet her soon, but first I must offer you my apologies. I've failed to find your Boxer manuals. They've all disappeared, and my scouts have returned empty-handed. But you won't need them anymore. The Boxers are here, they'll show you all their tricks!" Taking a large swig from his glass, he thumped on the stack of old books setting off a cloud of dust. "They're looting everything, including the garden flowers! In just a few days they'll destroy the Great Chinese Civilization! Smash and burn everything that's been touched by the foreign hand. They'll kill each other in order to destroy us. And the Big Fat Buddha will bless her brave spirit soldiers, turn every man into a eunuch and every woman into a palace whore."

"Will you be moving into the Legation then?" Antonio asked.

Wiping his sweaty face on the sleeves of his Jesuit robe, Ferguson gave him a cocky smile. "I'm not stupid, Dr. Maria. The Legation is unsafe, you know that well, don't you? There'll be a bloodbath soon, and personal scores will be settled. No one will escape, not even our dear old Polly."

"What personal scores?" He rose to pace the room, with Ferguson sitting on a trunk and drinking from the bottle. The heat spread like the flames of an oven, burning the soles of his feet and inching up rapidly. He picked up an empty water pitcher, and wondered where the gypsy would hide his treasures till the troubles ended. The young servant ran into the room and tried to attract his master's attention, but Ferguson waved him away and dropped his voice.

"Never mind the Boxers, it's better to talk about someone else."

Antonio raised an eyebrow.

"She's upstairs, your friend from Lisbon. Your *special* friend, should we say?" He smirked at Antonio. "Maybe she's the wife you left behind . . . ?" Coming up to Antonio, he laid a hand on his shoulder. "Don't worry, I haven't told her anything."

"Told her what?" He moved away from Ferguson.

"About your golden lily, the one and only one that you've had in China." He inched up closer to Antonio, and spoke into his ear, "The one you've had a fight with over her dead lover, the one who pretends to teach you *Nei ching*, the one that made you angry and punch the foolish Frenchman, the one with whom you've tried the Butterfly and the Pigeon, the Ox and the Monkey, tried all the thirty positions, haven't you!"

He pushed Ferguson away and started climbing up the stairs, just as the servant reappeared and tugged on his master's arm with great agitation.

"You can read your wife the *Memories of the Plum Cottage*. I can have the book sent up for you if you like. You can give her a taste of China that she's never had before." Dragged away by the young servant, Ferguson laughed deliriously, "Polly thinks she's come all the way from home just to win you back . . . poor girl . . . !"

Arees was sitting on the floor of an empty room and smoking. Antonio started to tell her how worried Polly had been at her absense, but she hushed him with a finger, drew him out onto the balcony and pointed through the casuarinas. A large crowd had gathered outside the villa, waving giant banners. They looked like a peasant army, armed with clubs, swords and spears and were advancing in a ragged line. Many were quite young, led by priests dressed in red and chanting, exhorting the crowd with their incantations. Hundreds of joss sticks set off a cloud of smoke above the crowd and it seemed as if a funeral procession had made its way through the wall of trees. The advance party had started a war dance, the peasants leaping up into the air and dropping down in grand acrobatic swoops.

"Boxers!" Antonio whispered.

They heard the servant scream as he dashed out of the parlor into the courtyard with Ferguson running after him, cursing the foolish boy and wrestling him down to the ground before he could scale the walls and land in the Boxers' laps. They were surrounded on all sides and there was no way to escape, except to hide inside a book box, hoping to fool the rebels and have them move on to yet another villa in search of villainous foreigners. The courtyard resounded with the crash of glass and porcelain as master and servant emptied the treasure crates that were large enough to hold them both.

A young rebel dismounted at the gate and walked into the courtyard flanked by a small group. Spotting Ferguson and the servant, they raised a cry of triumph, and within moments the Boxers were inside the walls. Antonio and Arees hid on the balcony and heard them go from room to room, smashing things, breaking down doors and windows. Pots and pans were thrown out of the kitchen, chickens and ducks cut loose from the coops, the birds darting out in a rush of feathers. Bricks and pieces of tiles flew all over the courtyard. The peasant soldiers kicked open the crates, and a jumble of ivory and jade spilled out of them.

There was a mad scramble with their leader shouting orders in a shrill voice to stop the looting, and soon a bonfire was lit with the soldiers lifting up the empty crates and hurling them into the flames. *Where's the gypsy and his servant?* What if they were hiding inside an empty crate? The young boy had stopped screaming. Antonio looked down from the balcony and found him kneeling before the garden shrine, held down by a Boxer's boot and praying for his life.

What will the gypsy do now — the scholar, the adventurer, and the merchant, who was blessed with the cunning of a fox? What bargain could he strike with the Boxers? Antonio waited to hear him speak in his loud and mocking voice, inviting perhaps a suitable response. Maybe the priests would start their chanting again and call off the attack, sparing his life.

They heard each other's nervous breathing, crouching behind the mahogany balcony rails. The horse head dagger pistol he had pinched from Cedric's collection of handguns gnawed at his side and Antonio took it out from his waist buckle. Down in the parlor, Ferguson sat on his thronelike chair, bound hand and foot, with the Boxers surrounding him. He was pleading with them to release his servant, who wailed loudly as a peasant made a move to thrust a spear into his heart. The Boxer leader stopped him, then silenced the boy with a single gunshot.

A young voice started to recite a list of crimes in Chinese, each one of them followed by a roar from the crowd. The gypsy replied after a short silence. He seemed to be denying the charges, offering long explanations for his behavior. What are the Boxers accusing him of? Putting his meager Chinese to work, Antonio tried to catch the words that spoke of profiteering and hoarding, hoodwinking innocents to part with their treasures, threatening all those who were witnesses to his crimes, and murdering a poor man by setting him on fire. With the list exhausted, a hush descended on the parlor. Then the Boxer leader spoke to the crowd, calling for a few volunteers. *He'll be tortured now . . .* Antonio whispered to Arees under his breath. Ferguson howled as his accuser read out the charges again, without waiting for answers. The crowd started to chant, and a roar went up with every confession, the priests spurring on the acrobats to perform their feats as a mark of celebration. The two on the balcony shut their ears with their palms as the howling grew louder. He wasn't offering any arguments but pleading now to be pardoned, appealing for his life and to be let off. Miserable shrieks and moans drowned out the young voice, appearing at times to be personal pleas for help from someone the gypsy knew.

There were no more words from Ferguson when the final verdict was read out. The crowd quieted down too, and a flurry of rain seemed to arrive from nowhere, rustling the casuarinas, and scattered bird feathers in the courtyard. Almost an hour passed without the noise of crashing things. The bells of the shrine rang softly in the breeze, adding a gentle refrain to the bonfire sputtering to a slow death under the drizzle.

Footsteps came up the stairs, as Antonio and Arees gathered themselves and rose to their feet. This was the moment that was bound to come, he knew, from the day he had taken shelter in the Legation, the moment when he'd have to face the enemy. He raised his pistol and took aim at the landing where the Boxer soldier would appear. Standing apart from Antonio, Arees pointed her Mauser at the landing too, giving herself the best chance to fell the intruder who was heading up steadily toward them, pausing for a moment as the chiming clock struck the hour.

Antonio saw the spirit soldier at the head of the stairs, dressed in peasants' blue with a black band around her head; a pair of almond eyes, and plaits dropped down to the back. The peasant who had once visited him dressed as a courtier. The rebel he had held in his arms. The woman who had made him feel helpless, the one he had loved like no other. A flush crept over Fumi's face as she observed the two of them, Antonio and Arees pointing their guns at her. He made a sign to Arees to stand still, then dropped his pistol to the floor and took a step toward her. Fumi's gaze flickered for a moment then she raised her hand to stop him, and pointed with her head toward the stairs. Glancing back at Arees, he hesitated then tried to speak to Fumi, who warned him with her eyes and motioned again for them to start walking down.

Smashed pieces of blue china crunched under their feet when they reached the parlor, watched closely by Fumi who walked behind them. What would she do, now that she'd killed Jacob's killers? How will she punish her lover, her *foreign* lover, and his foreign friend? What charges would she level against him? What exquisite torture did she have in store? He wondered if she'd be as brisk delivering her punishment to

Arees as she had with the servant. It might be impossible for her to save them, even if she so wished. The Boxer army couldn't let go of their catch, they'd take delight in torturing the woman, the devil's consort. He felt as troubled as when he had seen her for the very first time, possessed by the same urge to be with her again, to hold her one last time.

The room seemed peaceful after a storm, Ferguson's bloodstained robe serving as the only reminder of recent events. The throne chair was gone, taken away perhaps by the Boxers as bounty along with the dead foreigner to display at their public gatherings. The glass mirrors had been smashed, but the shards glinted in the sun like lanterns. The stack of drawers had been left intact by the intruders, he noticed through the open door of the library. Arees gave a start as they stepped into the courtyard filled with smoke from the smoldering bonfire, and pointed to Ferguson's servant lying face down in a pool of blood. A few scraggly peasant soldiers sifted through the wreckage, barely paying them attention, the priests and acrobats disappeared just as suddenly as they'd arrived at the villa. Fumi guided them through the open gates to the chair bearers sitting under the casuarinas' shade.

So this is the end . . . the act of mercy that's her supreme punishment. . . . Antonio thought.

"Wait!" He raised his voice to stop her before she could disappear back into the villa. She didn't answer him, but motioned to the bearers to leave. Sitting inside the sedan, Arees pressed him to hurry. He stood under the trees and called after Fumi, "Let me show you what I've learned." Trembling all over, he took off his shirt and drew the heart channel on his body with his finger, beginning at the eyes then swooping down to stab his chest.

Pinchback's bearers appeared to be wide awake carrying him and Arees away from Ferguson's villa. They rode in silence, without a grunt from their phantom carriers, galloping over deserted streets and wondering if they were being dispatched to a secret destination for the pleasure of the Boxers. Even with shutters down, Antonio could sense them leaving the narrow streets of the Tartar city away from the foreign Legation. Howling dogs chased the bearers as they leaped over narrow ditches and skirted fences like a flock of geese. It seemed a familiar journey, with the sun darting rays through the shutters into their coupe.

The lake carried the scent of the blooming plum trees when they arrived at the Summer Palace. The magnolia blossoms had come and gone, and a tent of green shade hung over every pavilion. With no sign of soldiers, the gulls had returned to nest by the shores, forming a line of surf along the calm waters.

The sight of the palace calmed Antonio. He recovered his voice and instructed the bearers to bring them over to his pavilion, spotting it easily among the trees. His steps quickened after they'd disembarked, leading Arees past the arched gate to the courtyard and to his lodge. Just as before, he expected his eunuch friends to rush out of the kitchen and welcome them, shying away perhaps from Arees and exchanging glances among themselves. Tian, he was certain, would be the more curious of the two, discreetly observing the wisps of smoke leaving her fine nostrils, as he feigned sweeping the lodge with his broom.

A flock of ravens feasted on worms in the courtyard, their croaking filling the pavilion with an eerie cacophony. Not a single leaf seemed to have fallen from the trees; the branches drooped tantalizingly low with swollen gourds and drew a homely pattern of light and shade on the ground. The teacher's chair faced the student's stool at the lodge's entrance, keeping a watch on the surroundings like a pair of stone animals. Entering the lodge, he found the vats empty, their bottoms caked over with ugly sediment and turned into a refuge of busy gnats. The kitchen was empty as well, just as he had left it after his attendants had disappeared, the stone-cold oven reminding him of his days of hunger.

Antonio wished he could show Arees the pavilion as it once was. Four full seasons flashed through his mind, and he saw himself in each one of them like an actor performing scenes from a Chinese musical show. The memory of each temple and tearoom, each bridge and terrace came flooding back to him, memories that seemed as ancient as the palace yet as alive as the gulls circling under the clouds. *You can stay here for as long as you need, till you've found what you're after . . ..* He wondered what his padre friend would've said had he seen him now. The sweet note of the konghou harp sounded like rain on the lodge's roof and blended with the flute, and he glanced quickly at the home of the American couple.

Why did Fumi send them to the Summer Palace? *It must be a hidden sign, a hint of things to come. Perhaps she wants us to escape the fate of the foreigners at the Legation.*

Arees called him from the lodge. He found her standing next to a coarsely built box, strapped hastily together with ropes, just like the ones Joachim Saldanha would bring over from time to time and leave with him for a few days before taking them back to his Macau museum. His mood lifted as he thought of his friend. Maybe he had come to look for Antonio, to remind him that Captain Jacque was still waiting in Tientsin to take him back on the *Warrior Queen*. Perhaps he was hungry and had gone out to look for the attendants. He remembered the Legation's fat teas: Joachim Saldanha wolfing down half a table before others had barely started, worrying his hostess about his insatiable appetite. *He's worse than a pregnant mother!* — Polly joked watching him eat, but he was making up for the past and for the days of hunger that'd follow. The box reminded him of Dona Elvira pulling the padre's leg for "scaring the poor Chinese with his stomach, happy to see him off with a few pieces of burnt log!"

Maybe my friend has left me a letter inside, Antonio thought as he opened the box, taking Arees's help to cut the ropes and prise the lid open. The room filled with a rotting smell and forced him to turn away for a gasp of breath. Arees screamed, banging the lid down, and fled from the room.

Antonio found Joaquim Saldanha inside the box, a gaping hole through his heart over the plain cross.

❋

Almost seven thousand miles separated them from the European coast, and a mere eighty from Tientsin. The Boxers were known to be active around the enormous walled city with its separate quarters for foreigners and the international port. Yet it was their only way out of China. They'd be safe if they managed to reach Tientsin, Oscar agreed with Antonio. Foreign ships would come to their rescue once they solved the tricky problem of navigating these eighty miles, steaming them away over the coast's unfriendly currents.

The Franklins joined hands with Antonio and Arees, burying Joachim Saldanha under the shade of a flowering narcissus, in the very same box in which they'd found him at the pavilion. Antonio kept the padre's cross to take over to his Macau museum. The American doctor was first to raise the matter of leaving the palace, a day after they'd arrived. "We'll stay, Boxer or no Boxer, but you must go," he said, with Lixia nodding in agreement. Arees objected: "It'll be risky for you to stay here, riskier than making the trip to Tientsin. The Boxers won't spare you just because you've saved hundreds of Chinese lives."

Lixia shook her head. "Not everyone is mad in this country. It's no worse now than before, when foreigners fought the Chinese for opium. We must wait till everyone's tired of killing."

Shall I tell them about Fumi, Antonio wondered, then decided not to. It'd be hard for him to hold back once he'd started, he'd shock the elderly couple with his outpourings. It would be awkward too to talk about her in Arees's presence. She hadn't asked him about Fumi ever since they'd left Ferguson's villa, although she must've seen enough to confirm what Polly might have told her.

With bridges destroyed, taking the train to Tientsin wasn't feasible any longer. Luckily the river was still flowing between the two cities, making it possible to travel by houseboat if one could find trustworthy boatmen. They conferred with Oscar and Lixia over a suitable plan to reach the Peiho River, before returning to their pavilion.

He felt strange sharing the lodge with Arees. She sat in the courtyard smoking, while he tossed and turned in bed. What does she think of her Candide now? He shut his eyes and tried to stop his mind from endlessly churning over the events of the past few days, to fall asleep before she came in, sharing the same bed like two strangers. His nightmares had gone, but he found it hard to sleep, fidgeting like a camp doctor on the alert all night.

Arees woke him, and led him out into the courtyard. She pointed to the plum tree, under which their visitor was sitting. With a shaven head and dressed in a white robe, he looked like a young monk. Antonio took a few moments to recognize him, then he called out to Tian. A rush of questions flooded his mind but he held himself back, waiting for his attendant to speak. The eunuch came up to him and stood with his face down.

"Why have you come?" He asked Tian, breaking the silence. "Why are you wearing a mourning robe?"

He looked fearfully past Antonio toward the lodge, and made a sign with his hands.

"What have you come to look for?"

Dropping his gaze back to the ground, the young eunuch spoke haltingly about a box that was inside Antonio's room. "It belongs to the padre."

"You mean Joachim Saldanha's box?"

Tian started to cry. "He had come here only to eat, and asked us to give him whatever we could. He ate his early and late rice with us, told us stories of the villages he'd visited. He stayed in the lodge for a whole week and then . . ."

"What happened?"

He wiped his eyes and looked despairingly at Antonio. "Boxers caught my uncle one day, when he'd gone out to the market. They called him a spy, helping foreigners and passing secrets to them. They tortured him and he confessed."

"Confessed to what?" Antonio brought his face close to Tian.

"That we were sheltering a dangerous foreigner in the pavilion, a devil worshipper, a Christian who was planning to kill our empress."

Antonio could imagine Boxer soldiers entering the pavilion, raiding the kitchen and dragging his friend out of the lodge. They wouldn't have found much to set to flames, disappointed too perhaps by the absence of treasures.

"The Savages didn't stop them when they came here. The padre was tying up his box to leave; he'd asked me to carry it out of the lodge with him. He thought my uncle had brought his friends over to help." Tian's voice dropped, watching the scene that reenacted itself before his eyes. "He tried to tell the Boxers that he wasn't their enemy; explained to them why he collected the statues, but . . ."

"Did they make Wangsheng fire the gun . . . ?" Antonio asked, his voice choking.

Tian nodded. "He didn't know how to. He'd never held a gun in his hand, but the Boxers taught him. They said he must atone for his sins." The eunuch bit his lips, then blurted out, "They made him kill the padre."

A white owl flew into the courtyard looking for a suitable perch, then flew back into the trees. Arees had lit a lamp, and asked Tian whether the older eunuch had managed to save himself from the Boxers. Tian shook his head. He didn't know; his uncle had gone away with the padre's killers. He hadn't seen him anywhere in the palace.

"Why have you come?" Antonio whispered to his young friend.

The eunuch raised his troubled eyes to him. "To tell you about the padre, and . . ."

"And what?"

"To go with you wherever you're going."

Antonio sat in the courtyard long after Arees had fallen asleep in the lodge and Tian inside the attendants' quarters by the kitchen. The owl had returned, unhappy with its nest in the trees. The plums had ripened in the summer and fallen to the ground, pecked by the raven, and started to rot. It wasn't after the sweet fruit, but the nest of scorpions under the twigs. He saw the bird's eyes glow.

He thought about the invisible empress. She had lived so near, and yet he'd never even seen her face. He wondered if it was true of everything he'd hoped to find in China, the invisible reminding him of what was still living and possible. The owl screeched, and he smiled to himself. *It has found its food.* The half moon cast a shadow over the pavilion, and kept him awake listening to the trees.

Whereas before he'd worry about their impending journey, the perils of traveling to Tientsin didn't occupy his mind. He thought instead about Tian. How he must've suffered at the loss of his uncle—his protector. The gruesome murder had changed him: he was no longer Tian-fen, the gifted one, the young eunuch who was full of mischief and wonder. The death of the padre had turned him, finally, into an eternal sufferer. The anguished face of Norma Cook, the dead pastor's wife, came to mind, pleading to him to let her die. Whereas in the past he'd worry over curing a patient, it troubled him now to think of those who must somehow go on living with their burden of loss.

Tian called them over to the arched gates in the morning, and they saw a mule cart waiting. The driver beamed and raised his whip to welcome them into the carriage. For most of the day, they rode in silence, passing bands of peasants fleeing their homes with bundles of food and bedding. Further they went from Peking, they were asked for news about the capital, and if the emperor was alive. To those fearing a general massacre, it didn't seem to matter who was fighting whom, who the victims might be—foreigners, Boxers or Chinese Christians. The carriage would be safer than covering the distance on a boat, Tian advised them, safer than having to rely on boatmen who were already mad at foreigners for threatening their livelihood with their railways. On shore they'd have to guard against petty thieves, and stay out of the way of marching soldiers.

Yet for the most part, their journey turned out to be just as uneventful as Antonio's trip on the carriage with Joachim Saldanha more than a year ago. With Arees and him resting under the thatched hold, Tian changed out of his funeral robe and sat next to the driver dressed as a simple farmhand. "No one should know that I'm a eunuch. Otherwise we'd be taken for palace royals escaping with treasures. Or spies, sent out by the empress to track her enemies."

"Where shall we take him?" Arees asked Antonio, as they waited for the driver and their young friend to return from the market with fodder for the animals.

"He has no family." He told her what Wangsheng had said about his nephew. "He lost everyone in floods."

"What will he do away from China? What use will anyone have of him?"

"He can come to Macau with us." Perhaps Dona Elvira would have use for him, Antonio thought. She'd think of something to keep him occupied, and out of the gaze of the curious. "Maybe he'll come back to Peking after the troubles are over."

They watched Tian and the driver as they made their way back, chatting merrily with sacks of grain thrown over their shoulders.

"What if there was nothing for him to come back to?" Arees sighed.

Both sat silently, imagining the Summer Palace in flames, the pavilions empty and scorched.

Unlike the fleeing peasants they avoided making nightfall. It'd take less than two full days to reach their destination, but the journey was prolonged by the only spectacle of war they came across, barely hours before arriving at the port city: the provincial armory had been set on fire, and blazed under the sun surrounded by open fields. A crowd had gathered around to watch the fireworks, and blocked their path. Shooting flames went up like rockets amidst thunderous explosions, and an immense column of smoke hung like a mushroom cloud over the charred depot. Antonio left the carriage, ignoring Tian's warnings, and joined the onlookers. The peasants were cheering the explosions, hoisting their children up on their shoulders to let them catch a glimpse of the streaking flames. The pack animals had broken rank to scamper away, raising a cloud of dust and chased by their owners. Uncertainty prevailed over the attack and the attackers. If Boxers were to blame, why didn't they loot the weapons? Few among the crowd had ventured close to the depot and returned with gory reports of mangled bodies of the armory guards who seemed to have been murdered in broad daylight before the arson.

"Tientsin is no Peking," Oscar Franklin had warned them. "Foreigners are the real threat there. You must avoid them and head for the port." Foreigners had more guns than the imperial army; more ships ringing the harbor, more hotheads among their civilians—the Tientsin Volunteers, who'd vowed to take on the Chinese singlehandedly. "The Volunteers will help you, but they won't take kindly to your friend," Oscar had said, gesturing at Tian. "They don't like foreigners who keep "too much touch" with natives."

The port area, normally bustling, was deserted, with a train of carriages waiting before the closed iron gates of the Jardine Matheson warehouse next to the customs shed. "They're waiting with boxes full of dead silkworms," their driver told Antonio and Arees. It was late already for Macau's silk fair, but the farmers weren't allowed into the port for fear that a Boxer or two might be lurking inside their carriages. Paul Simpson, baker turned Volunteer, received them at the porter's lodge after Arees had spent the better part of an hour arguing with the sentries at the gate. The young American, who commanded a substantial following among expats for his exquisite cakes, took less time to brief them than it'd take to fire up an oven.

"Everyone's waiting to leave 'double-quick,' after the holds have been loaded." Evacuees had arrived from all parts of China and were holed up in their "luxury suites"—the tiny rooms of the warehouse, waiting to catch a ship out. He eyed the meager belongings of the Portuguese couple with suspicion. "They'd be standing room only for those who arrive late."

"Loaded with what?" Antonio asked.

"Loot!" The young man laughed. "Before the Boxers can lay their hands on it!" Catching sight of Tian loitering among the crates, he dropped his voice. "Better ask your servant to hurry up and bring your things over from wherever you're hiding them."

"He's not our servant," Arees said.

"No?" Paul seemed surprised. "Who's he then?"

"Friend." Antonio spoke gruffly.

"That's the best loot in China, isn't it?" Paul grinned. "A personal eunuch to take back with you, and stun everyone at home!"

"How do you know he's a eunuch?" Arees asked.

"By the way he smells, of course!" He'd seen enough eunuchs sent to his bakery by their Chinese lords to buy Western cakes. "They leak, you know! Even their chief can't hide the rotten smell behind expensive perfumes." Changing his tone, he said sternly, "No servant or amah will be allowed on the evacuation runs. That's an order from our generals. If the Chinese want to leave China, they'd have to make their own arrangements."

Up from their afternoon siesta, the evacuees left their warehouse rooms to mill about a small hall set with tables for refreshments. Antonio watched them troop in, looking dazed in these unfamiliar surroundings, measuring up each other as they passed by the tables. Merchants stuck by other merchants; pastors formed a small circle at one corner, and consular officers preened around trying to appear as important as ever. The setting reminded Antonio of the Peking Legation, but the mood was sullen. Each table voiced its favorite grouse against the Chinese, for the unnecessary troubles brought on by the senile dowager. Some voiced more than a grouse or two, having faced the brunt of the revolt that was still ongoing, for losing valued property and servants. Many bemoaned the fact that they could've long been home had it not been for the timid allies, taking ages to wrest the Taku Forts from the Chinese and ensuring the flow of men and goods at the port.

"Not even steam could stop us being stalled!" A group of steel merchants from Sheffield pulled Captain Jacque's leg when he appeared and made his round of the tables. His *Warrior Queen* would be the first to leave Tientsin after the blockade had been forcibly lifted. Those assured of a berth were keen to keep the captain in good humor, to receive the favors of his table during their outward journey. Coming around to Antonio and Arees, sharing a table with a young German family, he smiled good-naturedly as Simpson introduced them as the "last-minute Portuguese."

"Where's the gravedigger?" Captain Jacque asked, then looked around the room, as if expecting to find Joachim Saldanha busy at the table of refreshments. He made fun too of his friend Dona Elvira—"If you're half as fussy about meals as she is, then we'll have to throw you overboard!" Taking their silence as a sign of anxiety, he sought to reassure them about the state of affairs.

"You're worried about your friends in Peking, aren't you?" He waved his hand in a dismissive way. "The siege will be over soon, you'll see. Allied troops have left Tientsin to liberate them. It's been done before. Just like the opium wars, all will be forgotten when it's over." He patted Antonio on the back. "I'll bring you back from Macau on my ship in the blink of an eye."

Antonio and Arees left the hall to look for Tian. They'd have to plan afresh if Simpson's words were true, if their young friend was refused a berth on the *Warrior Queen*. They might have to find a native junk that'd take them over to Macau. Or find a place to live in Tientsin till the troubles ended. It'd be a mistake to leave him alone in the port district—unescorted by a European he might be shot mistakenly by the allied guards as a Boxer spy.

They ran around stacks of crates in the transit sheds calling out for Tian, thinking he had hidden behind them in fear of the Bengal Lancers guarding the Jardine warehouse. The jetty leading up to the moored cutters was lined with crates too, waiting for coolies to arrive and begin loading the *Queen* at the crack of dawn. A pair of alley cats hissed at them as Antonio banged on the crates, wondering if Tian had pried open a lid and hidden inside one of them. They ran up the spiral stairs of the warehouse to the roof, then ran down and slipped into the master's garden that was used to entertain the harbormaster and other dignitaries. Their friend seemed to have disappeared into thin air.

Hysterical Volunteers, dubbed "wharf rats," were catching strangers and conducting sham trials, they'd learned from the evacuees. What if he'd fallen into their hands? Antonio shivered recalling the lynch mob he'd had to face off to save Wangsheng at the Legation hospital. It'd be foolish of Tian to leave the warehouse and venture out into the alleys of the old city. Maybe he was simply waiting outside the gates with their carriage driver, hoping for Antonio and Arees to return.

The sleepy Lancers were relieved to let them slip out of the warehouse, rather than face yet another argument with the memsahib. Outside, they faced the empty alleys. Piles of debris lay along the gutters. Smoke rose above single-storied homes, the darkness making it seem as if they'd been set on fire. They could hear their footsteps echo on the cobbled streets, having to hold on to each other as they came upon barricades guarding the dimly lit crossings.

"Tian!" Antonio called out at huddled forms on the pavements. One of them spat out a curse, then went back to sleep. They sensed someone was following them, and turned around to find their carriage driver. Coming up to them, he whispered to Antonio, afraid of raising his voice and arousing suspicion. Arees held out some money, but he shook his head. He said he'd come to give them a message from Tian.

"Where is he?" Antonio asked.

"A band of eunuchs were passing by the warehouse, and they stopped to talk to our Tian. They were going away to a place where no one could find them, to an ancient monastery. They'd be safe there, they said, and asked Tian to join them." He stopped to catch his breath, then spoke in a pleading voice as if he was Tian himself. "He told you not to be angry with him, and left you a gift." Antonio held out his palm. The driver hesitated, then passed him a piece of twig, polished to resemble a needle, one that'd make a seamstress proud and float on a bowl of water.

"Our Tian left with the half-men," the driver said, and bared his toothless mouth for a smile.

A junk flotilla left the harbor before the *Warrior Queen* could raise anchor, blocking her path with an advance party of sails. Captain Jacque's voice could be heard by everyone within a mile of shore, cursing the coolies and his men from his station inside the engine room. With passengers already on board and the harbormaster at hand to wave the vessel off, sounding of the bellows did little to comfort the remaining evacuees on shore left to await their turn as they returned to the warehouse to spend another day and night in their pigeonholes.

Among the last to settle into their cabin, Antonio and Arees went up to the deck to watch the sun risen behind the Taku Forts casting ominous shadows over a broad sheet of shallow water full of sandbanks. A pilot's ridge light beamed weakly at the mouth of the Peiho River. Sound of laughter came from the smokers' room. With Arees disappeared into the ladies lounge, Antonio stood alone on deck and watched the anchor rising from the muddy water. A midshipman waved at him from the hull, and he waved back. *How'd it feel to leave China after all that's happened?* he had asked himself the past few days after they had set out on their journey to Tientsin. Whereas in the past he might've felt remorseful, disappointed at having failed to achieve his mission, something appeared to put his mind at ease with the flow of events. He sensed the gentle ebbing of the past, as if he was returning home leaving the Portuguese doctor behind in this strange land. Just as he suffered for Fumi and grieved for Joachim Saldanha, they filled him with the will to keep searching for the secret of health and sickness. The shroud of a deeper mystery though, seemed to have lifted, the mystery that had chased him as a motherless boy down the Faculdade Medicina, driven him as far as China. He felt he had, at last, found his peace with the dead and the living.

A great tide of birds rose from the sandbars as their steamer lunged forward, thousands of them making a deafening noise. They heard the captain's call for a "good luck drink" at the bar, and the rush of deckhands setting places for the first of many memorable meals.

"You came to take me back, didn't you?" Antonio asked Arees, as they sat down under lively parasols.

"Yes." She sighed, then looked away at the receding line of junks following them out to sea. "But you are a different man now to the one I had known before."

He followed her gaze to the boats, brimming with peasants and their flocks, and imagined he could see his young friend among them, his arm around a glass jar that held the precious part he'd need to take to his grave to become a whole man in his next life.